PRAISE FOR *I AM DUST*

'Not going to lie, I had a tea[...] [...]l
thriller of love, loss, murder [...] [...]tting
what you wish for. Quite lovely in a dark, dark way
Sarah Pinborough

'A bold, original concept brilliantly executed by an author who is
unafraid to cross genres and challenge herself and her readers.
I adored it' John Marrs

'Ghost story, murder mystery, romance, this mesmerising and
entertaining book has it all … It's very spooky!' Emma Curtis

'Running its cold fingers along your spine, *I Am Dust* is a delicate
and mesmerising thriller' Matt Wesolowski

'Dark and haunting, this is another cracking read, which further
cements Louise Beech as one of the most original and exciting
authors of the moment' Claire Allan

'There are loads of twists and turns as the tension ramps up to
breaking point. I raced through, incapable of putting it down, and
strange things seemed to happen: gadgets broke inexplicably, and
there were odd noises through the walls. It's a novel that gets under
your skin' Gill Paul

'This book is about believing in yourself and finding out that you
had the power all along' Madeleine Black

'It's a darn good tale is what it is. Louise can, I'm convinced, write in
any genre, which makes her very special indeed. With *I Am Dust* I
think she's mastered the sense of place. I was in that theatre. I felt the
breath on my neck … It kept me reading until my eyes hurt and kept
me thinking about it long after I'd finished. A cautionary tale about
being careful what you wish for, I loved it!' Fionnuala Kearney

'Beech uses her in-depth knowledge of theatre life to great effect,
creating a work of almost tangible atmosphere and authenticity.
The timelines were handled brilliantly, the chemistry of physical

attraction and the pain of unrequited love actually hurt, and the loss of innocence was both poignant and layered' S.E. Lynes

'This book works: magically, emotionally and psychologically. There is meaning here – layers of it ... Every word is nuanced – I love how the author drew me in' Carol Lovekin

'Haunting, provocative and true to Beech's style: packed with pain and heart' Jack Jordan

'A captivating storyteller with the power to draw you into her fictional world and to make you emotionally invested in her characters ... an enthralling novel about magic, murder, secrets, and unrequited love' Louisa Treger

'A floating, lyrical, almost mystical read that is simply stunning' Jen Med's Book Reviews

'Atmospheric, haunting and sprinkled with magic – utterly breathtaking' Literary Elf

'It's spooky, mysterious, chilling and emotional' Off-the-Shelf Books

'Unnerving, scary, creepy and heartbreakingly sad, this atmospheric ghost story blew me away' Tales before Bedtime

'The writing is beautifully evocative ... Louise Beech clearly has a deep love of theatre and it just shines through on the page' Espresso Coco

'Beautifully written, evocative and powerful ... sheer emotional brilliance' The Tattooed Book Geek

'A spine-chilling, yet emotionally charged story ... the final scenes are heart-stopping in their beauty' Random Things through My Letterbox

'Immensely gripping, hugely addictive and fabulously atmospheric' Novel Deelights

'Louise Beech's most atmospheric novel to date'
From Belgium with Booklove

'Raw, emotive and powerful' The Book Review Cafe

'This novel is a real theatrical experience. Highly recommended'
The Book Trail

'Its sheer power, beauty and emotion will stay with me for a very
long time' Being Anne

PRAISE FOR LOUISE BEECH

'Tense, twisted and utterly compelling, written with such raw
beauty and unflinching honesty' Miranda Dickinson

'As twisty and deadly as barbed wire, this book will leave you
breathless' Erin Kelly

'Noirish psychological thriller with fascinating, disturbing
characters. Compelling, twisty, and seriously addictive' Will Dean

'Psychologically unsettling and with a sting in the tail, it's another
cracker published by Orenda' Russel McLean

'Beech has used her unique flair to construct a crime story that will
have you frantically turning the pages' Michael Wood

'Superb storytelling … claustrophobic, unsettling and intense' *Prima*

'A dark and atmospheric read which sends shivers down your spine'
Irish Independent

'Part psychological thriller, part literary noir and part tragic family
drama, its multiple strands slowly merge to reveal a captivating
truth' *Heat*

'Twisty, addictive and completely compelling, this powerful story
will keep you hooked and leave you haunted' *Best Magazine*

**Call Me Star Girl was winner of *Best* magazine's Big Book of the
Year 2019**

Also by Louise Beech

How To Be Brave
The Mountain in My Shoe
Maria in the Moon
The Lion Tamer Who Lost
Call Me Star Girl

I Am Dust

Louise Beech

ORENDA BOOKS

Orenda Books
16 Carson Road
West Dulwich
London SE21 8HU
www.orendabooks.co.uk

First published in the United Kingdom by Orenda Books, 2020
Copyright © Louise Beech, 2020

A catalogue record for this book is available from the British Library.

ISBN 978-1-913193-21-8
eISBN 978-1-913193-22-5

Resource: Image by acworks from silhouette-ac.com

Typeset in Garamond by typesetter.org.uk

Printed and bound by CPI Group (UK) Ltd, Croydon CR0 4YY

For sales and distribution, please contact info@orendabooks.co.uk

This is dedicated to the people who pick up the glitter.

And to a girl who *was* glitter: Allia Jen Yousef, or simply Jen.
I'll now have to wait until after the dust settles
to finally meet you.

I'm still here; I am dust.
I'm those fragments in the air,
the gold light dancing there,
that breeze from nowhere.

Dust – the Musical

Close my wounds,
keep me together;
give me strength
now and forever.
It stops.
The blood dries;
the panic stills;
the calm washes over me.
Saves me from my end.

Katy Beech

THE GAME

2005

YOU THREE
NEVER BE
UNDER ONE ROOF

This was one of the last messages before the three teenagers went their separate ways; one of the last messages of the game. Sitting cross-legged in a circle, Jess, Ryan and Chloe wore *Macbeth* costumes; Jess's red velvet dress was damp beneath her arms; Ryan wore his crown, as if he was saying that he was the leader tonight; Chloe wore her long witch robes, but she had flung the itchy wig into the backstage cupboard.

Their final show of the season had finished hours earlier, to rapturous applause. Now it was time to play the game one last time. When they began over a month ago, Ryan had called it a 'game', and he had told them the rules. But along the way they had bent them to fit their needs. 'We'll shut it down if it gets weird,' they had agreed. 'We're in control,' they had said.

Chloe knows now that they all lied.

Not only to one another – by saying they would end it if necessary – but to themselves. Over that summer, morbid curiosity, youthful bravado and teenage love had joined them on a dusty stage in a church. Now autumn was a breath away. Now the dying August sun could barely penetrate the boarded-up windows and light the room. Ryan had left a lamp on in the nearby backstage room, and it filtered gently through.

'Last time, then,' he said, positioning the alphabet letters in a circle.

'Last time,' repeated Jess.

'Last time,' said Chloe softly.

Ryan lit the three candles. The third one wouldn't ignite easily; he managed on the third match. Three, three, *three*. It had always been three. Chloe tried not to cry. So much ending. So much change. She wasn't ready. They put their fingers on top of the up-turned glass in the centre of the circle.

'Is there anyone here with us tonight?' asked Ryan, as he had so many times.

Nothing happened.

Chloe smiled, wondering if the spirits liked to tease, to make their audience wait. Eventually a slow, seductive scrape drew their eyes down – the glass moved from letter to letter, spelling out messages from beyond. Chloe smiled. She knew who was moving it so deliberately.

This was the one she most liked to talk to.

Then the glass stilled, but only for a moment, as though owner-ship had switched, and the new owner had taken a breath. She saw him. Like she had that first time, so long ago it seemed now. He was sitting behind Ryan. Cross-legged. A teenage boy. Grin-ning. Face bloody; the crimson flow from a ragged gash across his forehead pretty in the flickering light.

The glass continued moving. It spelled out the words:

YOURE READY

'We are,' said Ryan.

YOU ARE ETERNAL THREE

'We are,' said Ryan.

READY FOR THE POWERS

Chloe knew these words were the beginning of the end. The end of their friendship. The end of this. The end of childhood. Because they were all different now. She felt it as acutely as she had so many things this summer. Even though the spelled-out words were not spoken, Chloe heard them as though they had been. Many times, for her, the black-and-white letters somehow transformed into the voice of their creator.

YOU THREE

NEVER BE

UNDER ONE ROOF

It was only later – when Ryan and Jess had gone, and Chloe was speaking to the spirits alone – that she asked aloud why it was better they never meet again And the answer made her realise they never should.

Then slowly, she forgot it all.

Like a jigsaw broken up, piece by piece, the memories died. Chloe eventually forgot that summer, and Jess and Ryan and their words, and the spirits. But the love she had felt remained in her heart, as a feeling more than a physical memory – an ache, a pain that compelled her to return to the dark, secret habits again and again, until they were an addiction.

THE DEAN WILSON THEATRE

JANUARY 2019

There is a moment just before a show starts when the audience is united by a sharp intake of breath. A moment after they have turned off phones and settled comfortably in seats; a moment when darkness falls, and the stage is lit; a moment when they might wonder if they even exist anymore; when they forget everything for two hours.

In that moment, at the back of the auditorium, Chloe hopes over and over and over to experience the magic she felt when she first saw a musical with her mum; when she sang the songs to the brand-new show, *Dust,* here at the Dean Wilson Theatre, marvelling at the beauty of its lead actress and the passion of the story.

Now she works here as an usher and views the spectacle of the latest show each night, alongside up to five hundred patrons. She sits quietly in the shadows, her less-comfortable spot a flip-down seat near the technicians' box. Here Chloe can easily see if anyone turns a phone on. Here she can slip out if another usher radios to say there are latecomers needing to be let in. Here she has one eye on the stage and one on the audience, one ear on the musical numbers and the other plugged with an earpiece that punctuates her shift with announcements and instructions to hand out the right flyer at the end.

Tonight, though, Chloe's hope for the magic of *Dust* died with the first song, just as it has every night since this show opened ten days ago. *Forget Everything You Know* is a new musical set in a dementia hospital. It has so far received mixed reviews.

This evening, the lead actor, George Dewitt, has a cold, which can't be helped but means his song about childhood being more vivid than things from yesterday is raspy rather than haunting. The audience is small, their reaction muted. Chloe scans the backs of their heads, bored now in this second week of a show that the local newspaper has called 'tasteless but full of enthusiasm and the odd laugh'.

A voice crackles through the radio earpiece. Chloe can't make out the words, so she whispers into the mic, 'Can you repeat that, please?'

Another crackle. Nonsensical static.

Then: 'Never ... be... one ... roof...'

She frowns. What does that mean? Who said it?

Chloe steps out into the foyer and says more loudly into the mic, 'I didn't hear that fully. Can you repeat?'

Silence.

Bloody radios. Half of them don't work properly, but they're essential for communication between ushers, front-of-house duty managers, technicians and stage managers. Chloe is about to return to the auditorium when Chester comes out of the box office with six large posters under his arm. He was here when the theatre opened, as he happily tells anyone new. Slightly overweight and forty, he's a ray of light or an annoying gossip, depending on who you listen to. To Chloe, he's a joy.

'Did you radio me, Ches?' she asks.

'Me? No. Busy putting these up.'

'Who was it then?'

'I didn't get a message on mine.' He plonks the posters on a table. 'Maybe you're hearing things.'

'No, there was definitely some—'

'O.M.G,' interrupts Chester, his face bright with gossip. 'Have you *heard*?' It's a face Chloe knows well. He loves it when he's the only one with a nugget of information – some clandestine relationship among the cast or some scandalous sacking – and he usually strings out the sharing of it.

Chloe opens the theatre door to go back in, but can't help pausing. 'Heard what?'

Chester grabs her arm. 'It's coming back,' he hisses, eyes aglow.

'What is?' Maybe she shouldn't have asked. For some reason the words make the hairs on the back of her neck stand up.

Then duty manager, Cynthia, opens the box-office door, clearly not amused. 'Chloe, what are you doing outside the auditorium? How many times have you all been emailed about not leaving mid-show?'

'Sorry.' She sneaks back in and finds her seat in the dark.

The radio crackles in her ear again.

Chloe frowns, anticipating static and more curious words, but one of the technicians announces that there are five minutes until the interval. Thank God.

The cast start singing about incontinence. She wonders if this is a moment the local newspaper thought was tasteless, or funny. She can't wait until the end, although she's not looking forward to the bike ride home if it's still minus two and raining. The song reaches a squeaky climax; the lights come up in the auditorium; there's a spattering of feeble applause that fades into silence.

Chloe stands by the open door. Dressed in the customary black shirt, waistcoat and trousers – dark to blend in with the shadows – she holds out programmes and smiles at the patrons as they file past and towards the bar. Sometimes she feels like she doesn't exist. That she is as invisible out here as she is at the back of the theatre.

No one smiles back. Snippets of conversation catch her free ear.

'We should have gone to see bloody *Phantom* at the New Theatre.'

'Shall we escape and go to that place that does three-for-two on cocktails?'

'I suppose you could say it was topical.'

Chloe is supposed to convey such comments back to Cynthia for the show report, but she'll probably have forgotten them by the end of the shift. She has been an usher at the Dean Wilson

Theatre for six years. Staff and regular patrons affectionately call it the DW: it was named after the playwright who created the very first show – *Dust* – which opened the then brand-new building twenty years ago. Ten-year-old Chloe had nagged and nagged her mum to take her, saying she simply *must* see it, that all her youth-theatre friends were going, and she *had* to see what all the fuss was about.

She has never forgotten it, and still sings the songs.

Chloe's earpiece crackles and one of the technicians speaks. 'Three minutes until the end of the interval.'

Chester comes over and takes the remaining programmes and money pouch from her so he can cash up. Every night, three ushers sit inside the auditorium while one stays in the box office, dealing with latecomers, doing the timesheets, and any other job that comes up. Chloe likes to be inside the theatre, no matter how tiresome the show or how many times she has seen it.

'It's coming back,' says Chester with a wink, and hurries away.

Chloe shakes her head, laughing, knowing it will no doubt be gossip about something trivial. When clearance is given on the radio, she closes the doors, the lights dim, and the show continues.

Maybe if things had happened differently, Chloe might have been up there. In the spotlight. Assuming a persona. Speaking lines learned for months. Singing her heart out. Drinking in rapturous applause. It wasn't to be. She never believed herself quite good enough to pursue acting seriously.

Still, she often sneaks into one of the dressing rooms when the actors have left. There, Chloe stands in the dazzling mirror lights and imagines transforming into Fantine or Roxie Hart or Esme Black. There, she whispers the never-forgotten lines from her days at the youth theatre; from her days studying drama at university. There she sings lines from the title song of the first show she ever saw:

I'm still here; I am dust. I'm those fragments in the air, the gold light dancing there, that breeze from nowhere...

The hardest role Chloe has to play is the everyday woman she is – a woman once described as 'girl-next-doorsy but versatile' on a long-forgotten CV. Every actor learns early on where they fit in. There are those who can carry the iconic roles. And there are those who are forgettable enough to blend into a chorus line or crowd scene.

'Am I forgettable?' she often whispers in the dressing-room mirror.

She is scarred. Clearly. And not in some angst-ridden way. Not just emotionally. She is physically scarred. She could never play any roles that require her legs or stomach or arms to be on display. Never bare flesh. So instead she's writing a script on her laptop, hoping to create lines for another actor to perform one day.

Now, in the darkness at the back of the auditorium, she fingers the ridges on the skin beneath her trousers. The scars. Her history.

The radio crackles in her ear.

She frowns.

More strange words in the static.

'Never ... be ... under ... one ... roof...'

'Who said that?' she whispers into the mic.

'Never ... under ... roof...'

The words stir something black in her gut; ignite some long-buried memory.

'Never ... roof...'

Chloe rushes to the door, stumbling in the shadows. Outside in the foyer, she speaks into the mic. 'Is someone messing about on the radio?'

After a beat, Cynthia speaks. 'Must be yours. Nothing on mine.'

Then Chester says, 'Nor mine.'

Chloe wants to rip the thing out of her ear. But there are still twenty minutes of the show left. She goes back inside, returns to her seat. Tries to lose herself in the songs. Tries to concentrate on scanning the audience for illuminated phones.

Eventually gentle applause signals the end; a sitting ovation. Chloe hands flyers for an upcoming show about Brexit to the patrons as they quietly file out and escape into the night. The stage is lifeless without the lighting and action.

Once the auditorium is empty, she and the other two ushers – Paige and Nina – collect the rubbish and straighten up the chairs. Some bastard has left chewing gum on a seat.

'What's Chester going on about?' asks Paige. She's nineteen and a drama student, like most of the ushers here.

'What do you mean?' asks Nina. She's forty-two and an out-of-work actress who also waitresses and walks dogs.

'He's been going on about something coming back.'

'Bloody drama queen,' cries Chloe.

'Aren't we all?' laughs Nina.

'Wonder what he meant though.' Paige puts a coffee cup into the bin bag.

'You know Chester,' says Chloe. 'It'll be something and nothing.'

She takes the rubbish bags out to the skip at the rear of the building. To get there, she has to go backstage – an area reserved for authorised people; access is via a door with a keypad. It's Chloe's favourite part of the theatre. Here there are the four large dressing rooms. Here the actors bustle back and forth, speedily changing attire, hovering in the shadows until their cue. Here it smells of hot lights and sweat and old costumes.

Now the actors are removing make-up, enjoying after-show drinks and rushing off to greet families who have come to see the musical. Squeezing past the racks of costumes in the corridor, Chloe glances at the only dressing-room door with a name on it. The two words are etched inside a gold star; Morgan Miller. The room has been occupied by lead actor George Dewitt and as far as Chloe knows he hasn't made any complaints about it.

'Give him time,' Chester said at the start of the run.

But clearly the dressing room that has had so many other actors requesting a different one over the years doesn't faze George. He sneezes heartily as Chloe passes on her way back to the box office.

Cynthia asks the ushers how things were. Paige reports the comments she overheard. Chloe makes something up, since she has forgotten hers. Cynthia reminds them that they must check *all* the fire exits every single shift and says that there will be a big announcement next week.

Behind her back, Chester arches his eyebrows knowingly at them.

Chloe shakes her head at him.

She heads into the main foyer to escape. The red carpet is a little tired and the O on the Box Office sign keeps going out, but the pictures of the big actors who have been in shows here line the walls, fingerprints blurring their faces. Chloe recalls her first day, looking around at the posters and drinking in the atmosphere. She couldn't believe that she would be working at the iconic DW theatre. That was six years ago. It doesn't command quite the same respect today. Slumping sales and badly received shows mean audiences have dwindled and the décor needs a touch-up.

Chester grabs Chloe's arm, pulling her from her reverie.

'It's—'

'Don't tell me,' she laughs. 'It's coming back! OK, *what* is? Your sex drive? Your memory?' She shakes her head. 'Sorry, Ches. I'm just tired tonight.'

And a bit spooked, she wants to add.

'I never thought they'd do it,' whispers Chester.

'Do what?'

'Have it here again.'

'Have what?'

'*Dust.*'

'*Dust*...?' Chloe frowns. 'You mean...?'

'Yes, the musical,' he says, squeezing her arm.

'Here again?' A shiver runs up Chloe's back. She looks around, but the main doors are closed.

'Yes. It's coming in September.'

'Surely not? Isn't that ... well, bad taste or something?'

'How can they not?' demands Chester. 'Ticket sales have slumped so much recently. And how shit is *Forget Everything You Know*? How shit was that one last month? This will be a sensation!'

'I suppose. But...'

'What?' he asks.

'Well, look what happened last time...'

'That's why they'll all flock to it again, won't they? That show *made* this place.'

'For all the wrong reasons,' says Chloe, still cold despite a glimmer of excitement at the thought of maybe seeing *Dust* again.

'Who gives a crap about that. It was our first, our best, and if you think about it, it never finished its run.'

'Because someone died,' cries Chloe.

'Well, I can't bloody wait!'

'Is it really coming, Ches, or is it just gossip?'

'I saw it on Cynthia's computer,' he insists. Then more unsure, he adds, 'I *think*. But you heard what she said about a big announcement. The press will go fucking wild. I bet we sell out in an hour. And we work here. We'll see it all – be *part* of it.'

'It just feels so ... I don't know...'

'Oh, you'll change your mind when the atmosphere in here is electric again.' He pauses. 'You're *so* lucky – you saw the original.'

'So did you. You've worked here since the beginning.'

'I was ill that week.'

'Of course you were.' Chloe recalls his often-shared tale of woe, of how he had flu when *Dust* opened the theatre.

'You're one of the few here who saw it. Aren't you *excited*?'

Chloe isn't sure. She should be.

The songs have haunted her ever since.

But she can't help thinking that those lyrics belong only in her head now.

THE DEAN WILSON THEATRE

JANUARY 2019

When Chester has gone, Chloe heads backstage. She keys in the door code and then stands in the chilly concrete space between the dressing rooms; it's eerily quiet now the actors have departed. She fingers the row of costumes on the rack in the corridor, imagines them coming to life when no one is around, like the dolls in *The Nutcracker*.

Chloe smiles and shakes her head. An overactive imagination is a blessing when it comes to trying to write scenes in her room – here, it is a curse. And, oh, is she cursed with it. Her mum used to tell her frequently that she was born for the theatre – she used to say, when Chloe was younger and passionately performed her own little songs or skits, that she 'glowed'. She would applaud vivaciously; smile proudly.

Now Chloe glances at the Morgan Miller dressing-room door. She can never help but look at it. It is shut now and the lower points of the gold star are tarnished, as if it has fallen from grace. Over the years, many ushers have reported seeing curious shadows moving on the stairs; exchanged frenzied tales of sounds coming from inside this dressing room.

Singing.

Crying.

Shrieking.

Chester loves to spook everyone with the story of how he *definitely* saw Morgan's ghost here, dressed as the ethereal Esme, waiting to go on stage one last time. Some of the ushers don't like to come back here when it's empty, and persuade someone else to go with them. Chloe has no choice. Her bike is around the back. She makes hearty fun of those who need to pair up, but she can't say she hasn't felt things too: goose bumps when she looks at the Morgan Miller star; an icy draught on her neck when she passes this door; a soft rustle of movement that she can't be sure she has imagined.

The voice on the radio earlier was spooky. The words about being under a roof unnerved her. Thoughts of the incident that occurred in Morgan Miller's dressing room creep into her mind. She shakes her head to get rid of them.

She's about to hurry down the stone steps to the fire exit where her bike is chained when she hears it.

The creak of a door opening.

Chloe frowns. Stiffens. Waits. She is too scared to turn around and look back.

So don't, she thinks. *Don't.*

But she does.

The Morgan Miller dressing-room door is open. Chloe blinks, hoping that when she opens her eyes again it will be shut, just as she knows for certain it was earlier. No. It is wide open. Inviting. Gaping like the mouth in the famous *Scream* painting. She should run, but her feet are made of stone.

Another sound. A voice? Her name? Sung like the line from a musical? Why does the lilt of it stir something in her stomach? Some memory long gone.

No. She's hearing things.

But the door is real. Still open.

She goes towards it, her heart screaming not to.

The dressing room is empty. George Dewitt's things are scattered across the surfaces; ostentatious spectacles and scarves and make-up pots. The grey wig he wears in the show is perched on a mannequin's head. Someone has drawn black eyes on its face, giving it an evil look.

Chloe steps inside.

She never comes into this dressing room to stare in the mirror and imagine being on stage. She can't remember the last time she was in here.

Yes, you can, she thinks.

No. I can't.

The original poster for *Dust* hangs on the wall. It's yellowed at the edges and torn where its weight has pulled it free from drawing pins. It's forbidden for anyone to take it down. Chloe moves closer to it. A coating of dust on the surface traps the light, so it looks like it's sprinkled with glitter.

'I am Dust,' she whispers.

Surely it isn't *really* coming back. Chester has got things wrong before, like the time he told them all that Tom Hardy was going to be in a show and it turned out it was local actor Tom Hardling.

Dean Wilson wrote the show to open the brand-new theatre twenty years ago. It sold out in minutes. The lavish musical set in Victorian England told the story of Esme Black, a housemaid who fell for her employer, wealthy doctor Gerard Chevalier. But he loved Lady Louisa Pearse, a vivacious and flighty creature. While Chevalier and Louisa were kissing at a garden party in his house, Esme hurled herself from the balcony and died at his feet. After that, she haunted Chevalier day and night, until he succumbed, fell in love with her ghost and committed suicide to be with her.

There was a huge battle for the role of Esme; actresses slept with producers; agents paid money to those who might sway the decision; actresses made recordings of themselves crooning the melancholic songs and sent them to anyone who mattered. But after a two-minute, breath-taking audition that silenced the room, Morgan Miller won the role.

Chloe saw it the night it opened, snuggled up to her mum.

During the interval on the fourth night of the run – press night – Morgan Miller was found dead in her dressing room.

Hit over the head repeatedly with a heavy object.

The show shut down.

The killer was never caught.

The theatre stayed open, though, and became a place of macabre interest. Ticket sales flourished, and stayed high for a long time, even if the quality of the productions declined. Now though, nothing seems to bring audiences in, not even the exaggerated tales of how Morgan Miller haunts the shadowy passages backstage.

But Chester thinks it's coming back.

Dust.

If it did, who would play Esme Black? Does Chloe have the versatility, the passion, or the ability to do it? Could she portray shy, desperate Esme; and could she evoke the ghostly enchantress Esme, on the other side? Even if she could ... her body. Her damaged body. *No*. There's no chance. But how amazing it would be to *become* Esme Black. To be part of the show that made her fall in love with the theatre.

Chloe looks at the two faces on the poster.

A lank haired Morgan Miller looks into a mirror as the non-descript living Esme; but the reflection is the russet-lipped, golden-haired ghost who teases and taunts poor Dr Chevalier until he joins her in death. Chloe turns to the dressing-room mirror. She is also two opposing women. The one in the glass, with raven hair and neat eyebrows, smiles warmly and gives nothing away; the one with a heart beating too fast is afraid she will never be a success in the theatre.

But there is something else in the mirror.

On the mirror.

Small.

In the top corner of the glass, half hidden by one of the lights. How did she not notice before? Were they even there then? Chloe frowns at her own questions, wondering where they came from. They look like words written in black eye pencil. She moves closer, squints at the tiny capital letters. Then she gasps and leaps back:

YOU THREE NEVER BE UNDER ONE ROOF

What the hell? *What* three? It's just her.

But isn't that what someone whispered on the radio earlier?

Yes.

Again, a dark memory uncoils in her gut like a black ghost rising from a grave.

When did she last see those words?

Somewhere...

But *how* are they here on this mirror? Chloe looks wildly around. *Who* wrote them? When? She suddenly sees her friends from the youth theatre. Jess and Ryan. Jess Swanson and Ryan ... She can't remember. But she hasn't spoken to either of them for at least fourteen years. And why have they popped into her head? Why here? Now? What is it about these words?

YOU THREE NEVER BE UNDER ONE ROOF

Chloe has no clue what they mean.

You do, you just don't want to remember...

THE DEAN WILSON THEATRE

JANUARY 2019

Chloe opens her eyes.

Where is she? A floor, hard, cold. What's that? A dark shadow shimmers, moves closer. Someone leans over her, their face elongated, ghostly, menacing; their mouth moves around some words, a song, one she knows; a hand reaches for her throat.

No. It's just ... just Chester. Reaching to help her sit up.

'What are you doing down there?' he asks.

Chloe looks around. She's in the Morgan Miller dressing room.

'Must have been one of my blackouts.' She rubs the back of her head.

'Again?' Chester's face comes into full focus, his forehead creased with concern. 'You've had two this month. Shouldn't you see someone?'

'Ches, I *have*. They can't figure it out; said it's not gonna hurt me.'

'Unless it happens when you're high up somewhere ... or in water.'

'I never swim. And I hate heights.'

Chloe gets up, wipes herself down. She has been having blackouts for as long as she can remember. She thinks since she was a teenager, though she can't be sure. Experts call it syncope – a temporary loss of consciousness caused by a sudden lack of blood flowing to the brain. Chloe has had all kinds of tests to ascertain what causes it in her case – including an ECG – but the doctor say she's perfectly healthy aside from slightly low blood pressure.

She can go months without passing out; then it can happen three times in a week. She's never out for longer than a minute or two.

'I'm fine,' she insists to appease Chester.

Then she remembers.

The mirror.

The words.

YOU THREE NEVER BE UNDER ONE ROOF.

Again, the sickly feeling of something she can't quite explain engulfs her. She pushes Chester aside and approaches the mirror. Leans closer and squints at the top corner. Nothing there.

'What are you looking for?' asks Chester.

'I...' Chloe doesn't know what to say. She definitely doesn't want to say those creepy words aloud. Did she imagine them? Did she imagine the door being open? No. That was real. But the words? Can she be absolutely sure?

'Chloe?' Chester is studying her.

'What are you doing here anyway?' she asks, shaking her head.

'I forgot my headphones and the front doors are locked now. Let me get them and we should go. It's late.'

They leave the dressing room together. Chloe looks back one last time. For a fleeting moment she is sure the words are there again, in the top corner of the mirror, the small letters as menacing as tiny drops of blood leading to a body.

But she blinks, and they are gone.

THE DEAN WILSON THEATRE

JANUARY 2019

The following evening Chloe finds herself at the Morgan Miller dressing-room door again, fingers around the handle, as if she might go inside. With a gasp, she pulls her hand away, shaking it as though to waft away a fly.

It's deathly quiet. The show must be over. She looks behind her and cries out: something ghostlike is floating mid-air at the end of the corridor.

But it's just a white dress hanging from the costume rail.

What the hell is she doing here?

She came to get her bike. Yes, that's it. But she must have been standing here for twenty minutes. She looks at her watch. 11.15. How did she lose track of time like this? It makes no sense. The shift earlier was an easy one. Chester was quiet; no more mention of *Dust*. The audience was small, as usual. And the radios only broadcast messages about the intervals and latecomers. Nothing out of the ordinary and yet, standing here alone, Chloe feels fingers of icy dread scrape sharp nails down her spine.

No; the cold is real. The air is as chill as when she opens the upstairs freezer to get ice creams for the interval. Her breath mists the air like the effects in a bad horror film. She needs to get a grip.

And then she hears it.

Footsteps on the stairs.

Someone is coming down from the rehearsal room.

An actor?

'Who's there?' Chloe calls, still unable to move.

The sound stops.

'Is that you, Chester?' she cries, sure he's left already.

Are you though? You don't even know how long you've been here.

Silence.

Chloe moves away from the dressing-room door, towards the stairs. As she does, the footsteps begin again, this time hastily retreating.

Angry that someone is taunting her, Chloe chases them. But as she ascends the concrete steps, a choking cloud of pungent, lavender perfume engulfs her. Launching into a coughing fit, she has to grip the metal rail until she can breathe properly again.

When she finally reaches the top of the stairs, the corridor is empty. The nearby green room and rehearsal space are dark. But the essence of lavender lingers.

Chloe retraces her steps.

It must be *her*; it must be Chester mentioning *Dust* the other day combining with the overactive imagination she has had since she was small. She remembers at school when a group of popular girls laughed at her portrayal of Cordelia in *King Lear*. One of them – cocky Carrie Meadows – ended up with broken arm after hitting a wall. She swore Chloe did it. When her mum grounded her for a week, Chloe insisted she hadn't even touched Carrie. She hadn't. She was sure of it.

Wasn't she?

Now, Chloe stops in her tracks, aching at a sudden, vivid memory. Grandma Rosa had come to her bedroom one night after the broken-arm incident. She had kissed Chloe's head and told her she was a magic girl. Though she didn't say it in words, Chloe heard, 'You should always contain your anger, only ever lash out for love.'

She and Grandma Rosa often spoke to one another without words. Thinking of it now, Chloe realises it is odd, though it had felt so natural at the time. At a crowded Sunday lunch table, Grandma Rosa would ask Chloe to pass the mint sauce without opening her mouth. Only Chloe heard, and would hand it over.

Hadn't her grandma worn lavender perfume?

Yes. Is that why Chloe has just smelt it? She is missing her. Thinking about her. *Yes.* That could be it.

She looks around and realises that she is now on the stage. How did that happen? Chloe looks back, at the open stage door she can't even recall opening – almost expecting to see herself walking through it.

She walks to centre-stage and faces the rows of empty seats, gentle rays from the night lamp, which is always on, flickering over them. She looks behind her at the swathes of black curtain shrouding the brick wall – rows of tall, still witches waiting to cast a spell. There is nothing like it, being on stage. That gut-churning fear before going on; the buzz from an appreciative audience; the feeling of being bigger and brighter than any star in the galaxy; the relief afterwards. Chloe has only experienced it on an amateur set – only stood here and imagined it in a theatre like this.

How must Morgan Miller have felt? The weight of that expectation on opening night. The thrill of being the chosen one. The fear of forgetting those infamous lines. The relief at those early rave reviews. The glory of success.

And then it was over.

Then she died.

Chloe looks at her watch That can't be right. She looks again. It's 01.32. Almost the middle of the night. *How the hell did that happen?* She should go. She turns but something stops her. Some thing turns her head. Something drags her gaze upwards, to the back of the auditorium.

There's someone there.

There, as real as Chloe, yet as ethereal as a ghost: a woman – milky dress fluid, golden hair cascading, face obscured by a netted veil.

I'm still here...

Chloe imagines that the eyes beneath are grey but colour as she speaks. Imagines that the mouth beneath opens and familiar words pour out.

I am dust...

It's Morgan Miller.

And Chloe thinks: *I've seen you before.*

Then she blinks and Morgan is gone. No. Not gone. She was never there. *You imagined it.*

Chloe realises her trousers are damp and touches her thigh with disgust. Has she urinated in fear?

No. She can smell it. It's blood.

Blood?

Her scars are bleeding. Her wounds are open.

Then the night lamp goes out.

Blackness.

Chloe runs towards the light in the corridor.

She looks back just once and is sure for a moment that the lamp flickers back on – and that a large, black bird is standing on the ledge above it, feathers as sleek as oily water.

6

THE DEAN WILSON THEATRE

JANUARY 2019

As promised, a week later, Cynthia holds a meeting in the upstairs rehearsal room. Props from *Forget Everything You Know* litter the half-white-half-mirrored room; walking sticks, dressing gowns and worn slippers form small, random piles as though left by a group of elderly swimmers. In contrast, a glitter ball and two cheap fur coats have been abandoned on a table, possibly items from up-coming show, *Bright Lights, Bright Life*. White tape crosses mark the wooden floor, so actors know where they have to stand when they're on the real stage.

The ushers drag chairs noisily from the stack at the back of the room.

Nina grumbles that she's missing an important audition for this. 'I hope it's just about *Dust*,' she says glancing at Chester, 'and not redundancies, like six months ago.'

He hasn't mentioned the show for days, perhaps worried he had got it wrong after all. 'If they're getting rid of staff, it won't be me,' he whispers as they line their chairs parallel to the mirrored wall, doubling their number.

'What I'd do to play Esme Black,' sighs Nina, sitting down between Chloe and Chester.

'You're too old,' sniffs Paige.

'I'm only forty-two. My acting CV says I can do thirty-five to forty-five. Anyway, you're way too young. Esme is thirty in *Dust*.'

'Chloe would be perfect then,' smiles Chester.

'I doubt that,' she says, her chest tight at the thought of it. She knows every line; the original script book is on her shelf, dog-eared and yellowing. But after the other night with the lost hours and footsteps on the stairs and a woman (just a woman, *not* Morgan Miller) in the theatre, she doesn't want to think about the show.

'You've got that vulnerability,' says Paige. 'I never saw *Dust*, I wasn't even born, but I've always thought from the pictures that Morgan Miller lacked a softness. Yeah, she was magnetic and beautiful ... but in the script Esme is *sensitive*.'

'You can't diss Morgan Miller,' cries Chester, hand dramatically clutching his chest.

'Because she *died*?'

'No,' he hisses, 'because it's bad luck.'

'Oh, fuck off with your superstition,' laughs Paige. 'Nothing's gonna happen cos we bitch about her! There *is* no bloody ghost.'

Chloe nods more vigorously than she intends. Is she trying to convince herself? Since that strange night on stage, she's decided it was Chester mentioning *Dust*'s return that triggered her imagination. She was tired. She was spooked. The lights went out because there was a fault. That's the only explanation.

'They'd want a big star to play Esme,' she says. 'They wouldn't want a nobody like me.'

The door opens, stopping a united cry of 'Don't be silly!'

Cynthia comes into the room, her customary court shoes clacking on the wood, followed by a middle-aged woman with bright-orange hair and matching nails, who sits on the chair at the end of the row. Chloe is sure she has seen her here at the theatre a few times, her hair changing as often as an experimental teenager's.

'First of all,' says Cynthia, all business. 'This is Beth and in three weeks she'll be starting as an usher.'

'Hi, Beth,' everyone choruses.

She nods briskly at them all.

'We'll be interviewing for more ushers in the coming months,' Cynthia continues. 'You'll understand why when I tell you what's happening in September.'

Chester looks at Chloe, eyes wide; she shakes her head.

'Well, guys.' Cynthia smiles at them, clearly enjoying their rapt expressions. 'This is exciting stuff, it really is. I doubt a single one of you doesn't know about the show that opened this place – *Dust*.' She says it softly, with reverence, the way many do. 'There have been discussions for a good while about this, but I can now tell you that this year, on the twentieth anniversary of its opening, *Dust* will be returning.'

The ushers give an exaggerated 'ooohhh'.

Despite everything, Chloe's first reaction is excitement. She pushes away any niggling doubt ... simmering dread.

'I know, I know.' Cynthia laughs. 'It's going to be *huge*. This is why we'll be taking new staff on. The official announcement will be tonight at nine pm across all media platforms. Tickets go on sale first thing tomorrow. We anticipate them selling out in hours.'

'How long will it be on for?' asks Chester.

'Four weeks,' says Cynthia. 'Then it goes to the West End.'

'It's coming here first?' asks Chloe.

'Yes, it'll premiere here.'

'Wow.' Chloe knows it is usually the other way around.

'What date does it start?' asks Chester.

'The first show will be Thursday, the fifth of September. Press night will be Tuesday the tenth. The cast will be here rehearsing from mid-June, so the meet-and-greet will likely happen then too, and you'll get the usual chance to meet the actors.'

'Do we know who they are?' asks Nina.

'Yes,' says Cynthia. 'They'll be announced tonight too.'

'Who are they, then?' asks Chester.

'I don't know myself,' Cynthia admits. 'They want social media to go wild later so it's been kept very hush-hush. Only those at the top know.'

So only Edwin Roberts, the artistic director, thinks Chloe.

'There's not much more I can tell you,' admits Cynthia. 'Just that we have some very exciting times ahead. It's going to be hard work. The press will be all over this, especially in light of ... well, the show's history. Some may think ... well, that the show should not come back. I want you to remain professional at all times. Journalists may try and get inside stories from you, but send them straight to me. In the meantime, make Beth feel welcome. She saw the original *Dust*...'

'I actually auditioned for the role of Esme,' says Beth, a little smug.

'Maybe,' whispers Nina in Chloe's ear, 'but she didn't *get* it.'

'Did you meet Morgan Miller?' asks Chester, eyes wide.

'I did.'

'Wow. What was she like?'

'It was only briefly. For about five minutes, before she went in and did that killer audition that got her the role.'

Interesting choice of words, thinks Chloe.

'She looked like she knew,' says Beth.

'Knew what?' asks Chloe, thinking of her murder.

'That she'd get the role of Esme. She was pretty arrogant.'

'I thought she was absolutely mesmerising,' says Chloe.

Beth shrugs as though to say *whatever*. Then adds, 'I don't see how can anyone compete with an actress who literally died for her art.'

'I'm sure the new actress will be tremendous in the role,' says Cynthia. 'Anyway, while I have you, I want to talk about the new radios.'

Remembering the eerie words she heard on the airwaves a week ago, Chloe asks, 'Has anyone else been getting interference on theirs?'

No one answers. A couple shake their heads. Maybe she imagined it after all?

But then what about the words on the mirror?

What about the footsteps on the stairs?

The woman?

That horrible bird?

Chloe shakes away the questions and tunes out. She closes her eyes and hums in her head the chorus of the main *Dust* song: *Forever, together, we are dust. Pieces of everything; pieces of all of us.* For a moment she is sure it drifts in through the open door behind them, from the corridor where stone steps lead down to the dressing rooms, a haunting, lyrical, female voice. One she knows, first heard twenty years ago on stage. Chloe feels a whisper of breath on her neck and glances at Chester, but he's absorbed in whatever Cynthia is saying. Beth looks at Chloe and that's when she smells it.

Pungent lavender perfume. On Beth. Exactly the same as she smelt backstage the other night.

The song dies.

'I think that's it then,' concludes Cynthia, pulling Chloe back into the room. 'Thanks for coming.'

'Who do you think killed Morgan Miller?' asks Beth as they pack up.

'How would *we* know?' says Paige. 'I wasn't even born then!'

'Did you work here back then?' Beth smiles at Chester. 'I think Cynthia did, didn't she?'

'Yes,' says Chester. 'But I had flu that first week. I dunno who killed Morgan. They interviewed the caretaker – can't remember his name. He wasn't arrested. Ruined his life though. Shit sticks and all that.'

Chloe moves closer to Beth, trying to smell her scent. 'Why are you checking if Ches worked here then?' she demands.

'Just being friendly. I've been coming here a while, you know.'

'Thought I knew you,' says Chester.

'I always thought her boyfriend, Clive, was an odd one,' says Beth. 'I read about them. They were the golden couple until she got the role in *Dust*. Apparently, things got a bit fierier after that, and they fell out. Jealous maybe.'

'Best theory I read,' says Nina, 'was that she was into some sort of witchcraft and made a deal with the devil to get the role of Esme Black; she hadn't realised the price she would have to pay.'

'Silliness like that had better not make it to the newspapers,' calls Cynthia on her way out of the room.

'Were you backstage the other night?' Chloe hisses at Beth when Cynthia has gone.

'Me?' Beth frowns.

'Yes, *you*. I smelt the perfume you're wearing now.'

'No, I wasn't.' Does Beth sound like she is protesting a little too heatedly? 'And lots of people wear this perfume.'

'I doubt it,' whispers Chester.

'Why would *I* be backstage?' asks Beth.

Chloe shrugs, realising she is interrogating a new usher. She walks out.

Chester follows her down the stairs, and she's glad.

'What's wrong?' he asks. 'What was that about? You sound … I dunno, upset. You OK?'

'Yes,' she snaps.

'Sure?'

'*Yes*,' she sighs, more gently. 'Just tired.'

'Don't you wish you could have auditioned?' he asks as she unlocks her bike. 'For *Dust*?'

'No.' It's the truth. She couldn't audition, even if there was the chance. It's a role where her arms would have to be on display. 'I wouldn't have a hope in hell. It's going to be someone big, not for a failed actress who has to usher just to get near a stage.'

She is safe as an usher though, in her long-sleeved black shirt and trousers.

'Oh, Chlo,' sighs Chester, squeezing her arm. 'Don't say that; you're a beautiful actress. I saw your *Les Misérables* audition for that amateur group. You were so … understated.'

Chloe smiles. 'Understated doesn't cut it these days. And I didn't get the part, remember.' She had been glad, knowing she would have turned it down anyway. She had just wanted to see if she could do it. And it turned out she couldn't. 'I prefer to write now. I've nearly finished the first draft of my script.'

It's a lie. It's barely an idea. And she hasn't looked at it for a while. But she doesn't tell Chester any of that.

'Really?' he says. 'I'd *love* to hear it.'

'Maybe when it's done.' Chloe feels shy.

'What's it called?'

'I don't know,' she lies.

'What's it about?' asks Chester.

'Lost love.' She laughs, embarrassed, and wheels her bike outside.

'Like *Dust*,' calls Chester, as she rides away.

7

THE GAME

2005

It was Ryan who suggested the game; floppy-haired, adventurous, charismatic Ryan.

He was always their leader, always the one up for anything. The previous summer he'd had them spend the night in a supposedly haunted warehouse on the docks; the summer before that he'd insisted they camp in local woods where a dead baby was rumoured to have been found wrapped in a blanket covered with satanic symbols.

Jess more or less agreed to most things he said, though she'd flick her golden curls and shrug as though it meant nothing, not really. Chloe could see through her nonchalance; she saw how much Jess studied Ryan when he played the clown with other girls. Jess would probably have played any game he wanted.

But in the summer of 2005, he wanted to do something much darker.

The three of them – Jess, Ryan and Chloe, all recently finished with their GCSEs – were at the youth theatre on such a sticky, hot July evening that drama teacher, Mr Hayes, had thrown open all the fire doors, desperate for a breeze.

Chloe had joined the drama group six years earlier, straight after she saw *Dust* and fell in love with the idea of being on the stage too. Jess joined at the same time; she went to the same school as Chloe, though they weren't particularly close, not until acting lessons united them. Ryan came much later, changing forever the dynamics of their close twosome. He went to a different school, but Jess made sure she caught his attention with snug vest tops over her pert chest, and short skirts.

Chloe thought that boys were so predictable. So easily captivated by a hint of flesh. So easily seduced by a carefully chosen lipstick or the flutter of eyelash. She preferred a bit of mystery. A challenge.

Not Ryan.

On that sticky summer night, once the two-hour rehearsal for the summer show, *Macbeth*, was done, most of the drama group left promptly, gulping bottles of water and fanning themselves with scripts. Ryan caught Chloe and Jess on their way down the stone stairs towards the clunky, wooden doors.

'Don't leave yet,' he hissed. 'Wait around the back for me.'

The youth theatre occupied an old church on a busy street parallel to the docks, where cheap cafés and rundown pubs competed for a dwindling clientele. Viewed from across the road, the grey building could have been straight out of *The Exorcist* or *The Amityville Horror*. Ryan had made them watch a marathon of old films last week; Chloe had slept with the lights on ever since.

'Why?' demanded Jess. 'James might be taking me home.' James was another drama student she toyed with, if only to make Ryan jealous.

'Trust me,' he said. 'I've got plans for this summer, and you wanna be involved.'

Jess fake-yawned, but Chloe knew they would be meeting Ryan near the skip behind the church.

'Let's get some cigs first,' said Jess.

'See you in a minute,' said Ryan, heading around the back.

The two girls went to the newsagent's opposite, where the elderly man didn't care how old they were and often sold them vodka as well as cigarettes. Many nights they had come here, just the two of them, and shared a small bottle in the nearby park, Chloe afraid to drink too much, Jess more daring.

Crossing the road to go back, Chloe looked up at the church

as they approached it, at the boarded-up, dome-shaped windows – most of them broken – and the turrets with ornate crosses soaring from their peaks. A glossy black bird perched on one of them, squawking harshly.

What was the rhyme? One for sadness, two for joy? Chloe scanned the roof for a second bird. No. Just one. Wasn't it supposed to be a magpie in the rhyme? Chloe had no idea what they looked like, so maybe this was just any old bird. No omen. No darkness. No need to feel nervous.

At the back of the building, on a pile of newspapers, Ryan sat smoking. His floppy blond hair particularly irritated Chloe tonight. Maybe it was just the heat. She knew how quickly Jess was going to agree to whatever he wanted to do.

'Let's go inside,' he said.

Jess opened her cigarettes and lit one. 'How? Everyone's gone. It's locked.'

'There isn't a lock in the world that can stop me.' Ryan got up and led them to the side of the church; the gap between it and the next building was claustrophobically narrow. 'Look at that window there. See? It's low enough to reach and it's never locked. I know because it leads to the boys' toilets.' He dropped his cigarette and ground it out with his foot. Then he edged sideways down the gap and disappeared through the window.

Without a word, just as Chloe knew she would, Jess followed.

For a moment, Chloe stood alone.

Afterwards, she would see herself there, brow damp in the heat, faded jeans covered in hand-drawn doodles of flowers and rainbows, nail polish chipped. And she would whisper from the future to that young girl: *Don't follow them. Go home. See your mum. Learn your lines. Concentrate on your craft. Don't follow them.*

But she did.

She followed them.

She dropped onto the tiled floor of the boys' toilets and went out into the corridor.

'Hey, where are you?' she called.

No answer.

'Come on, guys. Don't mess around.'

Chloe had never liked the darkness that the boarded-up windows created. The place always smelt damp, and every floorboard creaked. She moved carefully along the corridor towards the theatre, opening the heavy door with an agonising scrape. This cavernous room was where parishioners once worshipped; where rows of wooden pews now served as seats for those watching a show rather than a sermon. The altar had been ripped out and replaced with a wooden stage, with crimson velvet curtains that took an immense effort to open and close. Here, on these boards, young actors craved the reverence once given to long-gone priests.

Chloe walked down the aisle towards the stage, afraid.

Breath on her neck.

She spun around.

Nothing. Just her overactive imagination.

But she often felt it in here.

She reached the stage and climbed the steps to the left. Someone had left the spotlight on, and it burned her face. She held up an arm to block it out and looked at the rows of empty seats. In the current show, *Macbeth*, Chloe was one of the unnamed witches. She rarely got glamorous parts, and though this was an important role she couldn't help but think that it was the story of her life so far: a nameless character. Jess was playing the ruthless Lady Macbeth with gusto. Ryan, of course, was Macbeth himself.

'Chloe!' Two hands grabbed her.

'*Shit.*' She fell to her knees.

Jess and Ryan helped her up, weak with laughter.

'Your face,' cried Ryan. 'Who the fuck did you *think* it was?'

'Nothing. No one.' Chloe's heart raced.

'You looked like that when we watched *The Exorcist*,' he laughed.

'Oh, fuck off.' Chloe stormed off the stage and sat in the front pew, arms crossed, scowling. It didn't feel natural to be so stroppy. She was always the smiley one. The *nice* one. The people-pleaser. But Ryan had been annoying her recently. 'Are you gonna tell us your plan then?' she demanded. 'If we get caught in here, we're in big trouble, you know.'

'Ooooh, *big trouble*,' mocked Ryan, from the stage.

Jess stayed there, at his side, a hand just inches from his, as though she might hold it if she dared; if they were alone. Sharing the spotlight, they could have been Romeo and Juliet. Cosette and Marius. Esme and Chevalier. Chloe ached with jealousy. It was another alien emotion. She seemed to be feeling so many recently.

'What's the plan for this summer, then?' Jess asked.

She finally moved away from Ryan and joined Chloe on the pews. Basking in his small audience's attention, Ryan paced the wooden floor, then stopped suddenly and turned to face them with a dramatic swing.

'We're going to play a game,' he said.

'A game?' Jess asked with a flirty smile.

'Not *that* kind of game.' He grinned at her. 'It is a bit sexy though...'

'Have you played it before?' Jess said, a suggestive tone to her question.

'I've done it on my own,' he admitted.

'And?' asked Chloe in spite of herself.

'Nothing happened.'

'You sure?' laughed Jess.

'You need at least two people,' explained Ryan.

'I've heard.' Jess again.

'More than two is even better. Three is perfect. Something to do with being connected to the divine or some shit. I thought of us...'

'I'm not spending my summer playing daft games.' Chloe stood up, sick of Ryan, sick of her own strange grumpiness. Why couldn't he fuck off and leave her and Jess to spend more time together? 'We're sixteen, not six.' She turned to leave.

'Did you hear about Daniel Locke and Harry Bond?' he asked.

Chloe stopped. She looked at Jess; she wasn't smiling now.

'What's that got to do with it?' Chloe asked softly.

Earlier that year, throughout April, Daniel and Harry had dominated the local news headlines. Daniel had died after walking out onto the A63 in the middle of the night; Harry had been in a secure mental-health unit ever since. The speculation about what had led to his tragic suicide included devil worship, drug abuse, demonic possession, and a bizarre game of dare.

'They went to my school,' said Ryan.

'*No*,' whispered Chloe and Jess simultaneously.

'Yes. And it wasn't any of the things they said in the papers.'

'How do you know?' asked Jess.

'And what *was* it?' asked Chloe after a beat.

'I know because I've spoken to the third person involved.' For the first time during his time on the stage, Ryan stepped out of the spotlight. For a moment, he was a silhouette. 'Three was what made it work, like I said.'

'Made *what* work?' demanded Jess

A master of any role he played, Ryan strung out the suspense; he walked slowly and purposefully down the steps and stood in front of the two girls, legs spread. 'There was a girl who never made the headlines: Amelia Bennett. She seemed to escape unhurt. But she wouldn't talk about what happened.'

'So how do *you* know?' asked Jess.

'I have my ways.'

Chloe shook her head at Ryan's cockiness.

'We got drunk together once, and she told me that there's always one person who gets out of it OK. One person who seems to have some sort of spiritual strength or magic, or whatever you want to call it.' He paused, then added dramatically, 'Apparently, they pay in other ways though.' Ryan laughed suddenly, making them jump. 'Look, I don't know if I believe any of that crap. But there's only one way to find out...'

'What did they do?' asked Jess softly.

'A Ouija board,' said Ryan.

'A *Ouija* board?' repeated Chloe.

She shivered; she had heard of one. Had been warned by her mum never to use one, especially not in the house, though when asked why, her mum couldn't answer. Chloe's cousin once said during a sleepover that she had known someone who used one, and they'd ended up being possessed by a demon. Though Chloe dismissed this as a ghost story invented to scare her, she lay awake all night afterwards. The words *Ouija board* had been whispered with reverence and fear by kids at school who shared tales of friends of friends of friends who had done them and been spooked. No one seemed to quite know exactly what had happened or could directly name those involved, but Chloe knew it was a bad idea.

'Isn't that what people use to speak to the dead?' asked Jess.

'Yes. And we're going to do it here.' Ryan gestured at the stage.

'How does it work? What do we do?'

'You can get an actual board game with a planchette and everything set out, but I'm not paying forty quid. We can improvise, make our own. We just need a glass, a flat surface, and some the letters of the alphabet written on pieces of ca—'

'But someone *died*,' cried Chloe.

'We don't know if that was really because of a Ouija board, or if Daniel Locke was just a troubled teenager. Unless I wanted to, nothing on earth would get me to walk in front of a fucking lorry.'

'You called it a game,' said Chloe. 'But that isn't how I've heard it described. It's not something fun. It's supposed to be dangerous.'

'I like "game"', grinned Ryan. 'Sounds, I dunno ... edgy.'

'How does it actually work?' asked Jess.

'We all put our fingers on an upturned glass and ask to speak to the spirits, and the glass moves from letter to letter, spelling out what the dead are saying.' Ryan paused. 'Are you two in?'

'Not me.' Chloe again made as if to leave.

Ryan shrugged. 'We can ask someone else.'

Chloe looked at Jess for back-up, but she couldn't take her eyes off him.

'I have to go,' said Chloe. 'If you guys wanna hang out and do something less insane this summer, let me know.'

She hoped Jess would follow her. She reached the door and looked back. The two of them were deep in conversation, oblivious to her aching heart. Chloe climbed out of the tiny window in the boys' toilets and edged along the gap. As she walked around to the front, she glanced at the steps leading up to the main doors.

What was *that*?

Chloe approached the black lump on the top step. When she realised what it was, she recoiled with a gasp. The bird. Its sleek, black wings were bent at an awkward angle like some sort of mechanical toy gone wrong, and its head was smashed and bloody. A dead eye stared coldly at her. Chloe looked up at the roof. Was it definitely the one from earlier? How horrible.

It filled her with sickly dread.

As she rode the bus home, she couldn't get it out of her head. And doing a Ouija board – or playing the 'game', as Ryan insisted on calling it – screamed trouble to her. But Chloe knew Jess was besotted with Ryan and would do absolutely anything he asked. She knew Jess would play his so-called game.

Recently she'd been watching Jess studying Ryan while he rehearsed for *Macbeth*. She knew what her gaze meant; even if Jess flicked her hair dismissively, her pink cheeks and that rapturous look belied the depth of her true feelings.

Chloe felt like this too.

For Jess.

Oh, Jess.

And she would do anything *she* asked...

8

CHLOE'S ROOM

JANUARY 2019

When she gets home – a flat shared with two students, James and Jennie – Chloe escapes to her room. She avoids the tall mirror on the back of her door, afraid she might see those seven words again; words that stir something sickly in her stomach. How is it that when she tries to visualise where she first saw them – long ago – they fade like old letters in the sun? Is it that she has forgotten them – or that she *buried* them?

Instead a face pops into her head – Jess.

Jess Swanson.

Gosh, Jess. Why her face? Why now?

Chloe sees her, pink-cheeked, blonde-haired, smoking a ciga-rette, and laughing at ... who? Of course; at Ryan. At some joke he's telling. This memory is vivid. It comes for the first time since ... when was it? A hot summer? Yes. Chloe smells the celebrity perfume Jess used to wear; the coconut conditioner that made Chloe breathless when she got close enough; the nail polish they took turns applying. What did the three of them get up to? Wasn't that the last year they went to the youth theatre?

Yes.

She suddenly sees them there, sitting on a dusty stage, candles flickering, an eternal trio of hurt. Because she loved Jess, but Jess loved Ryan, and Ryan loved only himself. The feelings are suddenly acute. Here. Now.

Still.

Hasn't she used such feelings in her new script?

Chloe reaches under her bed and pulls out the wooden box, now scratched and faded. She sits with it in her lap. Then she unhooks the latch and opens it. Inside are mementoes from the past; pictures she never bothered framing, tickets from her favourite theatre visits, flyers signed by actors and directors. At the bottom is the CD she wants. On the cover gold, swirly script reads '*Dust – the Musical*'. Chloe remembers how she knew all the songs. How she and Jess sang them together. How she would listen to the title track and imagine her and Jess together. In love. In the dark. Kissing.

Didn't they once kiss?

Maybe.

She plays the CD.

She turns the volume down after a while and starts checking the social media feeds on her phone, waiting for the big announcement at nine o'clock.

Then she goes back into the wooden box and takes out the knife.

DUST

Midnight for an hour,

I'm yours.

We dance in the shadows,

in the halls.

Midnight for an hour,

feel my touch.

When you dance with me,

I'm not lost.

I'm still here; I am dust.
I'm those fragments in the air,
the gold light dancing there,
that breeze from nowhere.
Forever, together, we are dust.
Pieces of everything;
pieces of all of us.
Dust.

When the dust settles,
and they all sleep,
we dance and love and kiss.
We live the dream.
You light me up
like a dawn I'll never see.
I light you up
and set you free.

I'm still here; I am dust.
I'm those fragments in the air,
the gold light dancing there,
that breeze from nowhere.
Forever, together, we are dust.
Pieces of everything;
pieces of all of us.
Dust.

9

THE GAME

2005

Chloe dreamed about the dead bird.

In the nights after Ryan suggested using the Ouija board, she woke in a cold sweat, despite the heat, sure the glossy, black creature was in her bedroom. She'd hear a scratch-scratch-scratching and a rustle-rustle-rustling and hide under the duvet until it subsided. Then it took hours to get back to sleep and she woke late, cranky, which was unlike her.

At breakfast, Chloe's dad laughed at her stuck-up hair.

'You get out of bed the wrong side, sweetheart?' smiled her mum.

'How could I?' snapped Chloe. 'There's a wall on the wrong side.'

Chloe arrived twenty minutes late to the next youth theatre drama group, and *Macbeth* rehearsals were already under way. Mr Hayes must have opened the fire doors again because a gentle breeze cooled Chloe's damp brow. Dust fragments danced in the stage lights. She paused at the back and took in the scene. As the lead character, Ryan marched the wooden boards, swathed in a stained, purple velvet cloak, chipped gold crown atop his blond hair. It occurred to Chloe – not for the first time – that this must be the one place he got attention. As one of nine boys, living in a three-bedroom council house with a single mum, it must have been crowded at home.

Jess was in the front pew, watching him – utterly entranced – and chewing bubble gum. She didn't even notice as Chloe slid into the seat next to her. Eventually Ryan finished his soliloquy, took an ostentatious bow and disappeared.

Jess seemed surprised to see Chloe there. 'Where were you?' she asked, blowing a pink bubble.

'I missed my bus.'

'We need to talk after rehearsals.'

Chloe would happily have talked to Jess for hours, about anything she wanted. She wished it was just the two of them; that Ryan would be spotted by a talent scout and fuck off to London or somewhere so she and Jess could have a wonderful summer together. When Jess was in the room – *any* room – Chloe didn't want to leave it. The way she felt about her was a little bit like pain; it hurt when she saw anyone else speaking to her, it hurt to know that it was unlikely Jess felt the same way; and it hurt to know that she would have to carry these feelings around inside her forever.

'Me and Ryan tried it,' Jess whispered, close to Chloe's ear, breath tantalisingly warm.

'Tried what?' Chloe burned with acute jealousy.

'The *game*,' hissed Jess. 'The Ouija board. We came back here the other night.'

Was that all they had done?

'Nothing happened,' said Jess as though answering the question. Chloe realised she was still referring to the Ouija board. 'We really do need three of us. Ryan keeps saying three is more powerful than two. He's right cos we tried for an hour. He brought a glass and some alphabet letters and the words "Goodbye", "Hello", "Yes", and "No" on bits of card. But nothing happened.' Jess nudged her playfully; Chloe loved the flirtatiousness of it. 'How can you *not* want to join us? We need you. *I* need you.'

Chloe knew when Jess looked intensely at her through darkened eyelashes that she would join them. This might be the only way to see her over the summer. In that moment Chloe would have jumped into a churning whirlpool of hot acid for her.

'I don't know,' she lied, enjoying Jess pleading with her.

'Stay, tonight, after this. *Go on*. I really have a feeling that you'll make the difference.'

'You do?'

'Yes. I can't explain it, but when me and Ryan sat on the stage the other night, I just knew it wouldn't happen. I kept thinking, *we need Chloe; then it will*.' Jess paused and touched Chloe's arm tenderly. 'Remember Ryan said something about one person being the sort of magic one? Well, I feel like that's you.'

The sort of magic one...

Grandma Rosa used to affectionately call her a magic girl. Used to talk to her in a way that was just between them. Chloe missed her acutely. It had only been a year since she'd died, and tears began to build at the thought of her. So Chloe lapped up Jess's words, not caring if it was probably just a way of getting her on board. 'OK then.' She pretended to give in reluctantly.

Chloe didn't say that she had done some research already. Not about Ouija boards. No. *That* she had decided to do another time. When she typed the two words into a search engine the other night, a bird suddenly hit her bedroom window, making her leap out of the chair with a shriek.

'Are you OK, sweetie?' her mum had called up the stairs.

'Yes! Just a ... a... spider.'

Chloe had deleted the two words. Waited for her heart to calm. Stared at the screen. Then typed in 'power of three'. She found a website dedicated to the number three, which it turned out was powerful for many reasons. Bad luck was said to come in threes, and spells were also more potent when recited thrice. The page mentioned the third dimension, the Holy Trinity, and the three witches in *Macbeth*.

I'm one of them, Chloe thought.

She had remembered when Mr Hayes told them at an early re-hearsal that the witches' speeches were full of numbers. They often chanted things three times. When they concocted their famous spell, they began with two references to the number three.

For a moment Chloe had imagined herself, Ryan, and Jess dressed up as the three of them, cackling around a Ouija board. She shook her head at the image and read about how three wishes are always granted in fairy tales; how three is a complete cycle, with a beginning, a middle, and an end; eternal; forever; always. She leaned closer to read a passage about how using three in some way means great power.

Chloe had whispered aloud the next paragraph, alone in her room, 'Those who form an eternal trio must understand its full potential and use it in the way it was intended. With this power, there is much responsibility. The power of three should only be used for good. If not, then the power of evil is tripled...'

Chloe had shut her laptop.

Shaken her head.

She preferred the idea of the power of two; her and Jess, no Ryan.

Now, Ryan joined Chloe and Jess in the front pew, velvet cloak gone, hair askew.

'She's going to do it,' smiled Jess, and Chloe buried the feeling that she had somehow been tricked, that Ryan and Jess had planned this all along.

'Ace. Let's do it tonight. The stuff is here.'

'Right,' interrupted Mr Hayes, clapping his hands with gusto. He was the typical drama coach, dressed as though playing the part of one in a film, with a curled moustache, ruddy cheeks, and an ostentatious quilted jacket, just too tight. 'I want to do the Lady Macbeth scene where she asks the supernatural spirits to give her the power of a man. Jess! You're up!'

At the end of the session, as the other students departed, the three teens hung around the back by the bins. Jess smoked and twirled her hair around her fingers. When he was sure the building was empty, Ryan led the way along the narrow alley and climbed in through the window.

Once inside the theatre, they filed along the aisle towards the stage, Ryan leading, as he always did, Jess next – neatly between the two of them – and Chloe last. Chloe felt for a brief moment like perhaps she was not last after all; that someone else had followed them into the room.

She turned. No one. The door was ajar though. Hadn't she shut it after them? She was *sure* she had. Distracted, she crashed into Jess, who crashed into Ryan.

'Fuck,' he cried. 'Watch where you're going!'

'Sorry,' said Chloe. 'I thought...'

'What?'

'Nothing.'

The three of them faced the stage. Costumes had been dumped on its edge; crowns and swords were scattered as though abandoned after battle. The velvet curtains hung askew, one a quarter across its rail, the other pulled back fully. Chloe wanted to straighten the loose one. The cheap LED floodlights were still on and the whole stage was coloured red. Like blood.

'Where's the stuff then?' asked Jess.

Ryan climbed the steps and disappeared behind the open curtain. Chloe heard him rummaging around, and she and Jess joined him. He pulled a sturdy glass tumbler and a shoe box from the metal cabinet where scripts and props were kept.

'Is it safe in there?' asked Jess.

'Where else should we keep it?' demanded Ryan. 'I'm not taking this shit home.'

'Why not?' asked Chloe.

'You're not supposed to.'

'Why?'

'You're never *ever* supposed to do a Ouija board in your own home.'

That was what Chloe's mum had said.

'But we won't be,' said Jess.

'I know.' Ryan spoke to her like she was a little kid. 'But I reckon that applies to where you keep anything you use. And if this really does work, well, I don't want it in my house. Do *you*?'

'No.' Jess shook her head vigorously.

'No,' agreed Chloe, thinking of the bird hitting her window. 'Why shouldn't you do one in your own home though?'

'If you get a negative spirit, it could haunt you forever.'

'But it's OK to do that *here*?' Chloe murmured the words.

'Better here than where I bloody live,' cried Ryan. He sat down, cross-legged, in the middle of the stage. 'Come on then. We need to sit in a circle. All of us.'

Jess joined him. He placed the glass upside-down, in between them. Then, from the shoe box, he took a stubby candle stuck to a white saucer and some matches. He lit the candle, and the flame flickered. Chloe looked back at the door, for the draught. But it was closed. She frowned.

'Come on then,' snapped Ryan.

She joined them.

'I bet Daniel Locke and Harry Bond didn't take it seriously,' said Ryan. 'I bet they broke the rules, and that's why one of them ended up dead and the other in a psych ward.'

'What *are* the rules?' asked Jess at the same time as Chloe said, 'Shit, I'm not sure we should do this.'

'We'll get to the rules,' said Ryan, dismissing Jess and glaring at Chloe. 'You don't *have* to do it,' he said to her. She wondered for a moment if he knew how she felt about Jess. 'We can get someone else to make up our threesome.'

He does, thought Chloe. *He knows it, and he knows Jess loves him.*

'Look,' he said, more gently. 'We can decide how we do this. All of us. It's up to us. I'll tell you the rules of how we're supposed to do it, and then we can discuss what we do if something none of us likes happens. OK?'

Chloe shrugged.

Jess nodded.

Ryan smiled.

'OK,' he said. 'This is just from what I've—'

'Hang on a minute,' said Chloe, frowning. 'You should *know* the rules. Didn't you guys do it already?'

Jess avoided her eyes.

'No,' said Ryan, clearly confused.

'But you told m—'

Jess interrupted her. 'I'm sorry. I told you we had and that it failed so you'd do it with us. I really want you to be part of this.'

Chloe didn't know whether to be angry that Jess had deceived her – or thrilled at how much she wanted her to be with them.

'You're here now,' said Ryan. 'That's all that matters. So – the rules. First of all, night is the best time to do it as there's less interference in the atmosphere.'

'By night, do you mean when it's dark?' asked Jess.

'Don't know.' Ryan clearly didn't like being interrupted. 'But it's dark in here, even if it isn't outside, and technically it's night.'

He took a pile of small squares of paper from the shoe box. As he spoke, he arranged them in a neat circle. They were the letters from A to Z, printed neatly in black capitals. Four large square papers came next and had the words 'Hello', 'Goodbye', 'Yes', 'and 'No' on them. These Ryan put in a square inside the circle; in the centre he placed the glass.

'Candles create atmosphere,' he continued. 'TVs and radios should be off. It's best to have the Ouija board in your lap, not on a table, but we can't do that. One person should be the questioner – I'll do that – though you can both ask me to ask stuff too. Another one of us should write stuff down, because apparently, it's very easy to forget what happens. I read this one story online where the kids who did a Ouija board said that once it was over, unless they all met up and talked about it, none of them could quite remember it properly afterwards.'

'How is that possible?' asked Jess.

'Dunno. But they swore down that it was like that. One of them said it was as though, when he saw the others, this curtain was lifted, and they could all remember.'

Chloe glanced at the velvet curtains.

'So who's gonna write?' asked Ryan.

'I will,' offered Chloe.

Ryan reached into the shoebox and took out a notepad and pen. Chloe took it from him.

'Who are we going to be speaking to?' asked Jess.

'What do you mean?' Ryan frowned at her.

'When you ask these questions – who do you ask?'

'The spirits. The dead. Those on the other side.'

'In heaven, you mean?'

'No, not there,' grinned Ryan.

Jess glanced at Chloe. The candle stilled.

'Where then?'

'Those who are just ... like... in between... who never really went anywhere... and those in...'

'*Where?*' asked Jess.

'Hell.' Ryan grinned. 'Your face! No, seriously, it's mostly just poor souls who don't know where they've gone after dying. But the reason we have to be careful is that, sometimes, dark entities can access us once we open this door – that's what they call it when you open yourself up by doing a Ouija board.'

'Shit.' Jess shivered.

'I don't even know if I believe it anyway!' laughed Ryan.

'Why are we doing it then?' asked Chloe.

'In case it *does* work. Look, we're following the rules to protect us. And if it does work and we don't like the way it is going, and a spirit seems evil or something, then we close it down. We're in control.' Ryan spoke as though performing a soliloquy. Chloe had to admit that, in the sputtering light, he was utterly mesmerising. 'If any spirits threaten us, we end it. This is all from what I read, OK? I'll have to try and remember it all. Here goes ... We should go into this with good intentions. We should be polite and respect the dead. We should know that the spirits can lie so not take every-thing seriously. We should avoid topics like asking when we might die – who wants to know *that*? – and we never use our own names. And we should never, *ever*, under any circumstances ask one of them to possess us.'

'Why?' whispered Jess, eyes wide.

Ryan laughed. 'Why do you think?'

'Oh.'

'When it's all over,' continued Ryan, 'we should never leave the board unless the spirit has said goodbye.'

'Aloud?' asked Jess, looking horrified.

'No,' laughed Ryan. 'By them moving the glass here to "Goodbye". If they don't say goodbye, well, that means they're still here ... and we can't just leave them like that...'

'So what do we actually do?' asked Chloe.

'First, we all put a finger on the glass,' said Ryan.

'Which one?' asked Jess.

'The one on your hand,' laughed Ryan, and she shoved him. 'Like this,' he said, putting an index finger on top of the glass.

Jess followed, putting hers next to his.

Chloe paused. She felt sure someone had inhaled next to her. She looked around. Had the curtain moved? Was that what she had felt? This was the moment when she should decide not to follow. To get up and leave.

But she didn't.

Chloe put her finger on the glass.

But she couldn't get the dead bird out of her head.

10

CHLOE'S ROOM

JANUARY 2019

Chloe lies on her bed and holds up the knife, moving it slowly so the lamplight slides along its sharp edge like a sunrise on an ocean horizon. The haunting lyrics from *Dust* die out. She puts the CD back in the wooden box, turns the radio on, and lies down again; not long until the cast for the new show will be announced.

In her hands, the knife is a danger.

It's absolute temptation.

The want is still there; the *need*. The desire to drag the blade across puckered skin, to sever flesh until blood flows, is still there. But she won't surrender. No; she has resisted for six months now and she can resist again tonight. Still, the silver shimmer as she holds the knife to the light and gets lost in its tease whispers words of warm willing – calls out to her, offers release.

Just like with the blackouts, Chloe can't remember exactly when the cutting started. Was she a teen? Yes. Maybe sixteen. She sees herself in a flash – hiding away in her bedroom, posters of The Pussycat Dolls and Kelly Clarkson plastered all over her walls, their albums playing on repeat, knife in her hand, drawing blood from her own thigh with a sharp gasp. Was that the first time? What had made her do it? How sad she is for that girl. Who *was* the young woman who did that? Not the happy, smiley kid she had been before.

Before what?

Before *what*?

That, Chloe can't recall.

The bleeding that randomly started the other night in the theatre had stopped by the time she got home. She had soaked her damp trousers, hoping to save them. She has never bled without cutting before. She was addicted to the sharp pleasure – the exquisite release – that self-harming gave for a long time; for years. When she was overwhelmed with feelings – that she wasn't good enough, didn't quite fit in, wasn't a success – that nick of pain, followed by a trickle of blood, released the emotion. Somehow, once the blood was freed, she felt better – euphoric even. But she had to do it again within days. When her thighs were a criss-cross of red, she cut her upper arms, and when they were a mess too, she cut her stomach.

The brain can't feel the two types of pain at once, so the physical hurt cancels out the emotional. After a while, though, she got used to the pain. The euphoria died. But by then, Chloe was addicted to the act.

She was never sure if she was trying to face her feelings – or obliterate them.

But it meant she could smile.

She could outwardly be the smiley, happy Chloe she had once truthfully been.

Now, she has gone from cutting every day to every other, from twice a week to once a week, from once to hardly ever, to never. With the help of an online support group, she has weaned herself off the bloody addiction. But she still needs to hold the knife occasionally; to squeeze it like a grieving mother might the bootie of a lost child. But there's always immense danger in doing so. The chance she might give in again.

The radio presenter – Stephen Sainty on WLCR – interrupts Chloe's thoughts:

'Let's get another song and then the big news of the day, including the latest from the Dean Wilson Theatre. You don't want to miss this...'

She puts the knife back in the wooden box, beneath her mementoes. Her mum and dad have never known about the cutting.

When she was younger, she refused to go to the beach on holidays, letting them believe it was typical teen angst – thinking she was fat. Now, in summer, when everyone else is wearing short or sleeveless tops, Chloe thinks she sees her mum staring at her long sleeves and trousers with sad eyes.

The *shame* is intense; it's as heavy as a cheap, itchy coat and can't be easily shrugged off. Some people at her online support group have reached a point of acceptance and display their limbs proudly, but Chloe isn't there yet. The ugly zig-zag of scars – some just white lines, others 3-D and less easy to conceal – are why Chloe has never had a long-term relationship. Who could possibly love her with skin like this? Who would understand, when she herself doesn't fully?

Two years ago she dated an actress who was in the Christmas show – Ellen, who played a flamboyant Tinkerbell – but Chloe froze when things went further than kissing, and neither of them addressed it. Ellen left to go and sing in London.

Chloe thinks again of Jess Swanson.

'*Jess*,' she whispers to the room.

She sees her gorgeous, smiling face in the flicker of candlelight. Hears the pop of pink bubble gum. Smells cigarettes and cheap perfume, and something she can't identify. Where were they? When *was* it? Why is Jess suddenly so vivid now when she hasn't been for years? Chloe wonders what Jess is doing now. She has searched for her a few times online in the past and found nothing. Did she go to RADA in London as she dreamed of doing? Or did she do something completely different – after all, we often don't end up living our childhood dreams. Did she find love? Get married? Have kids?

Would Jess mind Chloe's scars?

Would she kiss them better?

Stephen Sainty's words on the radio pull Chloe from the thoughts.

'Well,' he says in a rich voice, 'after months of wild speculation as to whether the Dean Wilson Theatre would do it, I can announce that, yes ... *yes*, they are. This evening I'm very excited to share with you that *Dust,* the musical that launched them, will return this September for the twentieth anniversary of the theatre's opening.'

Chloe sits higher up on the bed.

'It will run for a full month,' continues Stephen, 'and tickets will be on sale from nine am tomorrow. I never got to see it back in 1999. Did you? Were you part of the production? Did you go more than once? Did you know any of the cast? Do phone in and let me know if you were part of it in any way. I'd love to hear how you feel about its return.'

Chloe is curious too.

'Of course,' says Stephen more softly, 'we can't avoid mentioning the *real* reason the show has never been performed anywhere for twenty years – the fact that Morgan Miller, who took on the iconic role of Esme Black, was murdered in her dressing room during the interval on the fourth night. Do you think it's right that the show returns when her murder remains unsolved? Should the Dean Wilson Theatre leave well alone and have some respect for her family? Is this just a way to boost ticket sales after a disastrous run of mediocre shows? Call in and let me know what you think on the usual numbers, or message me on Twitter. Make sure you use the *Dust* hashtag. After the break, we'll have the list of big names taking part in the show. You don't want to miss that...'

Chloe checks Twitter on her phone for comments, using the *#Dust* hashtag.

Bring it back I say! Can't bloody wait! #Dust

Wonder which actress will dare take on #EsmeBlack #Dust

I won't go see it. Just horrible. #Dust

Disgusting. Next they'll be telling us Madeleine McCann is going to play the lead role. #Dust #DontBringItBack

Chloe is disgusted by the mention of that poor, still-missing girl. What is *wrong* with people?

Should she share what she thinks of the show's return? What would she say? Is she happy that it's returning? She's not even sure. She worries that it might ruin her memory of the original; that the new *Dust* won't come close to the magic she witnessed that first night at the theatre.

Stephen Sainty's rich voice fills the room again: 'OK, folks, it's time for the next big announcement of the evening, and you're hearing it first, here on WLCR. *So* ... who will take on the roles of Gerard Chevalier and Esme Black in *Dust*?'

Chloe realises she is holding her breath.

'I can announce,' says Stephen, 'that West End superstar, John Marrs – who has been wowing audiences for the past six months as The Phantom in *The Phantom of the Opera* – will take on the role of Gerard Chevalier.' Stephen pauses, as though for dramatic effect. 'Chosen for his ability to transcend any part he undertakes, agent Roberta Green said, "Marrs is perfect. He will resurrect Chevalier and bring his own, unique slant to the part." I agree. Not only will he bring in the crowds, but I reckon he'll make *Dust* his own.'

Chloe isn't sure; Marrs' scandalous affairs have dominated the headlines far more than his work recently. She can't deny that he will make a powerful Chevalier, but will he bring the magic? Yes. Yes, he will. She saw him in *West Side Story* five years ago and he made a passionate Tony.

She refreshes her Twitter feed.

O.M.G #JohnMarrs I definitely would! #Dust

This just got HUGE! #JohnMarrs #Dust

John Marrs couldn't carry a box of chocolates never mind the role of Chevalier! #Dust

Chloe wonders who'll carry Esme though.

'I know you're all wondering about Esme Black,' says Stephen. 'Well, that's the biggest surprise of all. Producers have gone with a lesser-known, rising star. Apparently, much like Morgan Miller twenty years ago, she blew them away with her audition. So, who is she? Her name is Ginger Swanson and she's a thirty-year-old actress whose other roles have included small parts in *Wicked* and *The Sound of Music*.'

Chloe has never heard of her, but she frowns at the surname. She refreshes Twitter again.

Who the hell is she? #GingerSwanson #Dust

She. Is. Hot. #GingerSwanson

Wasn't she that slag off #EastEnders #Dust

'Swanson has released a statement, saying that this is a life-changing opportunity for her,' continues Stephen, 'especially since the role is not only her biggest so far, but it will bring her back home. She said that she can't wait to return and show her home-town what she can do.'

Chloe's heart contracts. Hometown? It *can't* be. She types 'Ginger Swanson' into the search engine on her phone and waits for the images to load. Then she clicks on the first one, a black-and-white portrait on Wikipedia, and there she is, smiling enigmatically, head turned slightly away from the photographer, blonde hair teased into soft waves, lips moist and dark.

It's her.

Jess.

Jess Swanson.

Despite the differences – ones that could be due to subtle surgery – it is clearly the teenager that Chloe last saw ... when? When was it? Her mouth is perfect, much fuller than Chloe remembers; the eyebrows are sculpted into gentle arcs; the cheekbones are defined; the chin more pointed. But her eyes – those are the same.

I got lost in them, thinks Chloe.

I still am.

Jess Swanson, her first love, is coming back to Hull. To the Dean Wilson Theatre. Chloe can't quite believe it. Will she remember her? Then she feels a twinge of shame, of embarrassment. Jess – no, *Ginger* now – is returning as a star. As Esme Black. And

Chloe is just an usher with an unfinished script in her bottom drawer.

She reaches for the wooden box.

For the knife.

No.

No. Reach for something else. Reach for...

Chloe takes out her laptop, clicks on the file unopened for weeks. She looks at the title page. *She Haunts Me* by Chloe Dee. Why doesn't she finish it? Hell, she needs to start it properly. What is she afraid of?

Because I don't know how it's supposed to end, she thinks.

Jess Swanson is coming back.

Maybe she will find out.

11

THE GAME

2005

Once their three fingers touched the upturned glass, Chloe sensed that none of them were sure if they should proceed. She looked at Jess, face red in the LED lights, and then Ryan, frowning at the letters on the makeshift Ouija board as though willing something to happen right away.

Chloe pictured them again as the three witches in *Macbeth*. She knew all the lines, all the spells. But you never say the play title aloud in a theatre. Not ever. The reason you have to call it 'the Scottish play' instead is because it's believed that the witches' incantations were adapted from actual books of black magic; that they could bring real evil to life.

Was that what Chloe, Jess and Ryan were going to find?

'What now?' asked Jess.

'How am I supposed to write with one hand?' asked Chloe, realising how hard this would be.

'Can you two just *relax*?' snapped Ryan. His brow was damp, and Chloe wondered if it was more than the heat from the lights. 'We're not supposed to take our fingers off the glass at any point during this so...'

'Why?' asked Jess.

'It breaks the connection. So, if you need to do anything or ask something else, let's get it out of the way first.'

'Shall we turn the stage lights off?' said Jess, looking as flustered as him.

'That's bad luck too,' whispered Chloe.

Anyone involved in the theatre knew that you never leave a stage entirely dark. Superstition has it that mischievous spirits will play pranks on a darkened stage, so most companies leave a light on at all times.

'We've got the candle,' said Jess. 'And it's still light outside – not that much gets through the window boards.'

Sighing, Ryan got up and went to the small technician's table in the corner, behind the rows of pews. He flicked a switch and the room descended into sputtering shadows. All they had to see by was a line of fading sun between the window boards and the stubby candle's flame. In this dimness, everything looked different; more ominous; the colour of nightmares. Even the dust particles seemed to pirouette more malevolently.

Ryan rejoined them. 'Right,' he said with obvious impatience. 'Chloe, can you put the notepad next to you and write that way while the finger of your non-writing hand is on the glass?'

'I suppose. It might be a bit of a scrawl though.'

'We can write it up properly later,' Ryan sighed.

'How long will it take?' asked Jess.

'How long will *what* take?'

'This. I mean, how long do we have to do it for it to work?'

'It might not work this time,' said Ryan. 'It might not work *ever*. But we won't know until we try. It can take a bit of practice. We probably need to do it at least three times a week to really get things going.'

'So nothing's gonna happen tonight?' asked Jess.

'Look, I don't know. It might. Depends if anyone is...'

'What?' asked Chloe.

'*Open.*'

'You mean among the spirits?'

'No. Among us three.'

'Oh.' Chloe wondered if he had one of them in mind.

'Are we ready, then?' asked Ryan.

Chloe and Jess nodded.

'OK, fingers back on the glass.'

They placed them carefully, as if they were expecting a manicure. Chloe frowned. Was that an electric surge as her fingertip touched the cold base? Did she imagine it? Maybe. Her hair tickled her cheek as though someone had blown on her. She looked for the source of the draught, hating how dark the room was without the red floodlights. The door was closed. Had it been closed the last time she looked? She couldn't remember. Their three shadows swayed like bad, grey, drunken versions of the real them.

'Are you ready then?' asked Ryan.

Jess nodded. Chloe couldn't get over how hot her extended finger felt; she wanted to rip it away, not do this, not follow.

But *was* she following?

Why did it now feel like she was leading?

As if her finger had been there first?

'OK, we have to move the glass in a circular motion,' said Ryan.

In the candlelight, Jess's face was rapt. Chloe's heart felt tight with jealousy.

'Follow my guidance,' Ryan went on. 'We need to push it gently around the circle a few times to warm it up.'

Chloe felt the glass move and wondered for a moment if it was Ryan's doing, or if something had worked already. She could imagine that it would. The heat along her finger, the breath she was sure she'd felt on her neck earlier, the dead bird – it all had her believing something would happen. That *anything* could happen.

When they had moved the glass around inside the circle of letters a few times, Ryan stopped it in the centre, between the words 'Hello', 'Goodbye', 'Yes', and 'No'.

'OK,' he said and inhaled.

They inhaled with him; a collective preparation.

'Is there anyone here with us who wants to talk?' Ryan asked in his most authoritative tone.

Jess giggled. The sound was musical to Chloe, and she smiled too.

Ryan glared at them both. 'You have to take it seriously,' he hissed. 'It won't work if you don't, and if it does, you won't get good spirits.'

The girls fell quiet.

'Is there anyone here with us?' demanded Ryan. 'Is there anyone from the other side who wants to talk?'

Chloe imagined a ghostly voice filling the void. What would it say?

'If there's anyone there,' continued Ryan, 'make yourself known to us somehow. Move the glass and tell us your name.'

Chloe watched the glass, willing it *not* to move. She wondered if Jess did too. If it didn't move, they could just abandon this game and go off into the sunset together, leaving Ryan to find some other willing – or *stupid* – participants.

'Is there anyone there?' he asked again. 'Does anyone want to talk?'

A sound from backstage – rustling, like someone had shaken a carrier bag.

'What was *that*?' Jess pulled her finger from the glass.

'Damn,' cried Ryan. 'You've broken the connection now.'

'What connection?' laughed Chloe. 'We haven't connected with anyone!'

'We might have. How do you know?'

In the flickering light Ryan's face was for a moment pure evil; his eyes bloodshot, the lines beneath them black, his mouth a gaping hole. Chloe shivered despite the room being an oven after baking all day in the summer sun.

'I heard something,' insisted Jess. 'You did too – I saw you all jerk.'

She got up and went backstage. Chloe heard her rummaging around. Ryan still looked furious.

Jess came back, shrugging. 'I can't see what it was. But *you* heard

it.' She looked at Chloe. 'Maybe we should stop. What if it's ...
something ... ghostly.'

'If it's something ghostly, then we need to continue,' cried Ryan,
almost manic. He grabbed Jess and pulled her back onto the floor.
'Fingers on the glass. Come on. Both of you. Can't you *feel* it?'

'Feel what?' Jess whispered.

'I dunno.' He looked around at them. 'Something has shifted.'

'What do you mean?' asked Chloe, wishing she hadn't.

'I'm not sure. Come on. Keep your fingers on the glass, no
matter what.' He paused. 'Is there someone with us? Is there a
spirit here who made the noise just now? Are you able to move
the glass and spell out your name?'

Then the glass began to move.

12

THE GAME

2005

Chloe looked at Jess. Jess looked at Ryan. He avoided her eyes.

'That was you,' Jess snapped at him. 'Ryan! You moved it. I felt you do it.'

'Well, for fuck's sake, you two aren't doing much, are you?'

'You can't cheat,' cried Chloe.

'I'm just trying to get you two to take it seriously. You're not concentrating.'

'I am,' insisted Jess. 'I *want* it to work.'

'Come on then,' he said. 'Let's do this. No more messing.'

Chloe looked out at the rows of empty pews, at the black lines against grey. Was that someone in the back row? Someone watching them. She blinked and looked again. Nothing. No one.

'Is there anyone here who wants to talk to us?' asked Ryan again.

Chloe's finger throbbed now.

'Let us know somehow if there's anyone here?' he asked.

She didn't suppose it mattered how he worded it. A thought came suddenly to her that almost had her laughing out loud. She stifled it though. Ryan would lose it otherwise. What if the spirit was foreign and had no idea what Ryan was saying? Or did everyone speak the same language on the other side?

After ten more minutes of Ryan asking the question in different ways, he stopped. He looked at them. Shrugged.

'Guess it's not going to happen tonight,' he sighed.

'You said it might take a few times,' said Jess.

'I suppose.'

'Maybe you have to be patient,' she said.

Chloe realised he didn't want to be; he wanted what he wanted, right now. Though they didn't go to the same school as he did, Chloe had seen how he flirted with the girls here during rehearsals. How he made each of them feel like she was the only one sunbathing in the warm rays of his charm. How he had them fetching things for him, helping him with his lines at the click of a finger, lighting his cigarettes when he flashed a smile.

Chloe wished she had that ability with Jess. But it wasn't in her character: she was the happy-go-lucky one at school, the girl who was too sweet to be bullied, too soft to be chosen for sports teams, too nice to stand out. Forgettable.

'We'll just have to come again tomorrow night,' Jess said, and took her finger off the glass.

Chloe removed hers too. She was happy to come back. Not for the game, but for Jess. She started planning what she might wear. What perfume she might borrow from her mum to make Jess lean close and ask what it was, like she had once in biology.

'I suppose.' Ryan took his finger away too. He stood up and stretched.

'Shouldn't we pack it up then?' asked Chloe as he headed down the aisle, taking a cigarette from his pocket. 'We can't leave it here, can we?'

'Knock yourself out.' He was clearly done for the night.

Jess shrugged and followed him.

Chloe watched them leave. The candle flickered violently as they opened the door, then shut it after them. She wanted to call for them to wait, not leave her here alone with ... With *what*? It was just her. Wasn't it? She turned the main light on, hating the unpredictability of the shadows. Then she picked up the shoe box and knelt down to collect the letters and glass up.

A scream from the other side of the door stopped her.

Did the glass just move?

Who screamed?

The main light went out.

Chloe dropped the shoe box.

The door burst open and Jess came back into the room, breath ragged.

'There's a dead bird,' she cried, running onto the stage and grabbing Chloe's arm.

'What?' Chloe was cold, despite the warmth of Jess's touch. '*Where?*'

'On the windowsill in the boys' toilets. It's horrible. I can't climb out near that.'

'Was it ... black ... glossy?'

'Yes.' Jess frowned at her. 'How do you know?'

It doesn't matter, thought Chloe. *Because you're hanging on to me and I never want you to let me go.*

'I saw one,' she admitted. 'The other day. Dead as well. This is just ...*freaky*. Where is it now? Where's Ryan?'

'Getting rid of it.'

He came into the room and joined them on the stage. Jess let Chloe go. Chloe's eyes had become used to the dimness of the candlelight and the thin line of dying sun through the wooden window boards once again.

'I put it in the bin,' said Ryan. 'Come on, it's gone, you big wuss.'

'I'm not,' cried Jess. 'Chloe said she saw one the other day too!'

Chloe bent to pick up the shoe box and glanced at the Ouija board. She was right; the glass had moved from the middle. It now stood next to the letter Y. Then, before her eyes, it moved slowly on to the O. She tried to speak, to tell the others, to stop them arguing about how it was possible such a huge bird had landed and stayed on that narrow windowsill. The glass moved again, to the U. Chloe bent to get the notepad and pen. Still, she couldn't speak. It was as though her words were lodged in her throat to allow space for the ones forming before her eyes.

Now Jess was looking at her.

Chloe tried to blink, tried to communicate in some way what she couldn't say.

Look, it's working...

Look, I think I love you...

Look, it's working...

Jess finally looked at the glass. It moved from the U to the D. Chloe wrote the letters down. Jess tugged on Ryan's arm and he looked too. His mouth fell open like a door on an advent calendar. The glass moved from the D to the I. Ryan gulped and seemed also to be trying and failing to speak. It moved from the I to the D again. Chloe added the letters to her script. She held her breath. The candle danced. The glass moved, gathering speed now. When it was done, it returned to the middle.

They stared at it.

Their voices returned.

'Did I just see what I think I did?' whispered Ryan.

'Well, I saw it too,' cried Jess. 'Oh my God. It actually *moved*.'

'And we weren't even touching it.' Ryan bent down and put a hesitant finger on the glass. 'How the hell?'

'Maybe we all imagined it?' Chloe knew the idea was ridiculous.

'It's you.' Ryan looked at her.

'Me?'

'I knew it. You're the one we needed.'

'What do you mean?' she cried. 'I never touched it!'

Jess turned to her too.

'No,' Ryan continued, 'I mean you're the one with this spiritual ability thing. Like Amelia Bennett was supposed to have had. She was the girl who did the Ouija board with Daniel Locke and Harry Bond. The one who survived. You're *our* weirdo.'

'Thanks,' said Chloe.

'A witch,' said Ryan with a grin.

'I'm not a witch!' Chloe was outraged. She was the *nice* one; the sweet girl whose hair her mum plaited while they watched TV, who never answered back and tried to make everyone happy.

'Not a witch like in our play,' said Ryan. 'I read online that for this to work you need at least one person to be spiritually open – gifted, sensitive, psychic. Whatever you wanna call it. There were all these different words for it. Means the same thing though. Hundreds of years ago they'd have called you a witch.' Ryan studied Chloe as though seeing her for the first time. Jess followed his gaze, her expression unreadable. 'You made it work. We left the room and when it was just you, it happened.'

'But I didn't … It just…' Chloe looked again at the glass, now still. She shook her head. 'You said it was about the power of *three*. I looked it up. That's supposed to be where the magic is.'

'You still need one of that three to be … more *sensitive*.'

'What did it say then?' demanded Jess, interrupting him.

'What?' asked Chloe.

Jess motioned to the notepad in her hand. Chloe didn't want to read it aloud; she was afraid to. She simply held up the piece of paper. Let them look at it. But she looked too. And remembered what Ryan had said about 'Goodbye'. That the spirit must move the glass there or else they would still linger.

YOU DIDNT SAY GOODBYE

13

THE DEAN WILSON THEATRE

FEBRUARY 2019

Chloe tries to remember the goodbye she and Jess shared, long ago.

Was there a kiss? Was there even the word 'goodbye'? Didn't they all just go their separate ways and never speak again? Why is the memory so vague? When Chloe reaches her fingers out towards it – *towards the glass*? – the image breaks up like disturbed water. She needs to get the name Jess out of her head – that's not who she is now. She's Ginger. She's an actress. She's going to be Esme Black.

She's coming home.

'You're miles away.'

Chloe starts. Looks around. She's walking along the corridor towards the backstage door with Beth, the newest usher. It's Beth's first shift and Cynthia has asked Chloe to use the fifteen minutes before the shift starts to give her a tour of the building. *I think she might already know her way*, Chloe had wanted to say. The middle-aged woman has replaced the bright-orange hair dye with blue and made sure her nails still match. And she smells of vanilla tonight, not lavender.

'And she's back in the room,' Beth says.

'Sorry.' Chloe can't help but be brusque, still not sure she believes Beth wasn't backstage that weird night. Something about the woman just rubs her up the wrong way. She should try and be more welcoming though. 'You drift off easily when you're here sometimes. Wait until you're seeing a show for the twentieth time and you could be the standby actor.'

'I've been a standby for some big roles.'

'You have?'

Chloe taps in the door code and takes them both backstage. She has always loved how deceptively quiet the passage leading to the door is; how on the other side of it – backstage – the theatre really comes to life. The show starts in an hour. The place is electric with the hustle and bustle of stagehands doing checks, costume crew making last-minute repairs and fixing wigs, and the stage manager running things. The new show, *Bright Lights, Bright Life*, is a lively musical about the seventies disco era.

'What roles were you a standby for?' Chloe asks Beth, leading her through the crowd of backstage workers and towards the fire exit.

'I was on standby to play Ophelia at the New Theatre,' gushes Beth.

'Did you get to do it?'

'No. The actress was the healthiest one I've ever known!'

Chloe opens the fire door, revealing the darkened carpark and loading bay at the back of the theatre. 'We check all fire exits before each shift,' she explains. 'This one, and the two at the sides of the building.'

'Why?' asks Beth

'In case there's something blocking the door, or it's jammed. Wouldn't want our actors and patrons trapped inside a burning building.'

'Depends on the show,' laughs Beth.

Chloe laughs despite her irritation. Perhaps she has been too hasty in suspecting Beth was backstage that night.

They head back towards the front of the theatre. As they pass the Morgan Miller dressing room, Chloe tries not to look at the door. The lead actress – Anna Someone; Chloe can't recall offhand – is using it and so far, no complaints. It's empty. Beth pauses by the door and Chloe can't resist glancing at it. It's open. Messy inside. Garish, glittery costumes hang over the chairs, and chunky platform boots line the walls.

'Is it true?' asks Beth, peering inside.

'Is what true?'

'That Morgan Miller haunts the building. That staff hear her singing late at night.'

'I've never heard anything,' lies Chloe. She doesn't want to go in, doesn't want to look at the mirror; is afraid more words will appear at the top.

Beth frowns at her. 'You OK? You've gone really pale.'

'I'm fine.' Chloe tries not to think of the other incident in the dressing room. The one she has tried to forget. The one that happened before she saw those words on the mirror a few weeks ago. Her scars ache; they always do when she's tense.

'I've been in there before,' boasts Beth, smug.

'You have? When?'

'Way back, when it first opened. It was different then of course. The paint was new. Bright white. It wasn't as shabby as it is now.'

Protective of her beloved theatre, Chloe says, 'Well, what do you expect? That was twenty years ago. Guess I didn't need to show you the building. You know it already.'

Since the announcement three weeks ago that *Dust* was returning, the whole place has been buzzing. Tickets for the entire month-long run sold out the morning of release. Ushers – mainly Chester – have been frenziedly sharing tales of sightings of Morgan Miller, insisting they have seen her ghostly apparition wandering backstage. Nina said when she was leaving through the fire exit one night, she absolutely, definitely saw her, dressed as Esme, waiting in the wings to go onstage. 'She won't be happy that someone else is playing her role,' Chester said dramatically. 'She'll be here for revenge!'

'What were you doing in this dressing room back then?' Chloe asks Beth.

'It was when *Dust* was on.' Beth's voice breaks a little. 'I came here to find Morgan at the interval. I had some flowers for her – to show there were no hard feelings.'

'Hard feelings about what?'

'That she got the part of Esme Black. I auditioned too, remember.'

'Of course.' Chloe studies Beth. 'You *knew* her then?'

'Not really. Only from the auditions.'

'And did you give her the flowers?' asks Chloe.

'She wasn't here. I left them by the mirror. And just moments later, she was dead. Made me relieved I hadn't succeeded in getting the role.' Beth pauses. 'It's all a bit like ... you know, that *Scottish play*.'

'How?' asks Chloe.

'Well, the reason you're not supposed to say it aloud, is apparently because an actor died in the first ever production, cursing all future shows.'

Chloe feels sure, somehow, that she had heard another reason.

'Don't you think Morgan Miller's death might have cursed the new *Dust*?' asks Beth.

'Only if you believe that kind of thing.'

'I suppose. Do *you* think they should have resurrected it?'

Chloe doesn't answer. At first, she might have said no. She might have said no one should attempt to match it. But now it means Jess – no, *Ginger* – is coming back.

'Who do *you* think killed Morgan?' asks Beth.

'I've no idea. I was only ten when I saw *Dust*. Can't even really remember the murder part, I only know about it from reading things now.'

Beth shrugs.

'Poor Morgan,' says Chloe softly. 'She was only thirty.'

'About your age?' asks Beth.

'Yes. About my age.'

They head back to the box office, where Chester, Nina and Paige have arrived for the shift. The new radios have finally arrived too, and Cynthia is showing them how to attach the earpiece and make sure they're tuned to the correct channel. Chloe is glad they can get rid of the old ones. She was sick of missing out on messages that others insisted they had received; sick of hearing strange ones no one else did.

'Beth, you can tag along with Chloe on this shift,' says Cynthia, handing her a lanyard with her name on it. 'She'll show you what's what. Put a radio on and get used to all the messages we exchange, but don't use it yet. Just observe what Chloe does tonight, and you can work on one of the doors alone next time.' She then pats the pile of programmes and says, 'Right, we need to be ruthless about selling these. Our target is at least a hundred and fifty a night.'

'In your dreams,' laughs Chester. 'We don't even have that many patrons in!'

'That kind of attitude doesn't sell anything.' And Cynthia turns towards her small office, goes inside and shuts the door.

'I thought the news about *Dust* would mean tickets for our other shows would sell well too,' Chester says to Chloe. 'It's embarrassing having a half-empty theatre. Hey, did I tell you I might be in the newspaper?'

'Now what have you done, Ches?' smiles Chloe.

'*I've* been in the press a few times,' says Beth.

'This journalist rang me,' explains Chester. 'I wasn't meant to take it, but I answered the phone when the box-office guys weren't here. He wants an exclusive on what it's like to work in the most haunted theatre in the UK. His words, not mine. Of course, I'm happy to oblige!'

'Does Cynthia know?' asks Chloe.

'Nah. Why does she need to?'

'She did say at that last meeting that we should send all journalists to her.'

'Fuck that, I want my moment!'

Chloe laughs heartily and grabs her pile of programmes. 'Come on, we need to get selling.'

Beth follows her into the foyer, where people are beginning to arrive for *Bright Lights, Bright Life*. Some have clearly been to local charity shops and found faded seventies outfits to wear for the occasion. They buy ostentatious cocktails, and Chloe smiles, knowing they'll be dancing in their seats by the end of the show. The show is enjoyable and she's sad sales haven't been better – the cast are a lovely bunch.

The evening passes without much incident; the show starts on time, latecomers are few, the audience are a tidy one and bring most of their rubbish out with them, and a few of them give a standing ovation. The new radios appear to work well; voices are clearer over their airwaves. Chloe is glad. No chance of mishearing strange words.

After the shift, Beth thanks Chloe for being helpful. As the ushers leave, Cynthia asks Chloe to wait behind in the box office for a moment.

'You're one of our longest-serving ushers,' Cynthia says to her.

'Six years,' admits Chloe. Hadn't she intended it to be a year at the most – just until she found success with writing or acting? 'Chester's been here longer than me though.'

Cynthia ignores the observation. Chloe knows the two of them have clashed a few times over the years.

'I'm tired,' admits Cynthia.

'It's a long show I guess.'

'No, generally. I want to retire early, Chloe. At the end of the year, once *Dust* is over. I'm going to put your name forward to be trained as the next front-of-house duty manager. Would you be happy with that? I'd train you from June, I think.'

'I ... I guess, yes.'

But is she happy? This job wasn't meant to be her career. She loves this place with all her heart – the staff, the shows, the whole thing – but it was supposed to cushion her until she made it in some way.

'I was an usher for a few years first, as you know. I jumped at the chance when the last duty manager offered to train me up. You're very loved here, Chloe.'

'Am I?'

'Of course.'

'But ... I just ... pick up the glitter...' The words come out before Chloe can stop them.

'Pick up the glitter?' Cynthia studies her.

'Sorry. Yes. I saw Taylor Swift in concert, and she thanked everyone behind the scenes, those in the dark who we forget – the people who build the stage and do the lights, and pick up the glitter afterwards.' Chloe realises she is close to tears. 'That's all I'm here for. To pick up the glitter.'

'Oh, Chloe. You *are* the glitter.' Cynthia squeezes her affectionately and then turns to her computer.

Chloe heads backstage to collect her bike, throat still tight with tears. *Is* she the glitter? Maybe she *should* take the job. When Jess comes to the theatre, Chloe won't just be an usher; just a failed actress; just a failed writer. She'll be training for a job with responsibility. She'll be *someone*. She cringes at her desperation to impress a girl she hasn't even known as an adult.

It's quiet backstage. Chloe can almost imagine she hears the sound of the dust settling on the costumes. As she passes the closed door to the Morgan Miller dressing room, she averts her eyes and hurries down the stone steps to the back fire exit.

Her fingers are on the cold bike chain when she hears it.

14

THE DEAN WILSON THEATRE

A door opens – the familiar click of handle, followed by slow, ominous creaking.

'Is that you, Chester?' Chloe calls, knowing full well he has long gone. Maybe there's a stagehand still loitering. 'Who's there?'

No answer.

'Beth? Is that you?'

No answer.

Chloe unchains her bike with shaking hands, eager to get away.

And then she hears her name. She is sure of it. But who said it? Was it just inside her head because she's feeling tense? No. The voice is familiar – and yet she can't place it.

Then again – her name, lyrical, teasing.

No. She isn't going to listen. It's just her imagination. Like the other night. She pushes the fire door, ready to escape, but it's jammed shut. What? It *can't* be. She and Beth checked it earlier. She pushes again, harder. Still jammed. Shit.

Chloe...

No, no, *no*.

One huge push and the door opens, smashing against the wall. Heart pounding, Chloe shoves her bike through it, jumps on, and pedals as fast as her trembling legs will let her, up the street, into the darkness, afraid if she looks back she'll see Morgan Miller waving at her.

Once home, she puts her bike in the shed, nods at her flatmate James, who's making pancakes in the kitchen, and hurries to her bedroom. She leans against the door and waits for her heart to resume its usual rhythm.

She imagined the voice; she *must* have done. But did she imagine the voice on the radio that time? Did she imagine the words on the mirror? The bird inside the theatre? Did she imagine that long-ago incident in the dressing room that she pushes away so hard?

Is her imagination really that good?

She laughs out loud.

If it's that good, why isn't she a successful writer?

She sits on the bed and takes the embarrassingly few pages of her *She Haunts Me* script from her wooden box. She ignores the knife. She needs to get rid of it once and for all. She will, *she will*. Soon. One day. But now, she needs to think about finishing her script. She needs to find the ending. She needs to get into it fully, to complete it, and then maybe she can send it out to theatres. Is that really what she wants?

No.

She wants to perform in it herself. Maybe even at the Dean Wilson Theatre. On the stage finally. No scars on show, only her acting ability.

When Chloe opens the script, something else flutters to the floor. A piece of paper. She frowns and retrieves it. Reads it but can't understand what her eyes are seeing. The handwritten words there. Her *own* handwritten words.

YOU DIDNT SAY GOODBYE

Chloe drops it. She stares at it on the floor as though it might burst into flames, and then picks it up again. Where the hell did it come from? It stirs another memory. She wrote this; it's *her* handwriting. But how is it here? She hasn't seen it for a long time, she knows that much. The memory is becoming insistent; the youth theatre, Ryan, Jess, her. She can smell the dust, cheap perfume, a candle. She can feel the soft caress of a draught from somewhere. She can see red curtains, a sturdy glass, strange letters.

Chloe's mobile phone buzzes.

She puts the script and the note in the box and takes her phone from her pocket. It's a Facebook notification; a friend request.

From Ginger Swanson.

Jess.

Jess wants to connect. Why? Is it because she's coming home and thought of her? Chloe clicks on her profile. She browses the few pictures: Jess on a beach holiday, hiding from the sun under a parasol, large sunglasses on; Jess with a gang of women, clearly in some musical together, all dressed as showgirls; Jess with a man – dark, leathery, his arm loosely about her shoulder. There's a link to another profile, clearly the one Jess uses as a professional actress rather than to share personal snaps, where perfect pictures artfully depict her onstage.

There's one picture there that makes Chloe want to cry. The light catches Jess's eyes, making it appear that they shine with desire. Chloe pretends she's looking at *her*, through the screen, through *her*, seducing her, inviting her in.

She hovers a finger over the 'confirm' button.

She's going to have to learn to call her Ginger now.

She hovers a moment longer, and then accepts Ginger into her life.

15

THE GAME

2005

They studied the glass, expecting it to move again. Then they looked around at one another, eyes flickering like mischievous ideas in the candlelight; Jess, Ryan, and Chloe. The perfect three, and one apparently a witch. They looked again at Chloe's words written on the paper.

YOU DIDNT SAY GOODBYE

'Is that definitely what the glass spelled out?' demanded Ryan.
'You saw it!' cried Chloe, defensive.
'But we didn't know anyone was here.' Jess's voice was a rasp.
'*Who* didn't say goodbye?' whispered Chloe.
'Let's get back on it.' Ryan sat back at the makeshift Ouija board and looked at them both, hair ruffled. 'What are you waiting for? This is what we came to do – and it fucking worked!'
'I don't know.' Jess looked unsure. 'I didn't expect...'
Chloe wanted to stroke her hair, comfort her, calm her fears.
'Chloe,' said Ryan, looking intensely at her. 'I think *you* want to.'
Did she? It *had* worked with just her in the room. Terrifying as that was, didn't she feel a tiny bit powerful? A tiny bit magic? She could almost hear Grandma Rosa whispering, *You're a magic girl*. Maybe she *was* a witch? A named one, unlike the role she would soon undertake on this very stage. Maybe she could weave a spell and captivate Jess? Wouldn't *that* be something

She sat next to Ryan. 'Come on, Jess,' she urged gently. 'I'll only do it if you stay too.'

Did she mean that?

When Jess walked past her to sit down, Chloe imagined for a moment pulling on her ankle, toppling her down, into her lap, and kissing her. But would that ruin their six-year friendship? Would Jess be repelled? Never speak to her again? No one knew Chloe liked girls – or at least *a girl*. When Jess talked about boys she liked – including Ryan – and what she'd like to do with them all, Chloe just went along with it.

'I don't like how dark it's getting,' said Jess, hugging her knees. 'Soon one candle won't be enough. Are there any more? Can we put the big light back on?'

'It went out earlier when you two had gone,' said Chloe, glancing towards the door. 'Not sure if the fuse went.'

'For fuck's sake.' Ryan got up, went backstage and rummaged around. Eventually he came back with another two candles and lit them. They all shivered in perfect unison, as though it was a dance they had rehearsed over and over. The hypnotic glow made Chloe feel safe, like she belonged here, with the spirits.

'Let's just put our fingers on the glass,' said Ryan.

'If it can move by itself, why bother?' asked Jess.

Ryan looked unsure. 'I reckon we need to control it,' he said after a beat.

Or it might control us. Chloe wasn't sure where the thought came from.

Ryan placed his fingertip on the base of the glass. Jess followed. Chloe held back. She knew that this was her final chance to not follow. To get up and leave the room. But then it occurred to her that she wasn't following. Chloe had never so much as led a chorus. Never played the lead. She always went along with others. But tonight, she suddenly felt like she was the one who had really suggested they play this game. She put her finger on the glass.

'OK.' Ryan looked at them. 'Ready?

Jess looked afraid.

Chloe nodded.

'Is there anyone here…?' he asked the room '…who said goodbye to us earlier?'

Nothing. Just dying sunlight. Flickering candles. Held breath. Dust.

'We saw you move the glass. Someone is here with us. Tell us your name.'

Did Chloe feel something pulse along her finger?

'Tell us who you are.'

A movement. Jess gasped. The glass moved, just a fraction. Ryan's face glowed with excitement.

'Please tell us your name,' he begged.

The glass moved again. Chloe touched the pen to the paper, waiting for whatever story the glass created. Slowly, with a whisper of a scrape, it went towards 'Hello'.

'Hello,' whispered Jess, and then covered her mouth with her free hand.

'Shit,' whispered Ryan.

Chloe didn't write it down; no need.

The glass continued its slow journey.

'Are you moving that?' Jess hissed at Ryan.

'No!'

'You?' She directed the question at Chloe.

'No!'

The glass arrived at the letter I. Chloe wrote it down. Then it moved slowly from one letter to the next, to the next, their eyes not leaving it. Chloe recorded the words, seeing each one as a complete thing and knowing when to leave a gap; at the same time Ryan whispered them aloud.

I HAVE ALWAYS BEEN HERE

'Who *are* you?' asked Ryan.

Again, the glass moved, and Chloe wrote, and Ryan whispered it aloud, and Jess gawped.

ALWAYS HERE

'But who *are* you?' asked Ryan. 'Are you ... dead?'
'*Ryan*,' hissed Jess. 'Of course they are!'
'Tell us your name,' he said.

NEAR YOU

'I don't like it,' whispered Jess, looking around them.
'How near are you?' asked Ryan, grinning.
'*No*,' cried Chloe.
'Tell us your name,' repeated Ryan.
The glass moved; Chloe scribbled; Ryan spoke. The three candles continued their dance, dust spiralling above the flames. The scent of burning air merged with wafts of Jess's perfume, making Chloe dizzy. She shivered with both fear and excitement.

I SEE YOU I SEE YOU I SEE YOU

'They're just playing with us,' said Ryan.
'See if there's anyone else,' begged Jess, voice small.
'Aren't we supposed to make them say goodbye first?' Chloe whispered.
'Not until the end,' said Ryan. 'OK: Is there anyone else here with us?'
All the candles went out at once.
Blackness swallowed them whole.
'Shit, shit, *shit*.' That was Ryan. Chloe heard him fumbling for the matches.
'I don't like this!' Jess now. 'I'm fucking going home.'
A scratch of match against box and in the flame's flash Chloe

saw Ryan light the first of the candles with a trembling hand. For a split second, she saw it. Behind him. A shadow; a person. Someone with them. Her finger left the glass as she jumped up and backed away. The shadow raised a hand as though to point. At what? *No*.

At *her*.

'The connection!' cried Ryan.

'Fuck the connection! There's someone right there!'

'Where?' cried Jess.

Chloe blinked, rubbed her eyes. It had gone.

'It was there,' she insisted. 'It *was*.'

Ryan lit the other candles. 'Sit down,' he ordered.

In shock, Chloe fell back into her place. Jess was frozen; even her face didn't move.

'Your finger,' ordered Ryan. And Chloe placed it back on the glass.

Did she simply do it because Ryan told her to? Was it so she could stay with Jess? Or was it her own will? She couldn't be sure. But she stayed. She played.

'Who blew out the candles?' Ryan asked the board.

The glass shot across the floor to 'Goodbye'. A pause. Then it touched 'Hello'.

'Hello,' they all whispered.

'Who are you?' asked Ryan.

YOU KNOW ME

'Do we?' he asked. 'Tell us your name then.'

YOU KNOW IT

'Spell it out,' he said.

YOU WONT STAY

Chloe shivered despite the oppressive heat. She continued to write it all down while Ryan whispered the answers aloud as they appeared. Jess was as white as the paper Chloe wrote on.

'Tell us your name,' repeated Ryan.

I WAS ONE OF THE ONES

'One of what ones?'

THE OTHER THREE

'What other three?'

ETERNAL THREE LIKE YOU

'Tell us your name.'

TELL ME YOURS

'Don't,' said Chloe.

'Why?' asked Ryan.

'I don't know.' She didn't. Then she remembered Ryan had said they should never share them. 'He already knows it,' she added, shocked at her words. Where had they come from?

'Do you know my name?' asked Ryan.

Jess still hadn't spoken; still looked ashen.

I DO

'So what's yours then?'

COME BACK TOMORROW

'They're playing a game,' said Chloe. 'Are either of you exhausted?' She realised that she felt like she had just run twenty miles. Her whole body ached. Her head felt thick with fatigue.

'Yes!' Jess found her voice finally. 'I feel awful. And sick. Like I could throw up. Can we say goodbye now?'

'No!' cried Ryan, eyes wild. 'I'm just getting started!'

'I think we need a break,' said Chloe gently.

'One more question,' he begged.

'One more then.'

'Before we end for now,' he said, 'tell us how you died.'

'No!' cried Jess. 'I don't want to know!'

'OK, OK. If we come back tomorrow night, will you be here?'

WHEN SHALL WE THREE MEET AGAIN

'Yes?' asked Ryan.

IN THUNDER LIGHTNING OR IN RAIN

'What does that mean?'

Chloe lifted the pen off the paper at the last letter. She read it softly back. Didn't she know these lines? Hadn't she learned them by heart?

'Don't you recognise it?' she asked him.

She saw the realisation stain his cheeks with colour. Jess gasped too.

'*Macbeth*,' whispered Jess. 'Shit ... I mean ... *the Scottish play...*'

'The witches,' said Ryan.

'They *know* us.' Jess looked like she might cry.

'Let's say goodbye,' insisted Chloe.

'Push the glass towards "Goodbye" then,' sighed Ryan.

They did. Did Chloe feel it resist? Maybe it was one of the others; maybe Ryan still wanting to play. Once it was there, they all inhaled. The candles danced. And they let go of the glass, one after the other. Waited. Like something might happen. Chloe could almost see it. See the glass smashing into a thousand pieces and blinding them all. What a dark thought. Was it really hers?

The tension died.

'Is that it?' she asked.

'I guess so.' Ryan exhaled sharply.

'That was ... *intense.*' Jess sounded about ten years old.

'Are you OK?' Chloe asked her, concerned.

Jess nodded, still looking pale.

'What do we do now?' said Chloe. 'Should we cleanse ourselves or something?'

'Nah, we just make sure it's all packed away safely.' Ryan gathered the letters up in a pile and put them in the shoe box.

Jess suddenly jumped up, ran down the stage stairs and along the aisle to the light switch by the door, which she flicked on. The room flooded with warmth, but with the death of the shadows, Chloe felt uneasy; because that meant someone had flicked the switch off earlier.

Ryan blew the candles out and put them in the box too.

'Seriously, were you moving the glass?' Jess asked him, loitering by the door still, forehead shiny, clothes creased.

'Do you really think I could have made all that up?'

Jess shrugged. Chloe knew he hadn't; *couldn't.*

It had been too ... detailed.

'You're forgetting one thing.' He banged the lid onto the box. 'Were my fingers on it when it moved by itself?'

'It's just so freaky,' said Jess. 'Who do you think that person was?'

'Shouldn't we talk about who those three might be?' said Chloe. Surely the others were thinking of Daniel Locke and his friends like she was.

'We'll come back tomorrow to find out,' said Ryan.

'Shit, I'm not sure.' Jess stayed by the door like she longed to escape.

'It's not you we need. It's *Chloe.*'

'Thanks.' Jess looked hurt.

'If Jess doesn't want to come, then I won't either.' Chloe wanted to defend her friend.

Your love, you mean.

Ryan gave her a look charged with something she couldn't identify and then changed tactic. He put the box away in the cupboard behind the curtain, gave Chloe a meaningful look, and went down the stage stairs, blowing his blond fringe out of his eyes, swaggering, cocky. Chloe watched as he joined Jess by the door; watched as he leaned in, twirled her hair around the finger he had placed on the glass and said something in her ear; watched as she responded – giggled, melted, surrendered.

Don't fall for it, Chloe wanted to say.

Jealousy clawed at her chest.

Don't let him get away with it.

She glared at him, willing him to step away, to leave Jess alone.

Will it and it shall happen.

Push.

Where did that thought come from?

Ryan jumped back, away from Jess. 'What the fuck?' he cried, looking around.

'What's wrong?' Jess touched his arm, but he flinched.

'Someone pushed me!' he cried. 'Jesus. What *was* that?' He looked over at Chloe, still standing on the stage. 'Did you see anything?' His eyes flickered with fear.

'Me? No. Nothing.'

'We should go,' said Jess, and Ryan didn't argue.

They headed into the corridor. Chloe didn't want to stay here alone, even with the lights on, so she followed them without looking back.

Outside, at the bus stop, Jess lit a cigarette with shaky hands. It was dark now and the lighter's flame cast a soft, shimmering kiss on her mouth.

'Are we meeting again tomorrow night then?' asked Ryan.

'There aren't any rehearsals tomorrow.' Jess inhaled, hard.

'Does it matter?'

'I suppose not.'

'I'm not coming.' Chloe, again, was surprised by the words that left her mouth.

'Why?' Ryan stopped with a cig halfway to his mouth.

'I just ... look, it was interesting ... different. But none of us know what we've started. We did it, something happened, and that should be enough.'

'That's what's so ace about it,' cried Ryan.

Chloe saw the bus come around the corner. She put a hand out for it to stop. 'You coming?' she asked Jess.

Her friend shrugged; looked at Ryan.

'We're gonna hang a bit longer,' he said, eyeing Chloe. 'You go. See you tomorrow. Let's meet here at seven.'

Chloe ignored him, said goodbye to Jess and got on the bus.

It was the loneliest journey. Drunks got on and off. A group of teens hunched over a small games console, shouting at the screen. She was probably the same age as they were but felt a million years old; a million miles distant from them. That morning Chloe's mum had ruffled her hair and asked if she was OK, said she looked a bit down. Had anything happened? she wanted to know.

Had anything happened?

There weren't enough words.

'I guess she's just a proper teenager now,' joked her dad, kissing her forehead.

Or a witch.

16

THE DEAN WILSON THEATRE

FEBRUARY 2019

One of a theatre usher's main jobs is to stop patrons using a phone during the performance; this isn't just about stopping them taking pictures of the set, but about not distracting those watching the show, and more importantly those on the stage. Chloe hates confrontation and dreads seeing those tell-tale lights dotted around the auditorium. If she's not quick enough to get to them, sometimes a technician snappily announces on the radio that there's someone using a 'bloody phone'.

If an usher was caught with their own phone in the theatre during a shift, they would likely be instantly dismissed. But tonight, Chloe is taking that chance, though she did put it on silent, and she does pop out into the small vestibule between the two exit doors when she has to read and respond to the next message from Jess.

Or Ginger, as she is trying to get used to thinking of her.

Since she pressed 'confirm' on her friend request two weeks ago, they have chatted a few times. It took a few tense days. Though she had agreed to the connection, Chloe was too nervous to write to her; and Jess never sent anything either. Then – out of the blue one night – a small picture of Jess appeared at the top of Chloe's phone screen. It made her heart contract; a message.

Hi, remember me? I was Jess Swanson back in the day!

'I've never forgotten,' Chloe whispered to herself.

Except she has. A lot of it. But not the *feeling*.

Hi, she typed back, *of course! We went to the same school and youth theatre. Huge congrats on the big role! Can't believe you'll be in* Dust. *Amazing!*

It went from there – easy chitchat, not every day – maybe every other – not that Chloe was counting. Nothing deep, just exchanges of *hi*, gossip about people they remembered from school, and Jess asking what it was like to work at the DW and saying she was excited to be coming there. For some reason, when Chloe chatted with Jess, a void cracked open and memories Chloe hadn't known were there slithered out, like lava laden with debris – the dusty stage at the youth theatre, a box with letters and a glass in it, and three shimmering candles.

What did it mean?

What had they been doing?

Earlier tonight, when Chloe arrived for her shift, Jess sent her the most intriguing message so far:

What are you doing in two weeks?

Nothing, Chloe wanted to type. *Absolutely nothing if it involves seeing you in any way.*

There was no time to respond properly, so she hid her phone in her trouser pocket – something she had never done in six years – and went into the foyer to start work. Chester looked at her but said nothing; he was lucky he had never been caught on Grindr while at the back of the theatre.

Then, as she took tickets on the main door, Chloe felt her phone vibrate. She was dying to check it. Once the lights went up in the auditorium, and *Bright Lights, Bright Life* started for what felt like the hundredth time, Chloe tried to check her phone without anyone seeing. She could just make out the words of another message.

I'm coming home if you're around...

Now, midway through the first half of the show, she goes into the small vestibule between the exit doors and types: *I can be around yes.*

She waits to see if Jess starts typing back right away, knowing if she doesn't soon, she'll have to go back into the theatre. After two minutes and nothing, Chloe goes back into the dark, wishing she didn't have to. She feels the phone vibrate in her pocket and chances another look.

Fab! I'm home 2 March for a few days. It'll be weird. Been so long.

Chloe isn't sure if she's working then, but she'll swap if she is. Ring in sick if no one can cover it. Her heart races inside her chest. She's going to see Jess again. No, she's going to see *Ginger*.

At the interval, Chloe dashes to the toilets and in the privacy of a cubicle, she sends another message.

It'll be great to catch up. Can't wait. X

Within seconds Jess responds: *Let's meet at the DW. I wanna see the place.*

Disappointed, Chloe writes, *OK. Talk soon. X*

She returns to the foyer, distracted now; misses the 'one minute until the end of the interval' call on the radio and then just manages to shut the doors a split second before the lights come up. Beth – hair now a vivid yellow – sits on the opposite side of the auditorium, jumping up the millisecond someone gets a phone out. She'll soon tire of that. Against her thigh, Chloe's phone is quiet. She doesn't want her first meeting with Jess to be *here*. It isn't because she's ashamed of her much less glamorous life, though this is true; it's more than that.

An actual dread.

A feeling of intense foreboding.

Chloe shakes her head – she's just being silly.

It's probably because of all the gossip flying around the building at the moment. Last week, Chester said that he thought this 'new actress', Ginger Swanson, looked perfect for the part, but the role of Esme Black was like the Oscar curse. 'You know what that is?' he said. 'Loads of actors have won an Oscar only to have terrible luck afterwards. I reckon this show won't do Ginger any good in the long run.'

Chloe shrugged his words off, but she can't shrug off the weird things that have happened recently. The strange voice on the radio. The voice calling her name backstage. The words on the mirror. The footsteps. The bird. The spooky note between the pages of her script.

She wonders suddenly if it's because she has finally overcome her self-harm addiction. Has this somehow affected her mind? Has that lack of release done something to her? Is she seeing and hearing things because she no longer cuts? No – that's dangerous territory. If she blames that then she's giving herself an excuse to start again. God, she wants to right now. She fingers the scars through her trousers; wants to create more.

A voice in Chloe's earpiece rescues her. 'Five minutes until the end of the show.' One of the technicians. On stage, a woman hangs from a disco ball, singing about the night she learned to dance. Chloe knows all the words.

The radio crackles again. Someone else speaks. 'Never ... be ... under ... one ... roof...'

No. These are new radios. *No.* Chloe leaps from her seat and runs into the foyer.

'Who *said* that?' she demands into the microphone.

After a moment the technician asks, 'Said what?'

'About the roof,' stammers Chloe, embarrassed.

'You're hearing things,' he snaps.

She goes back into the auditorium, red-faced and unnerved. Every time the radio crackles, she tenses. But there are no more words.

When the show finishes, and the glitter is collected up, the ushers go to the box office as usual. Chloe is quiet, afraid that she's losing her mind. Cynthia doesn't look happy and keeps them behind.

'Right,' she says, holding up a newspaper.

Chloe knows what it is; she also knows that at her insistence, and probably because he was scared for his job, Chester gave anonymous comments instead of grabbing his moment in the limelight.

'One of you is responsible for this, and I think I know who.' Cynthia pushes her charcoal glasses up her nose and reads angrily from the double-page spread. "'A Dean Wilson Theatre staff member, who prefers to remain unnamed, said that he thinks the return of *Dust* will destroy all of those involved. He told us exclusively that the curse of Morgan Miller is alive and well, and it's true that she haunts the shadowy corridors of the theatre.'" Cynthia scans the page and continues at another segment. "'Our informant told us that he thinks Ginger Swanson is taking a huge risk in assuming the role of Esme Black. Not only does he think it could ruin her career, but that her very life could be at risk.'" Cynthia scans the page again. "'When asked who he thought had killed Morgan Miller, he revealed that the belief among staff was that a jealous actress who also auditioned for the role had taken the ultimate revenge. He added that he had a theory on exactly who it was but couldn't share it for fear of the repercussions.'"

Cynthia slams the newspaper on a desk and glares at Chester. 'Well?' she demands.

'Well, *what*? It wasn't me.'

'You're our only male usher,' she snaps.

'Did it say usher? No. *Staff member*. It was probably Edwin Roberts.'

Someone stifles a giggle.

'You're not seriously suggesting that the artistic director would say that kind of trash?'

'Why not?' Chester asks. 'Ticket sales of our other shows went up yesterday after it came out.'

'You are on very thin ice.' Cynthia is red with rage. 'I can't prove it was you, but I'm keeping my eye on you. And the rest of you – if I see anything like this anywhere, there will be trouble.' She goes into her office, slamming the door.

'Was it you?' asks Beth.

'As if,' he says. 'Was it you?'

'It bloody wasn't!'

When they're alone in the foyer, Chloe tells Chester he should be sensible now. He shrugs and says he might be. They huddle together by the garish *Bright Lights, Bright Life* poster.

'What's your theory, then?' she asks him.

'On what?'

'You know what. In the paper. This actress that apparently killed Morgan Miller. Who did you mean?'

He laughs. 'No one in particular. I was just shit-stirring.'

'Beth took flowers to Morgan Miller in her dressing room the night she died.'

'*Seriously?*'

'Yes. She told me.'

'Oh my God.' Chester looks genuinely shocked. 'It could have been her then.'

Chloe thinks about telling him about the night she smelt Beth's perfume backstage but decides against it. She can't be sure it was her, can she?

'Weird that she started here in time for *Dust* coming back,' says Chester.

'I suppose...' She lowers her voice. 'I'm meeting Jess.'

'Jess who?'

'Swanson. Or Ginger Swanson as she is now.'

'What?' He grabs her hand. 'You *know* her? You never said.'

'We went to school together,' she admits.

'You kept that quiet.'

'We've been talking on Facebook. The thing is...'

'What?'

'Nothing.' Chloe changes her mind.

'You *like* her.' Chester shoves her playfully. 'You do. I can tell. She your schoolgirl crush?'

She was more than that, Chloe wants to say.

'Oh my God,' he cries. 'You're going to have an affair with Esme Black!'

Chloe laughs. 'No, I'm not! We're just meeting. First time since...'

'What?'

'School,' Chloe says eventually.

'Your face glows when you talk about her.'

'Does it?' She puts her hands over her cheeks. 'You can't say anything to anyone. I *mean* it, Ches. You can't go to the press!'

'Never about you.'

'I had to tell someone,' she admits. 'I have this really odd feeling though...'

'It's called sexual arousal, darling.'

'No.' Chloe shoves him. 'I just mean ... I think we did things when we were kids. No, not like *that*. I mean ... things I've not thought about since. Things that are coming back to me. It's like I'd forgotten it all somehow. But weird things have been happening. And I feel like if we meet...'

'What?' Chester's voice is soft.

'I feel like something terrible could happen.'

'We all feel that way with someone new,' he says. 'And Chloe?'

'Yes?'

'We never forget. We *choose* not to remember.' He touches her cheek gently. 'Gotta go. Got a date with that slag who works behind the bar at Propaganda.'

Chloe watches him go. She hasn't the courage to leave via backstage tonight. She exits through the front doors, holding her coat tightly to her body against the icy wind, and goes all the way around the outside of the building. At the back, she unlocks her bike and pedals home, tears cold on her cheek and fears hot in her head.

17

CHLOE'S ROOM

FEBRUARY 2019

In her room, Chloe reaches into the wooden box and takes out her script. She hasn't written any more since she last held it. She whispers the title on the front: *She Haunts Me*. She read some of the pages the other night and wasn't happy with them. What is it so far? An idea. An outline. It's about a woman called Abigail who, after a family tragedy, goes alone on a three-month cruise to recover. There, each night in the piano bar, she watches the ghost dancers – the people paid by the ship to accompany solo travellers on the dance floor. One – a beautiful woman – is never asked to dance. Abigail is fascinated by her.

Tonight, Chloe is too distracted to write. She checks her phone again, praying for that little icon of Jess's face at the top of her screen. No – no more messages. Nothing from anyone, not even from Chester with updates on his date with the slag whose name she doesn't think he has ever shared. She shakes the pages of her script. Frowns. Nothing falls out. The note is gone.

YOU DIDN'T SAY GOODBYE

She searches in the wooden box, frenziedly pulling out the old photos, tickets and mementoes. No note. She looks around the small room, on her bedside table, under the bed. Nothing. Is she going mad? Did she imagine it? She must have done. She really must have done.

Beneath everything in the box, the knife glints; a silver smile. It whispers to her. No – it's more than a whisper. It's an instruction. One she hasn't thought of in so long. Cut, bleed, release. *Cut, bleed, release.*

No. *No.*

Find something to distract.

Chloe takes out her laptop and opens the *She Haunts Me* document. After a moment she starts typing. The words tumble from her. She cuts and spills blood onto the page. She severs flesh and feels. She doesn't stop until her fingers throb and there is no more, and she blacks out.

18

THE GAME

2005

Against her better judgement, Chloe went to the youth theatre the next night. She found Jess sitting on the front steps of the church, smoking and texting someone on her phone. Perhaps because of the heat – or perhaps to tease Ryan with the soft curve of her neck – she wore her yellow hair up, tied with the frilled scarf she'd bought the previous week. Denim shorts skimmed her creamy thighs; on the pocket was an intricate unicorn Chloe had drawn in physics when they were bored.

'Hey, you,' said Jess, looking up with a warm smile.

Chloe's breath caught and she couldn't respond straight away. She sat next to her and took a cigarette she didn't want.

'I didn't think you'd come,' she said eventually, though she had only turned up hoping Jess would. 'You looked really sick last night. Are you OK? Why don't we tell Ryan we wanna do something else?'

'I'm *fine*,' insisted Jess, stubbing out the cigarette with a scuffed trainer. 'Me and Ryan talked last night, and I reckon it was just the intensity of it. Anyway, he said...' Jess seemed to change her mind about sharing it.

'He said what?'

'Nothing.' She shrugged.

Until Ryan had come between them, Jess had never kept anything from Chloe. What had they got up to last night? The thought of them kissing was acutely painful. Before she could push further, Ryan turned up, all swagger and overpowering aftershave, wearing a white T-shirt and red jacket like a cheap, wannabe James Dean.

'What's up, bitches?' he joked, and Chloe wanted to hit him.

He headed around the back of the building, and Jess immediately followed. Chloe went too, last as always, watching Jess's ponytail swing. They climbed through the window and headed for the theatre.

Once they were inside, the air changed. Chloe was sure of it. She almost wanted to return to the corridor and walk back in to feel it again; a tightening. As if the space in the theatre was smaller than it had been yesterday. As if it had been waiting for them; as if it had not breathed since they left.

Ryan took the shoe box from the cupboard and laid the letters and words in two circles as though he had been doing so for eternity. Jess looked nervous but hid it with a too-big smile. The evening sun slanted between the window boards; dust danced there. Chloe thought of Esme Black's haunting song. *I'm still here; I am dust. I'm those fragments in the air, the gold light dancing there, the breeze from nowhere.*

Was that what happened when you died? Was that where you went?

'Let's get started,' said Ryan, sitting down and lighting the three candles.

Jess joined him. They shared a look that Chloe couldn't read.

She sat too. 'Aren't we going to talk about what happened yesterday?'

'What is there to say?' Ryan put a finger on the glass. 'It worked.'

'Maybe we should discuss it.'

'Later,' snapped Ryan. He handed Chloe the pad and pen.

'Did anyone else feel like they were being watched last night?' Jess put her finger next to Ryan's. 'At home I mean.'

He didn't answer. Which said everything. Chloe couldn't lie and say she hadn't felt that if she had turned around someone would be standing right behind her. So she also said nothing. She just put her finger on the glass. The three of them swirled it around a few times and then settled it in the middle.

'Is there anyone here with us tonight?' asked Ryan in the tone he'd assumed for *Macbeth*. 'If you are, move the glass and talk to us.'

Nothing. One of the candles flickered but not the other two. Odd. Chloe frowned. She leaned towards the flame, hypnotised. The heat stopped her when she got too close.

'We know there was someone here last night,' said Ryan. 'Are you with us again?'

Nothing. Chloe squeezed the pen, its tip against the pad.

'Is there anyone there?'

Slowly, the glass moved. They gasped in unison. Chloe couldn't help but be thrilled, despite her previous apprehension. For a moment, she was sure a tiny finger joined theirs on the glass as it scraped across the floor to the 'Hello'.

'Hello,' said Ryan. 'Who are you?'

STILL HERE

'Are you who we spoke to yesterday?'

FOREVER HERE

Chloe wrote the words down as they were spelled out.
'Tell us your name,' said Ryan.

YOU'RE MAKING ME KILL YOU

19

THE GAME

2005

'Shit,' whispered Jess. 'I don't like that.'

'Keep your finger on the glass,' hissed Ryan.

'I don't think it's the same person,' said Chloe.

'What? *Why*?'

'It's a different voice. Someone ... younger.'

'You can *hear* it?' Jess was studying her, eyes bright with nerves.

And Chloe realised she could. Shit – *she could*. Or was it her imagination? Was she just imagining the sound of a physical voice? As she had written each of those awful words, had she imagined she had heard them, softly, right by her ear, spoken by a small child?

'No, it's just an instinct,' she lied.

YOU'RE MAKING ME KILL YOU

'Shit,' whispered Jess.

'Tell us who you are,' continued Ryan. 'Are you a different person to yesterday?'

I WAS A BABY

'A baby?' asked Ryan.

NEVER GREW UP

'What happened?' asked Ryan.

YOU KNOW

'Do we? Tell us anyway.'

WOODS

'Which woods?' asked Ryan.

Chloe could smell talcum powder, and the kind of skin cream you put on a baby's body. These innocent odours merged with the thick, sickly sweet stench of blood, and crawled up her nose. A child's voice whispered *woods*, over and over, in her ear. She gagged.

'Are you OK?' asked Jess.

Chloe nodded, even as the horrible reek intensified.

'Which woods do you mean?' asked Ryan.

SCOUTWOOD

'Shit,' whispered Jess. 'We camped there last summer ... It's where...'

'Where that baby was found,' finished Chloe.

'Fuck.' Ryan looked nervous now. 'The one that had been ... *killed*.'

'It was wrapped in a blanket covered with all those weird Satanic symbols,' said Chloe.

'Are you Erin Moore?' asked Ryan.

Chloe could visualise the headline: 'Baby Sacrificed by Sadistic Satan Worshippers in Local Woods'. She remembered reading about how Erin had been cold, blue, and perfect, except for a neat cut around her neck. When Ryan suggested they camp in those woods last summer, she hadn't slept a wink. Kept imagining she could hear a baby crying.

YOU SLEPT WHERE I DIED

Where I died, whispered the child in Chloe's ear.
'We did,' said Ryan. 'We camped there. Shit.'

YOU'RE MAKING ME KILL YOU

'What do you mean?' demanded Ryan.
'Say goodbye to it,' said Jess.
Ryan nodded.
They all moved the glass towards 'Goodbye'. Chloe could feel it resist like it was stuck on the floor. They pushed harder. Looked at one another when it still resisted. Pushed harder. Chloe remembered yesterday. When she had wanted to push Ryan away from Jess. *Will it and it shall happen. Push.* And she did it again; she *pushed*. Not with her finger. Not with her body. With her heart.
The glass shot towards 'Goodbye'.
'Thank fuck,' said Jess. 'Can we stop now?'
'Hell, no,' said Ryan. 'It's just getting good.'
'I don't want to talk to dead babies,' she said softly.
'Me neither,' agreed Chloe, and Ryan looked at her with contempt, like he knew her real reason for siding with Jess.
'We can't just say goodbye the minute we don't like them!' he cried.
Jess didn't look convinced, but she kept quiet.
'Is there anyone else there?' asked Ryan. 'Anyone who isn't a dead baby?'
'Stop it,' hissed Chloe. 'Aren't we supposed to respect the dead?'
'Whatever. Is there anyone there?'
'Let's ask about the three,' said Jess.
'What three?' Ryan frowned.
You know which three, thought Chloe.
'That one yesterday who said they were one of an eternal three. They quoted the line from *Macbeth*. Sorry – *the Scottish play*...'

'Shit, of course. OK – are you with us? You said you'd come back and tell us who you are. Are you here now?'

ALWAYS

'That was fast. OK.' Ryan seemed to think. 'Did you die a long time ago?'

NO

'But you say you've always been here.'

NO ALWAYS WITH YOU

Ryan looked around at the girls. 'Always with me? Or always with *us*?'

ALL OF YOU

'When did you die?'

LAST YEAR

'How?'

CAR

'Were you driving?'

NO

'Were you in it?'

NO

'How did it happen then?'

WALKED IN FRONT OF IT

Chloe shivered as she wrote the words down. Once again, she could hear the voice as though he was whispering the words in her ear. A male. And then she saw him. Sitting behind Ryan. Cross-legged. A teenage boy. Grinning. Face bloody; the crimson flow from the ragged gash across his forehead pretty in the flickering candlelight. She had seen his face before, less broken, on the front of a newspaper. She knew who it was.

'Who are you?' asked Ryan.

DANIEL LOCKE

'Fuck.' Jess pulled her finger from the glass.

Chloe blinked and he had gone. But he was still here. She knew it even if she couldn't see him. She could *feel* it. His heat. His hormonal scent. Blood. She felt him get up and walk around behind them. What the hell did he want? Round and round the glass went, like a dark game of Scrabble, while dust danced in the candlelight.

'You're moving the fucking glass,' cried Jess, glaring at Ryan. 'You went to school with him. He died and they did a Ouija board too. You're pretending he's here to scare us!'

'You think it's me?' cried Ryan, red faced. 'Right – let's fucking test it. Prove it *ain't* me.'

'How?'

'I'll leave the room and you ask him a question only I know the answer to – if he gives the right answer, I can't be moving it, can I?'

'It might not even work without you here,' said Jess.

It will, thought Chloe.

'Only one way to find out.' Ryan stood up. 'Ask Daniel what his mum's name is. I know the answer. Do you two?'

Chloe and Jess shook their heads.

'OK. I'll be in the corridor.'

Ryan left the theatre, the candles dancing as he opened and shut the door. Chloe looked at Jess. Despite the orange glow, she looked as white as new snow.

'You OK?' Chloe asked.

'I feel a bit sick,' Jess admitted.

'We can stop. We should if you don't want to do it.'

'I'll be fine. Ryan *really* wants to do it. It's all he talks about when we're alone.'

'Jess, you don't have to do what he wants just to make him happy.'

'But I *like* him,' she said simply. 'So let's do this.'

'You think you can win him over by going along with it?' asked Chloe, struggling to keep her tears back.

'He likes his girls to be daring. Up for anything. I don't think I'm enough for him. I'm too ... I don't know... I'm nobody.'

'You are not nobody,' cried Chloe.

You are everything.

'My mum's always on about me *being* someone.' Jess shrugged.

Chloe knew this was true. She'd pushed Jess into acting lessons and demanded the absolute best from her, paying for extra singing lessons and insisting she diet.

'Because Mum never achieved much, she's relying on me to do well. She's always nagging me to rehearse, rehearse, rehearse. To be better than the other actors. Be *prettier* than the other girls.'

'You *are* prettier than the other girls,' said Chloe softly.

There was a moment then, a moment that fell into its place. It dropped quietly like a feather. They looked at one another. Chloe saw herself in Jess's eyes and wondered if Jess could see herself too. They each took a slow breath at the same time, and it felt to Chloe like they drank in atoms that would change them – strengthen them, join them. Chloe reached out and put the finger that had pushed the glass over Jess's mouth. She traced the dampness and then leaned forwards to put her lips there instead.

Then Ryan opened the door and yelled, 'What's the fucking wait?'

The spell was broken.

20

THE DEAN WILSON THEATRE

MARCH 2019

Chloe wonders if the currently trendy torn jeans are supposed to mirror self-harm scars; if they are some sort of statement about cutting. Are women wearing their lives? She bought a pair that in the changing room perfectly paralleled her scars and therefore hid them – until she stretched her arms, and the ragged gaps moved up. Chloe felt it was a triumph that she even bought them.

Now – sitting in the DW Theatre foyer wearing them – she is afraid they will gape and reveal everything she wants to hide. What had possessed her to choose them today? She takes her jacket off and places it over her knees.

Jess will be arriving in ten minutes – if she's on time, anyway.

Chloe hoped that, with it being daytime, the foyer might be less busy, but there's a tour of the building going on. They happen once a month. Today it's led by Edwin Roberts, the artistic director. He's explaining the process for choosing scripts with animated gestures, his customary fedora hat absent, his hair as wildly thespian as his hand movements. These tours are usually full of people morbidly fascinated by Morgan Miller's haunted dressing room.

'Are we going to *that* dressing room?' one of the group asks on cue.

'All in good time,' says Edwin.

Chloe turns her back to them and hunches over, pretending to read her phone. Except for Chester, she hasn't told anyone that she's meeting Jess today. She hasn't eaten a thing, sure she'll be sick if she does. For the fifth time she checks her lipstick in a small mirror. What time is it? Five minutes to go – *if* Jess is on time. Chloe knows without turning around that the box-office staff are watching her. She knows they're itching to ask what she's doing here on her day off.

The new *Dust* posters have gone up in the foyer. They are stunning: a simple black-and-white image of Ginger Swanson and John Marrs as Esme and Chevalier, swept up in a passionate embrace, is overlaid with gold lettering; it's very noir, very 1940s movie, despite the Victorian setting. Chloe knows the marketing team want to attract a new and younger audience. There is no need. It has sold out.

A tap on Chloe's shoulder.

She turns.

In that moment, the sun slants through the large window overlooking the street. It slips between two posters and she is blinded. She remembers sun through wooden window slats. Sees dust, dancing. Sees sixteen-year-old Jess, face pale, asking Chloe, 'Where do you think we go when we die?'

And Chloe blacks out.

When she comes around, faces lean over her, blurred at first and then emerging as though the lights have come up on a stage. Cynthia, her hair covering her face as she bends down. Chester, fanning Chloe's face dramatically. And Jess. *No, she's Ginger*, whispers a voice. Ginger is beautiful; her golden hair is a soft halo around her face, her sculpted lips speak incoherent words, and her eyes are bright blue with concern.

'Talk about falling at your feet,' Chester is saying, nudging Ginger like he's known her for years. 'Bet this happens to you all the time!'

Chloe gets up, rubbing the back of her head. How embarrassing. She must look an utter state.

'Jess,' she croaks.

There's a brief flicker of uncertainty in Jess's eyes; then she shakes her head, smiles warmly and says, 'No one calls me that anymore. They haven't for years. Please, it's Ginger or just Ginge.' And she helps Chloe to her feet.

When their hands touch, Chloe sees a glass tumbler with their fingers on it. It's gone as soon as it appears. She's going to have to call her Ginger now. After all, she *isn't* Jess; she isn't an insecure teenage girl. She's a woman who moves with the grace of someone totally confident about her beauty, a woman whose hand is warm. Chloe doesn't want to let go of it. But Jess – no *Ginger* – does.

'I often have these blackouts,' Chloe explains, blushing.

'Do you two know each other?' asks Cynthia.

'We did,' says Ginger. She's wearing an expensive-looking coat, the softest of pinks, and smells of exquisite perfume. 'Back at school.'

'Amazing,' says Chester. 'You've got loads to catch up on, then.'

'What are you doing here, Ches?' Chloe asks him, pointedly.

'Oh, I'm helping with the next backstage tour.'

Yeah, yeah, thinks Chloe.

'Anyway, I'm OK now,' she insists.

Cynthia heads back to her office; Chester leaves them too but glances back with a knowing look. Chloe feels stupid. Doesn't know what to say now they are alone. Ginger is so effortlessly gorgeous. The scars on Chloe's thighs and upper arms throb. She can feel the heat through her clothes.

'You really haven't changed,' Ginger says.

You have, Chloe wants to say. *But there's still something about you...*

'It's like I just saw you last week,' Ginger says.

Chloe smiles.

'It's weird,' starts Ginger, frowning.

'What is?'

'I can see all this strange stuff too.'

'What do you mean?'

'Like...' Ginger sits in a chair near the window; Chloe sits in the one opposite. A *Dust* poster hangs between them. 'Well, I can see you ... and me ... at the youth theatre. Really vividly. Remember that place? God, we were there for – what – five or six years?'

'Yes,' says Chloe.

'I've always been able to remember us at school quite clearly, and I've often laughed at what we got up to, but the youth theatre was a haze until ... well, until I walked in and saw you.'

Chloe feels the same. Flashes of memory appear – candles, always candles, and dust dancing.

'But weren't there three of us?' asks Ginger.

'Yes, there was Ryan too,' says Chloe.

'God, yes.' Ginger throws her head back and laughs. Her neck is long and swanlike. '*Ryan*. I had such a crush on him, didn't I? Probably made a real fool of myself.' She shakes her head. 'I wonder what happened to him. We could search for him, only I can't remember his surname.'

Chloe wants to ask if Ginger has searched for her; she wants to ask if she has a partner; but she can't. And she does not want to search for Ryan. The idea fills her with a curious dread.

'The three of us were together a lot, weren't we?' says Ginger.

'That last summer? Yes, I think so.'

'What did we get up to?' Chloe is sure Ginger is frowning as she speaks, but perhaps it's Botox that makes it difficult to tell. 'I haven't thought about it until now. But it's like, I don't know ... this door has opened, and it's because of you. Even saying that now gives me shivers. Like it means something more. God, how dumb do I sound?'

'Not at all,' says Chloe. 'I feel it too.'

She's tempted to tell her about all the odd things that have been happening recently; things that seem to point to their past. But she doesn't want to scare her away before they get to know one another again.

The backstage tour group emerge from the theatre, blinking in the glare of the foyer. A woman in a tracksuit spots Ginger and nudges another woman, who nudges another. They approach the two of them in the window.

'You're Ginger Swanson, aren't you?' says Tracksuit.

Even with the show months away, Ginger has become a superstar in her hometown. She is utterly captivating; she sits up straight, shoulders back, and nods and smiles.

'Oh my God. Me and my mum have got tickets to the show!'

More of the tour group approach, adding their thoughts to the conversation, shouting excitement, admitting they weren't sure about whether *Dust* should return, but now they can't wait. From the centre of the group Edwin Roberts calls for everyone to follow him up the stairs to another of the rehearsal rooms. He clearly doesn't realise who the commotion is for.

'What do you do here, then?' Ginger asks when they have gone.

'I'm an usher ... but I'm training to be a duty manager soon.' Chloe adds the second part in a rush.

'Do you still act at all?'

'No, but I'm writing my own show.' Earlier today, Chloe read through the words she'd written the night she'd blacked out, and even though she knows they are chaos, she thinks the story might be beginning to emerge. 'I'd really love to perform it somewhere myself, maybe.'

'I seem to remember that you were such a lovely actress.' Ginger studies Chloe. 'I always thought that, of all of us, you'd make it. That you had some sort of ... I don't know ... magic.'

'You did? *Really?*' Chloe could not be more surprised – or delighted.

'Yes, really. What's your show about then?'

'No, tell me about you.' Chloe is embarrassed to talk about her unfinished script. 'Did you go to RADA? What else have you starred in?'

'I did.' Ginger inhales as though preparing for a soliloquy.

Don't act or lie, thinks Chloe. *Just tell me it as it is.*

'We moved away straight after school, down to London. My

mum wanted to give me the best chance. You know what she was like. Pushy. I got my A levels and went to RADA. It's not been easy though. As you'll know, this is my first huge role. It's taken years of bit parts. I was Eponine in *Les Misérables* for one week when the actress got ill. That was when I thought it might happen, but it didn't...'

'It has now though,' says Chloe. 'You must be ecstatic.'

Ginger nods enthusiastically, but Chloe senses some trepidation.

'Do you want a coffee?' she asks, glancing towards the bar.

'No, but I'd love to see backstage. I know they'll show us when I come for rehearsals in May, but you must be able to show me.' She pauses, looking around. 'It's a bit run-down now, isn't it? Not how I remember it when we came as teenagers.'

Defensive, Chloe says, 'We've had a hard time recently, like many theatres have, but with *Dust* selling out they're going to do the place up next month. When you come back it'll be like a new theatre.'

'So? Can we go backstage?'

Chloe inhales. For a moment, the thought of taking Ginger there makes her want to leave. 'If you like, yes,' she says eventually.

'Fabulous.'

21

THE GAME

2005

Ryan returned to the corridor, slamming the door behind him. Jess leapt back from Chloe's finger. 'We're just warming the glass up,' she called after him, and put her finger back on it. Chloe put hers there too, but it was cold. It didn't pulsate beneath her touch like a warm mouth. In that moment she hated Ryan with every bit of her soul.

'Who's gonna ask the question?' Jess avoided looking at Chloe.

'I will.' Chloe's heart wasn't in it now. She paused. Shut her eyes. 'Are you still with us, Daniel?'

IM ALWAYS HERE

'Can we ask you something?'

ASK ME ANYTHING CHLOE

Jess's mouth fell open. Chloe hadn't picked up the pen, but she didn't care.

'What's your mum's name, Daniel?'

TELL ME YOUR MUMS NAME

'Don't,' said Jess.

'Why don't *you* tell *me*?' asked Chloe.

SHES CALLED LYNDA

Chloe looked at Jess – that was Jess's mum's name.

LYNDA IS A BAADDD GIRL

'Don't you talk about my mum that way!' she cried.

'He's messing,' said Chloe. 'Daniel, we'll say goodbye unless you tell us your mum's name.'

IF YOU DO ANYTHING YOU
CAN HAVE ANYTHING

'Your mum's name or we go.'

DO YOU WANNA DIE TOO

'Move the glass to goodbye,' said Chloe.

'It won't.'

Will it and it shall happen. Push. And Chloe did it again; she *pushed*. Not with her finger. Not with her body. With her heart. And the glass began to shift.

HER NAME IS STEPHANIE

The glass then stopped at 'Goodbye'.

They took their fingers away from it.

'Ryan,' called Jess.

He opened the door. 'Well?'

'Tell us his mum's name,' said Chloe.

Ryan flicked the light switch. 'Stephanie.'

The light flickered for a moment but stayed on.

'Shit,' whispered Jess. 'That's what Daniel said.'

'Now do you believe me?' Ryan asked.

Jess looked sheepish. She got up and went to him. 'I just had to know,' she said softly. Then she kissed him. Passionately. On the lips. Chloe could only watch, heartbroken. Was the kiss really for him or was it to show Chloe that what they had shared earlier meant nothing to Jess?

The game was over for the night.

But maybe another had started.

*

It was that night, at home, when the phone first started ringing. Not a mobile phone, but the house phone. It pulled Chloe from a restless sleep where hundreds of large birds were throwing themselves at the window. She went onto the landing. The phone continued ringing, and yet no one in the house stirred. She remembered how her mum always said that a phone call during the night never brought good news. She got to the table in the hallway and picked it up.

It continued ringing.

What the hell?

The receiver was actually in her hand.

But still it rang.

She put it to her ear. Static. Crackling. A voice. And still the ringing.

'Who's there?' she whispered, afraid of the answer.

'Never ... be ... under ... one ... roof...'

A flicker of recognition despite never having heard the words before. A sense of remembering something not yet happened. A feeling of absolute certainty that one day she would know what the words meant.

Chloe put the receiver down. It stopped ringing. As she walked up the stairs to bed, she didn't dare to look back, the sense that someone was watching was so strong.

She tossed and turned all night, haunted by visions of Jess kissing Ryan over and over, and hundreds of dead birds falling from the sky, and a ringing phone that never stopped.

22

THE DEAN WILSON THEATRE

MARCH 2019

Chloe and Ginger stand up at the same time, and manage to crash into one another. Both apologise and laugh. Chloe isn't sorry though. She wonders if there's a chance Ginger feels the same way, that she is flirting. No, it's probably nothing. Chloe leads the way along the corridor to the backstage door and keys in the code.

'It must be so mundane to you,' says Ginger as they go through the door. 'But all I wanted when we were teenagers was to be on the stage here. Do you remember? We used to act out scenes from *Dust* and pretend?'

'You always made me play Chevalier,' jokes Chloe.

'God, I was a pain, wasn't I?'

No. But you caused me a lot.

Now that the tour has passed through, it's quiet and cold. They are between shows, so the costume rails are empty and the concrete floor is tidy. All of the dressing-room doors are shut. The door that leads to the stage is ajar, black curtain just beyond. They are building a new set for the upcoming show about body image.

'This is it.' Ginger stands at the Morgan Miller dressing-room door. She touches the tarnished gold star with Morgan's name in the centre. 'They never took it down?'

'No. They've never taken the poster down inside either.'

'I want my name in this star now,' says Ginger.

'Do you think they'll change it?'

'I'm Esme Black now, aren't I?'

'Yes, you are.'

'Can we go inside?'

Chloe tenses. 'I don't like going in there. I rarely do.'

'Why?'

Chloe wants to appear brave. 'It doesn't matter. Go in if you want.'

I'll follow you, she thinks. *Like I always used to.*

Ginger opens the door. Chloe holds her breath, half expecting something to happen. Ginger's heels are sharp on the tiled floor as she sweeps into the space, but Chloe has the feeling that this bold body language is somehow forced. Ginger stands in front of the original *Dust* poster.

'It *was* magic, wasn't it?' she says softly. 'I think I saw it the night after you, didn't I? My mum said I sang the songs all the way home. And now...' She seems suddenly overcome with emotion. Chloe wants to put an arm around her. 'Now I'll get to sing them for real.'

'Is that why you auditioned? Because it's ... special to us?'

Ginger nods. 'It was to my mum, too,' she admits. 'She saw that they were auditioning for it in *The Stage* and rang me straight away. Said it could change my life. I already knew about it. My agent had told me.'

Chloe smiles. 'I remember her pushing you to be a big star. She must be so proud of you.'

'She is.' Ginger moves over to the mirror and switches on the surrounding lights, so that when Chloe joins her, they are both beautifully lit, flawless, side by side. 'She's a pain though. Never gives me a break. My dad's getting sick of it ... I think...'

'What?' asks Chloe softly.

'I think he's going to leave her.'

'I'm sorry.'

'Don't be. I'd leave her if she was my wife.' Ginger glances at her. 'Some of the biggest actresses didn't want to audition for Esme, you know. They thought the part was cursed. But I felt like ... I don't know ... like I'd been waiting all my life for it. That I had always known it would come to me. It might sound conceited, but I knew right away that I was going to get it. Before I even auditioned. In the taxi, on the way, I just *knew*.'

The mirror lights flicker. For a split second, Ginger's reflection changes. She is young Jess again, blowing a pink bubble, hair tied up in a scarf. The lights flicker again. Now she is Morgan Miller, head bloody, face deathly white. Chloe gasps. The lights flicker.

Just Ginger.

'Remember the Ouija board?' says Ginger suddenly.

'*What*?'

'It just came to me. We did a Ouija board that summer, didn't we?'

'A *Ouija board*,' Chloe repeats in a whisper.

She does remember. It's as though she has never forgotten. Chester was right. We never forget. We choose not to remember. Just as she has chosen to forget that first incident here in this dressing room; the blood, the vision. But those shadows are dissolving, forcing her to face it, and she knows why. Because Ginger is here. Jess. And the incident involved her.

'I can see it,' says Chloe. 'Now you've said it. These printed letters. Though it's like I'm looking at them through a dirty window, if that makes sense. There's a lot I'd forgotten until I saw you. It's like your presence has unlocked it all...'

'I agree.' Ginger touches the mirror – her two fingers, the real and the reflected, could be meeting atop a glass tumbler. 'I feel like, if we talk about the Ouija board, we'll remember everything.'

Chloe wonders if she will start to, but Ginger changes the subject.

'So, they never found out who killed Morgan Miller?'

'No.'

'I read this article online that said she was scared of something before she died. That people close to her said she had the dressing room blessed before she played Esme.' Ginger shrugs as though it is silly. 'What do you reckon happened?'

'Why would I know?'

'You work here. You must hear stuff.'

'It's an old case. There's been no new information about it for years, just endless speculation and exaggerated stories about her ghost. The caretaker and her boyfriend were cleared. Mind you, there's a new usher who...'

'Who what?'

'Oh, nothing,' says Chloe. 'She was just here around that time.'

'How do the people who work here *really* feel about *Dust* coming back?'

'They're excited. It will change everything.'

'And you?' asks Ginger.

'Me?'

'How do you feel about it?'

It brought you back to me, so I'm happy.

'Time will tell,' Chloe says. 'I guess you hold all the cards.'

A crash behind them. They instinctively clutch one another. The dressing-room door has slammed shut.

'What was that?' Ginger tries to open it. 'It's stuck.'

Chloe joins her. 'It can't be.' She pulls on the handle. 'Is that you Chester? Open it! This isn't funny.'

No answer. And she knows it isn't him. A memory flashes into her mind. Another time when a door wouldn't open. When it meant that she had to stay with Jess. And with Ryan. Don't forget Ryan.

'Does it always do this?' Ginger kicks it.

You shouldn't do that, thinks Chloe, not sure why.

'Only once,' she says.

'What do you mean?'

The dressing-room incident she has tried to forget. It won't stay buried. It's clawing its way out of the shadows. Not just coming back to her mind; coming *back*. The lights around the mirror fill with crimson, a gentle trickle that then swells. The room pulses red. It happened then, and it's happening now.

Ginger approaches the mirror, her face appearing burnt in the glow. 'What is *that*?'

'You see it too?' whispers Chloe.

'Of course, I do. It looks like blood. How the hell did it get inside there?'

The bulbs appear to pulse like rows of fat hearts. Chloe can hear them: *thump, thump, thump*. Or is that her own?

'It'll stop in a minute,' she cries.

And then Jess will appear, dressed as Esme Black, white nightgown covered in blood too, and her mouth will open, and black liquid will pour out like venom, and then Chloe will pass out.

But Jess is already here.

Ginger is already here.

'What do you mean?' asks Ginger.

And then it stops; the red drains away; the two of them no longer look bloody in the mirror. Chloe waits to see if Ginger appears as a ghostly, dying Esme. Nothing.

'Thank God,' she whispers.

'Do you reckon it's a fault with the lights?' Ginger goes to the door – it opens easily, onto an empty backstage. 'Maybe there was wind from somewhere that made it stick.' She comes back to the mirror. 'You OK?'

'Yes.'

'You sure?'

'We should go.' Chloe feels sick. 'We shouldn't both...'

'Both what?'

'Be in here.'

'Why?'

'I just ... have a bad feeling...'

'Don't say that.' Ginger looks distressed. 'I'm excited about being here.'

'Ignore me.' Chloe shakes her head vigorously. 'I didn't mean to ruin your moment. This place spooks me sometimes.'

'This room *is* eerie, but I'll change that.' Ginger pauses. 'It's you,' she says with a smile.

'Me?'

Ginger leans forwards and touches Chloe's face tenderly. 'You're a little bit magic. You always were.'

'Was I?'

Chloe puts a brave hand over Ginger's. Sparks pulse along the scars on her arm. Didn't she once feel the same buzz when they put their fingers on that glass all those years ago? Didn't they call her a witch?

Everything collides; the feelings she had for Jess when they were kids, the intensity of this longed-for moment, the sudden memory of another long-ago moment never grabbed, the sense of power that maybe she *is* some sort of witch, and maybe she can weave a spell and make Ginger hers at last.

She kisses her. Their tongues touch. Electricity.

Be mine. Chloe sets the rhythm; slow, teasing, patient. Ginger resists at first, then seems to accept it. *Be mine.* Chloe moves a hand along Ginger's spine, aroused at the gentle curve of her back, at the way she sighs into her mouth and then moves a little closer. *Be mine.* Ginger begins to lead, to kiss her back heatedly, to scratch her nails along Chloe's back; and Chloe follows, just like she always used to.

Ginger stops suddenly.

'I'm sorry,' she says, looking embarrassed.

'Why? I'm not.'

'I have to go.'

'Please don't,' says Chloe, realising how needy she sounds.

Ginger rushes from the dressing room without looking back. Chloe is glued to the spot in shock and hurt. She hears the back-stage door slam after Ginger. The desire to pull a blade along her flesh, to *cut, bleed, release*, is intense. She rakes at her scars. Then she looks at herself in the mirror.

'You're not magic,' she says to her reflection. 'You're utterly deluded.'

23

THE GAME

2005

At the end of the next Ouija board session – the three of them playing for the third time, three days after they started, Chloe realised – everything changed.

It began differently too. Chloe had always known Jess was in love with Ryan, but on this night, she arrived not just with him, but *with* him. Chloe got to the church first and was sitting outside on the front steps, trying to avoid the evening's searing heat, hoping the building's shadow and the stone under her bottom would cool her.

She hadn't intended to come that night. She hadn't heard from either Jess or Ryan until that morning, when they each texted saying it was time to do it again. Chloe ignored them for hours, wrestling with her longing to see Jess and the dread of seeing them together after their kiss – that steamy kiss that had tormented Chloe since.

Last night – after she unplugged the ringing phone when it disturbed her yet again – she had kicked the duvet off the bed, opened the window as wide as it would go, and tried desperately to sleep. But the kiss would not free her from its heat.

Now Jess and Ryan sauntered up the street, holding hands, Jess not meeting Chloe's gaze, her cheeks flushed. Chloe knew it then; the knowing simmered in the hot air around them, consuming her. Ryan and Jess had slept together. Jess was no longer a virgin. And she hadn't *told* her; she hadn't called her to share the very thing they had always talked about, the thing they had always imagined together, Jess describing the kind of boy she hoped it would be with, and Chloe vaguely agreeing.

Had Jess forgotten their almost-kiss three nights ago? Their *moment*.

Or had Chloe imagined it?

'Knew you'd come,' said Ryan, head cocked, grinning.

Chloe stood, at least as tall as he was, and said, 'No you didn't.'

'Can't you two get along,' sighed Jess.

'We do,' said Ryan, letting go of Jess's hand and heading around the back of the church. 'Chloe loves me to bits. Everyone loves a bit of Ryan.' He climbed in through the boys' toilet window, and Jess followed without looking back. Chloe swallowed her jealousy, and a heavy, aching sadness, and the anger that Ryan had taken her girl.

Inside the theatre, the stage was littered with dark capes and long, bedraggled wigs; at its centre was a black, plastic cauldron. There had been a rehearsal last night but neither Jess nor Ryan had come, each claiming to have a stomach bug. Chloe and the other two witches – twins, Elisha and Ella – had rehearsed a scene from Act Four, with Mr Hayes voicing Macbeth in Ryan's absence. 'How now, you secret, black and midnight hags! What is't you do?' he had bellowed. 'A deed without a name,' the three witches had cackled, Chloe the quietest, saddest witch of all.

Now she was an angry witch; angry at Ryan.

'Were you two really ill last night?' she asked as Ryan took the shoe box from the cupboard behind the curtain.

'*I* was,' said Jess. She loitered at the edge of the stage. 'I've been feeling sick ever since we left here the other night. And...'

'And what?' asked Chloe.

'Nothing.' Jess shook her head, pale in the dim light.

'Our house phone rings all night, every night,' said Chloe. 'But no one else hears it. I asked my dad, who's a light sleeper, and he hadn't. I had to unplug it last night.'

'I feel like someone's watching me all the time,' admitted Jess. 'And I don't think it's someone nice.'

'Me too,' whispered Chloe, feeling a barrier between her and Jess drop.

Ryan pushed the cauldron noisily to one side, making room for the Ouija board. 'You're imagining it because you're feeling spooked.'

'We didn't imagine the real name of Daniel Locke's mum, did we?' said Chloe.

Did she imagine the moment with Jess though?

'Fuck off, then,' snapped Ryan. 'Don't do it anymore.'

Chloe began to walk towards the door, her heart pounding.

'No.' Jess grabbed her arm.

Chloe looked at her delicate hand and then her beseeching face. And she realised – Jess was actually a little afraid of Ryan. She didn't want to be alone with him. Something had shifted; they may have slept together, but something else had happened too.

I need you, Jess's eyes said. *Don't leave me here.*

And Chloe couldn't.

Ryan laid out the letters and the words, then placed the upside-down glass in the centre. As he put a match to the three candles, Chloe turned out the light. They all sat. One by one they placed their fingers on the glass. A shiver went up Chloe's arm. She poised the pen ready to record what happened again. They moved the glass repeatedly in a circular motion.

'Let's get Daniel Locke back,' said Ryan.

'No, I don't want to.' Chloe shook her head vigorously. 'Let's just see who comes through naturally.'

'But then we get weirdos,' said Jess.

'And Daniel Locke isn't?' Chloe asked. 'He walked out in front of cars on a motorway!'

'Let's find out *why*.' Ryan studied them both. 'Let's find out what really happened.'

'I don't think I want to know,' said Jess quietly.

'Well, *I* do.' Ryan was adamant. He paused and then asked dramatically, 'Are you there, Daniel?'

The glass shot across the floor to the 'Yes'. Their three fingers almost came free. It stayed for a moment and then moved again, more languorously, as though toying with them, now it had their attention. Chloe recorded the words.

DID YOU MISS ME CHLOE

She felt sick. 'I don't like him using my name.'

'Why not?' asked Ryan. 'He likes you!'

'I don't want him to. He used it the other night too. It's a bad sign.'

'How?' asked Jess.

'I read online that if a spirit uses your name, it's dangerous, and you should finish the session right away.'

Jess looked nervous.

'This whole thing is dangerous,' cried Ryan. 'That's why we're fucking doing it. Fuck off if you don't want to. I'm sick of you complaining. You knew it was gonna be freaky shit when we started.'

Chloe took her finger off the glass. 'I'll go, then,' she said softly.

She walked down the aisle between the pews, without looking back, even at Jess.

'We don't need her,' she heard Ryan say to Jess. 'Daniel, are you still here?'

Chloe reached the door, tears threatening to fall. She was losing Jess. Staying here would not prevent that; she was under Ryan's dark spell, and he was under the dark spell of the game. She waited for Jess to call her name. Willed it to happen. When it didn't, she turned the door handle. Frowned. Tried again. It wouldn't move. She wriggled it harder. The door stayed shut.

'Shit.' It was Ryan, the word soft.

Chloe turned to tell them the door was stuck, but he and Jess were staring at the glass. It was moving slowly between letters. She could not help but be a tiny bit disappointed that it had worked without her there.

You're still here though, she thought. *You're in the room.*

The glass stopped moving.

'What is it?' asked Chloe in spite of herself.

'You can't go,' said Jess quietly.

'Why?'

'Because we'll all die,' said Ryan.

'What?' Chloe's breath caught.

'That's what he said.'

'You're making it up to get me to stay.'

'Open the door then.' Ryan looked at her; his eyes flickered with genuine fear. 'Daniel said he locked it. And he said ... he said ... we'll all die if we don't finish what we've started.'

Chloe tried the handle again, but it wouldn't open. She kicked the door.

'Come back,' begged Jess. 'I'm really scared now.'

What choice did Chloe have? She turned and walked back along the aisle. She had a morbid vision of heads poking out of the wooden pews as she passed them, faces distorted, eyes wild, possessed in some way. She sat down next to Ryan and Jess. Put her finger back – *where it belongs* – on the glass.

The door flew open, extinguishing the candles. Jess gasped. Ryan fumbled to relight them. The glass moved.

HELLO CHLOE

'Why me?' she asked. She could smell him again; hormonal, angry, close.

YOURE THE WITCH

'Only in *Macbeth*,' she said.

'The Scottish play,' corrected Jess.

'For fuck's sake,' snapped Ryan.

YOU WANT SOMETHING

'Me?' asked Chloe.

YES

Did he really know what she wanted? Could a dead spirit read her mind? It was a ridiculous question in light of all that had happened. Anything was possible here. It seemed so long ago that Ryan had suggested they play this 'game'. Did she wish she could go back and not follow? She wasn't sure.

YOU ALL WANT SOMETHING

'Do we?' asked Ryan, but as though he didn't want the answer.

I CAN GIVE YOU IT

Chloe could hear his voice again as the words were spelled out; in her ear, sneering, youthful, deep. She could smell aftershave – different from Ryan's – and she could see a dark shape behind him.

THATS WHY RYAN CAME

'What the...?' Ryan jerked back.
'What do you mean?' asked Chloe.

HE KNOWS

'What does he know?' she asked.

ME

'We know *that*.' Jess clearly wanted to defend him. 'He told us you were at his school. It's no secret.'

Ryan fell silent. He didn't look at either of them.

HE KNOWS WHAT HAPPENED

'What do you mean?' Chloe had given up writing down the words.

I TOLD HIM

Ryan was still quiet.

HE KNOWS THE GAME

'We know that too,' said Jess. 'He suggested it.'

DIDNT TELL YOU EVERYTHING

'What does he mean?' Chloe asked Ryan, but he avoided her eyes.

HE WANTS THE POWERS

'What powers?' asked Chloe.

ONES WE HAD

'You had?'

WHEN WE DID THIS

'What does he mean?' asked Jess.

'I'll tell you later. Let's say goodbye to Daniel for now and—'

NOT LEAVING

Chloe took her finger off the glass, willing Ryan to argue about it. He didn't. 'Tell us now. You said Daniel went to your school. What aren't you telling us?'

'OK.' Ryan took his finger off the glass too. 'I knew Daniel Locke more than I let on.'

'How much more?' asked Jess.

'He was my best friend.'

CHLOE'S ROOM

MARCH 2019

In her room later, Chloe opens her laptop so that she won't take out the knife. She reads again the words she spilled the other night, hoping to push Ginger's rejection from her head. But every time her mind wanders it takes her to that kiss, to the dressing room, to the slamming door as Ginger walked away. The humiliation of it eclipses even the horror of those rows of pulsating, blood-filled lightbulbs, and all the other sights and sounds she feels sure now are the result of Chester harping on about Morgan Miller.

Should she message Ginger? Ask why she ran?

No. She'll sound needy.

To rid herself of these images, she reads aloud from her script. It's better than she could have hoped. It's almost as though, in that frenzy of writing the other night, someone else wrote with her. Someone gifted. After a while she stops reading and begins typing again, without looking up, without lifting fingers away from keyboard, and without thinking. She is on the ship with her character Abigail, watching the ghost dancer in the piano bar who no one ever speaks to. In silence, Abigail takes the woman's hand, and they sweep onto the dancefloor, where their waltz is so beautiful everyone else steps back.

It comes to life.

Chloe forgets the knife.

She can hear music, feel the ship swaying, smell the woman's perfume.

It is the one Ginger wore.

THE GAME

2005

'Your *best* friend?' Jess asked the question with absolute disbelief. She took her finger off the glass. 'You told me last night about the powers, but you never said Daniel was your *best* friend.'

Ryan glared at her with dark eyes, obviously wanting her to stay quiet. So they *had* seen one another last night. They missed rehearsals and spent time together. Had they slept together? One of the candles died with a sizzle, as though invisible fingers had snuffed it out.

'What powers?' asked Chloe, trying to extinguish her hurt with a pinch.

Jess spoke over Chloe. 'Why didn't you tell us?' she asked Ryan.

'I thought, if I did, you'd refuse to do this,' he admitted.

'But why did you want us to so badly?' demanded Jess, her feistiness returning.

Chloe smiled to herself. This was the girl she knew and loved. This was the girl who Chloe had let contour her face with new make-up while they laughed at the extreme result; the girl who slept over and snored softly and stole the covers; the girl who got hiccups for ten minutes at a time.

'Because I know...' began Ryan.

'Know what?' asked Jess.

'What can happen.'

'So do we,' cried Chloe. 'People can die! Daniel Locke was your friend – your *best* friend – and he died. Aren't you even bothered?'

'Of course I'm fucking bothered.' Ryan pulled at his hair. 'It shocked me to my core.' He paused, looked sad – but it passed. 'I guess I was hoping to speak to him again. I guess I thought this was a way to ... reconnect. And...'

'And what?' asked Chloe.

'I saw what happened to him.'

'You mean on the road that night?' Jess looked ashen. 'You were *there*?'

'God *no*, I wasn't there. No, I mean I saw what happened to him *before* that. While they were doing... *this*.' He looked at the glass and the letters.

'Did you do a Ouija board with them?' asked Chloe, arms crossed.

'No.'

'How come?'

Ryan shrugged. Looked embarrassed.

Chloe saw it then. Somehow it landed in her mind, like a new, pencil written line in the margin of a script. She had a vision of Daniel Locke, all cocky, all that Ryan had tried to be with Jess, with all the girls. She saw Ryan in Daniel's shadow, following him, wearing a James Dean jacket because Daniel had one, smoking because he did, flirting because he did.

Chloe realised that sometimes Ryan followed too.

'You weren't needed,' she said, not unkindly. 'Why?'

Ryan got his swagger back; he sat up straight like he didn't care and held Chloe's gaze.

'They had three already,' he said. 'Danny said it had to be three, so I wasn't needed. He had Amelia Bennett, and she'd do anything he wanted. And Harry Bond's dad is that rich guy who owns the big car showroom. So nobody says no to fuckin' Harry Bond; he and Danny planned it in biology when I was away in Tenerife with my dad.' Ryan looked sad. 'I came back to school, and they'd already done it a few times.'

'Have you been to see Harry Bond in the mental hospital?' asked Jess.

'No.' Ryan looked shamefaced. 'Look, he wasn't my friend. It's not my place.'

'What did you mean about powers?' asked Chloe.

Jess looked at him. *She knows*.

'OK,' began Ryan. 'When they were doing the Ouija board, they got these ... powers.'

'You'll have to be more specific,' snapped Chloe.

'You could call them abilities, I suppose. Some spirit on there said they just had to ask.'

'For what?' asked Chloe.

'Whatever they wanted. This spirit said it could grant them anything. Harry Locke wanted to be able to control people. Get them to do anything he wanted. While they were doing the Ouija board, at school he seemed to be able to ask a person for something just once, and they did it.'

'Like what?' demanded Chloe.

'He got this girl to undress on stage, in assembly.'

'What the hell? No. You're lying.'

'I was there. I saw it.'

'Was she drunk? On drugs?'

'No. Harry said he whispered it to her before she went on stage to play in the school orchestra. And she just laid down her trombone and stripped. School went wild. Mr Phillips ran on stage to cover her up.'

Chloe shook her head. 'I bet Harry paid her, did something else to persuade her, just so he'd *look* like he had these so-called powers.' She paused. 'And what about your friend Daniel?'

'He wanted to get all As in his mock exams. His dad used to hit him with a belt when he didn't succeed.'

'And?'

'He got an A in every single one,' said Ryan.

'Maybe he just revised really hard?'

'I *know* that wasn't the case. He never went to the physics exam and still got an A.'

'Did the girl...' Chloe couldn't think of her name. 'Did she ask for anything?'

'Amelia. No. She didn't want to. She had this weird ... I dunno, psychic gift or something, like I told you. She has this air about her. I can't explain it.' Ryan looked at Chloe. 'The same as you have, I guess.'

Chloe shook her head. '*Me*?'

'Yeah. Danny told me that it first worked when there was only Amelia in the room. Like you, when it first worked for us. He said it would never work if she wasn't there. She was the gifted one.' Ryan paused. 'The witch.'

The word made Chloe nervous, the way we are when someone points out a truth about us that we don't like; a truth we don't want others to know; a truth we're afraid to look at more closely.

She tried to let Ryan's story sink in. It wouldn't. It sounded like those whispered rumours that get more and more outlandish as they are passed on. 'And what powers do *you* want?' she asked after a moment. 'Why are you really doing this?'

'Why is it about *me*?' Ryan spat at Chloe. 'We all had reasons we started this. Jess hoped I'd fuck her, and I have.'

'*What*?' Jess looked mortified.

'Sorry.' Ryan kissed her cheek as though that might appease her. 'I wanted you too. We wanted each other. That's why we both did this. You know how much I care about you.'

Jess blushed and said nothing.

'No, that's not all.' Chloe narrowed her eyes at Ryan. 'There's something else you wanted.'

'What were *your* reasons?' Ryan glared back, the knowledge black in his eyes. 'You must have had them too.'

The glass began to move then, its scrape seeming sharper to Chloe than previously. The three of them followed its tantalising trail, whispering the words aloud as they appeared. The two remaining candles flickered furiously.

IM STILL FUCKIN HERE

'Daniel,' whispered Ryan.

I KNEW YOU WANTED TO PLAY

'I miss you,' admitted Ryan.

FUCK YOU

Ryan looked crestfallen.
'Maybe he's different ... over there ... on the other side, wherever he is.' Chloe spoke kindly, feeling sorry for Ryan. 'We need to say goodbye to him. We all know it, don't we? This is getting out of hand, and we said at the start that we'd end it if we didn't like how it went.'

COWARDS

'He's just playing with us,' said Chloe.

ID LOVE TO PLAY WITH YOU CHLOE

'Say goodbye,' she urged them.
'Just to him?' asked Ryan.
'To *all* of them,' said Chloe.
'No.' Ryan shook his head.
'*Yes.* I think it's time to end it.'

I WILL END YOU

'Say goodbye,' insisted Chloe.
It was clear Ryan didn't want to stop; it was just as clear that Jess would still do what he wanted. Chloe put her finger on the

glass. She realised then that she could do this alone. It would work just for her. *Remember how*, she thought. *Will it and it shall happen. Push*. And Chloe did it again; she *pushed*. And the glass began to shift towards 'Goodbye'.

It settled there. She took her finger away. Waited. Nothing.

'There,' she said. 'We're done.'

Chloe stood. Another candle went out. Just one remained, fighting valiantly to stay bright, the last warrior standing. The late sun made dust dance between the window slats and the stage – fairies frolicking. Chloe felt like a weight had been physically lifted from her shoulders. The curious feeling that someone was standing just behind her abated. Had they closed whatever door they had opened? That was how the website she visited had described doing a Ouija board – you open a door. But once open, it was forever unlocked, even if you shut it. Once you had been through it, a part of you belonged there forever.

'So that's it?' Ryan sounded as whiney as a five-year-old.

'That's it. Let's pack it away.'

As Ryan reached for the glass, a low rumbling sound vibrated around them. His hand paused mid-air. Chloe would see it there like that, long after, as though he was a puppet on a string. They were all puppets. They were all on strings. She knew then – in a blinding flash – that they would all dance a dark dance until the spirits were done with them. They had tricked her. The weight was not gone. The watching someone had not left. The rumbling continued. Then smoke filled the air, billowing like bloated snow clouds.

Then she realised.

It was the cauldron. At the side of the stage. It was shaking and steaming and bubbling.

'What the fuck?' whispered Ryan.

Chloe approached it.

The movement stopped abruptly. She leaned closer and looked inside it. Nothing there.

'The glass,' said Jess.

Chloe turned. It was moving again. Fast. From letter to letter. They could hardly keep up, hardly string the words together. Chloe whispered it and felt like her voice changed. Ryan and Jess must have heard it too, because they stared at her, mouths open.

BY THE PRICKING OF MY THUMBS
SOMETHING WICKED THIS WAY COMES

'*Macbeth*,' said Jess. She didn't even correct herself.

OPEN LOCKS WHOEVER KNOCKS

'The witches,' said Chloe. She knew the lines by heart.
'Who *is* this?' asked Ryan.

DONT GO

'We are,' said Chloe. 'We're done.'

YOURE NOT EVEN STARTED

'Who are you?' asked Ryan, anyway.

THEY KNOW

'Who do?' he asked.

THE GIRLS

'And who are you?' he asked.

I AM DUST

Chloe shivered. She looked at Jess. Jess held the look. They both knew the three words. Had sung the line many times. Had acted out the role in their bedrooms, dressed in long nightgowns. Had said they would do anything to be the star of such an iconic show.

'Who *are* you?' repeated Ryan.

But Chloe and Jess didn't need to ask. They watched the glass move. Watched it evoke the name they were fascinated by. Watched it change everything.

MORGAN MILLER

26

THE DEAN WILSON THEATRE

MAY 2019

The DW Theatre green room is no longer that colour, instead it's now painted burnt orange. There are thick, cream curtains at the windows, new sofas, and chunky coffee tables offering platters of food. It's all been updated for the cast of *Dust*, who will be arriving at any moment for the meet-and-greet, with writer of the show, Dean Wilson.

This lively event is a big thing in the theatre; a time when staff gather to welcome the cast of a new show for the first time. It's hosted by the artistic director, Edwin Roberts, and usually happens on the first day of rehearsals, but because the marketing department wants to boost the show's media coverage they're holding the event two weeks early. Members of the press – both local and national – are here, standing around with their recording devices and eating vol-au-vents and crisps.

Chloe, Chester and Beth are the only ushers who could come. They group together by a yucca plant, eyeing the food, but not daring to eat it before the cast arrive. Cynthia keeps wandering over, reminding them to be careful if interviewed by any journalists. It is Beth's first meet-and-greet; her hair is the same orange as the new walls.

Chloe feels sick and tries to hide it with laughter.

It's been two months since she saw Ginger.

Two months since their weird experience in the dressing room. Since the kiss. Since Ginger quite literally ran away. There has been no contact. Chloe has desperately wanted to get in touch. She has written a private Facebook message and then deleted it, wondering if Ginger ever does the same. She has opened her wooden box late at night and wanted to slice her flesh with the knife; to watch the pain trickle away with her blood. Only writing the script has stopped her.

It's almost finished. She's not quite sure what she'll do when it's complete. How she will not think about Ginger. Not cut. Not bleed.

'I'm off to the loo,' says Beth, startling Chloe.

'I'm going to mention it to him,' says Chester when she's gone.

'Mention what to who?'

'Tell that hot journalist over there that Beth was here when Morgan Miller died,' he says.

Ever since Chloe told Chester that Beth was in Morgan's dressing room the night she died, he won't let it go. He cosies up to Beth at every opportunity and casually swings their chat around to that night. Oblivious to his motive for asking, she brags about how she would definitely have had the role of Esme if Morgan hadn't auditioned too; that the producers said she had star quality.

'Cynthia's watching,' hisses Chloe. 'Seriously, don't mention Beth. You could get in real bother.'

As though he's heard their conversation, the journalist by the window approaches, running his fingers through his hair as if he's on a catwalk. 'Are you both ushers?' he asks, looking up through his fringe, all Princess Diana.

Cynthia glares at them from across the room, a tuna and cucumber sandwich curling in her right hand.

Yes, just ushers, thinks Chloe.

'*She's* going to be a duty manager soon,' says Chester, overly dramatic as usual. '*And* she's writing a show. Tell them, Chloe, this could be your moment. She's going t—'

'Do you believe the theatre is haunted?' the journalist asks, ignoring Chester's words. 'Have either of you ever seen the ghost of Morgan Miller?'

'Oh, *I* have,' declares Chester. 'Every time I'm round the back. No one dares take the rubbish bags out alone, you know. We hear her singing. I'm very spiritual, you see. I could have been a medium. I—'

'Dean Wilson is coming tonight,' he interrupts. 'He's been a recluse since the original *Dust*. Do you think he feels guilty about Morgan Miller?'

Chester opens his mouth, but Chloe cuts in. 'You'll have to ask *him* that when he comes.'

'There must be lots of talk about her murder here,' continues the journalist. 'You guys must know more than most. Anything you'd like to share?'

'Well,' begins Chester, touching the man's arm and leaning close, 'there *is* this usher who—'

Chloe speaks over him: 'No, there's *nothing*.'

'But he—' the journalist tries.

'*Nothing*,' she repeats. 'Chester, we're going.' And just as Beth returns to the green room, Chloe drags him away.

'What?' he demands. 'I wasn't going to say her name, just tease them with a few hints.'

'You're obsessed.'

Chloe pulls him into the corridor as Cynthia makes her way across the room. They hide behind the pillar at the top of the stairs. Photos of the current show's cast line the wall; the *Dust* cast's pictures will be hung there too at the end of the meet-and-greet. Chloe has already seen Ginger's. It was in the box office yesterday, on top of the pile. For a split second Chloe was sure Ginger winked at her as she passed them. She is flawless in it; a goddess.

'Anyway,' says Chester. 'I have gossip.'

'What's new, Ches? You *always* have gossip.'

'But this is big. I saw it on Cynthia's computer.'

Chloe laughs. 'I have no idea how you're still here, snooping around like you do. Ches, you have to stop, I'd hate it if you left.'

'They're going to be filming a documentary,' he says.

'Who?'

'Some film company. About *Dust* – when the rehearsals start. I reckon it's because of the huge national interest. Because of the murder not being solved. And us being haunted, of course.' Chester claps his hands, face bright. 'We might be in it! I'll totally make sure *I* am. I might just *happen* to wander past when filming takes place, my hair all perfect and my walk all sexy. I'm going low carb from tomorrow. The camera puts ten pounds on you, you know.'

The sound of feet on the nearby stairs – heavy, light, heeled, scraping – interrupts them. For a moment, Chloe's heart stops. She recalls the footsteps that night backstage. How long ago that seems now. Chester squeezes Chloe's arm and peers around the pillar.

'It's *them*,' he hisses.

The *Dust* cast.

Chloe steps forwards too and peers down the stairwell. Leading the troop is Edwin Roberts followed by members of the executive and marketing team. Chloe feels sick. She knows Ginger is among them, somewhere. She recognises John Marrs first. In *West Side Story* his black hair was long and wild; now it's cut short for the role of Dr Chevalier. He looks like he has lost weight, his chiselled jaw now bladelike. Chester stares, mouth open. Chloe shakes her head at him, and they move aside for the procession as Edwin Roberts reaches the top step, fedora angled and face unreadable. He's closely followed by Dean Wilson, who they recognise from the black glasses he always wears in publicity pictures.

Last – like the superstar after the supporting act has finished playing – Ginger rounds the stairwell. Chloe sees her hands first; her long, red nails against the metal bannister. The fingers are white like she's gripping it for dear life. Is she nervous? Chloe remembers their fingers touching as they settled on an upturned glass, long ago.

Ginger steps into the corridor. Chloe smells her; it's the expensive perfume she tested the other day in Debenhams and can't recall the name of. They make eye contact. In the blue flecks of Ginger's irises, Chloe sees their past. She sees them singing the songs from *Dust* in a car on the way somewhere. Now, Ginger looks away first and follows the rest of the group into the green room.

'Honey, she *wants* you,' whispers Chester.

'She doesn't.' Chloe is embarrassed. He doesn't know about the kiss, or her rejection, or that they haven't spoken since that meeting in March.

'Come on,' he says, heading for the green room. 'We don't wanna miss this.'

Chloe isn't sure she wants to go in there. Isn't sure she can stand being just an usher when Ginger is there too, glamorous, admired, *somebody*; isn't sure she won't feel utterly worthless when all of the cast are introduced and welcomed. Chester looks back at her, hand against the door.

'I'm not in the mood,' says Chloe. 'I'll be downstairs.'

He looks disappointed but doesn't argue.

Chloe goes to the empty box office. There's no point going home and coming back in two hours for the evening shift. She picks up the glossy picture of Ginger and traces the curve of her face with a finger. She puts it back in the pile and tidies up the brochure and flyer cupboard to keep busy until everyone comes back. Cynthia is first to arrive, her face like thunder.

'Bloody Chester,' she sighs. 'You'd think he was one of the cast!'

Chloe decides not to ask and heads back up to the green room to relax before the shift.

'Can you make sure it's tidy?' Cynthia calls after her. 'Chester and Beth have made a start now the cast have gone to the rehearsal room for a meeting.'

Yes, I'll pick up the glitter, Chloe thinks.

In the green room, Chester and Beth are putting paper cups

and leftovers into a bin bag, him grumbling loudly about them just being a pair of skivvies.

'What am I, a fucking cleaner now?' he asks Chloe.

She gets a bin bag and helps them. 'So what was it like? What did you learn?' she asks.

'That John Marrs is *gorgeous,*' gushes Beth.

'Yeah, but he knows it,' says Chester. 'He's lucky that he doesn't have to compete with a dead actor. Everyone will compare Ginger to Morgan Miller, but no one remembers who played Chevalier last time, do they?'

'It was an actor called James McAllister,' says Beth. 'His career died after *Dust* ended.'

'Anyway, I think I prefer that Abel Thingy who's playing Esme's brother.' Chester chucks a load of sandwiches into the bag. 'Dean Wilson was dead nice, wasn't he? – So humble. Handled it really well when that journalist suggested he should feel bad about his show. And Ginger was lovely. Even when this other journalist asked if she was scared she'd end up murdered too.'

'They *said* that to her?'

'One did. He got some looks to be fair. But she just smiled and said she only had good feelings about playing Esme Black. I think she's gonna be amazing. I can see why you like her.'

'Chester!' Chloe shoves him.

'You *like* her?' Beth stares.

'They *know* each other,' says Chester.

'Not really.' Chloe tries to change the subject. 'What did Edwin Roberts have to say about the show?'

Among the discarded plates she finds a silver charm bracelet. She holds it up to the light. Trinkets dangle from it like small icicles; a witch's hat, a musical note, a star, and a theatre mask that makes Chloe's breath catch. She sees them all suddenly, in dying sunlight, clanking gently against a glass. She fingers the intricate theatre mask; why does it stir her so?

At that moment, the green-room door opens, and Ginger

comes in. She begins to speak and then sees what Chloe is holding.

'You found it,' she smiles. 'I panicked when I noticed it had gone. I've had it since—'

'You were sixteen.' Chloe remembers in a rush. 'You wore it all the time.' She hands it back to her.

'You bought me this one.' Ginger touches the mask.

'Did I?' Chloe sees it in her own younger hands. 'I did. Yes.'

Ginger smiles. She tries to fasten it around her delicate wrist but can't. 'These bloody nails,' she says. 'They do get in the way a bit.'

Chloe helps her. She knows that Chester and Beth are watching them but doesn't care. 'Can we go somewhere a bit private and chat?' Ginger says more quietly.

'You have your own dressing room now.'

'No. Somewhere else.' Is Ginger scared of that room? Is it any wonder?

'Are they all still in the rehearsal room?'

'Yes.'

'How come *you*'re not?'

'This.' Ginger holds up her hand, shakes the charm bracelet. 'OK, follow me.'

Didn't Chloe always...

27

THE DEAN WILSON THEATRE

MAY 2019

Chloe follows Ginger out of the green room and down the stairs, knowing Chester's face will be a picture. They go through the black backstage door and close it after them. For a moment, Chloe pauses. She hasn't been on the stage since that night when she thought she saw a woman at the back of the theatre. But she isn't alone now. It isn't the middle of the night.

The place is deserted; everyone is occupied elsewhere. The stage is set up for the current show, *Dark Dreams*, a musical about a woman's quest to make it in the modelling world. A mirrored path cuts the stage in two. Ginger marches along it to the centre. There, she spins, arms out, head back, her hair cascading like a gold water-fall. 'There's nowhere like it, is there?' she asks Chloe, laughing.

Chloe remains in the shadows.

'Come and join me,' says Ginger. 'You belong here too.'

Chloe shakes her head, suddenly shy.

'What happened to the girl who loved being centre stage?'

That was always you, Chloe thinks.

But she joins her; together they look out at the rows of red seats rising up towards the technician's box, and the flip-down usher seat where Chloe sits. Is that someone loitering at the top?

'What?' asks Ginger.

'Nothing.' It's nobody; just the shadows.

'I *did* want to contact you,' Ginger admits after a moment, the flamboyant façade dropped. 'I wrote messages a few times and deleted them.' Chloe smiles to herself. 'I was just ... look, I don't know if I'm ready for anything ... like *that*. You know – serious. I've had a few boyfriends, kissed a few girls, even, but my life has always been about this. The stage.'

'You don't have to explain,' insists Chloe.

'The thing is ... since I saw you again, things have been ... odd ... and it made me nervous to get in touch...'

'Odd how?'

'Remember when we met, and I said it was like a door had opened when I saw you?'

'Yes.' Chloe nods. 'I felt it too.'

'Well, I've been having these horrible nightmares since then.'

'About what?'

'It's hard to say.' Ginger wraps her arms about her body. 'They're vague. But *horrible*. Dead birds. Dead bodies. This ominous feeling. I wake feeling sick. I feel like...'

'Like what?'

'Like we need to remember.'

Chloe doesn't speak.

'We need to remember exactly what happened back then,' continues Ginger, and for a moment she is young Jess again, with pigtails and pink cheeks. 'With the Ouija board.' She pauses. 'That was weird, in the dressing room, wasn't it?' For a moment Chloe wonders if she means their kiss. 'The door shutting and the lights turning red. I feel like we imagined it ... *together* ... but also that maybe it's related to the past.'

'But why do we need to remember?'

Ginger thinks. 'So the horrible dreams stop. I've been trying to remember, but it's like ... I just can't *see* it all. And I know that the only way I will is with you.'

'You think so?'

'Yes.'

'Maybe we should get together and talk about it?' Chloe can't think of anything she would rather do, even if thoughts of the Ouija board fill her with a dark dread.

'Let's. I'm scared, but I think we should. How did we *forget*?'

'Don't people bury traumatic memories?'

'Maybe,' muses Ginger. 'But it's more like ... I don't know. It's like the synopsis of a play. We just can't see the actual script.'

'I agree. I can see bits clearly ... other stuff, not so much.'

'Look, I have to go back to London tonight, but I'm back in three weeks for rehearsals and I'll be staying at the Hilton. We can talk about it all then, can't we?'

'Yes.' Chloe is excited to imagine them together, even just as friends.

Ginger pauses. 'I think we should look for Ryan too.'

'Ryan?' Chloe sees him suddenly; a boy in a red jacket and jeans, hair ruffled. Ginger slept with him back then; no, *Jess* slept with him. She's sure of it. Ginger must remember too. You never forget your first. 'Why should we look for *him?*'

'There were three of us. Something big happened, I'm sure of it, and he's part of that. Can you remember his surname?'

'No.' Even if she could, Chloe wouldn't tell her.

'Shit. Maybe when we talk, we'll remember it. I know I had a crush on him.'

More than that, thinks Chloe.

The thought of him being back, coming between the two of them again, fills her with hurt. She won't let it happen.

'We shouldn't find him,' says Chloe.

'Why?'

'Do you remember ... "you three, never be, under one roof"?'

'*Shit.*' Ginger gasps and steps a little further away from Chloe, her eyes full of fear. 'I don't know what it means but, God, it scares me. Where have I heard it before?'

'I saw the words on a mirror.' Chloe doesn't tell Ginger it was in her dressing room. 'I think someone said it to us once.' She pauses. 'And I think it would be really dangerous to find Ryan.'

'Maybe you're right.'

Chloe hates to see Ginger looking so scared.

The door opens and they both jump with a shriek.

Edwin Roberts strides onto the stage, fedora in hand and hair as wild as a thorny bush. 'There you are,' he says to Ginger. 'We're all looking for you. We need a photograph of the whole cast. Can you come, darling?'

'Yes, of course, Eddie, darling.' Ginger assumes a professional, crisp air again. 'Are you still in the rehearsal room?'

'Yes. Come now, we're all waiting for you.'

She sweeps past and follows Edwin, who looks back at Chloe, an unasked question knitting his brow. And then Chloe is alone. She walks to the front of the stage. She can't look up towards the back, afraid of what she might see. What must it be like to have rows of captive faces awaiting your every word? She hasn't performed for any sort of audience since they were at the youth theatre, and that's so long ago now. What would she even say if the light swung her way?

You know what you'd say, she thinks.

But does she even know it by heart?

Chloe closes her eyes and pictures the script in her box.

She speaks.

Acts.

'The dancer who doesn't dance,' she whispers, nervous at first. 'Why does she haunt me? I am different with her. My body knows the moves, as if I'm guided by some higher hand. We are one when the music starts...'

Chloe pauses. She speaks more slowly, feeling the words. As all the best actors are supposed to, she draws on her own experience to bring the character to life.

'I'm changing, the way we change in water, becoming light, free, buoyant. As I change, I remember when she kissed me, surprising me, and made my pores tingle. She didn't laugh at my scars. She said we—'

'What's that?'

Chloe gasps. Ginger is standing in the wings, radiant against the black curtain.

'Nothing,' stammers Chloe.

'It's beautiful. Did you write it?'

'Yes,' says Chloe softly, embarrassed.

Someone calls Ginger's name. She looks back at the door, unsure. It comes again. She disappears. But Chloe can wait. Only three weeks, and she will be back.

28

JESS'S BEDROOM

2005

In Jess's room, under an original *Dust* poster that they'd both covered in pink lipstick kisses, she and Chloe admired Jess's new bracelet. Though silver, in the evening light that slanted through the open window it appeared to be gold. Chloe touched the single charm attached; a delicate witch hat with a frilled edge.

'My mum got me it,' said Jess, proud. 'She said she'll get me a new charm each time I star in a show. This one's to represent *Macbeth*.'

'I reckon you'll end up with thousands, then,' gushed Chloe. 'You'll need another bracelet.' She wondered if she could afford to buy her one.

It was the night after the Ouija board had spelled out MORGAN MILLER. Neither of them had mentioned it yet. After the actress's name appeared, everything had stopped. Cold. The glass hadn't moved another inch. Chloe had tried again and again to shift it, and Ryan had ranted at her, saying, 'Oh, *now* you want it to work!' She couldn't deny that she had been desperate to get Morgan Miller back.

Was it even really her?

They had to find out.

Even if it had been Morgan, she had disappeared as soon as she'd arrived, as fleeting as a lone flake of snow. They had left the theatre then, Jess going off with Ryan, leaving Chloe to wait for her bus.

Now she said to Jess, 'We need to do the Ouija board again.'

Jess fingered her bracelet. 'But you were the one who said it was getting out of hand. You wanted us to say goodbye and end it, re-member? And you said you're sick of the phone ringing all night.' She paused. 'Did it ring last night?'

'No,' admitted Chloe.

'Well, then maybe we should stay away.'

'But aren't you curious? I mean, it could really be *Morgan Miller.*' Chloe stretched up and touched the *Dust* poster where, as a lank-haired Esme, Morgan looked into a mirror at the more golden and glorious ghost of Esme.

'I bet it's not her. They can trick you, you know.'

'Who can?'

'Spirits,' said Jess impatiently. 'You're not the only one who did some reading, you know. They can play games. Pretend to be other people. Mess with you.'

'Then we do what we did with Daniel Locke,' insisted Chloe. 'We ask her questions we know the answer to, to check it's her. Come on, we've both read enough books about her.'

'I don't know.' Jess shook her head, her ponytail swishing. 'Maybe it's time to stop. After all, she came and then she disap-peared. I've felt so weird lately. Sick and tired all the time. Then last night I slept really well...'

'But we could find out what actually happened to her,' said Chloe.

Jess didn't speak for a moment. 'But even if she told us, who'd believe us? A load of teenagers on a Ouija board.'

'I don't care if no one believed us. We'd *know*.'

'Why us?' wondered Jess.

'What do you mean?'

'If it *is* her, why did she choose to speak to us?'

'Because we were asking?' Chloe shrugged. 'OK, I don't know. But I *want* to.'

'It makes me tired just thinking about it.' Jess untied her hair and lay back on her gingham pillows. 'We've got rehearsals tomor-row. Can we just decide then?'

Chloe joined Jess, lying on her back beside her. She loved this room. Loved being in it. Loved the way Jess arranged her perfumes and body sprays with the most expensive at the front. Loved that the sweet smell of her hit as soon as you opened the door. Loved sharing a bed with her on weekends, sleeping side by side, legs entwined, the bristle of two-day hair growth on Jess's an exotic irritation.

'Why didn't you tell me you'd slept with Ryan?' Chloe asked suddenly.

'I was going to. I just haven't seen you properly, have I?'

Chloe didn't want to know about it in detail, so changed the subject a little. 'I don't like how he speaks to you sometimes. I don't like how he treats you. What do you even see in him?'

Jess closed her eyes. 'There's just *something* about him.'

Chloe studied her; the spidery eyelashes that they always made a wish on when they found one; the neat, sandy eyebrows; the spattering of freckles Jess hated so much.

'He lied to us,' said Chloe, not giving up. 'He didn't tell us that Daniel Locke was his best friend. That's huge. He knew a boy who committed suicide! I don't trust him, Jess. He's doing the Ouija board for some reason that he won't share.'

'So let's not do it anymore.'

Now you have Ryan, thought Chloe, *you don't need to*.

'Where do you think we go when we die?' asked Jess, sleepily. 'What do you think there is?'

'I don't know. I don't really like to think about it.'

'I mean if we *have* been speaking to the dead, then what's it like for them?'

Chloe tried to imagine. Tried to visualise being on the other side; being here – still existing somehow in this world – but not able to speak to the ones you loved. Did the spirits wander among the living? Did they watch them? If so, what must it be like to witness others doing wonderful everyday things while you could not? Chloe hoped that when she went, she would simply go. Be gone. Not exist at all. Yet that was even harder to picture. Where did your soul go? Where did your feelings go? Your essence?

What would it be like to no longer love Jess?

29

THE GAME

2005

At the *Macbeth* rehearsals the following night, Ryan and Jess returned with gusto. When Ryan silenced the room with his dagger speech, any anger Mr Hayes had had about their absence was replaced with a satisfied smile. Chloe could not deny Ryan's stage presence. She sat at the back, out of his sight, not wanting him to see her admiration. Lit blood red, he was a living, breathing Macbeth, older than his years, haggard, driven to consider murder, descending into madness.

Jess sat stage left, face angelic with awe. The silver dagger glinted in the stage lights; something about it mesmerised Chloe. She imagined the blade in her own hands. How heavy it might be. How cooling to the palms. She knew it was real, a carving knife that Ryan had brought from home. Despite the fact that it could cause great injury, Mr Hayes had said it looked stunning and he would put it safely away after each rehearsal. Chloe blinked at the flash as Ryan held it aloft. Then frowned.

Why was it affecting her so?

Silence, followed by rapturous applause. Chloe joined in. It was only fair. Ryan deserved it. He and Jess were the kind of actors you couldn't take your eyes off when they performed.

'Just over three weeks until the show,' said Mr Hayes when the room fell quiet again. 'You need to attend *all* rehearsals from now on. Twice a week. OK, on a more serious note – has someone been staying behind when the building is shut?'

Chloe was glad she had sat at the back, hidden. Jess and Ryan were sitting together at the front, so she couldn't see their faces; she knew that Ryan would look composed, but was sure Jess looked nervous. No one in the theatre spoke.

'Well,' said Mr Hayes, 'I hope not. Some things have been messed around with.'

'Maybe it's that homeless guy who hangs around here,' said someone Chloe couldn't see.

'Maybe. We'll have to make sure the building is more secure. We can't run the risk of the set being destroyed or some important costume going missing. Right – witches! You're up!'

Later – long after everyone had gone – Ryan, Jess and Chloe loitered in the nearby bus shelter, fanning their faces with scripts in the evening heat. None of them had mentioned whether they were going back inside the theatre, yet none of them had put a hand out for any of the passing buses.

'So who wants to do it?' asked Ryan eventually.

Chloe glanced at Jess, who remained mute. 'I do. But Ryan – no more bullshit. You should have told us how well you really knew Daniel Locke. And you're only coming back in there with us if you tell us your *real* reasons for doing this.'

'Who fucking put *you* in charge?' Ryan stood up.

'I did.' The words came out of Chloe before she could think.

Ryan faltered. 'Well, what are *your* reasons, apart from the obvious?' He motioned to Jess with his eyes.

'I want to talk to Morgan Miller.' Chloe held his gaze, unafraid, bold.

'Shit, that was weird, wasn't it?' he said. 'You reckon it's really her?'

'Let's go and find out.' Chloe paused. 'But first ... why did you really want to do this?'

'OK, *OK*.' Ryan looked at his feet. 'I just want to be ... well ... *rich*.'

'Rich? How's a Ouija board going to help you do that?'

'You heard what I said about Daniel and his exams. And Harry being able to control others.'

'You don't need some spirit to help you get rich,' said Chloe. 'You're an incredible actor.'

'That's not enough though, is it?'

'*Yes.*'

'Oh, don't be fucking naïve, Chloe. It all comes down to money really. It doesn't matter how talented you are if you can't afford to go to the best drama school. I could be Richard fucking Burton, but I live in a council house with my single, drunk mother and eight brothers. I ain't ever going to RADA. It'll be a job in B&Q for me, if I'm lucky.' Ryan kicked a loose stone into the road. 'Jess's mum will make sure *she* goes to RADA. She makes sure she gets extra singing lessons and all that shit. Fuck, she'll probably pay for surgery, so she looks perfect too.'

'Don't talk about my mum like that.' Jess's voice was barely a whisper.

'That's not fair,' added Chloe, despite feeling compassion for Ryan for the first time. 'Jess can't help it if her parents are more comfortable.'

'I guess.' Ryan shrugged, deflated now. 'Sorry, Jess.'

Jess nodded, but still looked sad.

'Shall we go inside, then?' said Chloe.

'Let's,' said Ryan.

And they did – with Chloe leading.

The stage was how it had been left after rehearsals: the cauldron to the right, a pile of wigs and capes to the left, and the dust – as always – dancing in the dying sunlight through the wooden slats. Wordlessly, Ryan took the shoe box from the cupboard and set things up. Jess lit the three candles, and Chloe sat cross-legged next to them with the pen and notepaper. They looked at the up-turned glass and then at one another, faces orange in the glow. Then one by one they placed their fingers upon it. Jess's new brace-let tinkled against it like ice cubes in lemonade. They moved the glass in a circular motion for a while and then stopped. Looked around at one another.

'Am I still doing the questions?' Ryan asked Chloe. Something had shifted. He was unsure. Not Macbeth now.

She nodded. Let him do it. He had begun the game – let him think he was still its master.

He inhaled and then spoke. 'Is there anyone here with us?'

Nothing. The candles flickered in unison, three dancers hearing the same beat. Chloe looked towards the door, but it was closed still.

'Is there anyone here who wants to talk?' Ryan asked again.

They waited; breath held.

'If there's anyone there, make yourself known.'

Chloe felt a cool draught. She looked at Jess and was sure her face showed the same awareness of something. Then all three candles went out at the same time with a sizzling sound. The door was still closed. No one moved. Nor did the glass.

'I think someone's here,' said Ryan calmly. 'Tell us your name?'

The glass moved slowly. It did not scrape the way it had when Daniel Locke spoke to them. It was languid, lazy, somehow hypnotic. Chloe felt heat rise up her arm. She knew absolutely that if they had removed their fingers, it would still move. She whispered each letter as the glass touched them, wrote the words with her free hand.

I AM DUST

'Can you tell us your real name?' asked Ryan.

MORGAN MILLER

'The actress who died?' asked Ryan.

WE NEVER REALLY DIE

'What happens to us then?' asked Jess.

IM STILL HERE
I AM DUST
IM THOSE FRAGMENTS IN THE AIR
THE GOLD LIGHT DANCING THERE
THAT BREEZE FROM NOWHERE

Chloe could hear Morgan's voice as the words formed – so speedily now that it was hard to keep up. But it wasn't the song she had listened to on CD over and over, but Morgan's voice live, just like that night at the theatre, the first time she ever sang it for a paying audience.

'What does that mean?' asked Ryan.

'It's the song,' whispered Jess. 'You must know it. The theme to *Dust.*'

'Doesn't mean it's her,' he said. 'Everyone knows those words.'

'Well, you didn't,' said Jess, and Chloe couldn't help but smile.

'How do we know you're *really* Morgan Miller?' asked Ryan.

NOTHING IS EVER WHAT IT SEEMS

She was playing with them, but Chloe didn't feel it was malicious. Hadn't she read that Morgan liked to have fun, to play tricks on her fellow cast?

'She's an actress, remember?' said Jess. 'Maybe in that other place she doesn't even *know* who she is.'

'Morgan, how old were you when you died?' asked Chloe.

AGELESS

'I don't think it's her,' said Ryan. 'Shall we get someone else?'

WHO DO YOU WANT RYAN

He looked surprised. 'I ... I don't know.'

WHAT DO YOU WANT RYAN

'I want to know if you're really who you say you are.'

ARE YOU

'Yes,' he insisted. 'I am.'

NOT EARLIER

'What do you mean?' He looked nervous.

Though the glass had moved languidly at the start, now it zipped from letter to letter to letter, making Chloe dizzy. And she heard it all. Heard Morgan's soft voice as though she were sitting with them.

IS THIS A DAGGER
WHICH I SEE BEFORE ME
THE HANDLE TOWARDS MY HAND
COME LET ME CLUTCH I THEE

Chloe recognised the speech from Ryan's rehearsal earlier.

'Yes. I was Macbeth then.' He nodded, seemed relieved. 'Have you been watching us? Where are you right now? Who are you standing the closest to?'

She isn't standing, thought Chloe.

'You shouldn't ask that,' she said.

'Why not?'

'I just don't think we should. And don't ask so many questions one after the other. Wait for an answer to each one first.'

IM NEXT TO THE WITCH

Was that a breath in Chloe's ear? A lingering scent of perfume? A hand moving her hair?

Ryan smiled. 'Who do you mean, Morgan?'

CHLOE

'Told you,' he said.
'Fuck off,' she hissed at him.

CHLOE

'She likes you,' grinned Ryan.

CHLOE

'Who killed you, Morgan?' he asked.
'You can't just ask like that,' cried Jess.
'Tell us Morgan. You must know.'

I HARDLY KNOW YOU

'Is it really her, though?' Ryan sounded annoyed. 'I'm not con-vinced. We should ask her something only she knows. Like we did with Danny. You guys know all about her. What was her mum's name? Don't say it out loud now, just tell me if you know it.'

Chloe can't remember. She once read a biography where they mostly interviewed her mother, but she can't think what her name was.

'I know,' said Jess.

'Don't say it,' hissed Ryan. 'OK, Morgan, what's your mum's name?'

MUM

Ryan laughed.

DO YOU LIKE YOUR MUM JESS

'Yes, I do.' Jess looked put out.

I LOVED HER
IT WAS SIMPLE
SHE LOVED ME
IT WAS COMPLEX

'What does that mean?' demanded Ryan.

'It's from *Dust*,' explained Chloe. 'It's a song about Esme's mum.'

'I *love* my mum,' cried Jess. 'I'm sick of you all saying stuff about her.'

'I never have,' said Chloe.

'*You* did,' she snapped at Ryan.

'I'm sorry. I was just mad about mine.'

The glass moved again, pulling their fingers back and forth, back and forth, back and forth.

I AM DUST

'Yeah, you said that,' cried Ryan.

YOU ARE DUST

'What does *that* mean?' asked Jess.

BOYFRIEND GOT ME TO DO IT

'To do what?' asked Ryan.

HE KNEW WHAT I COULD DO

'Do you reckon she means that her boyfriend killed her?' wondered Jess.

'I'm sure it was proved that he wasn't there when she died,' said Chloe. 'He had a solid alibi. He always looks heartbroken in interviews, and it seems genuine.'

'Did your boyfriend kill you?' asked Ryan.

Nothing.

'Are you still with us, Morgan?'

Nothing.

'I think she's gone,' whispered Chloe.

The glass moved to 'Goodbye'.

'Now what?' asked Ryan

'I'm exhausted,' said Jess.

She looked it. Black shadows hung beneath her eyes like dark clouds too tired to move. Chloe realised she was tired too. She felt like she had been awake for days. This was what happened at the end of each session – a weariness that made muscles ache, bones throb, eyes heavy. Even though she could have talked with Morgan Miller forever, it was hard to find the energy to try.

'Let's go then,' she said.

They did. But once they were in the street, Chloe realised she had left her phone in the theatre. 'Shit,' she said. 'I can't leave it there.'

Ryan's bus rounded the corner. She knew Jess wanted to go and hang at his.

'I'll be fine,' she said, trying to sound braver than she felt. 'I'll catch the next bus.' She was disappointed that Jess didn't argue, went so easily with Ryan. Her heart ached as much as her other muscles did.

*

When Chloe got home it was dark. Her dad was watching some cop show in the living room. In the kitchen, her mum was sorting the laundry, separating pink socks from blue. She looked tired. Her hair hung like tights from a washing line on a still day. Chloe watched her folding the worn sheets and was suddenly overwhelmed with love for this woman who worked two jobs and yet always had time to talk.

'There you are,' she said when she saw Chloe. 'How was rehearsal tonight?'

'OK.' Chloe sat at the table.

'Just OK?'

Chloe suddenly wanted to cry. 'Mum, I feel ... *odd.*'

Her mum sat down and put the laundry on the table. 'You are odd, sweetheart. You're my lovely, odd girl, like no one else.'

'No, I mean ... *bad* somehow.'

'Oh, you're not bad. Why would you think that?' Her mum looked sad. 'It's hard being sixteen.'

'They said I'm a witch.'

Her mum laughed gently. 'Who did? And is that a bad thing?'

'Yes! Witches are always ugly and evil. Look at *Macbeth.* They're horrible.'

'There are white witches too.' Her mum looked serious now. 'They always said your Grandma Rosa was one, you know.'

'Did they?'

'Yes. You know how special she was. She'd just *know* things. Sense them. Like if I called her up, she'd tell me she had known I would. She said she saw ghosts too. We used to tease her, but she did have this curious knack of knowing things she shouldn't have.'

Chloe missed her acutely. It had only been a year since her death.

'Remember when she wouldn't let us set off for the airport that time?' said Chloe's mum. 'There was that horrible car pile-up that killed ten people. And she had known. We missed our flight, but at least we were alive.' She leaned over and touched Chloe's cheek. 'You're like her. I feel like she's still here because of you.'

'We used to talk to each other,' said Chloe.

'I know, sweetheart.'

'No, I mean ... without speaking. Across the table, when you and Dad were there.'

Chloe's mum studied her.

'I love you,' she said.

'I love you too, Mum.'

That night Chloe slept heavily. Dreams came hard. A black bird in her room somewhere scratch-scratch-scratching. Something under the bed rustle-rustle-rustling. And Grandma Rosa whispered, *my magic girl, my magic girl, my magic girl*, without moving her mouth.

30

THE DEAN WILSON THEATRE

JUNE 2019

Chloe is supposed to be restocking ice creams before the matinee of an amateur production of *Wicked*. The freezer is right near the rehearsal room fire exit, and it's the first *Dust* read-through. She can't resist opening the fire door a crack and peering through, heart beating fast at the thought of Cynthia finding her. They have all been warned to keep a low profile as rehearsals get under way.

'You should be as invisible around the building as you are in the auditorium,' Cynthia said at a meeting last week, with a stern look in Chester's direction. 'Do your usual jobs with as little fuss as possible. Help where asked, but do *not* make a nuisance of yourselves. There will be lots of people milling around with equipment, so don't get in the way.'

Could Chloe have felt any less important?

Pinch yourself, she thought. *You might not even exist.*

Now she puts a finger between the fire door and its frame, and spies on the cast. They sit around in a circle, scripts in hand, intense looks on faces. The large windows are all open; Ginger sits near one, her hair rippling like a golden waterfall in the breeze. Chloe recalls a similar heat long ago – the nights at the youth theatre when Mr Hayes flung open the fire doors to cool them down.

Chloe knows that Ginger will have already started doing research into the character and memorising the lines. That won't have been difficult – when they were kids, they knew them all. For Ginger it must be like returning to a beloved childhood fairy tale. It must feel like coming home.

Ginger was never as good at playing Esme Black the housemaid as she was the ghost; she could never quite be as nondescript as the former required, but was magnificent when she died and returned as her ghost, all breath-taking beauty and seduction. Chloe fantasises that they could *both* play Esme; they could split it. She would make the perfect housemaid, part of the shadows, like now, longing for someone she can't have. Ginger could take over when Esme resurrects as a ghost and finally wins Dr Chevalier's love.

'Who *are* you?' reads John Marrs, pulling Chloe from her reverie. He wears jeans and a red T-shirt, but even in this everyday attire, when he speaks, he *is* Dr Chevalier. 'I feel sure I know you, and yet you're a mystery to me. Can you speak, strange creature? Can you tell me your name?'

Chloe frowns. Hears a similar line. *Is there anyone here who wants to talk with us*? Is that Ryan's voice? Who were they speaking to back then?

'Come closer so I can look at you,' continues John as Chevalier. 'Come over here and whisper your name in my ear.'

Next to him, Dean Wilson smiles and nods. He pushes his glasses up his nose and looks proud. Pleased. No wonder. His show is back in a big way. Chloe realises that two of the documentary crew are filming from opposite corners. One of them now grabs a handheld camera and kneels down beside Ginger as though in utter reverence. She speaks. Electricity runs along Chloe's spine.

'You know who I am, my love,' she says, voice intoxicating. 'My name is right there on your lips, next to your own...'

Chloe smiles; they are close to the big song. Will Ginger sing it, or will they simply play it? She has not seen her to speak to since the cast returned yesterday. They have not even passed in a corridor. When she took the rubbish out last night, Chloe stopped near the Ginger Swanson dressing room, as it is now called; there is a brand-new, not-tarnished gold star on its door, with her name at the centre. Chloe touched the star, aware her fingers were greasy from the job. She left a single fingerprint over the S, as though to say, *I was here too.*

'I'm happy to sing it,' Ginger is saying now.

Edwin Roberts looks thrilled, says, 'If you're sure, darling?'

She nods. Even from this distance Chloe can see her eyes are glazed with tears. What a moment for her. The cameraman gets closer. An expectant hush settles over the room. All the singing lessons Jess's mum paid for were worth every penny. Beginning quietly, Ginger takes her rapt audience into the iconic chorus, breathy at first and then a deep, rich, warm vibrato.

I'm still here; I am dust.
I'm those fragments in the air,
the gold light dancing there,
that breeze from nowhere.

For a moment, Chloe thinks she hears another voice singing too; a ghostly echo.

A hand lands on her shoulder and she jumps back, covering her mouth to supress a gasp. But it's just Chester. She closes the fire door as quietly as she can, heart wild.

'You scared me.' She shoves him.

'What you doing? Ah, the rehearsals. I might go in and see if they want anything – like me!' He laughs heartily. 'Cynthia's looking for you. Come on, we've got to sell at least five million programmes. Look – you're melting the bloody ice cream.'

Chloe realises she has left the freezer top open. 'Shit, shit, *shit*.' She grabs two boxes of Vanilla, closes it, and follows Chester back to the box office, wishing she could stay and listen to Ginger all day.

Wicked drags relentlessly that afternoon. It's performed with zest by the young cast, but being a college production, the set is cheap and the props fall over at inopportune moments. Chloe turns her radio down low, nervous about hearing strange messages, and thinks about Ginger. About their kiss. The warmth of her mouth. The feel of her spine. Lost in thought, she almost misses the cues for the interval. Chloe and Beth then stand at the front of the stage, preventing patrons from climbing up the steps or stealing backstage. They often try, wanting to see the haunted dressing room for themselves.

'I reckon they'd be disappointed,' says Beth, her hair crimson today, lips matching.

'Who?'

'Audience members. If they got to see the dressing room. It's so much smaller and less glamourous than the press paints it to be.'

'It's nicer now,' says Chloe. It has been painted crisp white for Ginger, and the original *Dust* poster has been replaced with the new one.

'Yes. It is.' Beth leans closer, whispers, 'Never say anything to anyone, but I have something from the original room.'

'You do? What do you mean? How did you get it? What was it?'

Don't ask so many questions one after the other, she suddenly thinks. *Wait for an answer to each one first.* She has said that before. But when?

'When I went there ... *that night.*' Beth says the last two words with emphasis. 'When I saw Morgan Miller and—'

'Wait, you said you never *saw* her that night. You said you just left flowers in her dressing room.'

'That's what I meant.' Beth seems agitated. 'I mean when I *tried* to see her. And then I did, just for a second. Anyway, I took—'

At that moment, Cynthia marches into the auditorium. 'You shouldn't be standing chatting,' she snaps. 'Can one of you please stand stage left and the other stage right, like I've asked you to a *million* times.'

They split up and guard the stage separately.

After the shift, Chloe tries to catch Beth and finish their conversation, but Cynthia grabs Chloe first. 'I'm going to start your duty-manager training at the end of the month,' she says. 'Then, by the time *Dust* is on, you'll be in charge on some shifts.'

Chloe heads backstage with two greasy, stinking bin bags, excited at the thought of not having to do this anymore; of not having to pick chewing gum off the seats and popcorn off the floor and carry old beer to the sink. But then she loves it too. Loves the banter with the other ushers. And that would change.

Distracted, she crashes into someone near the dressing rooms. It's one of the film crew; a young man with a BBC lanyard and a bushy hipster beard.

'You're one of the ushers, aren't you? Can we do a short interview with you?' From the way he asks, he clearly expects her to respond with an eager 'yes'.

'With *me*? Oh.' The bin bag is dripping coke onto the concrete and Chloe knows she'll have to clean that up. 'I'm not sure. What do you want me to say?'

'Well, we'd like something spontaneous, you know, an everyday usher talking about how things have changed here with the return of *Dust*. We think you'd offer a nice contrast, especially in your uniform.'

'What do you mean?' Chloe looks down at it, at coffee stains and damp armpits.

'The plain-black kind of, you know, working-class apparel. A northern accent too – that would be great against the actors.'

'Ginger's from here,' says Chloe.

At that moment, Ginger comes out of her dressing room. She looks lovely; fresh, clean, immaculately dressed. Chloe is embarrassed about her appearance, about the sweaty hair on her forehead, about the mascara she knows is smudged at the corners of her eyes.

'*Ginger*.' The cameraman looks besotted. Chloe is forgotten.

'Seth,' she smiles. 'I'm done for the day, so I'll see you tomorrow, yes?'

When he's gone Ginger asks Chloe, 'Are you finished now too?'

'I just have to clean *that* up.' Chloe points at the coke spillage; it's like blood at a murder scene. 'Then I'm more or less done.'

'Do you want to meet for coffee? We can have that talk.'

'That talk?'

'About our past,' Ginger murmurs.

'Of course.' How could she have forgotten? 'Can you give me fifteen minutes?'

'I'll meet you in the bar?'

'OK.'

Back in the box office Chloe grabs the mop to clean up the coke spillage but Chester pulls her into Cynthia's empty office, his face full of gossip. He swipes his phone screen and opens Twitter.

'Look what's trending,' he cries. 'Someone sent a letter in.'

'A letter? To who?'

'Look – just bloody read it!'

The hashtag is #WhoKilledMorganMiller; and the latest posts all link to a newspaper article. Chloe clicks on one of them. Chester is trembling with anticipation next to her. The headline is 'New Clue in Morgan Miller Mystery'. She skims through, taking in random sentences, odd words. It seems the police have received a letter and an unnamed item from someone who claims to know the killer. The item apparently puts its owner in the dressing room with Morgan Miller that night. The letter is currently being analysed by a handwriting expert.

'It could be fake,' says Chloe. 'Everyone is mad for *Dust* at the moment. Everyone's contacting the press and posting stuff about their theories. For God's sake, I read something last night by a man who reckons Morgan Miller is still alive and living somewhere with Elvis and Hitler.'

'Doesn't sound fake. The posh papers are running the story too.'

'Wonder what it is?' muses Chloe.

'What *what* is?'

'The new evidence. The unnamed item.'

Chloe frowns. Remembers what Beth said earlier. *I have something original from the room.* Does she still have it? Or is it with the police now?

'What?' asks Chester studying her.

'Nothing.' No point telling him and having it blown all out of proportion. 'Anyway, I have crap to clean up and then—'

'Then what?'

'I'm meeting Ginger.'

'Ooooh. You go get yours, girl!'

31

THE DEAN WILSON THEATRE

JUNE 2019

Chloe wishes she had brought something to change into. She has tidied her hair and borrowed some of Chester's body spray, but as she approaches Ginger, sitting elegantly on one of the new barstools, her hair a cascade of curls down her back – her *beautiful* back – Chloe feels ugly. The scars on her thighs throb, reminding her of previous self-hatred, of insecurity about her looks, her abilities, her life. She takes the seat next to Ginger, but stumbles and briefly slips off the stool.

'You were incredible,' she says as she recovers herself.

'Was I?' Ginger smiles, a little shy maybe. 'When?'

Embarrassed, Chloe realises she'll have to admit she was watching the rehearsal. 'Oh, I heard you singing earlier. I was working near the fire exit. It gave me goose bumps.'

'Thank you. I can't describe how it felt. I still can't quite believe I'm here, playing Esme Black. It's utterly surreal. Like I'll wake up and...'

'And what?'

'And I'm sixteen again, and we're singing that song in my bedroom.'

Chloe smiles. Colin, the friendliest barman, comes up and asks what she wants. She orders a latte. Ginger has a black coffee in front of her. Chloe knows from an interview for a Sunday magazine that she is dieting for the role, avoiding all dairy, fat and sugar.

'They were good days, weren't they?' says Chloe.

'They were. Until...'

'Until what?'

Colin puts a steaming latte in front of Chloe. She sips it and waits for Ginger to respond.

'Until the Ouija board, I think. Then it all got ... weird. What do you remember about it?'

'If you'd asked me ten minutes ago, I'd have said not much. But sitting here with you, hearing you say those words, it all starts to take shape. Seriously, it's like it comes out of a fog. If I look at you, I can see more of it.' Chloe pauses, letting it in. 'Does that sound odd?'

'No. I feel that way too. Whose idea was it?'

'What?'

'Doing the Ouija board,' says Ginger.

Chloe looks around, realising that maybe they should have this conversation privately, but the foyer behind them is deserted. The main doors are locked open, letting the warm June day colour the floor with gold. It's that lull between the two shows; between the older patrons who prefer the matinee and the younger audience who come in the evening. Chloe wonders, would she really want to talk about this in Morgan's – no, *Ginger's* – dressing room, though? What might such a topic evoke in there?

'I think it was Ryan's idea.' Chloe sees him for a moment. Hears him. *We're going to play a game.* 'And we both went along with it. You did because you liked him ... and I did because...'

'Because?' asks Ginger softly, holding Chloe's gaze.

'You *know* why.' She says it more harshly than she intends.

As though to save Chloe's embarrassment, Ginger changes the subject. 'God, I had the worst dream yet last night. I woke up drenched in sweat. There were these birds, hitting the window. Bang, bang, *bang.*'

Chloe shivers because she too has been dreaming about them. But she doesn't interrupt Ginger.

'I even went and looked out of my hotel window at three in the morning, sure they would be piled up in the street. But there was nothing there. Then I dreamed there were these three witches chanting spells. This smoking cauldron. This ... ghost. This ... *woman*.'

'The witches is because of... the Scottish play.'

Ginger laughs. 'You still believe that old superstition? I do remember Ryan getting annoyed when I wouldn't say *Macbeth*. But fuck it. *Macbeth*.' Ginger says it boldly. For a moment, Chloe imagines them being struck down by lightning.

'That's what the play was that summer,' says Chloe. 'That's what we were rehearsing when we did the Ouija board.'

'God, yes. That would explain the dream. But the birds? Shit, that was eerie.'

'I think I used to dream about birds too.' Chloe isn't sure why she puts it in the past tense. She pauses. 'Wait. Maybe there *was* one. An actual bird. Yes. I think right before we did the Ouija board. I saw one. Black. Glossy. *Yuck*.'

'Shit, yes. Me and Ryan found one somewhere too. On a windowsill.'

'I can smell it,' whispers Chloe.

'My mum is quite superstitious about dead birds. Says it's an omen of death.'

'Well, it's definitely a bad omen for the poor bird!'

Ginger laughs, head back, and the sound is musical. Then in a switch as quick as a breath, she looks more serious. 'I just feel like ... something is coming.'

'Something *good*?'

Ginger doesn't respond; Chloe didn't expect her to.

'It's connected to those days,' Ginger says at last. 'What else do you remember?'

'Don't think I'm weird ... but can I touch your hand?'

Ginger nods. Chloe leans nearer and takes hold of her slender fingers. They warm within the protection of her own. And she begins to see something. She closes her eyes. Tries to let it in. This feels like something she has done before and yet never done. She sees the three of them, their fingers on a glass, the glass moving speedily between letters. She sees Ryan with a knife. No. Not just a knife. A dagger. In *Macbeth*. She sees it dripping with blood...

Chloe...

Who said that?

'Chloe.' It's Ginger. Chloe opens her eyes. Drops Ginger's hand.

'What was that?' asks Ginger.

'I don't know. I just thought I'd be able to see more if I touched you.' Hadn't Grandma Rosa often clutched Chloe's hand to her chest and told her things that then happened?

'And did you see anything? You looked ... *scared*.'

'No,' lies Chloe, afraid to share the image of a blood-soaked knife. It's probably her overactive imagination. Being with Ginger ignites her. It creates so many churning feelings, like the different ingredients in a magic potion. 'I think when we all did the Ouija board that we – I don't know – got cursed or something. Can you remember why we all stopped and never saw one another again?'

'No. That's the least clear of all. I sort of remember starting it. I can see the three of us with our fingers on that glass. I think one day it just started moving. And we got spirits. We spoke to dead people. Jesus, that sounds so crazy now. I can't believe I'm a grown adult sitting here saying that.'

'But we did.' Chloe finishes her latte. 'We *did*.'

'Who did we speak to?'

'Wasn't there some boy Ryan knew?'

'There was,' cries Ginger. 'A boy who had died in a car crash or something horrible.'

Daniel Locke. The name drops into Chloe's head. She must google him later. She feels sure he died in an accident. She won't mention him now. She'll see what the story is first.

'Do you think it would work if we did it now?' wonders Ginger.

'Yes.' Chloe knows it absolutely, and it terrifies her. 'But I never will.'

Edwin Roberts crosses the foyer then, his overly polished shoes catching the light as though winking at them. He doesn't look at Chloe but touches Ginger on the arm and says, 'Sorry to disturb you, darling, but would you mind meeting me and Seth for a quick chat. He's got a great idea about some footage of you outside the back of the theatre and the light is just right now.'

'That's fine,' she says, standing up.

Edwin heads towards the backstage corridor and Ginger follows. Halfway across the foyer, she looks back.

'What was it you were performing on the stage last time we met?' she asks Chloe. 'Was it the script you told me about?'

'Oh. Yes.'

'It was gorgeous. Can I read it?'

'Oh gosh, I don't know.' Chloe feels shy.

'What do you plan to do with it?'

Perform in it, thinks Chloe. *Be it.*

'I haven't really thought,' she says.

'I'd be honoured if you'd let me read it. See you soon.' And she disappears in a whirlwind of perfume and curls and shapely legs, in full possession of Chloe's heart.

32

CHLOE'S BEDROOM

JUNE 2019

When Chloe gets home, she goes to her bedroom and takes out her laptop. She types 'Daniel Locke' into the search engine. There's plenty of information, though most of the stories are at least ten years old. He died aged just sixteen in April 2005 after walking out onto the A63 late at night. One story claims he had been suicidal for weeks. Another says it was an extreme game of dare, something popular in the high schools at the time. Another says that he and two friends had been doing a Ouija board and been possessed by spirits.

Who were the other two?

Their names are in one of the stories – Harry Bond and Amelia Bennett. Chloe types each of them into the search engine. The stories about them are fewer, but they're there. And it is enough. Enough to learn that both of them are also dead. Chloe exhales and looks away from the screen for a moment.

Is that a bird on the windowsill outside? Staring in at her?

She blinks.

No; it's just the way the nearby tree has cast a shadow on the glass.

She looks back at the screen. Decides to read. According to one website, Harry Bond was in a mental hospital for a year, suffering from hallucinations and blackouts, and trying to harm himself in extreme ways. Chloe feels a growing unease as she reads on. Upon release, he stayed out of the headlines, until two years later when he too walked in front of traffic on the A63. Amelia Bennett doesn't feature in as many stories, but those available say she died just four years ago; it was suicide.

Chloe closes the laptop, realising her hands are trembling.

Three people who did a Ouija board too; all dead.

Three.

Didn't that mean something back then?

A knock on the bedroom door makes her shriek.

'What?' she cries, trying to control her voice.

'We're ordering take-away,' says flatmate James. 'You want owt?'

'No, I'm fine, thank you.'

Chloe breathes slowly. They are just *stories*. Exaggerated, like those surrounding *Dust*.

Do you really believe that?

She ignores her own question, puts the laptop away and pulls out her wooden box. She pauses before opening it, the way she always used to when she was trying not to cut. When she would count to ten, hoping the desperate need would pass.

'I will not cut,' she says.

'What was that?' calls James, passing on the landing.

'Nothing ... just, um, on the phone.'

Chloe closes the box. She needs to lose herself. To distract herself from the knife and swirling thoughts of blood. To bury the images of Daniel Locke and Harry Bond and Amelia Bennett, all cold in their graves, all young, all having dabbled with a Ouija board. She opens her laptop again and finds the *She Haunts Me* file.

Ginger said it was gorgeous.

Is it? Is it *really*?

It's finished now; Chloe knows that much. She wrote the final lines last night when she couldn't sleep. She wrote how Abigail falls utterly in love with Grace, the paid dancer. How they meet every night in the ship's piano bar and set the dancefloor alight. How one night she isn't there – and not the next, nor the next. How Abigail asks at the reception desk where she has gone, only to be told Grace was indeed a dancer, but she died ten years before, gone missing in the night, presumed lost at sea. How Abigail realises she's fallen in love with a ghost. How at the end, Abigail is standing on her balcony, staring at the sea, wanting to join her love...

Is it time to share it? To let Ginger read it?

That would be like baring her soul.

Her scars.

No.

For now, she reads aloud Abigail's final words:

'What if I let go? What if I fall? She is there, in the water, I know she is. What if I swim and don't look back, and swim and don't look back? Was I ever here, on this ship? Here and yet not here. There and yet not there. If I let go, what will there be? Only the music of the ocean – wordless, melodic, soothing – and the dance of the waves, and the two of us sinking, forever, together, to the bottom of the sea.'

33

THE GAME

2005

When Mr Hayes marched into the youth theatre on a sticky night, his face as thunderous as the August sky outside, Chloe was sitting on the edge of the stage, charcoal witch hat in her hand and matted wig on her head. Jess and Ryan were whispering by the door. Chloe had arrived at the theatre early and alone, and quietly recited her lines on stage, whispering, 'Fair is foul, and foul is fair. Hover through the fog and filthy air.' Now the drama students were scattered about the pews and floor. They perked up as Mr Hayes clattered up the steps to the stage.

'Attention, guys,' he cried, clapping his hands together. 'I was here last night to pick up those costumes that need mending, and I was *very* distressed to find that the knife we're using as a dagger is gone. I hope this is just a prank and that the culprit will now hand it over?'

The group looked around at one another, eyes wide. Jess and Ryan had come further into the room. Jess wore a white top Chloe hadn't seen before; it was wide-necked and her pink bra straps peaked out, both delicately cute and utterly erotic. Chloe pulled the wig from her head and tried desperately to do something with her now-sweaty hair.

'If anyone has it,' Ryan said, 'they'd better give it back, cos it's my mum's carving knife and I'll be in the shit.'

No one else spoke.

'Well, someone must know,' said Mr Hayes.

Silence.

'We're cursed,' cried someone.

'It's no laughing matter.' Mr Hayes shook his head.

'Well, *you* told us about that coven of witches who objected to Shakespeare using real incantations,' cried someone else. 'How they cursed the play.'

'Wasn't a real dagger used in place of the prop to kill King Duncan in the first ever play?' asked Jess. 'Didn't the actor die?'

Everyone nodded, vigorously.

'Maybe it's better that real knife has gone then,' she said. 'I did think it was too sharp. We should use a prop instead.'

'I guess we'll have to.' Mr Hayes didn't look happy. 'I don't like that a dangerous instrument has simply vanished into thin air though.'

'What shall I tell my mum?' demanded Ryan.

'I'll get her another.' Mr Hayes clapped his hands again. 'Right! Rehearsals! Ryan, you're up...'

After the session – when Macbeth's rusted, gold crown had been abandoned as though too great a burden – Ryan, Jess and Chloe climbed back in through the window, wordless, the agreement to continue the game unsaid but fat in the air between them.

As Ryan carefully set up the letters, Chloe wondered what they would do when the show was over. Would they still break in? Would they stop doing the Ouija board? She couldn't imagine *not* seeing Jess all the time. What if she went away to college in another city? Her mum often talked about there being bigger opportunities down south.

'Ready?' Ryan asked once their fingers were on the glass.

'Don't you think it's creepy about the knife?' Jess wanted to know.

'I'm just pissed off,' said Ryan.

'I don't like the idea of a missing knife.' Jess looked around them. 'Not with us doing this. The two things must be linked. Don't you think?'

'Forget it,' snapped Ryan. 'Let's just do this.' Then he asked, 'Is there anyone here with us tonight?'

The glass immediately shot across the floor.

'Shit,' said Ryan. 'This one's strong.'

Chloe didn't like it. A man. She was sure. She could smell him. Acrid, unclean, evil. His odour invaded her nasal passages, the back of her throat, her pores, as though to infect her. She whispered the words aloud as the glass spelled them.

THAT CUNT AINT COMING BACK

'What cunt?' asked Ryan, grinning.

'It's not funny,' said Chloe. 'We need to say goodbye. I don't like him.'

Ryan went on regardless. 'Who are you? Tell us your name.'

I AM GOD

'Oh *really*,' laughed Ryan.

'Stop it,' cried Jess. 'You told us right at the start that we should respect the spirits, never laugh at them. Look what happened to Daniel Locke!'

'You think he died because he laughed at some dead idiot?' Ryan sneered.

'I don't know, but I don't like this.' Jess's voice was small.

Chloe felt sick. The air around her was hot, tight, suffocating. She couldn't breathe. *Remember how*, she thought. *Push*. And Chloe did it; she *pushed*. And the glass began to shift towards 'Goodbye'.

Then it resisted.

Shit. This was one powerful spirit.

I KILLED MORGAN MILLER

Jess took her finger from the glass, her face devoid of colour. As her hand fell into her lap, the single witch hat charm on her bracelet caught the light, flashing at Chloe.

I KILLED THAT BITCH

'*You* killed her?' Ryan looked delighted.

SHES FOREVER HERE WITH ME

'Let *her* talk to us then,' said Chloe. 'She'll tell us what happened.'

I AM GOD HERE

'I don't believe him,' Chloe said to the others. 'I don't know why, but I just don't think he did it.'

'How do you know it's a him?' Jess still hadn't put her finger back on the glass, and Ryan was clearly too excited to comment.

'I just know. And not a nice him.'

'That's obvious,' said Jess with a shiver.

'I feel like ... he lived near here ... was horrible in life ... violent ... but nothing to do with Morgan, just playing with us.' Chloe spoke the thoughts as they came to her.

'How can you know that?' asked Jess.

'I don't know.'

I AM GOD HERE

'If you're really God,' said Ryan, 'then possess me, right now.'

Chloe pulled her finger from the glass too. 'That isn't even funny.'

'Well, this is getting dull now,' said Ryan. 'We're just asking stupid questions back and forth. We should have some proper fun.'

'No.' Chloe spoke in a low, firm voice. 'We are not doing *that*.'

'Fuck off then. Leave me and Jess to do what we want.'

'I'm not going anywhere.' Chloe held his gaze. The candles flickered, giving his irises a demonic streak.

'You can't really stop me,' he said.

I can, she thought.

Chloe closed her eyes, and – in her head – she saw Ryan quietly take his finger from the glass and stand and walk slowly along the aisle and out of the door, his face sombre and eyes unblinking.

When she opened her eyes, he had gone. Jess was staring, open-mouthed, at the door.

'Where did Ryan go?' asked Chloe.

'It was so weird.' Jess looked horrified. 'He just got up without a word, and his eyes, shit, they were just ... *dead*. Like he wasn't in there. I didn't even dare speak. No. It wasn't that. I *couldn't* speak.' She paused and Chloe was sure she could hear both their heart-beats, thumping in feral unison. 'I looked at you ... and for a split second ... you looked like...'

'Who?'

'*Morgan Miller.*'

'Shit.'

'But then it was gone. Like I imagined it ... Chloe?'

'Yes?'

'I'm scared.'

Don't be, thought Chloe. *I'm here.*

'What should we do?' Jess asked. 'Go after him? Bring him back?'

'No, leave him. If he wants to sulk, let him. We don't need him, do we?'

'But ... isn't it supposed to be three of us?'

Chloe looked down then; the glass sat next to 'Goodbye'.

'Whoever that man was, he's gone,' she said.

'Shit, what if he *did* possess Ryan and that's why he was all weird when he walked out?'

No, that was me, thought Chloe.

A slow scrape drew their eyes down again – the glass was moving. Chloe looked at Jess; Jess looked back, eyes wide. Neither had yet put a finger on it. It was both a surprise and expected.

Chloe mused how easy it was to get used to unusual things; how if someone had told her a month ago that she would sit in front of a freely moving glass that spelled out words spoken by the dead, she would have laughed. And yet it felt like she had been doing this since the beginning of time. Like everything that had happened previously was leading to this. So she whispered aloud the words as they formed, realising she hadn't written down a thing tonight.

JUST GIRLS NOW

'Who is this?' asked Chloe, though she knew.

WE ARE DUST

'Morgan, is that you again?'

I AM DUST

'It's *her*,' whispered Chloe, awestruck.

Jess smiled; her face was utterly beautiful in the gingery glow. This was perfect. Just the two of them. No Ryan to interfere and complicate their simplicity.

GOLD LIGHT DANCING THERE

'Hello Morgan,' said Chloe. 'Who was that other spirit just now?'

NOT WHAT HE SAID

'Did he kill you?' asked Chloe.

The glass remained still.

'Maybe she's scared of him. Maybe she can't answer that right now.'

'Can I ask,' whispered Jess, 'what is it like where you are?'
She rarely asked questions. Chloe smiled. Such a simple one.

LONELY

'Why?' asked Jess. 'Can't you see your family here on earth?'

SEE BUT CANT SPEAK

This was how Chloe had imagined it to be. Floating around in
an otherworldly place, not existing but not dead, there and yet
not there, and only able to watch those you love going on without
you. She felt an acute sadness for Morgan. Six years on from her
death and only ever mentioned in sentences including words like
'murder' and 'brutal' and 'unsolved'.

'We could pass a message on to your family,' said Jess, optimis-
tically.

'Not sure they'd believe us,' whispered Chloe.

MY BOYFRIEND

'Do you mean Clive?' Chloe knew he was still alive, that he had
been questioned extensively after Morgan died. Though their relationship had been described as volatile by the press, at the
moment she died he was with a group of people arguing in the
theatre foyer. 'Do you miss him?'

EVERY DAY

Chloe and Jess looked at one another, eyes moist.

HE GOT ME TO DO IT

Chloe frowned. 'Do what?'

WHAT YOU ARE DOING

'What's that?' asked Chloe.

SPEAKING TO THE DEAD

'You mean a Ouija board? You did one because of your boy-friend?'

YES FOR LOVE FOR LOVE FOR LOVE

'She must have done one *with* him maybe?' Jess paused as though she had thought of something. Chloe enjoyed having a moment to study her. A moment to imagine leaning in and kissing her on the lips. It would be her first kiss. 'Do you reckon you have to have *done* a Ouija board to be on the other side of one?'

Chloe thought about it. 'No. How could that baby we got have done one?'

'Suppose. Maybe its parents did?'

The glass moved again, in the slow and seductive way that Morgan often spoke. Chloe heard the whisper of her voice in her ear too.

THREE OF US

'Three?' Chloe felt tingles along her spine.

ALWAYS THREE BUT NOW YOU ARE TWO

'Can you really see us, Morgan?' asked Jess.

YES

'Why three?' asked Chloe.

THREE TO GET THE POWERS

'What powers?' Chloe looked at Jess. She knew they were both thinking about Daniel Locke, Harry Bond and Amelia Bennett; both thinking about Ryan's obsession with the powers he claimed they had.

WHATEVER YOU MOST WANT

'So we just ask?' said Jess.

THREE OF YOU

'If there are three of us?'

YES

'Were there three of you?' asked Chloe. 'When you did the Ouija board.'

YES

'And what power did you ask for?'

DUST

'Your role in *Dust*?' said Chloe.

I AM DUST

'You really think she got the role of Esme because she got powers on a Ouija board?' asked Jess.

Chloe didn't know what to say. *Did* she believe it?

She realised something then. 'You said there were three of you ... so there was you ... your boyfriend Clive ... and who else?'

The glass remained immobile; Chloe imagined Morgan had held her breath and closed her eyes.

'Who was the third person on the Ouija board?' repeated Chloe.

MY KILLER

34

THE GAME

2005

Jess gasped. Chloe's heart melted at her reaction. It was so vulnerable, her face alight with shock. It was Chloe's first response. Then she realised what Morgan had said.

'Her *killer*,' she whispered, and Jess mouthed it at the same time, their breath in the air together.

The glass didn't move. Chloe did. She reached out and put a finger over Jess's lips, the way she had when that moment fell into place the last time Ryan left them alone. She traced the softness and then leaned forwards to put her mouth there instead of her fingertip. Jess inhaled; Chloe was sucked in. She was lost. Their tongues touched, warm, nervous, then bolder. Chloe put a hand in Jess's hair, wanting to wrap the curls tightly around her fingers so she could never escape. *Be mine*, her heart whispered.

The glass moved.

Jess pulled back violently and watched the words form.

CUT BLEED RELEASE

'What does *that* mean?' she cried, not looking at Chloe. Then after a moment, 'I think I should go now.'

'No, don't,' begged Chloe. 'I'm sorry. We don't have to—'

Jess stood up, the candles swaying in her wake. 'Sorry, Chloe, no, I, um, I'm not ... that's not what I want...'

'I understand. We can forget it. We *can*!'

But Jess walked away, repeatedly saying sorry, still unable to look Chloe in the eye. The door closed gently but finally after her.

Chloe should have been afraid, being alone with the shadows and the spirits, but sadness was the more powerful emotion. And shame. Miserable, wretched *shame*.

The glass moved. Chloe followed its languid journey.

CUT BLEED RELEASE

'Cut, bleed, *release?*' she repeated softly.

CUT BLEED RELEASE

Chloe heard the words as though they were being sung. Heard Morgan Miller's syrupy voice swirling in the dust around her. Smelt her perfume as though she were gliding past. Felt the song was for her; *only* her. So lyrical. So tempting. So personal.

'What do you mean?' she asked.

IT HELPS

'Who was your killer, Morgan?'

WHEN THE DUST SETTLES YOU WILL KNOW

'What will I know? About your killer?'
Silence.
'*Tell me.*'

EVERYTHING

'Everything about what?'
There was no response. Chloe knew Morgan had gone, the way you know when someone sharing your bed has succumbed to

sleep. She felt as wretched as she had when Jess walked away. She wanted to die.

35

CHLOE'S BEDROOM

2005

When Chloe got home, she found her mum watching a documentary about the keto diet while her dad slept in the other chair. Wordlessly, she sat on the sofa next to her and snuggled in for a hug, the way she had when she was small. In this safe place, she could forget witches and spirits and daggers and blood.

'I like someone who doesn't like me.' The words choked Chloe.

'Ah, unrequited love,' sighed her mum, stroking Chloe's hair. 'Such sweet pain.'

'It's a...'

'Girl?' asked her mum.

'Yes.' Chloe was surprised, and then relieved. 'How did you know? I never said...'

'My darling girl, how did I know? Because you're mine. Because I gave birth to you and I love you and I *know* you like no one else. Of course I knew. Just like I know who she is.'

'Do you?' Chloe sat up.

Her mum nodded and touched her cheek. 'I think you should try and remain friends, sweetheart.'

Chloe remembered the elegant theatre-mask charm she had seen in the nearby jewellery shop yesterday. She decided now, despite her mum's advice, to save up the thirty pounds to buy it for Jess.

'I think she likes the boys,' said her mum.

'*Ryan,*' spat Chloe, the word, venomous.

Her mum looked surprised at the outburst.

'Sorry.' Chloe felt ashamed of her rage.

'No need. It's hard to see someone you love with someone else – especially a ... well, perhaps we could say unsuitable someone else.'

'It hurts,' she admitted.

In her room, Chloe knew – she could *see* it as though it was acted on a stage in front of her – that Jess had gone to Ryan's house. She could see them kissing on his bed beneath a James Dean poster. Rage simmered in Chloe's gut like boiling lava. Jealousy erupted from her throat in a stream of snarls. She had never felt like this.

It was terrifying.

'Never lash out in anger,' Grandma Rosa once said. 'Only in love.'

She had to control it. Temper it. Release it safely.

Cut, bleed, release...

Who said that?

No one. The words had dropped into her head. The words Morgan had said earlier.

Cut, bleed, release...

Chloe went to her special wooden box, one Grandam Rosa had left her, where she kept cherished items. She took out the dagger. It was an ordinary carving knife, belonging to Ryan's mum, but she would call it the dagger for as long as she, Jess and Ryan were together. She held it up to the light. She had stolen it the other night when she went back into the theatre for her phone; when she had walked along the aisle to the stage; when she felt breath on her neck. The sun had been dying but she could see in the dark. She found her phone.

And then she had heard it.

Chloe.

'Who said that?' she had whispered.

You know what you really came for.

Did she? Yes, she did.

You want it. You like it. Have it. Take away your pain.
'How?'
You'll see. It worked for me...

Chloe had found the key for the storage cupboard and taken the knife. It was as heavy as she had imagined. She had put a finger to the blade. Gasped when it nicked her skin. She was about to suck the blood away but enjoyed the feel of it gliding hot along her finger. Liked how her emotional hurt over Jess ebbed away with the flow. How the after-pain made her throb with relief, and something else. Something she had never felt before.

Power.

Yes, Chloe. Cut, bleed, release.

The dagger belonged to her now. Ryan – as Macbeth – would have to kill King Duncan in his sleep with another one. She wanted to feel like she had when she accidentally nicked her finger; that buzz of power; the sharp, exquisite pain followed by a rush of release; a release that let her pain over Jess ebb away.

Chloe put the blade to her thigh.

Cut, bleed, release...

She cut her flesh. Gasped. Watched the blood trickle. Felt the jealousy and rage flow with it, away, away, away.

Cut, bleed, release...

36

THE DEAN WILSON THEATRE

JULY 2019

In the final ten minutes of tonight's show Chloe decides that if Elvis were still alive, he'd sue the Dean Wilson Theatre for defamation of character. It's Saturday night, and the show is a one-off performance by a tribute act, Pelvis Presley, who in the weeks leading up to the show Chloe had felt sure was a comedian. Apparently huge in Japan, he flew onto the stage via hidden wires, wearing a cheap imitation of the iconic white, sequined suit, and burst into a drunk-sounding version of 'Suspicious Minds'.

Now he's crooning 'Can't Help Falling in Love' to a mortified audience member sitting in the front row. Beth has been dancing in her position by the door, hair now as violet as a field of lavender. Chloe catches Paige's eye on the other side of auditorium, and they smile. Nights like this – if nothing else – break the tedium of long-run shows, and it's definitely eased the tense, manic atmosphere in the theatre right now.

Chloe has been off work for a week with a nasty stomach bug that had her throwing up for three days. She can't decide if her nausea now is the remnants of it, or if it's because Pelvis Presley just slut-dropped and then staggered backwards against the stage. The radio crackles in her ear. She tenses.

'Five minutes until lights down,' says the techie.

Thank God. Though tonight's show sold out in hours, numerous patrons asked for a refund in the interval, and she dreads the complaints at the end. Cynthia will have plenty of feedback for the show report. As the lights in the auditorium come up and the smell of sweat drifts from the stage, Chloe opens the doors and hands out the *Dust* flyers, such a pointless promotion when it has sold out.

Chester is in the box office when they finish and is quieter than usual.

'You alright, Ches?' Chloe asks him.

He shrugs. He's not like himself at all. Cynthia is in her office, face unreadable. She ignores the ushers and types furiously on her computer. She was meant to have started Chloe's duty manager training two weeks ago, but it still hasn't happened. She apologised, said she was under a lot of pressure at the moment with the *Dust* stuff, and asked Chloe to give her a few weeks.

Beth is taking out her radio earpiece and rolling up the wire. Chloe hasn't stopped thinking about her words: *Never say anything to anyone, but I have something from the original dressing room*. Beth seemed so agitated when she questioned her about it. She needs to talk to her again, alone.

'Bye,' calls Beth, leaving despite the rubbish not having been taken out yet.

'Come with me and take this out, Ches.' Chloe shoves one of the bags at him.

With a sigh, he takes it and follows her into the foyer. When they are away from the box office, she asks him what's wrong.

'It's over for me,' he says as Chloe keys in the backstage code.

'Over? What is?'

'This. Here. Being an usher.'

'What the hell have I missed?' she asks. 'I was only off a week.'

'You don't wanna know.'

'I do.'

Pelvis Presley is in the dressing room on the left, talking on the phone to someone about an order of gold thongs. Chloe covers her mouth to suppress a giggle, and they hurry out the back to the wheelie bins. The summer evening is clammy, the sky not yet fully dark, thin ribbons of orange flickering behind the roofs. She suddenly recalls a similar sky above the church where the youth theatre was held. Sees a black bird watching her.

'Cynthia gave me four weeks' notice.'

Chester drops the rubbish bag into a wheelie bin; Chloe jumps from her reverie.

'Shit. *No*? You're *sacked*?' She can't believe it; he can't go. Not Chester. What will she do without him? '*Why*?'

'OK, so I might have told one of the film crew – that one who looks like a young Marlon Brando – that Cynthia fancied herself on the stage, just like most of us who work here. I mean, it's true, isn't it?'

'Is it?' asks Chloe.

'Yeah, she told me once. She said she always wanted to do it but never quite got her act together. She was here, of course, when *Dust* was first on, though she was just an usher then, like me. She covered my shift you know, that night. When I had flu and missed the show where Morgan was killed. I missed the whole damned four-night run.' Chester leans back against one of the wheelie bins, making the bottles clank inside. 'Anyway, I told the film guy this...'

'Why is that a problem?' asks Chloe.

'I might have suggested that Cynthia poisoned me, so I was ill, and she got to work all the *Dust* shifts.'

'Chester!' Chloe is genuinely shocked.

'I know, *I know*. He wanted a story and I gave him one. The thing is ... well, he may have then suggested that she had good reason to get rid of me.'

'What do you mean *good reason*?'

Chester fiddles with his cuff. 'That she might have needed to be there ... so she could kill Morgan.'

'Oh, Chester, that's too much, even for you.' Chloe shoves him. 'No wonder Cynthia gave you notice. How did she find out? What happened?'

He holds her gaze for a moment. 'The bloody film guy – Mr I'm an Even Hunkier Marlon Brando – told her what I'd said and asked for an exclusive interview. Said she might have been one of the last people to see Morgan alive. Asked if she'd ever been interviewed by the police.'

'Shit.' Chloe puts her face in her hands.

Since Chester showed her that breaking Morgan Miller murder story about a letter and new evidence a couple of weeks ago, it's featured in every single headline and hashtag. The Dean Wilson Theatre has received thousands of calls from journalists desperate for an exclusive; the film crew has interviewed every *Dust* cast member about their thoughts on what it might be, and who might have done it.

'That's irony for you,' sighs Chester.

'What is?'

'Didn't work *Dust* back then and won't be this time either. And it's far too late to get a ticket now.'

'That's not irony,' says Chloe, unable to stop laughing. 'That's you being a total shit-stirrer!' When she stops laughing, she pauses. 'You didn't *really* think that, did you?'

'Think what?'

'That Cynthia poisoned you so she could work instead?'

Chester shrugs. 'Don't think so. Never thought of it until Marlon Brando asked me.' He pauses. 'What if she auditioned like Beth did?'

'What? Cynthia? For *Dust*?'

'Yes. What if she was pissed off at not getting it?'

'Nah, she'd have said.'

'Would she?'

'Ask her.'

'Erm, like she's gonna talk to me. *You* ask her.'

'I'd like to keep my job for now, Ches, thank you.'

They pause. Look across at the almost-inky sky.

'I can't believe you're going,' says Chloe. 'I'll miss you so much. You've been here since the start. You're a part of the building. Can't you take it higher? To Edwin Roberts? You've been here longer than *he* has.'

'What? Give him a blow job in the staff toilets and hope he argues my corner? Don't think I'm his type.'

'You could say sorry,' suggests Chloe. 'To Cynthia.'

'Think that ship has sailed, darling. We should go back. Cynthia will be looking for us and you can't afford to get in trouble too.'

They head back inside. As they pass the stairs leading from the dressing rooms up to the rehearsal room, Chester pauses.

'Do you reckon they're all still rehearsing up there?' He grins at Chloe.

'You're already in trouble,' she berates him.

'So I've got nowt to lose, have I? Let's get our stuff, then sneak up and watch them.'

The idea is tempting. Chloe has only seen Ginger twice since they had coffee in the theatre bar, and those were brief moments between Chloe's shifts and Ginger's rehearsals. Ginger seemed distracted, and they only got to talk for a few minutes before she was called away each time. The second time, Chloe managed to tell her what she had read about Daniel Locke, Harry Bond and Amelia Bennett being dead – to Ginger's obvious horror – but as she began to describe how she thought it was curious that there had been three of them – Ryan, Jess and herself – years ago, just as there had been three of the dead teens, Edwin Roberts came and swept Ginger away for 'urgent discussions'.

Each night, after seeing Ginger, Chloe's dreams have been vivid and violent. Before falling asleep she fantasises about kissing her again. She slides a hand between her legs as she sees them in a passionate clinch, perhaps in Ginger's dressing room, perhaps against a backstage wall, but always mouths locked, hands hungrily exploring skin, bodies pressed close. Dark nightmares follow Chloe's sexual release; swirling images of black birds and smoking cauldrons and bloody knives have her even sweatier. She wakes with such a sense of dread that she tries to stay awake to avoid more dreams. In the blackness one night, she decided that she should speak properly to Ginger soon; it was time for them to recall everything.

'Come on, Chlo,' says Chester, making her jump.

They fetch their belongings from the box office, where Cynthia ignores Chester as they call goodbye, and instead of leaving, they go up the stairs to the rehearsal room. Sweet music meets them halfway up the steps. Ginger's voice eddies around them, the familiar words like a soft blanket on a cold night.

Then it stops, abruptly.

Chester opens the door a crack and they peer through, into the rehearsal room. The actors are now doing what's called a speed run of the main scenes. This is when they churn through at lightning pace – it isn't to rehearse as much as to reaffirm the muscle-memory of learned lines. Actors often employ unusual accents for their lines when doing this, switching between them to mix things up, and physically moving around the space at a fast tempo too.

Last week Chloe watched them doing a circle exercise, where the cast stand in a ring and someone jumps into the middle and says a random line from the show, cuing another actor. She loved how graceful Ginger was when she swept into the centre, pausing as though knowing all eyes were drinking her in, and then speaking two lines from the scene where Esme Black leaps from the balcony to her death.

'If I go, I go now so I fall right at his feet. If I don't, I stay here, forever in the shadows, never in the light. Look up, my darling Chevalier, see me here, see my love, see what I'll do for you.'

Now Ginger is racing between the other actors, chanting her lines as though to cast a spell, repeating them over and over: 'Never forget me, nor ever let me go. Never forget me, nor ever let me go. Never forget me, nor ever let me go.'

Chloe's heart contracts.

Never forget me, nor ever let me go.

'John Marrs thinks he's some kind of God,' whispers Chester, despite not having taken his eyes off him. 'He's not even all that.'

Two members of the film crew are in there too, trying desperately to follow the two main stars as they weave wildly about the floor. Chloe notices that each time Ginger sweeps past Marrs, she touches him in some way; his arm, his back, his neck. Is it just part of how they rehearse? Is she trying to recreate the chemistry they must share on stage? Or is it more? Chloe suddenly feels like she did when Ryan was the third person. Remembers that hot jealousy and rage.

Wasn't that when she started cutting?

It comes to her vividly.

Yes. *Yes*, it was.

'They're finishing,' hisses Chester, pulling them back from the door before Chloe can argue. They scuttle back down the stairs like two teens caught making out in a staff room.

As they pass Ginger's dressing room, Chloe pauses. 'I'm going to wait and see Ginger.'

'I *bet* you are. I might go and see if that slag is in Propaganda. Laters, Chloe.'

When he has gone, she waits by the gold star with Ginger Swanson in the centre of it. After a while, the door to the stairs opens and Ginger emerges. Sweaty hair is stuck to her face, but her cheeks are aglow as though she's just left a lover's bed.

'Hi,' she says, breathless, utterly beautiful.

'Hi,' says Chloe, feeling sixteen again.

'Were you waiting for me?'

'Yes.'

'I just need to freshen up and we can get a drink if you want? Or do you want to come inside and wait?' Ginger opens her dressing room door.

The last time they were in there together, the lights turned red.

The last time they were in there together, the door locked shut.

The last time they were in there together, they kissed.

Chloe goes inside.

37

THE DEAN WILSON THEATRE

JULY 2019

While Ginger showers, Chloe looks around the now crisp-white dressing room, ever anxious that something unexplained might happen. In place of the original, fading *Dust* poster is the new one, framed in gold and signed by both Ginger and John Marrs. Perhaps it will be sold when the show finishes. To distract herself from the thought of Ginger naked so close by, Chloe runs her hands over the sheer stockings on the back of a chair. She smells one of the scarves on a hook and frowns at a note on the mirror – dreading seeing the curious words she saw that other time – and then smiles in relief at the scrawl there: *Get coffee and plasters.*

There's a newspaper on the side. Chloe reads the headline: 'New Evidence in Morgan Miller Case Could Officially Reopen Investigation'. She skims the paragraphs and realises there's nothing new here. Nothing that hasn't been tweeted already. Inside, on the first page, is another headline, one that surprises her. 'Ginger Swanson Parents To Divorce'. Is nothing sacred? How must Ginger feel? Chloe remembers that when they first met at the end of March, Ginger said she thought her dad might be leaving her mum.

A door creaks. Chloe jumps, heart in her throat. Just Ginger, white towel around her damp body, another wrapped around her hair. Steam from the shower cubicle follows her in wafts like it too can't bear to let her go. She sees Chloe reading the article.

'Bloody paps,' she sighs.

'Oh, Ginger, I'm sorry.'

'It's fine.' She towels her hair in the mirror. 'After all these years together, eh? I understand it, I do. My mum isn't the easiest person to live with. Demanding, as you probably remember. But I'm still sad now it's really happened. She wanted something like this for me – *Dust*, I mean – and now I feel like it came at a price. Like I have everything, and she's lost everything.'

'I doubt it had anything to do with you,' says Chloe kindly. 'Kids always blame themselves for their parents' divorces, don't they?'

'I'm hardly a kid, am I?'

'I feel like we are.'

'What do you mean?'

'When we're together.' Chloe swallows the emotion down. 'I feel sixteen again. I was so...'

'What?' asks Ginger.

'Jealous of Ryan.' The words hang there, full of shame, painfully honest.

'Oh, he was nothing to me.'

'You slept together.'

'Did we? I hardly remember.'

Chloe watches Ginger fluff up her hair and then smooth some sort of product onto the ends. She watches as she leans closer to the mirror and rubs gloss onto her lips. If the lights filled with blood now, would she care? If a stuck door held them captive in here, would she fight it?

No. She never wants to leave. Let what should happen, happen.

Chloe approaches the mirror. Ginger looks up at her, lips slightly parted, a question in her eyes. Chloe feels brave. *Remember how. Will it and it shall happen. Push.* What does *that* mean? Where did those words come from? They seem familiar; send a thrill along her spine. So she does it; she *pushes*. Not with her finger. Not with her body. With her heart. And like a glass shifting across a Ouija board, Ginger moves. The question in her eyes dies, she stands, and she is the one to lean in and kiss Chloe.

As their mouths meet, Chloe is hit by two words that charge into her head.

Morgan Miller.

At exactly the same moment, Ginger whispers them into her mouth. 'Morgan Miller.'

'I think we got her.'

Chloe reluctantly breaks the union as it comes to her absolutely. Is it the physical connection with Ginger that provokes the memory and opens a door on a very clear image: the words *I AM DUST* being spelled out in capital letters on pieces of card?

'What do you mean?' asks Ginger.

'On the Ouija board. Back then.' Chloe doesn't take her eyes off Ginger's. 'It just came to me. It's being here, with you. I think she spoke to us. From the other side. What if she *told* us?'

'Told us what?' Ginger is breathing hard.

'Who killed her.'

Ginger studies Chloe and is the first to lean in and kiss her again. She tentatively teases Chloe's tongue, then pauses. 'We could have the story of the decade. What if she told us who did it and we've forgotten? We need to ... remember ... to talk...'

'We will.' Chloe touches Ginger's cheek. 'Soon.' She traces her tongue along Ginger's neck, enjoying her soft sigh. 'I always followed you.'

'Then why don't you lead this time?'

Chloe takes Ginger to the small sofa and kisses her until she surrenders, falling back onto the gilded cushions. She goes with her, hypnotised. Their hair tangles together against gold; raven and blonde, yin and yang, light and shadow. Chloe unwraps the white towel and kisses the creamy flesh beneath. Ginger moans. Then she reaches to unbutton Chloe's shirt.

'No, let me make you happy.' Chloe is thinking of her scars. Not ready to bare them yet. Afraid that it will end this glorious moment.

They kiss harder, hands hungry. Chloe's fingers find the spot that has Ginger gasping and clawing at her arm; the trinkets on her silver charm bracelet crash, matching the rhythm. Then, while coaxing her to exquisite pleasure, Chloe kisses Ginger's neck, chest, tummy – moving ever lower – and then gets lost between her thighs.

'I love you ... Jess ... sorry ... *Ginger...*'

'It's OK,' she sighs. 'Call me Jess.'

'I love you; I always have.'

'I know.'

Afterwards they lounge on the sofa. As if she's shy now, Ginger pulls the towel back around her body and tidies her hair. Chloe studies her, drinking in the scent of her, enjoying being so close. She smiles at the tiny charms about her wrist; the musical note, the star, the witch's hat, and the most special theatre mask. She wants to give her another charm. Perhaps one that symbolises *Dust*.

'You're mesmerising,' says Ginger.

'Am I?'

'You are ... Chloe?' she asks tentatively.

'Yes?'

'Can I read your script?'

'My...'

'That beautiful, *beautiful* script. Let me read it. I haven't stopped thinking about it since I heard you performing on stage.'

Right then Chloe would have let her read her most private and intimate diary. 'Yes. I'd love to know what you think. I can email you it tonight. Message me your address.'

'I will do. Thank you for trusting me with it.'

Chloe doesn't know what to say. What does it mean? Does Ginger like her the same way after all? Is there a chance for them? She wants to ask so many things but doesn't want to scare her away. Ginger's phone buzzes on the dressing table.

'Sorry,' she says, getting up. Chloe watches her frown at whoever is calling and then swipe the screen. 'Yes, it's me, I can't talk now,' she says quietly. 'I suppose, yes. OK. Give me ten minutes.' She hangs up and turns to Chloe. 'Sorry, I have to meet a friend.'

'No worries.' Chloe gets up too, disappointed.

'I might have time tomorrow during lunch to meet up if you're free. Will you be in the building?'

No, but I can be, Chloe thinks. 'Yes,' she says.

'We should talk more about the Ouija board. See if it jogs anything else.'

'How have your nightmares been recently?' Chloe asks her.

'Still bad. Yours?'

Worse when I've seen you.

'Yes, bad. We need to try and remember what Morgan Miller said to us, if she actually did speak to us. That sounds so insane said aloud, doesn't it?'

Ginger nods. 'No more insane than your effect on me just now.'

Chloe longs to kiss her again but feels shy now. 'Well, I'll let you get on,' she says, going to the door. She hopes it might be lodged shut, but it opens easily.

'Don't forget, send me your script,' Ginger calls after her.

'I won't.'

Later, long after midnight, Chloe reads through her pages, unsure, afraid of another person seeing them and tearing the words apart. But then she imagines Ginger and herself in the two female roles, learning to dance, having to rehearse together. And she emails it to the address Ginger has given in a Facebook message. She looks at the sent box for a while, almost willing it to bounce back.

Anxiety about having sent it keeps her awake. She reaches under her bed and gets the wooden box. At the bottom – beneath a history of mementoes – is the knife. She takes it out and touches the edge. An image emerges from the mists of her mind. The knife covered in blood. But not just from the tiny drop drawn by cutting. The blade is dripping with it. Onto a floor. Where? Where is the floor? Isn't it familiar?

It's the dagger.

Who said that?

You called it a dagger...

Chloe drops the knife. No, the *dagger*. Ryan's dagger. For *Macbeth*. How could she have forgotten all this time where it really came from? Has the intimacy with Ginger earlier freed something? She sees herself in the youth theatre, stealing it from a cupboard. Sees herself cutting that first time, angry, jealous. All these years, self-harming with *that* dagger.

You always knew, whispers that voice.

'I didn't,' she says aloud.

Eventually Chloe falls into a restless sleep where dreams of kissing Ginger are cruelly invaded by nightmares of bloody daggers and dead birds and unreadable words on a mirror.

38

THE GAME

2005

When Chloe silenced the house telephone in the hallway, she began to wonder if she really was some sort of witch. It started ringing again the night after the last Ouija board session, over and over and over. Eventually – when no one else stirred – Chloe dragged herself downstairs and stood in front of it, exhausted and afraid. She glared at it. And she *pushed*.

And the phone stopped.

She wondered if she had imagined the ringing earlier. Was she really the magic girl Grandma Rosa had called her? Was there such a thing? Were she, Jess, and Ryan just willing the glass to move when they used the Ouija board? Was it some sort of mass hallucination?

Standing in the shadowy hallway, shivering despite the August night, Chloe wondered if she had pushed Ryan away from Jess that time; if she had made him get up and walk away from the Ouija board two nights ago; if she had pushed against the spirits and forced the glass to 'Goodbye'?

She realised that throughout her life she had often *known* things. Known that some small event would happen before it did. Known what result she would get in a test. She had always put it down to coincidence. But Grandma Rosa had had it, this curious knack of knowing things she shouldn't have.

Chloe went back up to bed then but couldn't sleep. She thought about the dagger in the wooden box. About cutting. She had cut again earlier that night. After doing so, she felt wildly powerful, and then at peace. For a while. Now she was agitated. She hadn't heard from Jess and was too embarrassed to contact her.

Had she ruined everything by kissing her?

Chloe had relived it over and over – the warmth, the teasing, the thrill – until the shame of Jess's reaction flooded in, ruining the fantasy. She had loved it being just the two of them, speaking to Morgan Miller, candles flickering, no Ryan. The next rehearsal was in two nights and Chloe wondered if Jess would come. She knew she would stay afterwards, with or without Jess or Ryan. She *had* to speak to Morgan Miller. Had to try and find out who the killer was, and what she meant about knowing everything *when the dust settles*.

*

Two days later, before leaving for rehearsals, Chloe called goodbye to her mum and dad, and touched the tiny, silver theatre-mask charm in her pocket. Aunt Bess had sent some pocket money to spend 'during the school holidays' the day before, and Chloe had gone straight to the jewellery shop nearby. Part of her had known when she opened the pink envelope that thirty pounds exactly would be inside. Which had come first though – knowing about it or asking for it in her head? Because she had done. She had chanted the desire, over and over, as though casting a spell.

Thirty pounds, thirty pounds, thirty pounds.

Chloe's bus was late, and when she got to the theatre Mr Hayes was reminding them that they had just two weeks until the show. 'Since nothing else has gone missing,' he said with sarcasm, sweeping an arm over the piles of costumes scattered about the stage, 'we will crack on with our cardboard dagger and hope for the best!'

Jess and Ryan sat to the side, away from the pews, near a boarded-up window. Chloe was shocked by Ryan's appearance;

was it the dim light in here? No. His usually luscious locks looked like they needed a good wash, and he had deep lines etched below his eyes as though drawn with charcoal pen. She tried to catch Jess's eye to gauge if she still wanted to be friends but couldn't.

When the rehearsal was done and the group dispersed, Chloe told Jess and Ryan they should hide in the toilets, so they didn't have to break in. Ryan simply shrugged, no life in his eyes, and Chloe felt sure he wouldn't even stay. Jess looked at him as though trying to decide what she should do. Both of them joined her in the toilets, though, and stood in different corners of the tiled space, quiet until the building was empty. Then Jess took something out of her bag; a cutting from a newspaper.

'I saw this in my dad's paper,' she said, thrusting it at Chloe.

Chloe took it and read the headline. 'Ouija Board Triggers Demonic Possession in Teens'.

'It's about these about kids using one and ending up possessed. Read it. I reckon we should really think about this before we go on with it tonight.'

Chloe skim-read the article. It said that during the First World War Ouija board use had peaked as people tried to contact dead soldiers. Now the game was on the rise again as teens discovered it and were becoming addicted. Three teens in London – Chloe paused at the word 'three' – had reportedly been possessed by a spirit. One of them had used the board to try and influence the outcome of an audition for a school play.

The words at the end were most interesting though.

Chloe whispered them aloud. 'There is no scientific evidence that Ouija boards contact the spirit world, or that such a world even exists. The mysterious mechanism that powers the Ouija board is called the ideomotor effect and it's basically your body talking to itself. Like the sudden feeling of jerking awake from sleep, it's your brain signalling your body to move without your conscious awareness. In the case of a Ouija board, your brain unconsciously creates words when you ask the board questions. The muscles in your hands move the pointer to the answers that you unconsciously want to receive. In one Ouija board test, blind-folded participants spelled much more incoherent messages.'

Chloe looked at the other two.

'It makes complete sense, I guess,' she admitted. 'But how do we account for the glass moving by itself?'

'Could we have hallucinated it?' wondered Jess. 'I read about mass hallucination online. It's a real thing.'

Ryan was surprisingly quiet, face still pale.

'If it's not real and it's just us, then where's the harm?' Chloe realised just how much she wanted to talk to Morgan Miller. How desperate she was to play. It was addictive. She could feel its pull.

'Come on then,' said Ryan dully.

So they went into the empty theatre.

The sun was disappearing faster now it was August, and Chloe felt melancholy when she realised she would no longer see the dust dancing in its rays. Summer was dying and soon this would be over too – their final show and the Ouija board. She knew it.

She *knew* it.

Quietly, as Ryan went ahead, Jess said close to Chloe's ear, breath warm, 'I showed you that article because I'm worried about him. I was hoping we might stop...'

'About Ryan? Why?'

'He's ... he's been behaving oddly.'

'Oddly how?'

'He gets up in his sleep and walks around.' Jess paused and they watched him forage around in the cupboard.

Chloe realised Jess must have shared his bed to know he had been sleepwalking, and her heart ached at the thought; ached at the vision of them tangled up in his duvet. But at least Jess was talking to her.

'He says all this weird stuff.'

'Like what?'

Ryan looked directly at them then and Jess shook her head and joined him on the stage. Chloe followed. No. She did not. She may have gone last, but she did not follow. With hands that Chloe noticed were shaking, Ryan laid out the letters, as though for a game of cards. She suddenly felt sorry for him. He was not the boisterous and belligerent boy he had been, and that was sad. As annoying as that boy had been, she wanted him back.

'Did you tell Ryan what happened with Morgan Miller last time?' Chloe asked Jess as they sat in their usual circle.

'Yes.' Jess looked at him, as though checking his reaction, her face nervous.

'She said she did a Ouija board too,' explained Chloe. 'With two other people. And one of them *killed* her. We need to find out who that was.'

Ryan barely looked bothered.

Then, once the candles were lit and dancing their eternal dance, he said, 'I think it's time.'

'Time?' Jess repeated.

'To ask for what we really want, and then we can finish this once and for all.'

'What we really want?' Chloe felt nervous.

'The powers,' whispered Ryan, his face alive for the first time all evening. 'Jess told me Morgan Miller said you need three to get the powers. You just ask. That reinforces what we knew about Danny, Harry and Amelia. We want those powers. That's why we really did this. And I think it's time.'

'We?' Chloe shook her head. 'You mean *you*.'

'But what powers do you want?' asked Jess.

'You know.' He looked at her. 'Money. Wealth, beyond my wildest dreams. Then I can be the biggest actor the world has ever known.' He paused, breathing hard, and looked at Jess. 'You know what you want.'

She glared at him. 'I want more than just *you*,' she said angrily.

'You do?'

'Yes. You have no idea.'

Chloe looked at Jess, her face radiant with life in the fiery light.

'But that's my business.' Jess folded her arms.

Looking put out, Ryan said, 'I guess we don't have to share what we want. We can ask for it without saying what it is and maybe the spirits will just *know*.'

'I just want to speak to Morgan,' said Chloe. 'She came to us.'

'If we *really* believe it,' whispered Jess.

'I do. And there must be a reason. Look, we might able to find out what really happened the night she died.'

'It doesn't matter if we want different things from this now,' said Ryan. 'We all have an aim.'

'But the powers,' whispered Jess. 'Daniel Locke *died*. And we can't forget that Harry's in an asylum.'

'Amelia is OK,' said Ryan.

'But she didn't—'

'Let's just do it,' snapped Ryan.

'If we get that horrible man again, I'm leaving,' said Jess.

'We'll ignore him,' said Chloe.

They placed their fingers on the upturned glass. Whatever that newspaper article had said, Chloe was sure all three of them believed what they were doing. Was that the driving force? That they *believed*?

'Is there anyone with us?' asked Ryan.

Chloe realised she hadn't bothered with the notepad and pen – but she didn't need them. They were all adept now at reading the words as the letters created them; like a second language. And surely she would never forget something as intense as this. How could it not stick in her head forever – the playful flames, the smell of Jess's perfume, the warmth of the late summer night?

'If there's anyone here, let us know,' said Ryan.

And she arrived. Chloe knew it. The glass didn't move but she felt a gentle vibration in her buttocks as Morgan Miller walked across the stage behind them. The curtains moved too, the motion sending the candles into a frenzy.

'She's here,' Chloe whispered.

'But ... the glass...' Jess was staring at it, still immobile.

Then it moved.

I AM DUST

'Hello Morgan,' said Chloe and Jess, smiling at their natural unison.

'We need to know more about the powers,' said Ryan.

'Ryan.' Chloe sighed. 'Give it a rest. Can we not just talk to her?'

'What made you do a Ouija board?' he asked gruffly.

HANDS JOINED WE FLY
NEITHER FIRST NEITHER LAST
WE GO AS ONE

'What the hell does that mean?'

'It's from *Dust*,' said Jess. 'When Chevalier finally joins Esme on the other side to be with her forever.'

'What does that have to do with my question?'

'Remember she said she used the Ouija board with her boyfriend, to prove her love for him.' Chloe took over. 'Maybe she's referring to that? Morgan, who was the other person you were with? Can you tell us their name?'

FIND MY EARRING

'Your earring?' Chloe fingered the theatre charm in her pocket. She needed to get Jess alone later. To talk to her. Tell her they could forget the kiss, be friends, that she could accept just friendship if it meant not ruining things and losing her. Give her the gift. 'Can't you just tell us the name of that third person?' she asked aloud.

IT WAS MY MOTHERS

'The earring?' asked Chloe. In a flash, she saw it; a delicate, silvery stud with a single, dangling, tear-shaped pearl. She saw Morgan's slender hands touching it. Saw the other ear without one.

ONE IS NO GOOD WITHOUT THE OTHER

'When did you lose it?' asked Chloe.

WHEN I DIED

'When you were killed, you mean,' Ryan said.
Chloe tutted at him. 'What happened, Morgan?'

IT FELL OUT

'In your dressing room?' asked Chloe. 'That night?'

TOOK IT

'Who did?'

KILLER

'Tell us their name? Who *was* it?'

CANT

'Why?' asked Chloe, desperate.
Nothing.
'She's just playing with us,' sighed Ryan. 'You know what women are like. Tease you with stuff and then don't tell you.

Morgan, was it someone you knew and you're being loyal to them or something?'

NOT WHO I KNEW WELL

Chloe frowned. She needed to hear the exact way the words were being said to interpret them properly, and Ryan kept putting her off with his brusqueness. It was all about that subtle nuance. 'But you said they did the Ouija board with you so you must have met them more than once?'

FIVE TIMES

'Five times?'

FOUR TIMES ON OUIJA BOARD

'And?'

ONCE THAT LAST NIGHT

'What happened that last night?' asked Jess.

JEALOUSY

'Jealousy?' repeated Chloe. 'Someone was jealous of you?'

WE BOTH ASKED FOR SAME

'You both asked the Ouija board for the same thing?' Ryan leaned forwards, interested again. 'I never thought of that. What would happen if two people asked for exactly the same thing? After all, only one person can have a role in a show...'

I AM DUST I AM DUST I AM DUST

'Someone wanted it too,' whispered Chloe, realising. 'So it must have been...'

'A woman,' finished Jess.

SHE HAS MY EARRING

'Who was she?' asked Chloe.

NOT DUST

'Then who?'

A door slammed somewhere and all three of them pulled their fingers off the glass.

'Shit.' Ryan looked from Jess to Chloe, and back to Jess.

They waited for another sound; breath held.

'Do you think that was a ... *human*...' whispered Jess. 'Or...?'

Footsteps followed. Two sets. Slow. Were they torturously teasing or was it someone in an unfamiliar place, not sure which door they wanted?

'*Hide*,' hissed Ryan, standing up.

'But... the stuff?' Jess motioned to the glass, letters and candles.

'No time.' He headed for the curtain.

Chloe and Jess followed him, trying hard to tiptoe with speed across the wood. They cowered together behind the red velvet, listening hard. The theatre door opened with a creak. The lights clicked on.

It seemed an age before a male voice laughed and said, 'Look at this fucking place.' More footsteps then, possibly along the aisle, and then another male voice said, 'Fuck me, I never even knew this was here. It's *perfect*. We can hang in here any night we want.' They must have reached the stage because one set of footsteps halted, quickly followed by the others. 'What's this stuff?' asked the first voice. The sound of cautious steps on the wood. 'What weird shit is it?' asked the second voice. Rolling glass then and a smash as it must have fallen off the stage.

Chloe.

Who said that?

Chloe.

Then she knew. It was Morgan.

Don't let them destroy your magic...

Chloe stepped out from behind the curtain before she could think, Jess's hands trying to pull her back, Ryan's gasp hot on her neck. Her body moved as though not her own, and the words came out that way too.

'What are you doing with our things?' she asked the two men who were bending over their letters.

One had rotten teeth and he smiled a jagged, yellow smile. Chloe could hear all the terrible intentions fighting for space in his head. The other was small, less smiley, his thoughts less visible.

'What do we have here, then?' asked Yellow Teeth, moving closer.

It was then Chloe found out that she really *was* a witch.

39

THE DEAN WILSON THEATRE

AUGUST 2019

It is another two weeks before Chloe and Ginger get a chance to talk privately again. With conflicting schedules, they pass one another in the cold corridors and hidden passages of the theatre, exchanging shy smiles, Chloe desperately trying to read Ginger's face. Once, Ginger is wearing the Esme Black ghost costume and sweeps by, creamy skirts rustling, lace veil flowing, making Chloe feel like she might disappear, as though she were never here at all.

Each time they pass – fingers brushing fingers and film crew often in Ginger's wake – Chloe longs to ask if she has read her script yet; longs to hear that Ginger loves her words and thinks she has talent. It's a childish desire, one wrapped up in the need to know there's a chance her love is requited. That night, in the dressing room, she told Ginger – Jess – that she loved her. She said the words out loud, and now they exist beyond her heart, dancing like dust in sunlight.

But Chloe has no idea how Ginger feels. No idea if their passion was just a moment of curiosity for her, or if it was the beginning of something more. Chloe can only close her eyes and relive their kiss in the dressing room. Only picture again and again Ginger saying, 'You're mesmerising.' Only hope that when they meet again to chat, they can continue what they started; that it can become about them and not just the past they are trying to remember.

The night has arrived for this chance.

Tonight, they are meeting in the bar for a drink after Chloe's shift and Ginger's rehearsal. It's two hours away; Chloe just has to get through the tedium of a show that – despite the frenzied press coverage of *Dust* and therefore the Dean Wilson Theatre – has sold abysmally and is half empty. *No Greater Love* is set during the First World War and attempts to address the complexities of same-sex love during a time when it was taboo. Unfortunately, the play is clichéd, sentimental and badly acted. Edwin Roberts sent an email to all staff last week, urging them to promote it among their friends and share it on social media. Despite *Dust* being sold out, he's clearly concerned that this success isn't having an impact on ticket sales for other shows. *Dust* is all that people want.

Chloe makes her way down the darkened auditorium steps to tell yet another patron to turn off her phone. The light from numerous mobile devices is a sign of one of two things – a show so spectacular that photos simply *must* be taken; or a show so dismal that the person is bored. As she returns to her spot in the shadows, Chloe realises with emotion that in just over a month this very stage will be home to *Dust*. She is sure the ushers will have to stop many a photo being taken then.

The radio crackles. Chloe stops beside her seat, heart beating. It's been forever since she heard those ominous words – *Never ... be ... under ... one ... roof...* – but still she tenses every time there's a message.

'All ushers please flyer *Dust* at the end,' says Cynthia, despite the ridiculousness of promoting a sold-out show. Chloe wonders why on earth they don't flyer all the shows that *aren't* selling.

Chester is on the opposite side of the auditorium and does a 'Fuck, I'm bored' face at her. She laughs. Then remembers he will be gone in two weeks and deflates. Beth – her hair midnight blue this week – is quietly tidying the flyers up.

The ushers finally saw the model box for the *Dust* set last week. This is a scale mock-up of what the stage will look like and is created for every show. Even with computer graphics and high-end 3D design, nothing beats the physicality of this model; there's no better way to test out the logistics of the space – to get a godlike perspective.

It was beautiful.

The show will have a rotating set, built on a revolving platform. This device means there are quicker changes between scenes, and it works perfectly when a show has only a couple of locations. In *Dust* there is just Dr Chevalier's luxury house and his garden. The rooms are mainly white with flowing curtains at tall windows and vases of white roses on every table. The garden is brick walls covered in a creamy, climbing hydrangea, and trees alive with white blossom.

As the ushers crowded around, Chester touched a tiny tree, his eyes moist, perhaps realising fully then that he would not witness the iconic show returning. Beth said it was more 'modern-looking' than the original. Construction on the real set will begin when *No Greater Love* finishes next week, so the cast and crew have plenty of time to do the technical rehearsals, which is when the lighting, sound, and scenery and costume changes are tested for any problems.

Chloe can't wait to see it for real.

Can't wait to hear the music again.

The radio crackles. She holds her breath. 'Five minutes until the end,' says the techie.

The show finishes to light applause and mostly derogatory comments from patrons on their way out. The ushers pick up the rubbish afterwards.

When Beth and Chloe reach for the same coffee cup, Chloe speaks before she can think. 'What was it you had from the original dressing room?' She has kept this question to herself for so long, the curiosity is burning her.

'*Sorry?*' Beth frowns. Is she playing for time – trying to come up with some lie?

'You told me you had something from the original Morgan Miller dressing room – remember? I just wondered what it was … if maybe…'

'Maybe what?'

'Well, with the investigation all over the papers again, what you have might be a clue.'

'A clue? What are you *implying*?'

'Nothing,' insists Chloe a little too passionately.

'It was tiny, just—'

'What's going on?' Chester saunters over, always an ear for gossip.

'Nothing.' It is Beth who's insistent now, before moving away to another pile of rubbish.

'Nothing,' repeats Chloe, not needing any more drama.

In the box office, Cynthia is still cool with Chester. He has tried to put things right by telling the Marlon Brando guy that he was exaggerating, but the damage is done. Cynthia rarely opens up, but Chloe found her crying in her office one night. When Chloe asked if she was OK, she admitted she was sad about the Chester dismissal but had had no choice when he'd violated staff privacy and gone against her orders, yet again.

'Yes, I covered *Dust* for him back then,' she said sadly. 'But I felt bad that he never got to work it when he'd been so excited. I still can't believe he'd think anything malicious.' She paused and in that second Chloe wondered if there *was* a chance that Cynthia went to Morgan's dressing room that night. Was it a feeling or just a wondering? Could she see it or was she merely imagining it?

'I'm sorry we haven't got around to your duty-manager training,' Cynthia says now, when Chloe goes into her office to hand over keys. 'All this recent drama and *Dust* so close and everything else ... well, I've been overwhelmed. Can we postpone it until after *Dust* is done?'

If I'm still here.

The thought pops into Chloe's head. *Still here?* Is a better job on the horizon? Could it be to do with her script? What if Ginger loves it so much, she helps her get it out into the world? Chloe smiles to herself, picturing it, the two of them in the starring roles.

'That's fine,' she says to Cynthia. She hoped to impress Ginger by being more than an usher, but now maybe her script will do that.

'We'll discuss it in October.' Cynthia turns back to her computer.

'What were you two on about?' asks Chester in the box office. Beth has gone, leaving no chance to resume their earlier chat.

'Just my duty-manager training.'

'You wanna go for a drink? I could do with one.' Chester looks fed up and Chloe's heart melts.

'I would but...'

'But what?'

'I'm meeting Ginger.'

'Get you! Where? *Here*? Oooh, I'll come and third wheel!'

Chloe laughs and shakes her head.

'Can you put a good word in for me with that Abel guy?'

'I'll see.' Chloe pauses. 'Are you OK? I mean, *really*?'

'No,' he admits, deflated. 'I haven't got another job yet. And I just can't imagine not coming here anymore.'

Chloe wants to tell him that she has a feeling she won't be here either soon, but keeps it to herself. 'I'm going to miss you so much.'

'You know what I'd love?'

'What?'

'If I solved the Morgan Miller murder before I left.'

'Oh Ches,' laughs Chloe. 'You'll only end up in more bother.'

'Doesn't matter, does it? I'm going anyway. Might as well go out with a bang!'

When he has gone, Chloe reaches into her bag and takes out a small velvet box. She unwraps the soft, grey tissue inside it to reveal a tiny charm; a silver, smiling ghost. It's for Ginger. To symbolise *Dust* and to add to her others. Chloe changes into a more attractive ensemble than her usher uniform – a creamy, ruffled blouse and grey trousers – tingling with excitement at the thought of seeing Ginger in five minutes.

And hopes she'll like the gift.

40

THE DEAN WILSON THEATRE

AUGUST 2019

Ginger is already in the bar, sitting on a stool, ever elegant, even in jogging bottoms and a fitted pink T-shirt, and with her hair clipped up in a messy bun. As Chloe approaches her, heart hammering, she realises that Ginger can't be embarrassed about being with her if she's happy to meet in such a public place. She could have suggested somewhere more fashionable on the marina, far from here. And Chloe doesn't mind now if staff see them. She wants to sing her happiness at being with Ginger to all.

'Hi,' she says, sliding into the next seat.

The show finished half an hour ago now, so the place is almost empty. An older couple sit on the bar stools opposite, and a group of women sit in the chairs in the window.

'Hey, you.' Ginger's smile is intoxicating. 'What are you drinking?'

Looking at Ginger's glass of Prosecco – and smiling when she remembers the Sunday mag story that she's supposed to be avoiding sugar – Chloe says, 'Same as you.'

'Colin,' Ginger calls to the barman, who promptly arrives with an adoring face. 'Another one of these please.' He looks at Chloe with a knowing smile.

'So how were rehearsals?' asks Chloe.

'Intense. We all know it now, and we're desperate to get on the actual stage for dress rehearsals. It's not the same doing it with the set taped on the floor.'

'It's being built next week, isn't it? *So* exciting. I can't wait to see you as Esme, in full costume, on stage, under the lights. Oh, Ginger, this must be like a dream for you!'

'It is.'

The Prosecco arrives, and Chloe sips it. She notices that there's a newspaper on the bar. The headline is 'Ginger Swanson Parents Blame Dust for Divorce'. 'Oh my God,' she says, picking it up. 'Are they still writing about it? How crass. And to blame the show. Are you OK? I felt like you were blaming yourself last time.'

'Oh, it's fine.' Ginger waves a dismissive hand. 'You know what the papers are like. It's a story and it'll sell. They don't know the truth. That my mum and dad were never what you'd call a perfect match.'

Colin approaches to take Ginger's empty glass away, but she asks for another. When he returns with it, he points to the newspaper story and asks, 'Would you mind signing that for me?'

Wordlessly, Ginger finds a pen in her bag and signs it with a dramatic flourish, across the word *Dust*, as though to emphasise its importance to her. Chloe notices another headline and pulls the paper towards her: 'New Clue in Morgan Miller Case Revealed To Be Earring'.

Chloe almost falls off the stool. She sees – as clearly as though they are also in the newspaper – other words. FIND MY EARRING. What do they mean? Then she sees the three of them; herself, Jess, and Ryan. Sitting cross-legged. Fingers on an upturned glass. FIND MY EARRING.

'Are you OK?' Ginger's words pull her back into the present.

'She told us.'

'Who did? *What*?'

'Morgan Miller. On the Ouija board. Back then.' Chloe skim-reads the article while Ginger continues asking questions. The item sent to police from someone claiming to know who killed Morgan was a single pearl earring. It's being tested now for evidence, and hopes are that whoever sent it in will be named within weeks. 'She told us that we should find her earring,' cries Chloe.

'I just remembered it. The word earring must have triggered it. And it says here that's what the police have.' She looks at Ginger.

'Shit.' Ginger looks at the newspaper. 'I can't exactly remember, but you do, and it can't be a coincidence.'

Chloe thinks again of Beth. What had she said earlier before Chester interrupted them? 'It was tiny, just—' Tiny? Just *what*? She remembers that night backstage, the lavender perfume.

'Do you think we should contact them?' wonders Chloe.

'The police?'

'Yes.'

'God, no.' Ginger looks aghast. 'Imagine how we'd be treated? Two grown women saying they used a Ouija board fourteen years ago and think they spoke to Morgan Miller, and she told them to find her earring? We'd be a laughing stock. I'm an actress. I can't have that kind of scandal attached to me.'

Chloe is stung.

It would be OK for *her* to have such a scandal attached to her?

More gently, Ginger asks, 'Why do *you* think we can't fully remember what happened back then? I'm sure Ryan once said it was common, that teens forget using the Ouija board until they meet up again, but it must be more than that?'

Chloe thinks about it. 'Maybe it's like PTSD or something. You know, when something is so traumatic the person buries it. And then later in life, something happens that brings flashes of memory back to them.'

'You don't sound convinced.'

Thinking of Chester saying that we choose what we remember, Chloe says gently, 'No. I think we *chose* to bury it...'

'Why?'

Chloe decides not to answer. 'Look, what *do* we remember about when we used the Ouija board?

'I remember Ryan suggesting it. I remember rehearsing for *Macbeth*. And now...' Ginger pauses, her voice breaking with obvious apprehension. She takes a large gulp of Prosecco. 'You found out that those three teens did it before us and they're all dead. Chloe, that chills me to my bones. Tell me exactly what happened to them?'

Chloe describes how Daniel walked out onto a busy road, that not long after that Harry did the same, and that just four years ago Amelia died by suicide. She doesn't mention her unease upon reading that Harry had suffered hallucinations and blackouts, and was an extreme self-harmer. It's too familiar. Too close. Too painful. Too unsettling.

'Shit,' whispers Ginger. As she reaches with a trembling hand for the glass, she almost knocks it over. '*Shit.*'

'I know,' murmurs Chloe. 'I *know.*'

'I wish we had never...'

'What?'

'I don't know.' Ginger looks like a five-year-old waking from a nightmare. Then she shakes her head. 'So we know we spoke to Morgan.' She glances at Chloe. 'I think *you* triggered that memory. But who killed her? How can we remember if she told us that?'

'Let me touch your hand again,' says Chloe.

Though she knows that they need to remember, Chloe suddenly wants to forget about the past and enjoy this. To enjoy Ginger sitting here, beautiful and real. She wants to bury the words she said to Chester before Ginger arrived here at the theatre, how she'd felt that if they met again, something terrible would happen. She wants to forget the creepy words on the dressing-room mirror and the voice on the radio and the haunting sound of her name floating out of the dressing room. She wants to forget everything and kiss again. She wants to know how Ginger feels but is afraid to ask.

'OK,' says Ginger.

Chloe touches her hand. Holds it to her chest the way Grandma Rosa did when she was small. Last time, she saw the dagger, dripping in blood. This time she sees Morgan Miller. Alive. Real. Now. Walking past the bar, her hair in rollers as though for the show, her lips crimson red. The vision is so vivid that Chloe can't understand why Colin the barman and Ginger don't turn and watch her go by.

Chloe.

She realises then.

'I know you,' she says aloud.

'Of course you do.' It's Ginger, face creased with concern, glass now empty in her hand. 'It's me.'

'No, the voice. One I've been hearing. It's her. *Morgan.* It's been her the whole time.'

'You're creeping me out.' Ginger pulls back in her seat.

'*I* am?' Chloe feels sad.

'No, all of it.' Ginger pauses. 'You have always been a bit magic, though.'

The word falls heavily; *magic.*

'Shit, you...' Ginger begins, but then looks nervous.

'I what?'

'I don't know if it's that word – *magic* – but it just ... it just triggered this memory. There was a time, back then ... there were these men. They broke in or something and you...'

'*What?*'

'Sent them on their way.'

Chloe feels sick. She doesn't want to talk about it anymore. She wishes none of it had happened. But if it hadn't she wouldn't be here with Ginger now. She just wants them to go back to her dressing room. Wants their yin and yang hair to entwine once more.

'I have something for you,' Chloe says, remembering.

'You do?' Chloe can't read Ginger's face.

Chloe takes out the velvet box and puts it in Ginger's perfectly manicured hand, the red matching her long nails.

'What is it?' she asks.

'Open it.'

The tissue paper rustles as she reveals the miniature ghost.

'Oh, Chloe, it's beautiful.'

'To represent *Dust*. I remember your mum said she would always buy you one for each show you acted in.'

'And she did,' says Ginger, holding up her arm. The tiny charms shiver at the motion. 'You clip it on,' she says.

Chloe attaches the ghost to the bracelet, placing it next to the theatre mask she bought all those years ago.

'I'll treasure it.' Ginger touches it tenderly. 'It was very thoughtful of you.'

'Oh, it's nothing,' Chloe lies.

'No, it's a great deal.'

Chloe finishes her drink and finds the courage then to say, 'I don't suppose you've had time to read my script?'

'Yes, I did.' Ginger continues to study her bracelet and Chloe can't help but feel she doesn't want to look at her. 'I printed it out and read it on my breaks.' She still won't look at her.

Chloe's heart sinks. Ginger doesn't like it after all. Is she trying to be kind? To not say what she really thinks. But she said it was beautiful when she saw Chloe performing it onstage.

'You can tell me the truth.' Chloe tries not to sound put out. 'I'm a big girl.'

'Has anyone else read it?'

'No.'

'You've not sent it anywhere?'

'No.'

'I wouldn't yet. I thought it was … *quite* good.'

Quite good? Chloe knows an insult when she hears it. She has read enough reviews of shows here to know a veiled slur.

'Oh.' She doesn't know what else to say. She can't decide if she's more hurt about the words she toiled over being so casually dismissed, or by the thought this might mean Ginger doesn't care about her.

'Look, I'm no expert.' Ginger shrugs.

'You're an actress and you read scripts. You must know which ones you'll consider doing and which you won't. Is mine one you'd take on?'

Ginger doesn't answer. Colin drops a glass and it shatters, making them both jump.

'Sorry,' he says, disappearing, presumably to find a brush and pan.

The silence then is vast. Chloe notices their black silhouettes in the glass of the nearby *Dust* poster, so it appears that Ginger and she are Esme and Chevalier's shadows. They are alone now. All the patrons have left.

'You said it was beautiful,' whispers Chloe, desperate to fill the quiet void. 'That day...'

'Maybe that was the *way* you performed it.'

'It's fine,' lies Chloe. 'It's only a first draft.'

'Exactly.' Ginger seems to latch on to the excuse. 'It is. And I mostly liked it. I thought Abigail was engaging and some of the scenes were good, but it needs more polish. That's all. Maybe we could go over it together one day?'

'I'd like that.' Chloe thaws a little. Maybe she's being oversensitive. She knows literary critique is essential for improving work. And this could be a chance for them to see one another more.

As though hearing her thoughts, Ginger says, 'The only thing is that rehearsals are about to get even more intense now, so it could be a while before we can meet properly like this. I'm sure you understand?'

But what about our kiss? Chloe wants to ask. *What about the other night?*

'Of course,' she says instead.

'I know we'll cross paths around the place.' Ginger's phone buzzes in her bag and she takes it out and reads a message, her face expressionless. 'Sorry, I have to go now.'

Are they not even going to talk about what happened between them?

'Ginger,' ventures Chloe. 'About ... you know...'

Ginger puts a warm hand on Chloe's arm. The ghost and the theatre mask settle cold against her skin. Chloe studies them to brace herself for what's coming. 'I find you attractive,' Ginger says softly. 'I think in different circumstances, maybe we could, you know, but now … well, I have so much on…'

Different circumstances? Isn't this the *perfect* circumstance? Both of them here, in the theatre they dreamed as teens of performing in. It's as though it has been written in the stars. But apparently Ginger can't read the heavens; she gets up and puts her bag on her shoulder. 'I have to get changed. I promise we'll catch up again when this is all over.'

'We're closing now,' says Colin, wiping the bar down.

Chloe stands too and the room begins to sway. Ginger's face stretches white and ghostlike in front of her. The ceiling with its strings of gold lights blurs; the walls close in.

And Chloe blacks out.

When she comes around Colin is fanning her with a stained tea towel, and Ginger is holding her hand. She doesn't want to let it go. Wants to say, 'I don't care if you hated my script and I don't care if you're busy now, I'll do anything if we can just see each other again, the way we did the other night.' But she is mute. She sits up, rubs her head. 'I'm fine,' she insists, embarrassed. It's been months since a blackout happened. In fact, the last time was when she first saw Ginger.

Colin scuttles back to the bar.

'You really should see a doctor about this,' says Ginger.

'I have,' she sighs. 'It's just something that happens now and again.' She shakily gets to her feet again.

'You sure you're OK?' Ginger obviously wants to get away.

'Yes. You go.'

Chloe watches her head for the corridor that takes you backstage. A large curl has fallen from Ginger's bun and swings enticingly. Chloe remembers when she approached the mirror that night. How Ginger had looked up at her, lips slightly parted, a question in her eyes. What was it she had done then? *Remember how. Will it and it shall happen. Push.* The words had seemed familiar; sent a thrill along her spine. And she had done it; she had *pushed*. And Ginger had moved towards her.

Now, just as Ginger reaches the doors to the corridor, Chloe *pushes*.

Just to see.

Just to try it again.

The moment is one of comedy.

And Chloe laughs. She can't help it. Ginger flies forwards and lands in a heap in front of the doors, the contents of her bag scattering on the floor, more curls falling free from her bun. Then Chloe feels terrible and hurries over, picking lipsticks and tampons up and handing them to her.

'What the fuck?' Ginger wipes her knees and stands. 'It was like ... like someone *pushed* me. But ... how?' She is trembling. Then she looks at Chloe. Two emotions flit across her face. The first is recognition; she remembers something. The second, Chloe has seen on her face once before. A *long* time ago.

It's fear.

And Chloe realises then that she prefers this fear to when Ginger couldn't look at her at all.

41

THE GAME

2005

Yellow Teeth edged closer to Chloe. The heat in the theatre built to fever point, as though the empty cauldron nearby was smoking again. She heard Ryan and Jess approach from behind the velvet curtain. Perhaps they felt they should support her; perhaps they felt the power of three against two was enough; perhaps they too felt the fire of outrage at these two intruders daring to smash their glass and disturb their time with Morgan Miller.

'Come on, let's leave 'em to it,' said the smaller of two men.

'They're just fucking kids,' said Yellow Teeth, eyes still on Chloe.

He gathered up some of their letters and threw them in the air with a challenging grin. As they scattered, Chloe saw a picture from one of her favourite childhood books; she saw the scene from *Alice in Wonderland* where Alice is attacked by playing cards. It's at that moment in the story that Alice wakes up.

Chloe felt like she woke.

'Pick them up,' she told Yellow Teeth.

He grinned again. 'Make me.'

Chloe...

Will it and it shall happen. Push.

Had Morgan Miller said those words to her all along? Chloe felt her spine uncurl, strengthen. And she did it; she *pushed* with everything she had, and Yellow Teeth's face changed for a split second – from leering to pure horror – before he flew backwards and off the stage, landing heavily against the front pews, broken glass crunching beneath his splayed boots. Chloe was as surprised as he was. She gasped. Turned and looked at her friends. Jess stared at her with an emotion she had never seen in her eyes before – fear. Chloe looked back at Yellow Teeth.

And she remembered.

Carrie Meadows. Mocking her portrayal of Cordelia in *King Lear* at school. How she had flown at a wall, broken her arm. And Chloe swore she hadn't done it.

But she had. *She had*.

She had *pushed*.

'Fuck.' Yellow Teeth touched his right arm and then got up clumsily, groaning as he did. Shards of glass came away from his jeans, tinkling melodically as they fell. 'What the—'

His sidekick looked from Chloe to him and back again, the confusion on his face comical. 'What the hell happened?'

'*She* did,' cried Yellow Teeth. He was angry but didn't direct it at her; he hardly dared look at her. 'I think you broke my fucking arm, you little freak.'

'You came into *our* theatre,' said Chloe calmly.

'Let's go,' said the smaller man, heading for the door.

'I should break her fucking face,' cried Yellow Teeth, still cradling his arm. But he didn't approach the stage. He followed his friend. When they were at the door, he finally dared to look back. 'This isn't over,' he said.

I think it is...

'I think it is,' said Chloe.

They left, slamming the door after them.

'Shit, Chloe, what did you *do*?' Jess touched Chloe's arm, looking as afraid as she was intrigued. 'You scared the hell out of me! What *was* that?'

'I don't know,' she admitted. 'It was like I pushed with my head instead of my hands. I don't feel very good now though.'

She didn't. Her skull felt it was going to implode and she couldn't stop shaking. She sank to the floor. Sat among the scattered letters – a T, I, W, H and C. She frowned. Moved them around. WITCH. She looked up at Jess.

'You *are*,' whispered her friend.

Ryan still hadn't spoken. He gazed at her with tired eyes, his face haggard.

'I honestly don't know how it happened.' Chloe's teeth chattered, and the words came out as small bullets. 'I feel sick. I need to go home.'

'No.' Ryan found his voice at last. 'We aren't finished with Morgan. We want to know how to get the powers.'

He began to arrange the letters in a circle. Chloe didn't have the strength to stop him. She squeezed her aching temples.

'We just need to get her back,' he continued.

Chloe had been desperate to talk to her earlier but now she needed to escape, get some air, cool down.

'We don't have a glass,' said Jess, perhaps hoping this would stop him.

He went back to the cupboard and when he didn't find one, he went into the little room backstage, where Chloe knew there was a sink. He came back with a glass, put it in the centre of the letters and sat down.

'I don't know how you did that,' he said to Chloe, 'but you're a fucking witch and that means we can get the powers.'

'What if I don't want them?' Chloe staggered to her feet. The pain in her head was blinding now.

'Of course you do. We all know what you want.'

'Do we?'

Jess looked uncomfortable.

'You want *her*.' Ryan motioned his head towards Jess. 'I get it. It's fine.'

'I don't,' lied Chloe softly.

'Why'd you kiss her then?'

The question hung in the air with the dust fragments. Jess had told him. The scars from Chloe's recent cutting session throbbed.

She wanted to shed blood now. To let her hurt seep away with it. How could Jess have shared that with him? They were friends. Or were they? After all, she had stepped over that line.

'I don't care,' said Ryan. 'You're welcome to her; you can both lezz it up all you want; I just want the powers.'

Now Jess looked hurt. And Chloe couldn't help but be glad.

Then the glass moved.

All three of them watched it, mouths open. It was no surprise now, but it never failed to remind Chloe that this was truly an extraordinary thing; that one day – if she remembered it by then – she might question if it had happened at all. She remembered what Jess's newspaper had said earlier. That your brain unconsciously creates words when you ask the Ouija board questions; that the muscles in your hands move the pointer to the answers you unconsciously want to receive. Had they been doing that? But the glass was moving alone. How could the theory explain *that*?

Jess joined Ryan on the floor, sitting opposite him as though to create distance. Chloe remained on her feet, desperate to leave. She looked at the door – then at the two words being spelled out.

YOURE READY

'Ready?' asked Ryan. 'Who is this?'
'I don't think it's Morgan,' said Jess.
'Who then?'

HI RYAN

'Danny?'
'Daniel Locke?' asked Jess.
Ryan nodded.

YOURE READY

'For what, Dan?'

THE POWERS

'I know. But how? Tell us *how*. Morgan Miller said we needed three of us and we just ask. Can we ask you?'

Chloe couldn't stay any longer. The room was spinning; the pews bent and warped as though they were a burning photograph in a house fire; Jess and Ryan's words slowed down, sounding like an old-fashioned record played at the wrong speed. She was going to be sick. She raced for the door and made it into the corridor at the side of the theatre before throwing up all over the concrete.

She was leaning against the wheelie bin at the back when Jess climbed out of the window and came to her.

'It stopped,' she said simply.

For a moment Chloe wished they had never begun. That they could go back to a time before the Ouija board. That they had said no to Ryan's idea, and instead spent their summer singing their favourite musical numbers and trying on clothes they would never buy and trying to get a tan in the back garden.

'The glass stopped moving as soon as you left.'

'Maybe it's a sign we should stop,' said Chloe.

'No, it's sign that you have some sort of gift.'

Jess studied her. Despite Chloe's hurt at the betrayal, at Jess having told Ryan about their kiss, Chloe still ached with love for this girl. If she did indeed have some sort of gift, why couldn't she rid herself of the feelings? How simple life would be if she could. Which incantation might break the spell?

'Ryan's still trying to talk to Daniel,' said Jess, taking a cigarette from the pack in her dungaree pocket and lighting it. 'He's obsessed with these powers.'

'You said earlier that he walked around in his sleep.' Chloe took a drag of the cigarette, hoping it would make her feel better. 'That he said some weird stuff. Like what?'

Blushing, Jess said, 'It was at his house. His mum was away and we ... well, I stayed over. Anyway, in the middle of the night I woke up and he was just standing in the corner, not even moving. I was totally freaked out. Then he started walking backwards. I couldn't see his face in the darkness, and I don't know why, but I was glad. He kept saying...' Jess inhaled hard on the cigarette. 'He kept saying "I can't do that, I can't do that, I can't do that."'

'What do you think he meant?'

'Dunno. It scared me though.'

A sound in the passage then, and Ryan appeared.

'We need to meet after the next rehearsal,' he said, taking the rest of Jess's cigarette without asking. 'Finish this thing.'

'I still feel crap,' said Chloe. 'I'm going home.'

And she headed out to the front of the church. She looked up at the boarded-up, dome-shaped windows – most of them broken – and the turrets with ornate crosses, just as she had when Ryan first suggested the game. Then, a glossy, black bird had perched on one of the crosses, squawking; now there were three of them. A trio, all the same size, all quietly looking down at her.

Jess rounded the corner. 'I'm going home too,' she said.

Chloe looked back up. Now there were two birds. She smiled. 'OK, let's get the bus.'

One arrived a minute later, and as they sat down inside, Chloe looked back and saw Ryan watching it leave. Despite everything, she felt desperately sad for him. Poor Ryan with his single mum, yearning for more. He was such a brilliant actor – why couldn't he see that and be happy?

'What powers do you want?' Chloe asked Jess. 'Ryan thinks you want him, but it's something else, isn't it?'

Jess shrugged. Then she turned it on Chloe. 'What do *you* want?'

Chloe ignored the question too. 'I'm sorry.'

'What for? I should be sorry. I've been horrible. I shouldn't have told Ryan about ... you know. It just ... came out. I was still processing it, I guess.'

'No, I shouldn't have kissed you.' Chloe felt ashamed again. 'I just ... well, I like girls. I like ... *you*.'

'Why didn't you tell me? We're friends. Don't we share everything?'

You haven't been, Chloe wanted to say.

As though realising, Jess added, 'I've let Ryan get between us, I know. And you're right, he doesn't treat me very well. But I can't help how I feel about him.' She fiddled with her dungaree strap. One of her purple nails was chipped. 'I like boys, Chlo. I'm not saying I couldn't get with a girl – and I did enjoy our kiss. I *did*. But I don't think I'm gay.' Quickly she added, 'I don't care that you are. I just don't want anything more than friendship with you. You are mesmerising though.'

'Am I?'

'There really is something special about you.' She paused. 'I just don't wanna fuck you.'

Chloe laughed heartily, and it felt good, despite her headache. 'Can we put it all to one side. Forget it all and just be the friends we are?'

'Of course.' After a moment, 'Are we going to finish it?'

Chloe was blank. 'Finish what?'

'The Ouija board. Do it one last time?'

Chloe...

She was so sure she heard her name being called that she turned and looked behind them. But the seats were all empty.

'Chloe?' It was just Jess.

'I feel like ... we *should*.'

Then she remembered the theatre-mask charm in her pocket. They only had a few minutes until Jess's stop, which was two before her own. She took out the small packet.

'This is for you,' she said. 'Don't worry, it's nothing heavy. Call it an early birthday gift if you like.'

Jess laughed. 'My birthday isn't until February.' She took it though; opened the tiny packet and smiled. 'It's gorgeous. I *love* it.' When she held the silver charm up, Chloe was sure for a second that it winked at her. 'Clip it on for me, would you?'

Chloe attached it to the bracelet, next to the other trinket, the delicate witch hat with the frilled edge. She saw then – as clear as if it was actually there – a miniature ghost, also silver, shimmering in the weak bus lights.

'Shit, my stop,' cried Jess, jumping up and ringing the bell. The bus stopped with a violent heave. 'Thanks, Chlo, I love this.' She held up her arm, shaking her wrist, jingling the mask and hat together. 'See you at rehearsals!'

And she got off.

*

At home, Chloe opened her laptop and typed 'Am I a witch?' Thousands of sites came up. 'Thirteen Signs You're A Witch'. 'How To Know You're A White Witch', 'Why White Witches Rule'.

She clicked on one and read the first paragraph:

> **Powerful Signs that You Are a White Witch**
> A white witch is someone who practises magic for the greatest good of all. A young white witch may be aware she sees and knows things and be afraid of this. But she shouldn't be. It's within her power to will things as long as it is with good intention. She is magic. She makes people nervous. She can move people. She can strike down a malicious person with the force of her rage too. She is dust.

Chloe blinked. Read the last line again. But she had imagined it. The words were: 'She is eternal.'

Was she really a witch?

She read again the line about 'good intention' and could hear

Grandma Rosa as clear as though she was in the room. *Never lash out in anger, only lash out in love.* If she was a white witch, then she had failed. She had lashed out in anger. Both at others and at herself. Wasn't self-harm the most brutal of lashing out?

The urge to do it burned. But then, suddenly, Chloe was so exhausted she could barely reach for the dagger in the wooden box. Instead, she collapsed in her bed and passed out in seconds.

And she didn't leave it for almost two weeks.

42

THE DEAN WILSON THEATRE

AUGUST 2019

Chloe carefully opens one of the doors and sneaks into the back of the auditorium. The swell of music is a physical thing that steals up the aisle steps and teases her with words she knows well. She smiles and whispers along.

'Up here, or at your feet, wherever I am, I'm yours, wherever your heart beats...'

The stage is ready for *Dust* and – with only two weeks until it opens – there is a tech rehearsal going on. Chloe first saw the completed set yesterday, but it was empty then, not lit, not boisterous with movement and sound. She spied on it from the wings, a beautiful, lifeless shell. Now it is alive with actors and wardrobe assistants and the stage manager and Edwin Roberts, red-faced and frantic. Now the air is hot with flood lights and the scent of sweat and conflicting perfumes. Now the LED lights subtly change the shade of white walls and flowers and curtains, signifying the emotions of the scene. Now Chevalier's pretty summer garden moves gently in the breeze.

Ginger is singing 'Up Here', the song before Esme jumps from the balcony and lands at Chevalier's feet; the song that she hopes will win him over once and for all, before she ends her life for him. Her voice is the best Chloe has ever heard it; tenderly tremulous at times, soaring when the verse needs it. She must have practised and perfected, and practised and perfected.

'I don't fall, I fly, I don't die, I'm free, wherever your heart beats...'

As she watches from the shadows, Chloe realises there are tears on her cheeks. Tears of pride, and of absolute love. Despite her hurt at Ginger's critical appraisal of her script, and despite her being so dismissive when they last parted, Chloe can't help but be emotional. She knows what this must mean to Ginger; she can only imagine how it must feel. She sees the two of them as kids, singing this song, pretending Jess's bed is the balcony and falling onto the floor.

But this isn't Jess now. It isn't even Ginger.

This is *Esme Black*.

The transformation is complete. Despite this not being a dress rehearsal, she is in full costume. Still a housemaid, she wears a white smock and cap, muted make-up, her golden hair in a smooth bun. But as she jumps from the balcony – it's positioned so her actual fall isn't seen – a small change takes place, hinting at what is to come.

The stage spins, revealing Esme on the ground, Chevalier leaning over. She lifts her head and the cap has fallen so her curls now cascade free. The lights change, adding angelic hues to the gold. The audience will know she has died. And Esme sings the final line of the song, before the stage fades to black, and it is the interval.

'*Wherever your heart beats...*'

'Let's take a break,' cries Edwin, clapping his hands.

Ginger is helped up and disappears.

Chloe realises it's two weeks since they had that drink together and, in that time, they have only passed one another in the corridors twice. Chloe hasn't been around as much. Since they started building the stage, there haven't been any shows on; but today the ushers have been called in for a last meeting about the imminent *Dust* run. Chloe looks at her watch. It starts in one minute. She wants to find Ginger and tell her how wonderful she was – say that even if she doesn't like her script, it doesn't matter, that she thought she was incredible – but there isn't time.

Chloe leaves the auditorium and heads upstairs. The rehearsal space is now free again, and Cynthia is waiting for them, sitting on a chair in front of rows of others, folder on knee. The cue marks for the actors are still in place on the floor. Chester, Nina, Paige, Beth and the other ushers are there, gossiping among themselves. Despite not needing the information this meeting will provide, Chester has come because it's his final day on the rota and they're going out for drinks later at Propaganda.

Chloe takes a place on the end, next to Chester. She sneaks a look at Beth, hair bright purple today. She hasn't stopped thinking about the earring; the single pearl that the press revealed was taken from Morgan's dressing room that night. She has wanted to ask Beth again about the tiny item she took, but her brusque reaction to being questioned last time has deterred her. Today she feels buoyed by the glorious scene she just witnessed onstage and is determined to ask Beth again.

But what if she won't answer? Does Chloe tell someone else? Share her suspicions?

'Right, this is it, folks.' Cynthia interrupts Chloe's thoughts. 'In two weeks, we open. *Two weeks*! I've no idea where time has gone. It feels like days since the announcement. First, I want to thank you all.' She doesn't look at Chester. 'You've all worked so hard and put up with a lot, especially with the film crew in your way, and endless journalists trying to get a story. Edwin Roberts wanted me to thank you too.'

'Bet he didn't,' whispers Chester.

'As you know,' continues Cynthia, 'we officially open on Thursday the fifth of September.'

Paige and Nina clap their hands wildly. Beth glances at them with distaste. Chester looks sad. Chloe wishes he was staying.

'Will the media be here?' asks Beth. 'I know the official press night isn't until the tenth of September, but I bet they won't be able to wait.'

Chloe wonders if Beth asks because she has something to hide from them? She realises now that Beth has kept well away from the film crew recently, and – unlike Chester – has avoided speaking to any journalists.

'The box-office staff told me that a few journalists they know have tickets for the premiere,' admits Cynthia. 'If any of them harass you for stories, the same rule applies as it has for the last few months – send them to me.'

Chester raises his eyebrows at Chloe.

'I'm gonna make sure I look my best for the whole run,' says Paige. 'Make sure my hair's always done and I have full make-up on. You never know which agents or producers might come.'

'Doubt they'll be interested in an usher,' says Beth.

Is she bitter? wonders Chloe. *Could that bitterness have made her capable of murder?*

'They might be,' says Nina.

'Most of all,' interrupts Cynthia. 'Enjoy it. Be professional at all times; be helpful and happy. You're experiencing a historical time in our theatre – in our city. It's going to be fantastic.' She pauses as though to let it sink in. 'OK, the next time I see you all will be opening night. I want you in half an hour earlier than usual. See you there.'

Chloe suddenly feels overwhelming sadness – for the fact that it's Chester's last day, for the fact that she won't be here now for two weeks, for the fact that she won't see Ginger in any way until then. She looks up and realises she's the only one in the rehearsal room. Damn; no chance to question Beth. Maybe she's in the box office.

She finds Chester alone there, opening the 'Good Luck' card they have all signed for him.

'Where's everyone gone?' asks Chloe.

'They're getting changed and coming back to go out for my drink thing.' He reads the card, his eyes filling with tears. 'Shit. I can't believe this is it.'

'Oh, Ches.' Chloe puts a head on his shoulder. 'This isn't it for us. We'll see each other all the time. And anyway...'

'What?' he asks.

Chloe was going to say that she has a feeling she won't be here for much longer either but doesn't.

'I have gossip,' he says, perking up.

'What now?' she laughs.

'Seriously, I do. So, I looked at the list of people who have tickets for the first night.'

'Why? Must have taken you ages. That's five hundred people.'

'I was bored. The box office was empty.'

'You weren't bored,' laughs Chloe, 'you were up to mischief.'

'Anyway, guess who's coming that night?'

'Oh, God. The Kardashians? Prince William?'

'I wish.' Chester pauses, holding her gaze with wide, dramatic eyes. 'Clive Jacobs and Paul Thomson.'

'I don't even know who they are?'

'Clive was Morgan's boyfriend, remember? And Paul Thomson was the caretaker here. You know, the one who was questioned by the police. Why are two of the original suspects in Morgan's death coming to see the show?'

'Erm, maybe they like the theatre?'

'Whatever.' Chester waves a hand. 'God, I wish I had a ticket for that night.'

'They were both cleared, remember,' says Chloe.

'I don't even think it's either of them, to be honest.'

'Don't tell me. It was Harold Shipman. Charles Manson.'

'I think it was Edwin Roberts,' whispers Chester.

'Don't be ridiculous.' Chloe laughs. 'It was a woman, anyway.'

'How do you know that?' Chester frowns at her.

Chloe realises what she has just said. 'I ... just a *feeling*.'

'A feeling? Why? Which woman?'

'I don't know.' She tries to change the subject. 'Maybe because of the earring.'

'Anyone could nick an earring, man or woman. Could have been both.'

'Both?'

'A man *and* a woman. What if two people killed her. Your woman and a man. Maybe Clive Jacobs was let off, but he was there, except with someone else, so the evidence didn't point to him?'

'Chester, with your imagination, you should write a play.'

'I might.' He pauses. 'How's yours going?'

Chloe shrugs, not wanting to talk about it. 'I'll see you in a bit. I'm just going to the toilets to touch up my make-up and get changed.'

Chloe spends a few minutes fluffing her hair up and applying more mascara and lipstick. On her way to the box office, she pauses, and looks towards the backstage door.

Chloe...

That voice. Morgan Miller. But if it really is her, *why*? Why does she want Chloe? Why has she been calling her these recent months?

Chloe...

She heads backstage. On her way past the door that leads to the stage, she pauses. Is Morgan Miller still really here? If so, how must she feel about the new stage? About the reimagined set. Does she like it? Does she wish she had finished her run twenty years ago? Does she wish she could take part now?

Chloe opens the door and walks through. She passes the curtain and steps out, into the *Dust* world. No one is here. She walks carefully into Chevalier's drawing room, touching the soft curtains and vases of white flowers. She steps into the garden and smells the plastic climbing hydrangea, laughing at her own silliness.

She imagines being the star.

Esme Black.

No. Imagine being the girl in your own show – Abigail.

Who said that? Is it Morgan? Chloe looks up at the back of the auditorium, as if she might be there. No one. Is she just hearing things? What if Chloe *could* perform her own play, here on this very stage? How would that feel? But it's no good. It needs work.

You don't believe that, Chloe...

She faces the empty auditorium and whispers the final lines of her script: 'Only the music of the ocean – wordless, melodic, soothing – and the dance of the waves, and the two of us sinking, forever, together, to the bottom of the sea.'

What was that? Footsteps? Someone real or just a ghost?

Chloe leaves, afraid of being caught. She loiters for a moment at Ginger's dressing room door. Despite everything – despite her coolness, despite her abrupt dismissal at their last meeting – Chloe can't change how she feels about her. She decides to knock and tell Ginger how stunning she was. To tell her she's going to wow them. That she outshone even Morgan Miller; that she *is* Esme Black, and it's as though she was always supposed to be. There won't be another opportunity before opening night.

Just as she is about to knock, Chloe hears voices.

Ginger and Edwin Roberts. Probably chatting about the show. None of her business; she'll come back another time. She turns to leave, but then three words stop her. Three words that Ginger says to Edwin. That Chloe recognises. That she *wrote*.

She Haunts Me.

43

THE DEAN WILSON THEATRE

AUGUST 2019

Why is Ginger talking to Edwin Roberts about her script if she didn't like it? Is she going to laugh with him about Chloe's lack of talent, tell him that she has audacity to write her own show? Though she fears the hurt it will cause, Chloe lingers a moment longer. She needs to hear. She puts an ear to the wood.

'You mean it's by Chloe Dee? The *usher*?' Edwin is saying.

'Yes.' Ginger sounds excited.

'She let you read it?'

'Yes.' Ginger's voice trails off as though she has moved further from the door. Chloe strains to listen. 'She's got a bit of a thing for me, the darling girl. We were friends at school – I told you that. We did a drama group together as kids.'

'I've always thought her a little odd,' says Edwin, and Chloe can picture him, hair sprouting from his head like overgrown thorn bushes, hat in hand. 'Maybe *that*'s why – cos she's a bloody writer. So, she can act, eh?'

'Well, a bit. She's not especially good.' Tears tickle the corners of Chloe's eyes. 'But her writing – it's just incredible.'

Chloe frowns. *Incredible*? So Ginger did like it after all. But why did she lie in the bar? Say it was 'quite good' in that patronising way. It makes no sense.

'Eddie, the way she writes. It's just … exquisite. It's like she pours her whole heart onto the page. I tell you, at times, I cried.'

Chloe puts her forehead against the cool surface of the door to try and calm the confusion of emotions within. Ginger loves her script; she loves her words. But why did she say otherwise? To hurt her? But why? What has she ever done to deserve that?

'I *must* read it,' says Eddie.

'But it's hers.' Ginger sounds conflicted. 'I can't share it without her permission, can I?' She pauses, and Chloe wonders if they are looking at one another, smiling. 'We do need to find a way.'

'What do you mean? Why?'

'Because I want to play the main character – Abigail,' says Ginger.

'Abigail...' repeats Edwin, as though testing the name out.

'Yes. She'd be perfect for me. She's troubled, intense, passionate. So much to get my teeth into. And it would be a perfect follow-up to *Dust*. Eddie, I don't think Chloe would let me though. I think she'll want to play her. There's the other female lead, Grace, but I want a big star to play her. Alongside me.'

'And, darling, it doesn't matter how good a writer Chloe is, if she's a mediocre actress, she'll ruin her own work.'

Ginger remains silent, and Chloe realises that Ginger doesn't think she is mediocre. Chloe knows – like she always *knows* – that Ginger is afraid of Chloe performing Abigail. She doesn't want Edwin to see Chloe play the part. She knows that she will do it how it should be done. That she will win them over. The betrayal hurts more than any before.

'I know,' agrees Ginger. Does she even feel guilty? 'How can we ensure the role is mine? She wrote the script. We can't just ... steal it.' She pauses. 'Can we?'

Can we?

'She hasn't let anyone read it as far as I know,' says Ginger. 'And she hasn't sent it anywhere either.'

'There are ways.' Edwin sounds excited too now. Chloe knows he is desperate for another hit show to continue the *Dust* success; she knows that the one following it has had dismal ticket sales so far. 'Send it to me. We can tell Chloe that we need to shape it, polish it, improve it. That this is the necessary process if she wants it on the stage. Then it becomes a joint work. Then we take over a little more and her name becomes merely a credit. And then we could suggest you play the main role.'

Silence from Ginger. Is she feeling terrible at the thought of doing something like that, or is she nodding along? 'I think it could be even better than *Dust*,' she says eventually. 'The final scene where Abigail jumps into the ocean to be with Grace ... oh, I cried my heart out...'

Fuck you. Chloe wants to scream. *Fuck you. You don't even have a heart...*

She has heard enough. She needs to cut. She needs to bleed. Release.

She turns and bumps into Chester.

'Are you OK?' he asks. 'What are you doing?'

'Nothing.' She pushes past him and heads for the back door.

'Chloe! Where are you going? Aren't you coming for drinks? *Chloe*!'

She pedals home with his cries of 'Chloe' tugging on her heart-strings, tears as hot as the August night on her cheeks.

Once in her bedroom, she takes the knife from her wooden box. She has not cut for a year now. She holds it up so that it shimmers in evening sun, still spellbinding after all these years.

Don't do it. You're healing. Your scars are looking good now.

Cut, bleed, release ... rage...

Don't do it.

She cuts.

But it doesn't work.

The hurt doesn't trickle away with the flow of crimson. She remembers suddenly that she first started cutting when she was angry that Ryan might steal Jess from her. But Jess was never hers. Ginger isn't hers. The script is though. The script is all she has. Many times, she has reached for it instead of the knife. She wrote scenes until her fingers throbbed and she blacked out. She lost herself in the prose to ease her turmoil. It was there when nothing else was.

She reads the final words again.

'What if I let go? What if I fall? She is there, in the water, I know she is. What if I swim and don't look back, and swim and don't look back? Was I ever here, on this ship? Here and yet not here. There and yet not there. If I let go, what will there be? Only the music of the ocean – wordless, melodic, soothing – and the dance of the waves, and the two of us sinking, forever, together, to the bottom of the sea.'

She will *never* let anyone else say them.

44

CHLOE'S BEDROOM

2005

After the *push* incident – that was what she called it afterwards – when the two men broke into the theatre, Chloe was ill for almost two weeks.

She fell into her bed that night and stayed there for thirteen days; it felt like an eternity. It was a tornado of fever and nightmares and hallucinations. Birds scratched under the bed. The telephone rang all night, and she had no energy to even try to silence it. Her mum fussed and brought food she could barely eat, and drinks she devoured as the August sun cooked her room. Her dad, who rarely took much notice of illness, sat quietly with her at times. At some point a doctor came. To Chloe, he was a blurred phantom, a distorted voice who prescribed more liquids and bed rest.

Her mum put a cold flannel on her forehead, and Chloe cried; cried because she loved her and felt so lost, so sad, so ill, so hot; cried because she was afraid she was going mad. She longed to tell her mum what they had been doing that summer, but the confession stuck in her throat like dry crackers. She longed to cut her thigh again; to feel that exquisite pain followed by the rush of release; to feel alive. To *cut, bleed, release* ... But she hadn't the strength to reach for the dagger, let alone use it.

To add to her misery, Chloe knew she was missing the final *Macbeth* rehearsals. Her mum told her a few times that Jess had rung but that she had said to stay away in case it was contagious. 'I'm not ill,' Chloe wanted to scream. 'I'm haunted. I'm possessed. I'm a witch and I don't want to be.'

But she just cried again.

Sometimes Morgan Miller came into the bedroom.

She stood by the door where the sunlight didn't quite land, reaching out for the dancing dust fragments, eternally Esme Black in her flowing white robes. It took Chloe's breath away. She had felt her near them when they did the Ouija board, but never seen her like this. Never seen that her eyes were grey but coloured as she moved. Never seen that her hair shimmered as though electricity pulsed there. Was Chloe imagining it? She *must* be. Was the Ouija board making her ill so that she was hallucinating? Or was it just *her*?

I am dust, whispered Morgan. *When the dust settles, you will know. I am dust. When the dust settles...*

Then Chloe would fall asleep and dream about Jess: Jess in her arms; in her bed. She dreamed once of a spell that would make Jess fall in love with her, but the words flew just out of reach. Was *she* writing it? Or did Jess whisper it to her?

On this Friday ... so bright ... the hour of Venus ... blessed night ... perform this rite ... let her love me...

'Are we going to finish it?' Jess had asked on the bus, about the Ouija board. Were they? Should they? Now she had seen her, Chloe desperately wanted to know who had killed Morgan. They were so close. Morgan had told them the culprit was a woman who had used a Ouija board with her; a woman who took her earring. Chloe didn't care what Ryan wanted – didn't care about his stupid powers – but she felt if they finished the game, maybe life could return to normal – whatever that was.

One morning, Chloe woke and waited. Waited for the nausea. Waited for the birds beneath the bed. For Morgan. For the phone. But there was just silence. Calm. Nothing. She sat up. It had passed. She was no longer hot. She still felt weak as she stood up but was surprisingly clear-headed. Strong. As though she been cleansed by the fever.

Her mum must have heard the movement; she rushed into the

bedroom. 'You're OK,' she gushed, touching Chloe's forehead and fussing. 'I was so worried, sweetheart. I've never seen you so ill. You had these awful episodes. You were clawing at me and asking over and over if I could hear the birds or the phone or Morgan Miller.'

'I must have been dreaming,' said Chloe. 'What day is it?'

'Friday.'

On this Friday ... so bright ... the hour of Venus ... blessed night...

Her dream? The love spell?

'Which Friday?' asked Chloe, realising something.

'The twenty-sixth of August.'

'No.' Chloe looked at her calendar; at the single red word written there on that day. *Macbeth*. Shit. The show. It couldn't be today. 'But it's the...'

'I know. Don't worry, sweetheart. They won't expect you to perform. I've been updating Mr Hayes on how ill you've been, and he said if you were still ill tonight, they would somehow make do with two witches.'

'You can't have two,' cried Chloe, getting up. 'You need *three*.'

'Where are you going?'

'To have a shower.' Chloe knew they would be doing a final rehearsal this afternoon before the big night. 'I *have* to get to the theatre.'

'But you haven't eaten for days,' cried her mum, following her onto the landing.

'Will you make me an omelette or something then, please? I'll eat it when I'm dressed.'

'OK. But I'm worried about you. Should we get the doctor to look you over fi—'

'I'm fine.' Chloe slammed the bathroom door.

45

THE GAME

2005

When Chloe walked into the theatre, it felt like she was coming home after years. Like she had been away for much longer than two weeks and was returning a new person. And with the illness behind her she felt invigorated.

The stage was set for *Macbeth*. Since so many scenes took place at night and in gloomily lit castle rooms, it was an inexpensive play to put on. The backdrop was painted black, with grey sheets hanging here and there, and the cauldron pushed to one side. Ryan and Jess were rehearsing the scene where Macbeth declares that he no longer intends to kill Duncan. Lady Macbeth, outraged, calls him a coward.

'When you durst do it,' said Jess, face flushed in the lights, velvet dress threadbare yet stunning on her. 'Then you were a man. And to be more than what you were, you would be so much more than the man.'

Lady Macbeth was questioning her husband's manhood as she gained more control over him. It was Chloe's favourite Jess moment, not only because she was captivating, but because she outshone Ryan. She felt a brief pang of jealousy at the pair of them, but it passed. She had missed them – *both* of them.

Then she felt powerful. Like Sleeping Beauty, waking after a hundred years, having survived the third of the three wishes at her christening. Chloe might not have a lead role in the show, but she realised she didn't want to recite anyone else's words. She wanted to recite her own; *write* her own. Create a spell. Perhaps that's what all lines in plays were; spells.

She Haunts Me.

The words came to Chloe then. What did they mean?

The scene ended and Mr Hayes applauded, breaking into her thoughts. The rest of the room clapped too. Mr Hayes saw Chloe, looked surprised, and came over. 'Good to see you,' he said. 'How are you, dear? Your mum was terribly worried. Are you here to see the show tonight?'

'No, I want to perform.'

'*Perform?*' He looked doubtful. 'Are you sure you're up for it?'

'I'm sure, I feel good. I know my lines. Please, I want to.'

Jess joined them. 'You're back,' she smiled, and it was the old Jess. The Jess before Ryan and Ouija boards and kisses.

'I am. To play my part. Please let me, Mr Hayes?'

'Oh, do let her,' cried Jess. 'It won't be the same with two witches!'

He laughed heartily. 'I guess not. OK then. You'll need to do a few run-throughs though.'

Chloe didn't mind. She would do anything. They rehearsed hard all afternoon. Then it was time for something to eat before the big night – a treat of pizza that Mr Hayes laid on for everyone. Chloe sat with Jess and Ryan in the back pew, her appetite back with a vengeance. Ryan picked at his food and told Chloe he was glad she was better.

When he disappeared to the toilet, Chloe asked Jess, 'Have you seen much of him?' She was afraid to ruin their happy reunion, but curious.

'A bit, yes. Not, you know, sexually or anything. He's hardly been interested in that recently. He's still obsessed with doing this one last Ouija board session. When we came off stage earlier and he saw you were back, he grabbed me and told me that it was meant to be. You were here for that reason.' Jess paused. 'Is it true?'

'I don't know,' admitted Chloe. 'But I woke up feeling better this morning. And then I realised what day it was, and I knew I had to come. I have to talk to Morgan Miller.' She thought about telling Jess what she had seen while she was ill, but something stopped her. 'I haven't stopped thinking about her. You?'

'I guess. I reckon if we do it one more time, Ryan will shut up, and we can get on with ... well, with whatever life holds.'

Whatever life holds.

At 6.30 the theatre opened, and the audience – mostly families of the performers – filed into the pews. Chloe peered around the curtain and saw her mum and dad in the fourth row, reading the black-and-white programme Mr Hayes had put together. She caught their eyes and waved, knowing how concerned her mum had been.

Backstage, Mr Hayes ran around as though his backside was on fire, helping to style hair and calming last-minute nerves. The whole cast was squeezed into a tiny room with just one mirror, so it was bedlam. Chloe and Jess shared an excited 'this is it' look while Ryan stared at his gold-plated, cardboard dagger with ill-disguised disappointment.

Then, at exactly 7.32, the lights on the pews went off and the LED lights shone on the stage. The audience fell quiet and the wind machine whirred into blustery action for the first scene, in which the witches chant their opening lines during a storm.

The show had begun.

It went well. More than well.

Ryan outdid himself. His despairing delivery of the 'tomorrow and tomorrow and tomorrow' speech seemed to come from another man; a man who had reduced the entire cast to a handful of dust. Chloe heard the audience gasp a few times. She could hardly believe it was him. Why did he long for endless money when the talent he had was priceless? Was she naïve to think that this alone would get him what he wanted?

Jess, of course, was beautiful.

Chloe watched from the wings as she shone. 'Come, you spirits that tend on mortal thoughts,' she cried. 'Unsex me here, and fill me from the crown to the toe, top-full of direst cruelty.' She *was*

Lady Macbeth, willing to do whatever was necessary to seize the throne; the real steel behind Macbeth.

And then it was Chloe's favourite of her own scenes: the three witches in the cavern, chanting spells around their cauldron – lit red in the middle – with rumbling thunder from the sound machine nearby. Chloe's solo line was 'Tis time, 'tis time!', which she cackled with relish. Then all three circled the cauldron, reciting 'Double, double, toil and trouble.' Chloe wasn't sure when smoke began to rise from it, but it buffeted and spiralled as though a fire had ignited there.

Was this a new effect that had been put in place during her absence?

No – Elisha and Ella, her fellow witches, looked just as confused. The audience must have thought it part of the show though as they ooo-ed softly.

Then Chloe saw Morgan Miller at the back of the room.

Standing behind the pews. Wearing white. Smiling. Glowing. Encouraging. As clear as when she had appeared in Chloe's room while she was ill. Morgan smiled. Chloe gasped. Then words came out of her mouth; words she did not control.

'On this Friday...' she whispered. 'So bright ... the hour of Venus ... blessed night ... perform this rite ... let her love me ... let her love me ... let her love me...'

The other witches looked unsure and paused in their incantations. Chloe knew without turning that Mr Hayes was glaring behind the curtain. Then Elisha – perhaps hypnotised by Chloe's words – repeated them too. Finally, Ella joined in. When they were done, a breath in unison, and the three of them concluded with, 'Double, double, toil and trouble; Fire burn and cauldron bubble.'

The show went on. The audience clearly thought it was part of the script, perhaps modernised, adapted. When her scene was done, Chloe staggered off stage, feeling light-headed again now.

'What the hell was that?' hissed Mr Hayes.

'I ... don't know...' It was the truth.

'Are you ill again? I should never have let you perform. Thank God that's your last scene.'

'The audience were loving it,' said Ella.

'Yeah, they were captivated,' said Elisha.

Chloe collapsed on a beanbag in the small room, her heart racing. What had she said? Was it a spell? Hadn't she pictured Jess when she said it? She wasn't sure how long she sat there, young actors racing by, changing costumes, but before she knew it the audience were applauding vigorously, and she had to go back on stage for the bows.

Chloe caught her mum's eye. She was crying, looking proud, mouthing, 'You were amazing.'

Afterwards, the high. The room buzzed. Chloe told her mum she would be staying behind to celebrate with the others, then joined them, laughing and high-fiving. Later, still in full costume, crown atop his unruly hair, Ryan found Chloe in the girls' toilets.

'You can't come in here,' she cried.

'That spell you did. Did you make it up? It was pretty cool.'

'I don't know,' she admitted, not able to meet his gaze.

'It was about Jess, wasn't it?' He said it kindly for once.

Chloe didn't respond.

'You can't force someone to love you, you know,' he said. It sounded so mature that she finally looked at him. 'If you do that kind of spell you're never, *ever*, supposed to ask for the heart of someone specific.'

'*What*? How do *you* know that?'

'I was in a play last year. The lead character did something like that, and she just ended up *three* times more in love with the man she wanted. And he never loved her back. It's not ethically right or something. Doing love spells. I was the man.'

'It was only words,' whispered Chloe, not believing that.

'I know you don't like me much,' said Ryan.

Chloe shrugged. She realised then what he really wanted – to be liked, to be adored, to be loved. That was the true reason for his pursuit of making it as an actor. 'You're not so bad,' she said.

'My friend died,' he said sadly, taking off his crown and looking at it. 'My dad's hardly around much now. My mum drinks and has too many kids. Is it so wrong for me to want something that's just mine?'

'No,' said Chloe softly.

He looked at her, that glint back in his eyes. 'Now I think we do should do some real magic,' he said. 'Don't you?'

'Is Jess up for it?'

He nodded.

And they all stayed behind one last time.

46

THE DEAN WILSON THEATRE

SEPTEMBER 2019

The Dean Wilson Theatre foyer is as beautiful as the *Dust* stage; all creams and whites and golds. The usually bare dining tables are covered with linen cloths; on top small jars of amber lights twinkle. Gilt-framed black-and-white shots of the last dress rehearsal line walls softened by white drapes that move like ghosts every time the doors open. From the ceiling, strings of lights add to the atmosphere. It's opening night. It's packed. And the atmosphere is electric.

Chloe keeps thinking about the dead bird on her doorstep.

The film crew get shots of the crowds and interview random patrons, who are more than happy to gush for the cameras. Cynthia is wearing the frilled shirt and bow tie she always saves for special events, and is rushing around, making sure everything is just as it should be front of house. The ushers on shift are wearing crisply ironed shirts – they've had three emails this week reminding them to be smart tonight – and they mill around the foyer, smiles on faces and glossy programmes in hands.

Chloe stands in front of the box office and looks at the front cover again – it's the black-and-white image of Ginger and John Marrs as Esme and Chevalier swept up in a passionate embrace, and is overlaid with gold lettering, just like on the posters. Cynthia has explained that they expect to sell a lot – to fans hoping to get them signed by the actors – so Edwin Roberts has decided they should be ten pounds instead of the customary five.

'That's pretty steep,' said Beth, flicking through it.

'Fans will pay it though,' said Paige.

Chloe imagined Chester having plenty to say about that and missed him desperately.

'You're quiet, Chloe,' Cynthia said then. 'You sure you're OK?'

'Yes,' she lied. 'Just a big night, isn't it?'

Now she opens the programme and finds the page about Ginger. Reads the biography describing her ascent to fame because of the iconic show. Looks at the pictures of her at various stages of rehearsals. Touches her beautiful, lying, devious, *betraying* face and tries to bury the anger churning in her gut.

We can't just ... steal it. Can we?

'She's gorgeous, isn't she?'

Chloe looks up. 'I'll have three,' gushes a man in a *Dust* T-shirt. 'My mum and her carer didn't get a ticket so I'm getting them one. Do you reckon the actors will come out and meet fans afterwards?'

'We can't promise anything,' says Chloe, forcing a smile. Cynthia told them earlier that the cast said they might pop out, if all goes well, but it isn't set in stone.

Chloe doesn't want to see Ginger. She can't bear to. She's glad she has been away from the theatre for the last two weeks. She doesn't know what she might have said or done if she'd seen her. And she doesn't know what will happen if she sees her tonight, so she plans to get away as quickly as possible afterwards and avoid backstage in between. She hardly even wants to see the show now; it's ruined for Chloe before it even starts.

The dead bird comes to her again. Black, stiff, eyes cold and wide, on the step as she opened the door to leave the house that afternoon. She couldn't bear to touch it and had housemate James put it in the bin. She hasn't dreamed about birds for a while; she wonders if Ginger has.

Now, her scars ache. Every night for the last two weeks she has cut again, desperately wanting to calm the fiery rage, to release the pain of the only woman she has ever loved betraying her in such a cruel way. *Cut, bleed, release...* Lying on sheets speckled with blood, she recalled being in Jess's room, way back, while they were using the Ouija board. Talking about what it must be like to be dead. Wondering where the soul went. Where feelings went. Your essence. And Chloe had wondered what it would be like to no longer love Jess.

Does she know now?

She hates Ginger right now with every bit of energy she has. She's angry. Hurt. But does she love her?

Yes. *Still.*

And she hates them both for it.

To distract herself from these thoughts, Chloe joins Beth at the main doors.

'Are you excited?' Beth asks, her hair ashen grey now, perhaps to tie in with *Dust*.

Chloe just wants to weep.

'Yes,' she lies. 'You?'

'God, yes. I never thought they would beat the original, but I think they just might have done.' Beth sells two programmes to a family. 'You're going to ask me if I took that pearl earring, aren't you?'

'No,' says Chloe, not even sure if she was.

'The item I took is probably way less valuable. And I still have it – it hasn't been sent in to the police. It was just this little goblet trinket.'

Chloe suddenly sees Ginger's charm bracelet. Their whole history dangles from it; the *Macbeth* witch hat; the theatre mask; the tiny ghost. How could she even think of stealing her script? *How could she*? After all they have been through.

'I think it might have come off a costume,' continues Beth. 'It was lying there on the floor. I just wanted a memento, I guess.' She looks at Chloe. 'I was with Morgan when I took it.' Beth pauses. 'It was me, that night.'

'*What*?' Has Chloe heard her right?

'Backstage,' Beth says. 'That night. Just before I started working here. Yes, it was me.'

'Oh. *That.*' And Chloe realises Beth means the footsteps she heard backstage that time. 'It was? But why were you there?'

'I don't know. I wanted to ... see her dressing room. Because, yes, I was there the night Morgan died. I might have been the last to see her alive. But I didn't kill her.'

Does Chloe believe her?

Edwin Roberts squeezes past them. Usually, on such an important night, he might tell them not to stand gossiping, but he clearly can't look at her. *Yes, you turn away,* thinks Chloe. *You turn away.* The strength of her anger is so great that she fears she'll set the programmes on fire.

'I reckon you should look at Chester more closely,' says Beth.

'Sorry?' Chloe frowns.

'Ever questioned him?'

Chloe laughs. '*Chester*? No. He wasn't even there that night.'

'He wasn't *working* that night, you mean. Doesn't mean he wasn't there. He could have got in. And if you wanted to kill an actor, wouldn't it be easier *not* being on shift?'

'That's ridiculous. He doesn't even have a motive.'

'All I'm saying is that he's trying very hard to deflect it away from himself. He's accused just about everyone. Got himself sacked in the process.'

At that moment, Cynthia emerges from the throng, face thunderous. 'How many times have I told ushers *not* to stand gossiping. If Edwin sees you, he'll go mad. Get mingling, get selling, and get smiling.'

Chloe weaves through the crowds. She recognises a few journalists. She wonders if Morgan Miller's boyfriend Clive is here; if the caretaker whose name she can't recall now is. The *Dust* theme song filters through the speakers, prompting smiles from the patrons. Ginger's melodic voice taunts her. '*I'm still here; I am dust. I'm those fragments in the air, the gold light dancing there, that breeze from nowhere.*'

Then she sees Chester.

'What are you doing here?' she cries, beyond happy to see him.

'EBay,' he laughs. He's dressed in a red waistcoat and matching polished shoes. 'How could I miss this?'

'EBay?'

'People have been selling their tickets there. I paid stupid money, but I don't care. I'm here.' He squeezes her arm. 'I'm actually going to see bloody *Dust*!'

Chloe can't help but be infected by his joy. He has been everything to her this last week, coming over, offering his shoulder. She told him what she heard Ginger say. She had to tell someone, and it had been impossible to hide her pain when he asked why she hadn't come for his leaving drinks. He insisted Chloe send him her script, assured her no one could take it, and that he would say he had read it long before anyone else.

But it wasn't whether or not Ginger could succeed in stealing her work that kept Chloe awake at night.

It was that she could even *think* of doing it.

'Have you got your phone on you?' asks Chester now.

'Of course not, you know we're not allowed.'

He gets his out, swipes, and taps the screen. 'Look at the news today,' he says, showing her

'"Who Will Die?"' she reads aloud. 'Is that seriously an actual headline?'

He nods. 'They're speculating about whether someone else will die tonight when *Dust* opens. Sick, eh? And then on the next page they've released some of the letter that was sent to the police with that earring.'

'What does it say?' Chloe leans closer to Chester. For a moment she thinks of what Beth said earlier: *He's trying very hard to deflect it away from himself.* No, that's ridiculous; he's just a gossip.

'Something about how the person who sent the earring to the police has kept it in all this time and just can't anymore. He or she thinks justice should finally be done. Police think it's written by a man though.'

'That could suggest a woman killed Morgan, then.'

'How so?' asks Chester.

'It could be the killer's boyfriend or husband who sent the letter. Maybe he's known all these years that she did it and finally decided to tell the police.'

'I suppose. It's trending too.' Chester shows her his Twitter feed – the most popular hashtags are #Dust #DustIsBack #WhoKilledMorgan and #WhoWillDieTonight. Someone has posted a picture of Ginger with blood dripping from her chest and written 'Morgan's killer is coming for you'.

What is wrong with people?

'Jesus,' whispers Chloe.

'What are you going to do?' asks Chester, putting his phone away.

'What do you mean?'

'About Ginger? The script.'

'Just do my job and go home.'

'For a whole month? What if you see her?'

'I don't know.' Chloe shrugs. 'I'll deal with that when it happens.'

'I still can't believe it. What an absolute bitch. You should actually report her. And Edwin Roberts. That's the real scandal. The fucking artistic director talking about nicking someone's script.'

'Please, Chester, you *must* keep this to yourself.' Chloe grabs his arm. 'I mean it. I'll decide what I'm going to do when I get a chance to think.'

He nods. 'How can you not absolutely detest her?'

Chloe looks at him. Remembers how it felt to *push* Ginger that time. Remembers the fear in her eyes. Remembers the buzz. Thinks that if she *pushed* even harder, she might do more damage. Would she do that? Then the radio crackles. Words whisper softly in Chloe's ear. 'Never ... be ... under ... one ... roof...' She frowns. Who said it? Is she hearing things again?

Now she feels ... *ready*.

'Are you OK?' asks Chester.

'I think so.' Maybe she imagined the words. Maybe she has all along. 'Look, I'd better get on.'

'OK. That slag from Propaganda is supposed to have a ticket. I'll go find him. See you at the interval.' Chester disappears before she can ask if he knows whether Morgan's boyfriend or the caretaker are in the crowd.

The radio crackles again and Chloe waits, ready. But it's just the techie announcing that they are ready to open the auditorium. Cynthia radios that ushers should get into position. Chloe is on the main doors, taking tickets. The announcement on the tannoy follows, voice excited: 'The theatre is now open if you would like to take your seats for *Dust*.' Despite all that has happened since Chester said, 'It's coming back', despite the strange voices, despite Ginger ripping her fucking heart out, Chloe shivers. This is it. The big night. This is her theatre, and this is her favourite show.

She opens the doors. Smiles. And takes tickets from excited patrons. Unlike usual – when people hang around in the foyer until the last minute, drinking – they're desperate to see the set and pile through the doors, gasping when they first see it. A beautiful middle-aged woman, her hair piled up on her head, smiles radiantly at Chloe as she hands her ticket over.

'Lynda Swanson,' she says. When Chloe doesn't respond, she adds, 'Ginger's mum.'

'Of course.' How could Chloe not have realised? 'Oh my God. It's been years. You must be so proud.'

'I am, darling. She was born for it, wasn't she?' And she sweeps into the theatre.

When the techie says on the radio that there are just three minutes to go, the foyer is completely empty. A *Dust* flyer skims the floor, caught in the breeze from the doors as they open.

There's a latecomer. A man. He looks unsure. The suit is designer, and the aftershave preceding him smells expensive. He reaches into his trouser pocket, retrieves his ticket, and approaches Chloe. That walk. A hint of arrogance. A hint of teenage swagger despite looking early thirties. The floppy hair now less thick but sharply cut. The face. He looks at Chloe and he clearly recognises her, just as she does him.

Ryan...

And she still can't think of his surname. Did they ever know?

'I came to see Jess,' he says, even though she hasn't said a word.

'Ginger,' says Chloe softly.

'Ginger,' he repeats. His eyes are sad, more lined now.

'She's very good.'

'I knew she would be.'

Chloe has a million questions. What did you do with your life? Where have you been? Did your dreams come true? You look wealthy, but are you happy? Can you remember what happened when we used the Ouija board? But there's no time now. The radio crackles. She anticipates those words again. She's ready. But the techie just says that there's one minute to go.

'It's good to see you,' he says. 'I didn't know you worked here. You look well.'

She takes the ticket from him.

Their fingers touch.

And Chloe sees it all. She sees it the way you see highlights from a previous TV episode when you're waiting for the next one. She sees the three of them. The dusty stage. The Ouija board. The last time they did it. God, she sees it all.

'That's so weird,' whispers Ryan. 'I just...'

'I know. Me too.'

'What *was* that?' He studies her and smiles. 'You always were a witch.'

'I was, wasn't I?' She smiles too. 'You're in the front row. Lucky you.'

He nods. 'I had to be. It's good to see you. Have to catch up properly at the interval. Or afterwards?'

On the radio, the techie says it's about to begin. 'You'd better go in,' she says.

He nods at the programmes; she tells him how much and he gives her ten pounds.

'Isn't she beautiful?' He looks at the glossy cover.

'She is,' says Chloe.

Then she closes the doors after him, and the show begins.

YOU THREE NEVER BE UNDER ONE ROOF.

But now they are.

Now they are, and it's *her* roof.

47

THE GAME

2005

Sitting cross-legged around the Ouija board, Jess, Ryan and Chloe were still in costume; Jess's red velvet dress was damp beneath her arms and the two charms – the witch hat and theatre mask – tinkled when she moved; Ryan had put his crown back on as if he was saying that he was the leader tonight; Chloe wore her long witch robes but she had flung the itchy wig in the cupboard.

When they began over a month ago, Ryan had called it a game. He had told them the rules, but along the way they had bent them to fit their needs. 'We'll shut it down if it gets weird,' they had agreed. 'We're in control,' they had said.

Chloe knows now that they all lied.

Not only to one another in saying they would end it if necessary, but to themselves. Morbid curiosity, youthful bravado and teenage love had joined the three of them, on a dusty stage in a church. Now autumn was a breath away. Now it was too late in August for the dying sun to penetrate the boarded-up windows and light the room. Ryan had left a lamp on in the nearby backstage room, and it filtered gently through.

'Last time then,' he said, positioning the letters.

'Last time,' repeated Jess.

'Last time,' said Chloe softly.

'Exam results tomorrow.' Ryan lit the three candles. The third one wouldn't light easily; he managed on the third match. Three, three, *three*. 'I'm fucked. We should've done this *before* we did our exams, and I might have passed them all.'

'You don't even know that you've failed yet,' sighed Chloe.

'Of course I fucking did. Thank God I'm good-looking, eh?'

'My parents are selling our house,' said Jess. 'My mum wants me to go to college in London, so I have a better chance of making it as an actress.'

'Lucky you.' Ryan couldn't hide the bitterness in his voice. 'I'll be stuck on that fucking council estate with my family for years.'

'You're leaving?' Chloe could hardly say it. 'You never told us.'

'Yeah, they only just told me.'

Chloe studied the two charms on Jess's bracelet so she wouldn't cry. So much ending. So much change. She wasn't ready. Jess had asked Chloe earlier about her improvisation during the witch scene, saying maybe she should write her own show. 'Imagine if you did,' she'd gushed. 'You could write it and I'd star in it.' And as much as she adored Jess, she had thought, *No: my words, my role*.

'You ready?' asked Ryan.

No, Chloe wanted to say. *No, I'm not*.

'Right, let's just ask for Danny Locke and the powers, shall we?' Ryan put a finger on the upturned glass. 'That's what I really want.'

'We can get to that,' said Chloe. 'I want to talk to Morgan Miller again. One last time. Don't you guys? The last time we had her here, she told us a *woman* had killed her. A woman who used a Ouija board with her and who wanted the role in *Dust* too. Who has her earring. We need her to tell us her name. If it's going to be the last time we do this, I want to know.'

'She's right,' said Jess. 'Let's ask for Morgan.'

'OK.' Ryan paused. 'She might not even come.'

'She's already here,' said Chloe.

'How do you know?' asked Jess.

'I saw her. When I was on stage.'

Jess stared at her. Was it in awe? Disbelief? Admiration? Whatever it was, Chloe enjoyed the moment. Then Jess smiled – she looked like an angel in the glow – and Chloe smiled back. And they both put their fingers on the glass at exactly the same time, neither leading, neither following.

'Is there anyone here with us tonight?' asked Ryan.

Nothing. Chloe smiled, wondering if the spirits liked to tease, make their audience wait.

'Is there anyone here to talk to us? Morgan Miller – are you there?'

A slow, seductive scrape drew their eyes downward – the glass was moving. Morgan. Chloe smiled. Only Morgan moved it so deliberately. Subtle perfume lingered on the air. Shadows moved behind Jess.

I DONT FALL I FLY
I DON'T DIE IM FREE

'Wherever your heart beats,' finished Jess and Chloe together.

'Let me guess,' said Ryan. 'Another song from *Dust*.'

'It's her,' said Jess excitedly.

Chloe was thrilled too. She still couldn't quite believe the iconic star was talking to them, three everyday teenagers.

'Hi Morgan,' she whispered.

I AM DUST

'You are,' Chloe smiled.

YOU WILL BE DUST

'That's what I want,' said Jess.

'What do you mean?' asked Chloe.

Jess looked for a moment like she had regretted her words. 'That's it,' she admitted eventually. 'I want to play Esme Black one day. In *Dust*.'

'But I doubt the show will ever come back. When it shut down,

Dean Wilson became a recluse and said he'd never let it be staged again, didn't he?'

'Things change, don't they?'

YOU WILL BE DUST

'Will I really, Morgan?' cried Jess.

'You got the powers, Morgan' interrupted Ryan. 'When you did the Ouija board. You said we just had to ask. We were gonna ask Daniel but we're asking you now. Give us the powers. We know what we want.'

WHEN THE DUST SETTLES YOU WILL KNOW

Chloe knew that was meant for her. Morgan knew what she wanted tonight. Was she going to speak directly to each of them in turn?

MONEY NEVER GAVE ME MORE
THAN MY HEART WOULD LET IT

What does that mean?' asked Ryan.

A LESSON IN THE CURRENCY OF LOVE
DON'T FORGET IT

'It's from *Dust* again,' said Chloe. 'From the song about Chevalier's greed as a young man.' She realised it was meant for Ryan. A warning about the power he was hoping for. But would he listen?

'I'm asking you, Morgan,' continued Ryan. 'I need more money than I've ever seen or held. I know I can act, I know that, but I want the chances that Jess's mum gives her, that all the rich kids have. I want to go to London too. Follow my dreams.'

SOMEONE ELSE IS HERE FOR THAT

'Someone else?' Chloe's heart sank. 'No, we want you to stay. *Please*, tell us who killed you, Morgan?'

'Who else is here for that?' asked Ryan.

WHEN THE DUST SETTLES YOU WILL KNOW

'Can't you tell us now?' begged Chloe.

'Who's here for that?' repeated Ryan.

And then Chloe knew. She could feel it. Morgan had gone. The glass stilled, but only for a moment, as though ownership had switched, and the new owner had taken a breath first.

She saw him. Like she had that first time, so long ago it seemed now. Sitting behind Ryan. Cross-legged. A teenage boy. Grinning. Face bloody; the crimson flow from the ragged gash across his forehead pretty in the flickering light. Daniel Locke. Ryan's best friend. The glass moved.

YOURE READY

'Is that you?' asked Ryan. '*Dan*?'

YOU ARE ETERNAL THREE

'We are.'

READY FOR THE POWERS

'We are. But how? Tell us *how*. Morgan Miller said we needed three of us and we just ask. Can we ask you?'

SPEAK IT ALOUD

'That's all?' Ryan looked thrilled.

'You really believe it can happen?' asked Chloe. 'Just like that?'

'I don't know,' said Jess, unsure. 'It can't be that simple.'

'But he *died*,' said Jess. 'He asked for the powers and he died.'

'That was suicide,' said Ryan. 'Doesn't mean it was directly to do with the powers he got. Not really.'

'Do you really believe that?' Chloe shook her head.

'He was just a troubled kid,' said Ryan. *Like you*, thought Chloe. 'He might have done that anyway, even without the Ouija board. Don't we only ever do what we really want to do? No one forces us.'

NO ONE HAS TO DIE
SPEAK IT ALOUD

'I will, Dan,' said Ryan, his face manic in the glow. Chloe felt a strong breeze around them and wondered if the others did too. Before they could argue with him, Ryan spoke. 'I want wealth. Riches beyond anyone's wildest dreams.'

JESS SPEAK IT ALOUD

As though hypnotised, Jess said, 'I want to be Esme Black. One day, I want to play her and be a superstar.'

They both looked at Chloe.

'I only want to know who killed Morgan,' she said, softly. 'I don't care about any powers. I just want her to come back and tell us. Are you still there, Morgan?'

Nothing. Then the glass moved violently.

ALL THREE

'Chloe did hers earlier,' cried Ryan. 'On stage. Her spell. She asked for Jess.'

Choe glared at him.

'What?' Jess frowned. 'Asked for *me*?'

'That's all three of us,' cried Ryan manically.

'No, it isn't. I didn't—' The moving glass interrupted Chloe's words.

IT IS DONE THEN

Ryan smiled.

THERE IS A PRICE

'You never told us that,' he said.

SHAKESPEARE ALWAYS HAS A PRICE

Ryan gulped. 'And what is it?'

NEVER SEE THESE TWO AGAIN

'*What?*'

YOU THREE
NEVER BE
UNDER ONE ROOF

Chloe knew the words were the beginning of the end. The end of their friendship. The end of this. The end of childhood. She felt it as acutely as she had felt so many other things this summer. She looked at Jess. Her lip was trembling. Chloe longed to calm it with a kiss.

Remember her, she thought. *Drink in her face. Cherish this moment.*

Even though the spelled-out words were not spoken, Chloe

heard them as though they had been. She heard Daniel. The letters had transformed into the voice of their creator – calm. In control. Enjoying.

'Never see Jess and Chloe again you mean?' asked Ryan.

NEVER

Ryan looked at them both. Chloe saw a host of emotions pass across his face – fear, sadness, indecision, and finally acceptance. A decision. He stood.

'You *can't*,' cried Jess, taking her finger from the glass.

He shrugged. 'You're going to London anyway. I wouldn't see you, would I? It was nice. You were a really great fuck, you know.'

Her mouth dropped open.

LEAVE NOW

'Have a good life, Chloe,' said Ryan.

And he walked down the stage steps and along the aisle between the pews.

'Ryan,' yelled Jess. 'Wasn't I more than a fuck?'

He reached the door, turned and looked back. For a moment, his eyes looked yellow; like pools of hot lava. One of the candles went out. The other two waved in the draught. Then Ryan was gone. Jess looked at Chloe, absolute shock bright in her eyes. Neither of them said a word. The glass moved again.

YOU WILL BE DUST

'He's talking to me, isn't he?' whispered Jess.

Chloe nodded, unable to speak.

LEAVE NOW OR NO DUST

'How much do you want it?' asked Chloe, afraid of the answer.

Jess looked at her lap.

'You never told me *that* was your dream,' cried Chloe.

'Did I really need to *say*? Didn't I show you with every action and every song? You know me like no one else – you must have known.'

Chloe, the girl who felt like she often *knew*, had been blind to this most obvious fact.

'You're going to go, aren't you?' she said.

Jess stood up.

'Please don't,' said Chloe. 'You don't need some power to get what you want, Jess. You have that within you, I know it.'

Jess walked wordlessly away.

'Come back! *Please!*'

But she had gone. It was just Chloe. Then the glass moved.

48

THE DEAN WILSON THEATRE

SEPTEMBER 2019

After twenty years, a frenzy of social-media coverage, exaggerated headlines about Morgan Miller's ghost, and 'exclusive' stories about the new casts' scandals, *Dust* begins six minutes late due to a torn dress.

Then that moment comes when the audience is united by a sharp intake of breath; the moment after they have turned off phones and settled comfortably in seats; the moment when darkness falls, and the stage is lit; that moment when they wonder if they even exist anymore; when they forget everything for two hours.

Chloe has hoped over and over, for years, to experience in that moment the magic she felt when she first saw *Dust*. Now the familiar music soars just before the lights come up, and goose bumps climb her spine. Despite Ginger ruining the lead-up to this longed-for moment, she sits forwards on her seat in the shadows and anticipates Esme Black's first appearance.

Ginger *asked* for this.

For this night.

Back then, when they were kids.

As Chevalier sings, '*Money never gave me more than my heart would let it, a lesson in the currency of love, don't forget it*', Chloe can't stop thinking about it. Ginger – no *Jess* – asked for this role all those years ago, that last night on the Ouija board. She agreed not to see Chloe or Ryan again – the price to fulfil her dream of being Esme. Of resurrecting *Dust*.

How could Chloe have forgotten?

Was it seeing Ryan that completed something and freed the memory? If they were all supposed to be apart forever to achieve their dreams, what does tonight mean? What might happen now they are all under one roof again?

Chloe shakes her head.

Enjoy the show, she thinks. *You can't change anything now.*

It's hard to watch the audience as vigilantly as she should. Quickly, knowing Esme will be onstage in a few minutes, Chloe scans the heads and spots Chester on the far left. As though sensing her gaze, he turns and catches her eye. They smile. His first time seeing the show. Chloe is so happy for him. She wonders where Clive is. If he came. She wouldn't know him if she saw him.

She then finds Ryan on the front row. She wishes she could see his face. Is he nervous about what the night might hold, or is he entranced by the show?

The radio in Chloe's ear crackles. 'Never ... be ... under ... one ... roof...'

Is she imagining the words? Did she imagine the vision earlier? Imagine seeing that final Ouija board session as clearly as a film. Seeing Ryan walk away, and then Jess. Seeing one candle burning. The radio crackles again. Chloe tenses.

'Someone's taking pictures audience right,' snaps the techie.

That's Beth's side. Chloe watches her go down the steps and tell the patron to stop. Another tries on Chloe's side, and she rises to warn them. As she returns to her seat, one of her favourite songs begins; 'Amongst the Ashes'. Esme sings it while cleaning Chevalier's home and longing for him.

And Ginger makes her first ever entrance in *Dust*. The audience applauds; they usually wait for a song to be over but can't seem to contain themselves, and they clap over her opening lines. Ever the professional, she continues as though she hasn't heard, but Chloe knows she must be thrilled to hear it.

'I'm as grey as the ash that I clean at his feet, I'm the aftermath of fire, flames he never sees...'

Ginger is utterly beautiful. There is no denying it. No trying to get over it. Beautiful. Even though the role at this stage demands she be plain, modest, humble, Ginger manages to outshine the simple maid costume, to outglow the shadowy lighting. John Marrs as Chevalier is more ostentatious in a purple top hat and coat, gold pocket watch in hand, but Ginger steals the limelight.

'I'm the aftermath of fire, flames he never sees...'

Chloe realises that Ginger has never really seen *her*. Jess might have done, long ago, but she was prepared to turn her back on their friendship for power. Ginger came here for what *she* wanted. Now she's prepared to steal Chloe's script to try and continue her moment of fame.

'I'm the aftermath of fire, flames he never sees...'

Hot rage consumes Chloe. She read once that when a mother sees her child in pain, she feels it in her Caesarean or vaginal scar. Now, Chloe feels her anger at Ginger in the recent scars on her thighs. She scratches at them and feels dampness beneath her fingertips. She's bleeding. Shit. She goes out into the foyer where it's light. It just looks like she spilt coffee. No choice but to let it stain.

Cynthia emerges from the nearby box office. 'What are you doing, Chloe? You can't be out here, even for a minute, tonight. If anything goes wrong...'

'I was just ... overwhelmed for a moment.'

Chloe returns to her seat. On stage, Ginger is about to jump from the balcony and die at Chevalier's feet. The atmosphere in the auditorium is electric. In Chloe's ear, the radio crackles. 'Five minutes until the interval,' says the techie. She wonders for a moment if she could *push*. Ginger leaps. The stage spins around and Chevalier is holding her tenderly, amidst white flowers. No. Chloe would never do anything like that.

Would she?

The lights come up. The first half is over. People rush to the bar, raving about the show as they pass Chloe on her door, buying more programmes and asking repeatedly if the actors will be coming out to meet fans afterwards.

Chester grabs her arm, making her jump. 'Oh, my fucking God,' he says. 'I'm just … speechless. Seriously, I know Ginger's a bitch, but fuck, she's good, isn't she?'

'She is,' admits Chloe.

'Is she better than Morgan Miller?' he asks. 'Come on, dish the dirt.'

'I don't know. What's better? She's *different*.'

'So Simon Cowell would say she's made the role her own?'

Chloe laughs. 'Look, if I don't see you later…' she begins.

'What do you mean? We *have* to have drinks after this.'

'No, I don't think I'll be here.' Chloe doesn't know what she means; what she's saying. Then she does. 'I'm going to confront Ginger.'

'You are?' He grins.

'I am.' She realises that she is.

'Oh God, I need to be there.'

She laughs. 'No. You don't.'

He pauses, and then kisses Chloe's cheek. 'Confront her, but don't let yourself get hurt. That's usually what happens. You're the sweet one. The lovely one. And it could be *you* that ends up the most hurt.'

Is she sweet? Lovely? She doesn't feel it right now.

'I won't, I promise.'

'Hey, I got a job interview. For the duty manager at the New Theatre. Get me!'

'Oh, good luck, Ches.' She hugs him, hard. Knows somehow that he will get it.

'You have to continue my search for Morgan Miller's killer now,' he says seriously. 'I'm entrusting you with the mission. How can I when I'm not here?'

'If I ever do find out, you'll be the first one I tell,' Chloe says affectionately.

'And Twitter will be the first one I tell,' he grins.

She feels desperately sad as he disappears into the crowd. She turns, and Ryan is there, programme held tightly to his chest. 'Now I know why she wanted it,' he says. 'The role of Esme. It was made for her.'

No, it was made for Morgan, thinks Chloe suddenly.

'And did you get what *you* wanted?' she asks him.

'You know, I'd sort of forgotten it all,' he says. 'Maybe forgotten is the wrong word, because now it's like I never did. I was a little monster then, wasn't I?'

'Not really,' laughs Chloe.

'Well, I got the money. All the money I wanted. I won it.'

'Shit, really?'

'Yep. Twenty million on the lottery. But it made me lazy. Having so much stole my ambition. What are you gonna strive for when you can buy it all? I've never been on the stage since we did *Macbeth*.' He laughs then and says, 'God, Jess would kill me for saying that word aloud here.' He pauses. 'Can you take me backstage so I can see her? Just for a second.'

'I can't,' says Chloe. 'I'd be sacked.'

'But I was her friend. You were too. Back when we were kids with dreams. I just want to wish her well.'

Chloe realises she wants to witness Ginger's face when she sees Ryan. She can't wait until later to confront her. She has always loved this, being an usher, being here, but fuck it. Fuck being an usher tonight. She's a writer who has written a script and she won't have it stolen. She looks at her watch. Only ten minutes of the interval left. She rips the earpiece from her ear, wraps it around the radio, and puts it in a bin. Fuck it if she gets sacked. She's not here to pick up the glitter tonight. She *is* the glitter tonight.

'Let's go,' she says.

'Really?'

'Yes. I just have to get something.'

Checking Cynthia isn't inside, Chloe grabs her bag from the

box office and leads Ryan along the corridor to the backstage door. She keys in the code and opens the door onto madness; actors rushing around, stage managers swearing, piles of abandoned clothes, and sweat heavy in the air. They push through the throng and stand at Ginger's dressing room door.

My dressing room...

Was that Morgan Miller above the din?

Ryan touches the gold star, clearly impressed. He looks at Chloe, as though to check, so she nods, and he knocks on the door. She touches the knife in her bag. No, the *dagger*. It was Ryan's once upon a time. Now she isn't even sure why she has it. Can hardly remember putting it in her bag. Did she bring it to give it back to Ryan? Did she know – somehow – that he was coming tonight? She really isn't sure. She fingers the blade.

Chloe...

She smiles. Yes. Morgan is here too.

I'm the aftermath of fire, flames he never sees...

Is that Morgan singing the line that was hers first?

Well, Ginger is going to *see* Chloe now.

Chloe is the aftermath of fire.

Ginger opens the door.

49

THE GAME

2005

YOU THREE

NEVER BE

UNDER ONE ROOF

Chloe wanted to get up and chase Jess; to go home with her, stay over at her house, see her in the morning, and the day after that, and the day after that, just to cancel the price of the powers. But she couldn't move.

Another candle died. The final flame valiantly danced on. Should she stay here? She knew you should never use the Ouija board alone, but she looked down at the glass, put her finger upon it, and she waited, afraid. Then it moved again. Slowly. Seductively. Was it *her*? Morgan. Had she spelled out the phrase about never being under one roof or had that been Daniel?

It occurred suddenly to Chloe that word *spelled* had double meaning – a magical spell and a spelling of words. That's what this game had been – both.

'Is this still you Daniel?' she asked softly.

I AM DUST

'Morgan.' She smiled, not afraid now. 'I shouldn't be doing this alone. It's one of the rules.'

TWO OF US

'Yes. I guess there are.' Chloe paused, thought. 'Can you see other spirits who speak on here? Did you see Daniel Locke?'

I PASS THEM

'Are you always here? Where do you go when you're *not* here?'

HERE IS NOT HERE

'Do you sleep or anything?' asked Chloe. 'Do you ever get hungry?'

NEVER

'Do you miss the stage?'
The glass stilled. Chloe waited. Eventually it moved again.

I WAIT FOR MY CUE AND SING SING SING

'At the Dean Wilson Theatre?' asked Chloe.

YES

Chloe felt sadness but it wasn't her own; she felt it like it was mist in the air, damp, heavy, suffocating. It was Morgan's, she was sure. She wondered if any of the people at the Dean Wilson Theatre ever heard her singing. She had read about the place being haunted and now she imagined it was true. She saw Morgan dressed as Esme, waiting backstage, hair like a wedding veil around her glowing face.
'And you miss your boyfriend, Clive?' she asked.
Stillness again. The sole candle flickering bravely on.

ALWAYS

'And he never hurt you? Only loved you?'

ALWAYS

Chloe took a breath. 'Please, can't you tell me who killed you, Morgan?'

NOT YET

'Why not yet?' Chloe tried to control the impatience in her voice.

YOU ARE NOT READY

'I *am.*'

THERE WILL BE A DAY

With other spirits, the glass had sped across the boards, hot beneath their fingers, from letter to letter; messages from some place beyond here. With Morgan it was gentle. Now even more so.

'So you *will* tell me?' said Chloe. 'One day?'

YES

Chloe realised she believed her, and that she must accept it. 'OK. I won't ask you anymore. I guess you'll find a way to tell me.' She took her finger from the glass. Just to see. 'I should say goodbye now, shouldn't I?'

NEVER BE UNDER ONE ROOF

The glass moved faster now, as though free from the limitations of her finger, as though Morgan felt this was urgent.

'You mean me, Ryan and Jess?' she asked, dread clawing at her heart. 'I doubt we ever will be now. They're obsessed with these powers. I'm not.'

YOU HAVE THEM ALREADY

'I do?'

YOU DO

'Were they right? Jess and Ryan. Did they need me? To do this.'

THEY DID

'But I'm not ... *bad* in some way, am I?'

ONLY DO GOOD

Like Grandma Rosa had said.

BAD COMES BACK ON YOU

'OK. I only wanted to find out about you, you know.' Chloe said sadly. She paused, then asked, 'Tell me why we should never be under the same roof, Morgan?'

MURDER

'Murder?' Chloe whispered. She felt sick.
Then she blacked out for the first time.

50

THE DEAN WILSON THEATRE

SEPTEMBER 2019

Ginger clearly expects someone else to be on the other side of her dressing-room door. The radiant, painted smile dissolves like a watercolour in a rainstorm. She is dressed now as ghost Esme; her hair a golden waterfall beneath the veil, robes virginal and flowing, face made-up with gold. She looks from Chloe to Ryan and back to Chloe again. Emotions race across her face, white clouds chased by black. But this is not the actress, Ginger – this is young Jess, seeing Ryan. Her eyes briefly light up, but realisation of something darker quickly dims them.

Is she remembering that final Ouija board, just as Chloe did when Ryan turned up, out of the blue, after fourteen years?

'Ryan,' she says, and she could be sixteen years old.

'Jess,' he says, sounding equally young.

Will she correct him? Will she say, 'No one calls me that anymore. They haven't for years. Please, it's Ginger or just Ginge,' like she did to Chloe when they first met again? No. She leaves the word 'Jess' in the air between them. Despite her anger, Chloe is acutely jealous. Like she was back then. It only feeds the rage.

'What the hell?' Ginger laughs, and the mask is back in place. She is the actress now, vivacious, professional. 'How are you even *here*, Ryan?' She raises her eyebrows flirtatiously. 'You look great!'

'I *had* to come and see the show.' He smiles. 'You look gorgeous. And on stage you were just amazing. I can't believe you did it. You *really* did it.'

'Thank you.' She flicks her hair, trying without success to look modest.

'You'll have to sign my programme.' He holds it out.

'Well, of course I will. I'll get a pen.'

It's as though Chloe doesn't even exist.

Once again, like years ago, she feels invisible.

'Did *you* enjoy it?' Ginger asks Chloe warmly, seeming to remember she's here. She obviously has no clue that Chloe overheard the conversation with Edwin about her script.

Chloe can't bring herself to speak. She simply nods.

A voice filters through from the dressing room behind them and for a moment Chloe thinks someone else is in there; Morgan Miller? Then she realises that it's just the pre-show call coming out of the speaker. 'Ladies and gentlemen of *Dust* this is your five-minute call. Five minutes please.'

'Do you want a quick drink with me?' Ginger asks Ryan. 'I've only got five minutes as you heard, but come in for a moment. I wouldn't normally, but my mum brought me some champagne earlier. I can at least open it and have a sip and toast to you being here.' He shrugs and goes into the dressing room. Ginger follows him and then pauses and looks back at Chloe, at her uniform. 'Do you have to go back to work? Maybe we can meet after and celebrate?'

Chloe...

She smiles. 'I don't work here anymore,' she says.

'You don't?' Ginger frowns. 'Why the uniform then?'

'I just handed my notice in.'

Chloe follows them into the dressing room and closes the door.

51

THE DEAN WILSON THEATRE

SEPTEMBER 2019

'What are you doing?' asks Ginger.

Chloe leans against the dressing-room door. 'I thought we could talk.'

'Talk? About what? I'm on stage in...' she looks at the clock '... four minutes.'

'Why don't you open the champagne?' Chloe points to it.

'What do you want to talk about?' Ginger looks pale.

Chloe...

'Everything. The three of us being under one roof again, maybe?'

'Shit,' says Ryan. 'That phrase.' He whispers it slowly too. 'I remembered it when I arrived in the foyer and saw you, Chloe. Something about how the three of us shouldn't ever see each other again.'

'You three,' says Chloe, 'never be under one roof again.'

'That was it.' Ryan looks uneasy.

'Don't be nervous. I'm not.' Chloe looks at Ginger. 'You remember it too, don't you?'

She doesn't respond.

'The powers,' whispers Ryan. 'I remember it all now. You wanted this, Jess. This role. But didn't we have to...'

'Yes,' says Chloe. 'Stay away from one another. But here we are.'

She looks around the room. Pots of make-up and creams litter the dressing table. Numerous vases of colourful flowers fight for glory, the cards in them wishing Ginger luck and love. Unopened, the champagne awaits celebration. In the mirror, the three of them stand in a circle as though they are about to sit down, put their fingers on a glass and speak to the dead.

What would happen if they did that now? Would Morgan talk to them? Would Daniel Locke still be around, or has he gone elsewhere?

Something small glints in the mirror lights. Chloe goes to it. The charm bracelet. She picks it up. 'You don't wear it anymore, then?'

'Yes, just not on stage.'

'Do you feel guilty when you look at my ghost?' Chloe fingers the charm.

'Why would I feel guilty?' Ginger shakes her head. 'Right, you need to leave now.' She marches to the door. 'I have to go back on stage. You too Ryan. This was nice, but I have a job to do now.' She twists the door handle. Frowns. Tries again. 'What the fuck? Did you lock it, Chloe?'

'Not me, no.'

Ginger bangs on it. 'If anyone's out there, this isn't funny.'

'I don't think it's anyone out there. Remember last time?'

'Last time?' asks Ryan. 'What do you mean?'

'We got locked in here,' says Chloe. 'I think it was Morgan Miller.'

'And now?' Ginger looks horrified.

Chloe shrugs.

Ryan marches to the door and tries it. 'It *must* be locked from the other side. Come on, open it! Who's out there!'

'When Ginger and I first came in here the door locked like that,' says Chloe. 'And then...' She looks at the mirror lights. They begin to fill with crimson liquid. Then the room pulses red. 'And then *that* happened...'

'What the fuck?' Ryan goes to them. As he leans close, he looks like he's blushing in the glow. 'Is it a trick? Are you two in on this?'

'Not me,' cries Ginger. '*Shit*, I'm gonna miss my cue!'

'Maybe Morgan never wanted you to take her role,' says Chloe.

'Quit with the Morgan Miller crap, will you? We're not kids anymore. That stuff was just dreamed up by a load of hormonal teenagers with overactive imaginations.'

'How do you explain *that* then?' Chloe points to the red light-bulbs.

Ryan is still studying them.

'I'm as grey as the ash that I clean at his feet, I'm the aftermath of fire, flames he never sees...'

The words drift out of the speaker. It's Morgan. Instantly rec-ognisable, her tone less sweet than Ginger's, but richer, fuller. The three of them look at one another.

'Someone's *doing* that,' insists Ginger. 'Playing her version to unnerve me. Well, it won't work. I've made that role mine. *I'm* Esme Black now.'

'Did they never find her killer?' asks Ryan, almost to himself.

Chloe shakes her head. 'Maybe Morgan thinks you stole this show from her,' she says to Ginger. 'Like you're trying to steal mine.'

Ginger starts to say something but then shuts her mouth.

'I handed my notice in, you see. Because I'm going to devote myself to writing.'

'You've been writing?' asks Ryan, turning away from the bulbs.

'Yes. I wrote a script. Ginger read it. Didn't you?'

'I did.' Her voice is shaky. 'It's quite good.'

'Yes, that's what you told me. To my face anyway. To Edwin Roberts? Well, that was an entirely different description. Some-thing about me pouring my whole heart on the page.'

'How do you...?'

'Know? I heard.'

'Heard?'

'You and Edwin. In here, talking.'

'Oh, that.' Ginger tries to laugh it off. 'I was just trying to sell it to him. To help you out.'

'Really? Help *me* out?' Chloe frowns as though trying to

recall what she heard. 'What was it Edwin said? Oh yes... "We tell Chloe that we need to shape it, polish it, improve it. Then it's a joint work. Then we take over and her name becomes a credit. And then we suggest you play Abigail." Remember that, Ginger?'

'But Edwin suggested it, not me,' cries Ginger.

'But you didn't argue. You were silent. *Silent*. And that said it all.'

'I would have let you audition too, and they would have picked the best one for the role. That would be fair, wouldn't it?'

'*Let* her audition,' says Ryan, softly. 'Fucking hell, Jess.'

'I think you've forgotten what fair even means.' Chloe has to compose herself. Has her friendship with Jess – because it's with Jess, really – come to this? 'What have you become? What has a hunger for fame *done* to you? You're not the Jess I used to know. You're not the Jess who slept over on a weekend and shared your dreams about making it as an actress and made wishes on my eyelashes and promised we'd be friends forever.'

Ginger looks sad.

Chloe rolls up a sleeve. The scars there are healing now but still a criss-cross of old, fading pain. Ryan stares with the fascination of a teenage boy, any fear or good manners put aside. Ginger tries to hide the repulsion in her face, but her acting skills fail her.

'Yes, I did that,' says Chloe. 'I destroyed my body for years. I started because of my anger and sadness at you and Ryan sleeping together all those years ago. I became addicted to the pain. I only managed to stop a year ago.' Chloe lets her sleeve fall back. 'And then you betrayed me, and I cut again.'

'But I haven't,' cries Ginger. 'I *didn't*.'

'I put my pain on the pages of that fucking script. It helped me stop cutting. It got me through life. And you're not going to steal it, you two-faced bitch.' Chloe goes into her bag and takes out the dagger. It looks bloody in the red glow. Ginger gasps. 'This is what I used. Recognise it, Ryan?'

'I do.' He comes over, stares at it. Then laughs. 'You had it all this time?'

'It isn't funny,' cries Ginger. 'Why the fuck did you bring a knife into my dressing room? You're crazy!'

'Not just any knife,' says Ryan. 'The *Macbeth* knife. Shit, my mum went mad about me losing that.'

There's a sharp rap on the door then. 'Ginger!' comes a voice. The stage manager.

She runs to it. 'It's stuck! I can't get out! You *have* to open it!'

'The show's about to start!' The door handle rattles.

'I *know*! You have to get me out!'

'I'll get someone,' comes the voice, sounding far away now.

Ginger turns back to them, her face ablaze. 'Jesus Christ, it's my opening night and I won't be on stage for the second half! I'll be *ruined*! My career is over!' She marches over to Chloe but stops a few feet away from her when she sees the dagger again. 'This is your fault, you fucking witch. Coming in here and making shit happen.'

'I don't make anything happen,' says Chloe. 'You asked for this.'

'It was always you. You caused all that crap on the Ouija board.'

'No, it was my idea, remember?' says Ryan, still flushed in the red lights. 'You can't blame Chloe. I suggested it. I wanted to mess about with it. You never could make your own decisions or take responsibility for yourself.'

'Who the fuck do you think you're talking to?' Ginger turns on him now. 'You're the nobody loser. You always were. So jealous of my talent.'

Ryan shakes his head gently. 'You're wrong. I was never jealous of your talent. I was jealous of the money and support you had. I was a better actor than you and it killed me that I knew you had a much better chance of getting somewhere than I did. And I got the very thing I wanted, but it was my undoing. So did you, Jess.' He looks at Chloe then. 'But you'll never be the actress Chloe always was, and I think you know that.'

Chloe is speechless.

He thought I was talented?

'She stole the show in *Macbeth* that night,' continues Ryan. 'When she improvised, and the other witches just followed her ... shit, it was electric. That's what you call true talent. Being able to lead, unrehearsed, and the other actors follow without question.'

Chloe still can't speak.

But I always thought I followed.

'If she's so talented, why isn't *she* in *Dust*?' Ginger is incandescent with rage.

'Maybe she didn't want to step into a dead woman's shoes,' says Ryan. 'Maybe she decided to write her *own* show and say her *own* words.'

'Ha! Her *own* words! What, some piece-of-shit script about a woman jumping from a ship for a woman she'll never really have? Is it an autobiography, Chloe?'

'A woman you want desperately to play,' says Chloe.

'Whatever. The pair of you are riddled with jealousy over my success. Wait until the newspapers find out you broke in here with a knife!' Ginger runs to the door again and bangs on it. 'For God's sake, open it, someone!' Panting, she turns back to face Ryan and Chloe, and rips the veil from her head.

Then, once again, music filters through the speaker, a ghostly echo making it all the more eerie.

'I'm still here; I am dust. I'm those fragments in the air, the gold light dancing there, that breeze from nowhere...'

'It's my song now!' cries Ginger.

'When the dust settles, you will know...'

'That's not a *Dust* song,' says Ryan.

'No, that's just Morgan,' says Chloe. 'It's something she used to say to me.'

'I don't fall, I fly, I don't die, I'm free, wherever your heart beats...'

'Long before you came here,' says Chloe, approaching Ginger, 'you appeared to me, in this room, as a dying Esme. I've just realised that it was a premonition that you would get this role. And I don't know why, but I think Morgan doesn't like you. She never wanted you to play Esme.'

'Well, I am,' seethes Ginger. 'It's *mine*! I earned it!'

'No, you made a deal. You sold a part of yourself to get the role.'

'Fuck you. It's not my fault you were so easy to manipulate. It's not my fault you were so desperate for anything that I *let* you fuck me. This isn't about a script. This is because you love me, and I don't love you, and I never fucking will.'

Remember how. Will it and it shall happen. Push.

The familiar words send heat along Chloe's spine. And she does it; she *pushes*. Not with her finger. Not with her body. With her heart. And Ginger flies back, hits the opposite wall, and then crumples in a heap on the floor. The new, gold-framed *Dust* poster falls beside her, smashing with a thick crack.

'What th—' Ryan's eyes are wide.

Then rage heats the rest of Chloe's body; rage like the aftermath of fire. With the knife in one hand and Ginger's charm bracelet still clutched in the other, she goes and stands over her.

'Please, Chloe, put the knife down,' cries Ryan, somewhere behind her.

It is hot in Chloe's hand. Ginger pulls herself to her feet, not taking her eyes off Chloe. They simmer with realisation, and then fear.

'*You*,' she whispers. 'The time I fell...'

'Yes. I *adored* you, Jess. I really did. But you're not taking my script.'

Chloe remembers the moment that fell into place all those years ago; the moment she first leaned forwards to put her mouth on Jess's. She had put a hand in Jess's hair, had wanted to wrap the curls tightly around her fingers so she could never escape. *Be mine*, her heart had whispered. Now she puts a hand in her hair again, wrapping the curls around her hands once more, and she raises the knife.

Darkness then. Chloe is dragged into a blackout as though by multiple pairs of hands. Before they steal her fully, she sees blood. The dagger and blood, just as she saw it that time in the bar with Ginger.

And Morgan Miller in the mirror...

52

THE GAME

2005

Chloe opened her eyes. Above, dust dancing playfully in a circle. Nearby, one candle burning still, its flame reflected and blurred in the upturned glass. She sat up. It was just her on the stage, the letters scattered like white rose petals to her left. Had she messed them up with her fall? How long had she been out?

Was Morgan Miller still here?

No. The air was too still. Even the candle barely moved. She had gone, Chloe knew it. Perhaps forever. She wanted to cry. She had never felt so alone. The show was over. No more rehearsals. The game was over too. No more magic. Ryan and Jess had gone, and she knew – like she always knew – that there was no point in chasing them. She didn't mind letting Ryan go, but her heart hurt when she thought of never seeing Jess again.

Forever, together, we are dust. Pieces of everything; pieces of all of us...

The song words came to her. How could Chloe ever sing them alone? If she did, she'd only ever hear Jess, her voice more beautiful; only ever feel Jess, her presence eternally there. The scars on Chloe's thigh throbbed; the dagger was waiting. It was time for her to leave too. She stood.

Should she say goodbye? What was the point to an empty room?

'Goodbye Morgan,' she whispered anyway.

Nothing. Chloe left the candle burning to light her way and descended the stage steps. She looked back, knowing nothing would have moved. She saw them in a flash, the three of them, in a circle, lost in the game. She saw them in character; the king, the king's wife, and the witch. She started down the aisle between the pews. What was it Morgan last said? The question popped into her head – the answer followed.

MURDER

Had she meant her own? Already – as though the night was being swallowed by dirty water – it was hard to recall. Already, the details of the Ouija board were fading like dreams did over the day. Hadn't Ryan, or maybe Jess – it was hard to recall now – said that when the game was over, those who had played often forgot what happened? Chloe wanted to forget it; and she wanted to remember every detail.

She closed the theatre door after her, climbed through the toilet window, stole along the dark passage, and emerged at the front of the church. She looked up at the turrets, at the inky sky beyond, at the stars scattered like distant Ouija board cards.

And slowly, in the weeks after, she forgot it all.

Like a jigsaw broken up, piece by piece, the memories died. Chloe forgot their words and the spirits and Morgan talking to them. She forgot Ryan and the upturned glass and how to *push* and where the knife had come from. Jess remained in her heart though, a feeling more than a physical memory, an ache, a pain that compelled her to continue cutting.

Like Esme Black, Chloe woke from her fall a different person.

Like Chevalier, she was forever haunted.

53

THE DEAN WILSON THEATRE

SEPTEMBER 2019

Chloe opens her eyes. Above, dust dancing playfully in a circle. Nearby, the cracked *Dust* poster and Ginger's charm bracelet on the floor, the ghost looking her way. She sits up. She is on the dressing-room floor, but it's empty now and the door is wide open, looking out onto a quiet, empty corridor.

What happened?

Where the hell did everyone go?

Chloe tries to remember the last thing she saw. There was blood, she is sure of it. Ginger. Ryan. But where are they now? Where's the dagger? Did they take it? What time is it? She looks at the clock – 12.45. It's been hours. She has *never* blacked out for this long. The show will be long finished, the theatre probably deserted now. How could they have just left her on the floor like this all that time? Maybe they tried to rouse her and couldn't. But didn't Cynthia wonder where she had gone and come looking for her?

Maybe she thought Chloe had gone home.

Chloe picks up the bracelet, grabs her bag from the floor and stands. She expects to feel dizzy and is surprised at how alert she is. Maybe she hallucinated the blood. Maybe she saw it the way she has seen so many other curious things recently. Ryan and Ginger are clearly not injured. Maybe they tried for a while to rouse her and then had to go. Maybe Ginger got on stage in time after all; maybe Ryan went back into the theatre to see the rest of the show.

Did they forget her, lying here? But wouldn't Ginger have come back at the end? To freshen up? Maybe not. Maybe they all partied the night away, and went back home or to hotel rooms, and forgot about her. Though she's relieved not to have hurt anyone after all, Chloe feels sad that they would do that. The rage has died now, and she feels calm. Sad but calm.

Is she maybe still unconscious and dreaming?

No. This feels too real. She is too ... *here*.

Chloe takes her phone from her bag – still switched off for her shift earlier – and turns it on to see if anyone has messaged, asking where she is. It won't turn on. Surely her battery can't have died without her knowing. Maybe it broke in the fall. Damn. She should just leave. Go home. Charge it up. It's late now.

She looks down at her uniform. Remembers her radio in the bin. Will she even have a job tomorrow? Probably not, after abandoning her shift on such an important night. Does she still *want* it? Without Chester? She's not sure.

You have your script.

Yes, the script. Her show. And she knows it's more than *quite good* and that Edwin Roberts has probably read it too now. She can go to him and tell him she knows what he and Ginger were plotting. Then he'll have no choice but to do whatever she wishes, or she'll expose his corruption.

Chloe steps out into the corridor. The silence is thick.

She sees it then, almost like a vision – a poster for *She Haunts Me* on the opposite wall. The title is silver; the background is the hundred blues of a sparkly ocean meeting a starry sky; in the foreground is a woman on the balcony of a ship, facing away from the camera. Is it *her*? Or is it Ginger? Chloe can't tell. She blinks and the poster is gone.

She puts a hand on the door that takes her out back to her bike. And then she hears it. Singing. Is it Ginger? Still here after all?

It's coming from the stage.

Chloe abandons the exit and goes to the backstage door, which is closed now, and she listens.

'Forever, together, we are dust. Pieces of everything; pieces of all of us...'

She smiles. And opens the door. Morgan Miller is on stage. Dressed as Esme Black, in the original costume. It all comes back to Chloe. Her first trip to the theatre, seeing *Dust* with her mum, except now she's watching from the wings. She half imagines that if she looks out into the audience, she'll see herself and her mum sitting there, faces entranced. But the seats are empty. It's just her and Morgan. She really must have fallen and hit her head hard to be seeing this. Morgan stops singing and turns around. She shines like she is lit from within.

Is she real though?

'I always come here when they've gone,' she says.

'Really?' asks Chloe, stepping closer. 'Every night?'

'Where else would I go?'

Chloe doesn't know what to say. 'How are you ... *here*?' she asks after a long pause. 'I mean ... I've heard you, before now, when I was working. I thought I saw you up there, once. But I've never *seen* you, not as real as this.'

'I don't think *Dust* will ever resume now,' says Morgan, ignoring the question. She glances at the Chevalier house behind them. Without the special lighting, it is shadowy, like a spooky mansion in a gothic novel.

'What?' Chloe is confused. '*Why*? Didn't it go well? The audience seemed to love it at the interval. I thought the first half was wonderful. And Ryan said it was incredible...'

'It's not about how well it went. It never should have happened at all...'

'Why? What do you mean?'

'Remember what I promised you?'

Chloe wants to ask more about *Dust*. Did Ginger make it back on stage for the second act? Was her performance not up to scratch after the argument in the dressing room?

'I've been waiting here so I could tell you,' says Morgan.

Chloe realises. 'That's why you're here? Seriously? To *tell* me...'

Morgan nods. She wanders into the Chevalier house. 'I think you're ready now. You weren't then. You were just a child. And besides, if you'd known then, it would have changed everything for you.'

'Why?' Chloe goes to the Chevalier doorway, watches Morgan run her hands over the drapes at the window. She realises Morgan is wearing the single pearl earring. Her other ear is unadorned.

'You'll know when you know.'

'Who killed you, Morgan?'

'Like you, we messed around with a Ouija board.' She stops at the vase of flowers and pretends to smell one. 'The three of us. In the weeks before I got the part. But *she* wanted the part too. She was just a friend of Clive's; I didn't know her that well. She was this actress he'd taught. He was a drama teacher, you see. She had more ambition than talent. I only met her a handful of times when we used that stupid Ouija board – and then again the night I died...'

'Who was she?'

'We both asked the spirits for the role in *Dust*.' Morgan moves into the garden, gravel crunching beneath her satin-shoed feet. 'We knew it was going to be huge.'

'How?' Chloe follows her. 'It was new. It'd never been seen then.'

'The spirits told us. They said we only had to ask – so we did. I asked first. Maybe that's why I got it...'

'No, you got it because you were an incredible actress. You'd got that big award for *All About Eve* the year before, hadn't you? Why did you, of all people, need a Ouija board to get anything?'

'Even award-winning actresses feel insecure, Chloe.' Morgan pauses. 'She asked for the part too. Then the spirit said there was a price. He said none of us should ever be under the same roof again.'

Chloe shivers and wraps her arms around her body.

'I knew I couldn't do that – not see Clive. I loved him and he loved me. But our relationship started to become tense. We argued a lot. What we had done affected us. It felt like we were ... *cursed*.'

'Who *was* she, Morgan?'

Morgan looks up at the balcony where Esme falls to die at Chevalier's feet. Then she looks at Chloe. 'Come back to the dressing room with me, and I'll show you what happened that night.'

'What do you mean?'

'You'll see it, just as it happened.'

'I'm... *scared*.' Chloe is curious, but also wants to run, escape, go home, not see.

'Don't be. You're safe. We're only watching a long-gone event. I see it all the time. Now I'll show you. You always wanted to know. Now you will.'

Morgan leaves the Chevalier garden and heads backstage. Chloe watches her leave.

She is alone on the stage. What if the next time she's here it's to be in her own show? Could she do it? Is she good enough? Chloe anticipates Morgan's voice, telling her she is. But she is left with only her own. 'Yes, you're good enough,' she whispers.

And then she follows Morgan.

54

THE DEAN WILSON THEATRE

1999

It is Morgan Miller's dressing room again. The door is shut, and the original star is back, not tarnished though, but polished gold with her name in the centre. Chloe approaches the door, heart wild in her chest. Reverently, she touches the star, expecting it to disappear beneath her fingertips; but it remains, original, perfect.

Should she knock? Just go in? Or leave now and never know?

Chloe turns the handle and opens the door. Laughter inside, sweet and high. A heavy scent of flowers. The original *Dust* poster on the wall, not yet faded. Everything pure white – the walls, the dressing table, the floor, the bouquets of roses. And there at the dressing table, incandescent in the glow of the mirror lights, Morgan Miller. It must be the interval because she is wearing her ghostly Esme Black costume and applying gold eye shadow. Tiny, delicate pearls dangle from each ear.

Can she see Chloe?

'Morgan,' she whispers.

She turns, as though maybe hearing her, then frowns and resumes her make-up. A ten-minute call filters through the speaker; it's like déjà vu. Chloe's anticipation is so intense she wonders how Morgan can't feel it simmering in the atmosphere too. Chloe approaches the flowers. Everyone must know Morgan likes white roses. The most ostentatious display has a card in it that simply says, *Love Eternal, Clive*. Has he been here already? Delivered them by hand?

Morgan starts to sing. *'Never forget me, nor ever let me go...'*

Chloe smiles.

Then there is a knock on the door.

'Come in,' calls Morgan cheerily.

It opens and Beth enters. She's younger, her hair longer and streaked with pink and blonde. In her arms are flowers – blood-red roses. She can't know Morgan that well. Chloe realises she has her hand over her mouth as though to stop herself speaking. Does she want to scream, to warn Morgan what's to come? Is Beth the killer after all? Did she lie all along?

Morgan is frowning at Beth. 'It's…?'

'Beth,' she says, a little haughtily.

'Oh, yes.' Morgan nods. 'You auditioned too, didn't you?'

'Yes.' Beth pauses as though the words take effort. 'You were amazing.'

'Thank you.'

Beth thrusts the flowers out at her. Morgan takes them with a gracious smile. Chloe can't help but laugh when she dumps them on the dressing table near a Coke can and some make-up-soiled tissues.

'Wow – is that the award you got?' coos Beth.

That's when Chloe first notices the bronze statue near the mirror. Laurence Olivier as Henry V is immortalised on its side. Morgan received it for her supporting role as Karen Richards in *All About Eve*. Chloe freezes as Beth picks it up; she knows it was used to murder Morgan.

'I guess no one else had a chance of beating you when you have *this*,' says Beth, as though forgetting Morgan is there. Perhaps remembering, she looks up and adds, 'Sorry, did I sound bitter? I'm not.'

'I have to get ready.' Morgan's tone makes it clear their chat is over.

But Beth doesn't put the award down. Chloe moves a little closer and remembers this is just a scene, just some curious flash from the past she is witnessing, and there's no point in trying to intervene if anything happens.

'Has it been worth it?' asks Beth.

'What do you mean?' Morgan turns around in her seat.

No, Morgan, don't speak to her like that, thinks Chloe. *Just let her leave...*

'It hasn't made you popular. Lots of actresses hate you.'

'I don't let that bother me.'

Beth takes a step closer. 'Not sure I believe you.'

Morgan holds out her hand. 'My award?'

Beth looks at it and then Morgan. She raises it. Chloe inhales. Then, finally, she hands it over. Chloe breathes a sigh of relief. On her way out, Beth pauses by the door, having seen something on the floor. It's a tiny silver goblet, perhaps from a costume. She picks it up and slips away. Morgan shakes her head at herself in the mirror.

A voice filters through the speaker. 'Ladies and gentlemen of *Dust*, this is your five-minute call.'

Then there's another knock on the door.

Chloe holds her breath.

'What now?' calls Morgan, clearly not happy at being disturbed again.

The door opens.

'Oh, for fuck's sake,' she says. 'I told you to stay away.' She stands. 'I want you to leave, right now. Clive told you, we don't want to see you anymore.'

Chloe watches the visitor enter the room. She knows her; she saw her earlier. She knows she will kill Morgan. And she knows why Morgan never told them back then, on the Ouija board. Chloe wants to escape, run, go home, and not witness the murder of Morgan Miller.

55

THE DEAN WILSON THEATRE

1999

Lynda Swanson closes the door after her. She is exactly how Chloe remembers her from back then, when she and Jess were just ten. She always dressed as though she was about to go on stage. Whether she was driving her and Jess to youth-theatre rehearsals or doing laundry, her hair was always coiffed, her lips always red. And she was always telling Jess to work harder, be the prettiest, the best; Lynda was the personification of the pushy mum.

Tonight, Lynda is wearing a black dress that hugs her curves and killer heels that strike with each step she takes towards Morgan. 'I don't care what Clive said,' she says.

'How the fuck did you manage to get backstage?'

'It wasn't difficult. This woman with pink-and-blonde hair held the door for me. Must have thought I was one of the cast.' Lynda pauses. 'I *should* have been, shouldn't I? We both know the part belonged to me. You cursed me.'

'What are you talking about?' Morgan speaks angrily, but there's fear in her eyes.

Chloe understands it.

The Ouija board. The effect of using one. The nightmares. The darkness.

'You know exactly what I'm talking about,' says Lynda.

She always was daunting. Jess cowered under her glare. Chloe remembers Ginger saying in the theatre bar that her parents were getting divorced; she remembers all the stories about it in the papers. She thinks that Lynda's husband – what was his name? –

must have realised long ago that she was the killer. When they split up, he must have decided to tell the police. Maybe he didn't have the courage to do it in person, so he sent the letter. Sent a clue he knew they might eventually link to her.

The pearl earring.

Chloe looks at the earrings now, shivering like two wilting snowdrops as Morgan moves.

She wants to stop this before it happens.

But she can only watch.

'You made sure I was ill the day of the auditions, didn't you?' says Lynda, standing right behind Morgan so they are both reflected in the mirror, one seated, one towering.

'How the hell could *I* have done that?'

'I have no idea, but I was as sick as a pig that day, and I never am. I couldn't even get out of bed.'

Morgan stands up, but in her satin, Esme Black slippers, she's tiny next to majestic Lynda. Chloe moves closer, cries, '*Please*, stop now,' but they can't hear her.

'Why is everyone so bitter about me and this part?' demands Morgan. 'Why can't you just be happy for me? It ages you, you know. Being bitter.' She touches Lynda's powdered cheek. 'You should watch yourself. Everyone knows you lied when you said you were thirty-two on your CV.'

'Fuck you.' Lynda swipes her hand away.

'No, fuck *you*.'

'Is Clive here?'

Morgan frowns. 'Of course. He came to wish me luck earlier. He's been to every performance so far, and he wasn't going to miss press night.'

'So we three are under one roof again.'

Morgan turns white.

'Didn't that spirit say we shouldn't ever be?'

'It was just a stupid game,' whispers Morgan.

'You got the role though, didn't you?'

Chloe is glued to the spot. She suddenly remembers a night with the Ouija board when Daniel Locke told Jess her mum was a bad girl. Another moment comes to her, when Morgan asked if Jess liked her mother. Subtle clues there all along. Scattered breadcrumbs leading them to Lynda Swanson, but they didn't pick them up.

'If we hadn't done that Ouija board,' says Lynda, 'you'd never have got it.'

'Yes, I would. I *earned* it. I gave *everything* at that audition.'

'So did I!' screams Lynda. 'I starved myself so I'd be the perfect size. I rehearsed the lines over and over and over. I lived and fucking breathed them. I neglected my ten-year-old daughter for that role! I'm a better actress than you!' She pauses, breathing hard. 'When I brought Jess to see *Dust* the other night, she agreed that I would have been magnificent. And Clive said I'm his most talented student.'

Morgan's face changes. It is ice cold. 'No, he didn't. He thinks you're desperate. He said you're all ambition and no talent.'

'You fucking bitch,' says Lynda, in a low, menacing voice.

When it happens, it's fast. Lynda grabs the nearest thing and launches at Morgan. It's a wild, whirlwind of war. Swinging arms, one attacking, two defending. Blood flying, ruining the pure-white walls and roses. Lynda smashes at Morgan's head – over and over and over – until she falls. Then there is stillness. Silence, except for Lynda and Chloe breathing heavily in unison.

'Shit,' whispers Lynda. She looks at the bloody Olivier award in her trembling hand and puts it back on the dressing table. '*Shit.*' She bends down to Morgan with a sob, but it's obvious from her shattered skull that she is gone. Esme Black's ghostly costume is crimson now. Lynda's hair is splattered too. One of the pearl earrings has come out and lies next to Morgan. Lynda takes it. Then she looks up, seems to realise someone might come at any moment.

'I can't believe it was *you*,' whispers Chloe. 'Did Jess ever find out?'

Asking questions is pointless; Lynda doesn't even look at her.

She starts to leave, but then, perhaps realising how flamboyantly – how memorably – she's dressed, she grabs a bath robe from a hook, wraps it around herself, and pulls the hood low over her face. She takes her spike heels off, grabs the Olivier award, and carries them, hidden beneath the robe. Chloe follows Lynda as she weaves through the busy corridor, no one taking any notice of a woman who looks like a cast member between costumes. Lynda slips away through the back fire exit. Chloe watches for a moment, wants to scream that she should come back, own up, face things.

But it is done.

It is done.

When Chloe returns to the dressing room, it is Ginger's once again. The new *Dust* poster is on the floor, cracked, the flowers are colourful again, and a champagne bottle awaits celebration.

Morgan sits at the dressing table, no longer bloody.

She turns to Chloe and says, 'The dust has settled, and now you know.'

THE DEAN WILSON THEATRE

SEPTEMBER 2019

Chloe closes the dressing room door and leans on it. It was Lynda Swanson. All this time. Was poor Jess waiting in the audience that night, left alone after the interval when her mum committed that atrocious act and escaped? No, she hadn't been at that final show. Lynda must have returned to have her say, alone and angry.

Chloe sits next to Morgan and looks at them both in the mirror. She realises they are the same age, both thirty – Morgan forever, Chloe for just a while longer. How must it feel to be eternally young? It's what actresses in Hollywood crave, and Morgan has achieved it. But the price? No one to see it. And loneliness. Absolute loneliness.

'Wasn't Lynda ever questioned by the police?' asks Chloe. 'She auditioned alongside you; she *must* have been a suspect.'

'She was, briefly, but her husband said she was home all night.'

'So he knew, and he protected her. But Clive must've had his suspicions that she killed you.'

'Oh, he did. I'm sure he did.'

'Did he never tell the police that? Insist they check her alibi?'

'No.' Morgan shrugs. 'I actually think he was scared of Lynda. Scared that what we did on the Ouija board might come out and somehow ruin him. Scared that he'd be implicated, even if they proved it was her. And how could he be sure? He didn't see her do it.'

'An usher here said she heard a rumour about witchcraft helping you get the role, so I guess the Ouija board stuff got out anyway.'

'Not to the papers, I don't think.'

'Did they ever find the Olivier award?' asks Chloe. 'What did Lynda do with it?'

'No. She threw it in the River Humber.'

'Clive must have been upset to have been a suspect,' says Chloe.

'He was. It wasn't for long though. Too many people saw him at the interval – he was arguing passionately with someone about my acting skills. His loyalty to me saved him, in a way.'

'He was here tonight, wasn't he?' says Chloe. 'My friend Chester said his name was on the ticket list.'

'Yes, he was.'

In the mirror, Morgan looks sad. How hard it must be to see the man she loves and not be able to touch him, talk to him, kiss him. How would Chloe feel if Ginger could no longer see her? Does she still care about her?

Yes. Despite everything, yes.

Still.

'Do you know if Clive talked to Lynda tonight, during *Dust*?' asks Chloe. 'He must hate her.'

'He didn't. He avoided her, and she avoided him.'

'I wonder if Ginger ever discovered what her mum did. Do you know? I guess you can see stuff like that.'

'I don't think she did,' says Morgan. 'That's why I didn't want to tell you back then, when you were kids. It could have destroyed Jess. Would have ruined her life. And if I'd told you, I know you'd have felt compelled to tell your friend. But now you can't.'

'You mean because Ginger and I have fallen out?'

Morgan doesn't respond.

'I guess I understand now why Lynda was so pushy,' says Chloe. 'Why she was so obsessed that Jess make it. She knew it was too late for her, so she channelled every bit of her ambition into her daughter's career. And it worked, didn't it? Ginger ended up bringing *Dust* back. How ... poetic.' Chloe pauses. 'Don't you *hate* Lynda? Haven't you wanted to, I don't know, get revenge somehow?'

Morgan shakes her head. 'No. I haven't felt anger since I died. Her time is coming though.'

'Is it?'

'Yes. I see it. The police will be at her door by the end of the week. And her husband won't defend her now.'

'Shit. Poor Ginger.' Chloe wonders why she feels so calm. She should be wishing Ginger ill. But she doesn't. Where did that raw anger go? Did it just die out, like fire? 'I hope it doesn't ruin things for her.'

'She'll have enough on her plate,' says Morgan.

'Was it because of Lynda that you came to us through the Ouija board? Because her daughter was there?'

'No. It was because of you.'

'*Me?*'

'You called me,' says Morgan.

'I didn't though. It was Ryan.'

'But I *heard* you. You bewitched me, Chloe.'

'*Me?*' Chloe remembers then. 'You got me to cut myself, didn't you? You invited me to take the dagger that time.'

'I've regretted that ever since.' Morgan looks sad. 'I self-harmed as a teenager. I never should have suggested it to you. I thought it might help ease your pain the way it had mine. But it was cruel of me, I guess ... I don't know, I wanted us to have something in common.' Morgan pauses. 'I taught you to *push* as well. I knew you'd be able to.'

'You can do that too?' Chloe pauses. 'How did you know I'd be able to?'

'You're a witch.'

'Am I really though?'

'It's just a name,' smiles Morgan. 'Some call it psychic. Sensitive. Open. I like to call it gifted.'

'*You*,' whispers Chloe. 'You have the gift too.'

Morgan nods. Chloe studies them both in the mirror again. Is it just the row of lights that makes them glow? She leans closer.

Despite the lateness of the hour, the intensity of the night's events, she has never looked better. Maybe she should get one of these dressing tables for her bedroom.

Morgan smiles at her. 'Yes, you're beautiful,' she says.

'My skin hasn't looked this good since I was sixteen. Wow, if Jess could see me now. No, if *Ginger* could see me now. Why was I so insecure then? I was gorgeous, wasn't I? Why do we never realise that when we're teenagers?'

'You still are gorgeous,' says Morgan.

'I loved Jess so much. Why did she have to betray me? *Why?*'

'That's what ambition does to some people.'

Chloe fluffs her hair up in the mirror, laughs, and pouts like a Hollywood goddess. As she does, her black sleeve drops to her elbow. She frowns. Leans closer.

'What is it?' asks Morgan as though she already knows the answer.

'I don't understand...'

'What, Chloe?'

'My scars. They've... *gone.*'

Is it just her reflection? Is the intensity of the glow washing away the criss-cross of pink and white ridges? Chloe looks at her real arm. Touches the exposed flesh. It is perfect. Not scarred. No longer a map of her pain. Tears spill down her cheeks. It's all too much. She can't take it in.

'How on earth did it happen?' she sobs. 'I'm ... *clean*. Did you do it, Morgan, you witch? Is this like when the lights filled with red? Am I just *seeing* it? It's a cruel trick if I am.'

'No, you're healed,' says Morgan warmly.

'How? *You?*' Chloe feels light-headed. The two of them blur in the mirror. 'I'm so tired,' she says. 'It's been such a long, strange night. I must have hit my head really hard earlier. I think I might be imagining you, imagining my scars are gone.' She pauses. 'I might come in tomorrow, officially give my notice in, see Edwin Roberts. Maybe see Ginger, find out what happened before I blacked out. Will you be here?'

'I'm always here,' Morgan smiles.

Chloe shrugs. 'Well, I'm exhausted now. I just want to go home and eat something fattening and have a hot bubble bath and sleep for a long, long time.'

'You can't,' says Morgan gently.

She takes Chloe's hand in hers. Chloe expects it to be the cold flesh of a dead ghost, but it's warm, like her own. They are the same. Ginger's bracelet — which Chloe is still holding – tinkles between them, the ghost charm shivering at the movement. 'You can't ever go home, not to that one anyway.'

'What do you mean?' Chloe puts a hand to her chest, feels her heart pulsing beneath. 'Why not?'

'Because you're dead, sweetheart.'

57

THERE AND YET NOT THERE

What if I let go? What if I fall? She is there, in the water, I know she is. What if I swim and don't look back and swim and don't look back? Was I ever here, on this ship? Here and yet not here. There and yet not there.

'Where do you think we go when we die?' asked Jess, sleepily. 'What do you think there is?'

'I don't know. I don't really like to think about it.'

'I mean if we *have* been speaking to the dead, then what's it like for them?'

Chloe tried to imagine. Tried to visualise being on the other side; being here – existing still somehow in this world – but not able to speak to the ones you loved. Did the spirits wander among the living? Did they watch them? If so, what must it be like to witness others doing wonderful everyday things while you could not? Chloe hoped that when she went, she would simply go. Be gone. Not exist at all. Yet that was even harder to picture. Where did your soul go? Where did your feelings go? Your essence?

What would it be like to no longer love Jess?

If I let go, what will there be? Only the music of the ocean – wordless, melodic, soothing – and the dance of the waves, and the two of us sinking, forever, together, to the bottom of the sea.

Chloe leans nearer and takes hold of Ginger's slender fingers. They warm within the protection of her own. And she begins to see something. She closes her eyes. Tries to let it in. This feels like something she has done before and yet never done.

What if I let go? What if I fall? She is there, in the water, I know she is. What if I swim and don't look back and swim and don't look back? Was I ever here, on this ship? Here and yet not here. There and yet not there.

This was how Chloe had imagined it to be. Floating around in an otherworldly place, not existing but not dead, there and yet not there, watching those you love going on without you.

If I let go, what will there be? Only the music of the ocean – wordless, melodic, soothing – and the dance of the waves, and the two of us sinking, forever, together, to the bottom of the sea.

Chloe reached out and put a finger over Jess's lips, the way she had when that moment fell into place the other time Ryan left them alone. She traced the softness and then leaned forwards to put her mouth there instead of her fingertip. Jess inhaled; Chloe was sucked in. She was lost. Their tongues touched, warm, nervous, then bolder. Chloe put a hand in Jess's hair, wanting to wrap the curls tightly around her fingers so she could never escape. *Be mine,* her heart whispered.

Only the music of the ocean – wordless, melodic, soothing – and the dance of the waves, and the two of us sinking, forever, together, to the bottom of the sea...

58

THE DEAN WILSON THEATRE

SEPTEMBER 2019

'Please Chloe, put the knife down,' cries Ryan.

Chloe moves closer to where Ginger is still in a heap on the floor, cracked *Dust* poster at her side like a remnant of a marital dispute. Ginger pulls herself to her feet, not taking her eyes off Chloe for a second. They simmer with realisation – and then fear.

'*You*,' she whispers. 'The time I fell...'

'Yes. I *adored* you, Jess. I really did. But you're not taking my script.'

Chloe inches even closer, puts a hand in Ginger's hair – wrapping the curls around her fingers – and raises the knife. Ryan is glued to the spot, his face a ghostly mask of speechless shock. The knife cuts the air between the women, as close to Chloe's face as it is to Ginger's, dividing them equally. With an animalistic grunt, Ginger grabs Chloe's arm to stop her. The knife moves back and forth, back and forth, higher, lower, trembling as each woman pushes with all her strength.

It is the battle following a war.

There's hammering on the door then. Voices on the other side. Something heavy heaving against it. The sound seems to break Ryan's trance. Chloe has the knife at Ginger's throat. There are tears on her cheeks as though this is not what she really wants. There is blood. Blood dripping over the knife, down Chloe's hand, onto the floor. Ryan yells again for Chloe to put it down.

Shocked at the blood, Chloe lowers the knife. Ginger seems to find strength to fight. She grabs the nearest thing – the unopened champagne bottle on the dresser – and hits Chloe on the head, hard.

Everything stops.

The war is over. The battle ends. Chloe falls backwards. Hits the ground.

The door opens at the exact moment of impact; the stage manager falls into the room, followed by Edwin Roberts, his hair a tangle.

'She had a knife at my throat!' shrieks Ginger, still backed up against the wall, eyes horrified at the sight of Chloe on the floor with blood trickling away from her head. 'I had to stop her!' She seems to remember the champagne bottle, bloody in her hand, and drops it on the dressing table with a look of repulsion. 'I didn't mean ... I ... it was ... I thought she was going to *kill* me...'

'Call an ambulance,' cries Edwin, kneeling beside Chloe's inert body.

The stage manager takes out her phone and goes into the corridor.

'Is she...?' Ginger moves closer to where her one-time friend lies.

'I don't know.' Edwin rolls Chloe over into the recovery position, checks her pulse, listens at her mouth. 'Have you called them?' he yells into the corridor.

'They're on their way.' The stage manager is in the doorway. 'Ten minutes.'

Ryan puts a hand on Ginger's arm but she shrugs him off. 'She cut me,' she cries, hand over her neck.

'It's not deep.' Ryan studies her. 'Just a nick really.'

'She could have done it again and *killed* me!'

Quietly, right next to Ginger's ear, he says, 'She had lowered the knife.'

They share a look. It's clear Ginger realises the implication of this; that it was not self-defence. She was no longer in danger. She could have pushed her away, got free, when the knife was away from her neck. Ryan shakes his head gently and then turns to Edwin, who's still kneeling beside Chloe.

'She had a knife at her throat,' Ryan says to him. 'What else could Ginger do? It was self-defence. She had to do *something*, or Chloe might have killed her.' He pauses. 'Is she ... is she ...?'

Edwin doesn't speak.

'No,' cries Ginger. 'No, no, *no!*'

'What happened here?' asks Edwin, standing up.

'She just turned up, and she had a knife.'

'Jesus.'

'We never should have done it!' Ginger kicks the broken *Dust* picture, looking at Ryan.

'Done what?' asks Edwin.

'Done the ... when we were...' Ginger can't finish. Ryan understands though.

'What about the show?' calls the stage manager from the doorway.

'We'll have to cancel it.'

'For *good*?'

'God, no,' cries Edwin, as though the suggestion is ridiculous. 'Just tonight. Get them to make the announcement.' The stage manager nods and disappears. 'On the first fucking night too. The press will love this.' He seems to think again. 'No matter, it's all press.' Some of the actors gather in the doorway, gasping and flapping. John Marrs pushes through them, dressed as Chevalier, demanding to know what the delay is. Edwin slams the door on them all.

'You expect me to perform tomorrow?' Ginger is aghast.

'Of course.' Edwin sweeps his arm dramatically around the dressing room. 'This is *Dust* 2019. We don't shut down for *anything*. You're not dead, are you? That cut's just a graze. A demented usher broke into your room and tried to kill you and you defended yourself. This fan witnessed it. The police will see that. And the show goes on.'

'Are you insane? My friend is dead.' She kneels beside Chloe, sobbing into her hand. Ryan hovers nearby, trembling, clearly in shock.

'She wasn't your friend when you sent me her script.' Edwin shrugs. 'If you don't show up tomorrow, we'll get another actress. One bigger than you. Now, where is that ambulance?' He opens the door. 'Let me through,' he orders the crowd still huddled there, all trying to see what's going on. 'Lock the door after me,' he tells Ryan.

'What did I *do*?' cries Ginger. She puts her head on Chloe's still shoulder. 'This is your fault too, Ryan. We should never have messed about with that fucking Ouija board...'

'No, this is because of *you*,' he says. 'You betrayed her.'

'No! I'd never have done that!' Ginger leaps up and pushes him back.

'Oh, you would.' Ryan resists her shove. His voice is ice cold. 'She should have stabbed you to fucking death.'

Ginger shakes her head and then begins to pace, her flowing robes whispering against the floor. 'You three,' she whispers, 'never be under one roof.' She repeats it, over and over, and then puts her face in her hands.

'Three came in,' says Ryan quietly. 'Only two leave.'

'You'll defend me, won't you?' Ginger pleads. 'I had no choice, Ryan. She had me by the neck and I hit her. I didn't know it would kill her, I just wanted to stop her.'

'She *had* stopped,' says Ryan. 'We both know it.' He pauses. 'It was murder, not self-defence. But I won't tell them that.'

Ginger nods but her face is drawn, and her eyes are haunted, fearful – guilty.

'I was really happy to see her earlier,' he continues. 'I couldn't believe it was her.'

Ginger sobs into her bloody hand and says, 'I'm sorry.' Then she bends down, kisses Chloe's forehead and says again, 'I'm sorry.'

'Will you still go onstage tomorrow?' asks Ryan after a moment.

Ginger goes to the mirror and powders her face as though to get ready for the next act. She adds red lipstick as though to strengthen her mouth for any words she must say and fluffs up her hair. Then she turns to Ryan. 'What choice do I have?'

When the paramedics come into the dressing room, Ryan and Ginger are sitting on either side of Chloe, as though she's merely sleeping, and they are watching over her until she wakes.

59

THERE AND YET NOT THERE

'I don't want to be dead.' The words come out as the tiniest whisper, and Chloe is sure Morgan can't possibly have heard them. She starts to say them again, but Morgan speaks.

'Most people don't,' she says gently.

'But my heart is still beating.' Morgan let's go of Chloe's hand; Chloe keeps the other on her chest and can feel her heart pulsing beneath.

'It's beating here,' says Morgan. 'Just not there.'

Chloe shakes her head; her reflection mirrors the denial. 'But, look – I'm there, I exist.'

'Here,' repeats Morgan. 'Not *there.*'

'But I'm real. I'm breathing.'

'Only here.'

There and yet not there... A line from her own script.

'No. I can't be dead. How can I be? We were fighting, and then I blacked out like I often do. I lowered the knife. But, God, there was blood, wasn't there? What the hell happened?'

'Look in the mirror,' says Morgan.

Behind them, in the glass, Chloe watches the final scene unfold; sees Ginger grab the bottle and hit her; watches herself fall; sees her last breath. She watches with great sadness as Ginger and Ryan sit beside her lifeless body while paramedics try and revive her. She longs to climb through the glass like Alice and go back to the beginning of the *Dust* interval and never go to the dressing room with Ryan.

'I wasn't *really* going to kill her,' Chloe cries, pushing her chair back from the mirror. 'I was just so angry. I loved her and I hated her. I wanted to scare her. But I stopped, I did, I'm sure of it.'

'You did,' Morgan agrees gently.

'And she still hit me? Still killed me?'

'Who knows how she felt. She must have been very scared. She didn't know if you might attack her again, did she?'

'I thought I'd just blacked out.' Chloe's feelings of distress and sadness are somehow less; softer, as though felt through a filter. Is this what being dead feels like? Then she realises something. 'Why didn't the dressing room look bloody when I came around then?'

'You just saw it how you had last seen it.'

'When did it happen? How long ago?'

'There, it happened at nine-fifteen on Thursday the fifth of September, twenty-nineteen. Here, there is no time, as such. Here it's always just … now.'

Chloe won't accept it; she can't. It isn't possible. She can feel the breath in her lungs and the hair on her arms. 'But I haven't said goodbye to anyone. I'm too young. No. I'm *not* dead.' She stands up. 'I'm going home. No, not home; I'm going to see my mum and dad.'

'That's what I found the hardest,' admits Morgan, still golden gorgeous in the glow of the mirror lights. 'Never getting to say goodbye to anyone properly. But there are ways you can. Love lingers. It's still there even if you're not.'

Chloe marches to the dressing-room door. 'No. I want my mum. I'm going to her.'

'Chloe, sweetheart, stay here,' begs Morgan 'For now. *Please*. If you go out there, into the world, you'll see them, but they won't see you, and it hurts. It hurts so much. I'm warning you. I did it. Stay with me and wait for them to call you.'

'Call me?' Chloe pauses at the door.

'Yes.'

'Like on my phone?'

Morgan shakes her head. 'That doesn't work here. They might call you somehow though, and you'll know when it happens.'

Now Chloe is afraid to leave the dressing room. What if it's true? What if she *is* dead and she goes home, and her mum can't see her? Doesn't respond when she speaks? It will be unbearable. Maybe she should wait. Just another hour.

'Sometimes my mum used to look up when I went there,' says Morgan as though she knows Chloe's torment. 'She'd tell my dad later that she had been sure she smelt me. She got so upset about it that I stopped going. I hated seeing her so tormented. Sometimes it's kinder to stay away ... unless they come looking for you.'

'My mum *will* come looking for me,' cries Chloe. 'I know she will. But will she know how to? Oh God. Will she? Does she know yet that I'm dead? I can't bear it – does she?'

Morgan ignores the questions, and says, 'I responded to you on the Ouija board when you called because you bewitched me – and I came back when *Dust* returned because I knew you'd be here with me soon.'

'You *knew* this would happen?'

Morgan nods. 'Sit here,' she says kindly. 'Days there pass in just a moment here. It won't feel like long.'

'You knew I was going to ...' Chloe can't say it.

'Yes. I knew. Back when you were sixteen. I've been waiting. It hasn't been so long for me. Come, sit.'

Chloe sits back down. She and Morgan are beautiful in the mirror; flawless, aglow, eternal. Then in the glass, the room dissolves and behind them both, Chloe sees Ginger crying into one of her Esme Black dresses, staining it with inky mascara. There is a pile of newspapers on the dressing table; the headlines are 'Dust Death Doesn't Stop Show', 'Cursed Dust Still Wows Sell-Out Audiences', 'Morgan Miller Murder Solved after Twenty Years' and 'Dust Star Daughter of Morgan Miller Murderer'. Ginger picks up the story about her mum, stifles a sob, and throws it into the bin. She looks at her wrist then; the charms on her bracelet tinkle softly. She touches the tiny ghost and looks up at the mirror. For a moment, Chloe wonders if she can see them and wants to reach out and touch her.

'How does she have her bracelet and yet I do too?' asks Chloe, looking at it in her hand still.

'You only have it *here*,' says Morgan.

'But you have one earring in. Why don't you have your other one *here*?'

'This is the way I *see* it.'

'Lynda kept it all this time,' says Chloe, realising. 'Her husband sent it to the police when they split. You'd think she'd have thrown it away like the award she killed you with.'

'She kept it in a compartment in her jewellery box. Now and again she would take it out and look at it. I could never tell what she was feeling.'

Chloe looks at the mirror, wondering how many times Morgan must have sat here, watching events unfold. 'Did you show me Ginger in the mirror?' she asks.

'No, that's you.'

'And Ginger hasn't gone to prison?'

'No,' says Morgan. 'Ryan supported her self-defence story.'

'And is he OK?'

The mirror mists over and a new scene emerges – Ryan walking into a room Chloe doesn't recognise. It looks a little like the Dean Wilson rehearsal space, but larger. There's a row of people on chairs with scripts; one of them asks Ryan to stand on the marked spot and begin when he's ready. Ryan composes himself for a moment. When he looks up, he is young Ryan, full of swagger, magnetic, utterly mesmerising.

'Oh my God, he's auditioning for something,' cries Chloe. 'I'm so glad. After all these years. Good luck, Ryan.' She pauses. 'But...'

'What, Chloe?'

'What about me now? I must be hated. They must know I went after Ginger with a knife. My poor mum will be ashamed of me.'

'Your mum is only proud. Chester and Ryan made sure everyone knew that Ginger tried to take your script. The papers spoke kindly about you, said you lost your mind after your childhood friend did that to you. You can see your mum if you want...'

Chloe shakes her head. She doesn't know if she can bear to. But the mirror mists over again, despite her grief, and there, beyond the glass, her mum kneels at a white headstone. Her knees are muddied by the fresh soil and she places a bunch of pink roses in the centre of the grave. Then she weeps; quietly, with agonising dignity.

Chloe does too.

She and Morgan sit in silence for a while. Chloe supposes there is no word for how long, since there is only here now.

After a hundred heartbeats, Chloe says, 'What really happened with Daniel Locke and Harry Bond? Do you know? Why did it all end so tragically for them? For Amelia Bennett. Why did all three of them die and yet ... Ryan is OK. And Ginger.' She looks at herself and Morgan in the mirror; realises it has ended for them too.

'It's about the kind of person who is drawn to the kind of darkness a Ouija board represents,' says Morgan. 'They held their own fates in their hands. Really, troubled teenagers have no place playing with something they don't yet understand.' She pauses. 'Would you like to see them?'

'No,' says Chloe firmly. 'But tell me ... are they OK now?'

Morgan nods.

'When this run of *Dust* finishes,' she says after a beat, 'and it returns—'

'It's coming back?'

'Yes. But when it does, it won't be with Ginger.'

'Poor Ginger.' Chloe pauses. 'Poor *Jess*. That's who she really is. They're all going to forget me anyway, aren't they?'

'Never.' Morgan smiles. 'When you're famous, you never die.'

'But I'm not famous.'

'Oh, you are. Your show is.'

'My *show*?'

Morgan nods. Chloe looks into the mirror again. The dressing room behind them is a rainbow of flowers, so many that she's sure she can smell the sweet aroma; no, it's just her imagination. Sadness seizes Chloe at the realisation that she will never again smell a new perfume or a lover's skin; Ginger's skin; no, *Jess*'s skin. A young woman – one she doesn't recognise – answers the door and receives another bouquet. She is fresh-faced with her hair scraped back, clearly about to put her stage make-up on; a young, everyday girl who Chloe would have chosen for the role if she'd been able to.

Behind her, instead of the *Dust* poster, is the one Chloe saw earlier; *She Haunts Me* is written in silver, her name just above it; the background is the hundred blues of a sparkly ocean meeting a starry sky; in the foreground is a woman on the balcony of a ship, facing away from the camera. This girl, in this dressing room, is now painting her face to become Abigail.

A haunting melody drifts from the speakers.

'Only the music of the ocean – wordless, melodic, soothing – and the dance of the waves, and the two of us sinking, forever, together, to the bottom of the sea...'

'This song,' breathes Chloe. 'It's...'

'Yes, it is,' says Morgan. 'You wrote those words. They've made your show into a musical. It hits theatres on the fourth of February twenty-twenty-one. It's even bigger than *Dust*. You've left your beautiful imprint on the world, Chloe. They sacked Edwin Roberts after Chester and Ryan reported him, and the new artistic director took on your script.'

'Did Ginger audition for it?'

'No. I don't think she felt it was the right thing to do. She'll get plenty of work still, though she's not as loved by audiences as she'd like to be after what happened with you.'

'That makes me sad,' admits Chloe. She remembers her rage. But all that's left is calm now. 'I still love her. I think I always will.'

'Really, it's the only thing that never dies.'

Morgan begins to sing 'I Am Dust' as more scenes flash before them in the mirror. A kaleidoscope of past and present unfolds, like a slideshow of holiday snaps: Chester in all his tuxedo finery, opening the theatre doors for eager patrons; Ryan, Jess and Chloe sitting around cardboard letters and a glass, youthful in the candlelight; Chloe falling with Ginger onto the dressing-room sofa, hypnotised, their hair tangled together, raven and blonde, yin and yang, light and shadow; Ginger whispering, 'I'm sorry, I'm sorry, I'm sorry,' to a picture of Chloe in the newspaper; Lynda Swanson, ever glamorous in a packed-out courtroom; Chloe's mum watching the closing scene from *She Haunts Me* with tears on her cheeks.

'I wanted to play Abigail in my show,' says Chloe sadly. 'I never quite believed myself good enough, but I still dreamed of doing it.'

'You would have been sensational. But it wasn't meant to be that way. You left your words. They're forever.'

Forever. Such a long time.

'But I don't want to sit here like this forever.' Chloe is tired of the visions. 'I don't like watching but not taking part. I want to *talk* to them. To my loved ones.' She pauses. 'This can't be it. There *must* be somewhere else.'

'There is.' Morgan holds her gaze, her eyes sad.

Of course.

'Why didn't you go there?'

'I lingered here too long.' Morgan plays with her right earlobe as though missing that pearl earring. 'I couldn't leave my loved ones. And the longer I've stayed in this in-between place – not here or there – the harder it is to go where we're supposed to.'

'How do *I* get there?' asks Chloe softly.

'You know how. You wrote it; you wrote Abigail sinking to the bottom of a beautiful ocean. Open up to it. Like when you used to black out – those were your practice runs. Go with it. Say it. Whisper those words. You know what they are.'

Does she? *Yes.* She does.

'But stay a while,' says Morgan. 'The stage is all ours here. Out there we can perform whenever we want to. I've been waiting so long to have you sing with me too.'

'I'm not going yet,' says Chloe softly. 'I need to say goodbye first. I need to wait for them to call to me...'

60

THE DEAN WILSON THEATRE

FEBRUARY 2021

'Are you there, Chloe? Will you come and talk to us?'

When she hears the words – like a favourite song playing after a long time – Chloe knows who it is. Morgan disappears from her side and Chloe is in the dressing room still, but it's the one she saw in the mirror earlier. The one with her silver-and-blue *She Haunts Me* poster on the wall, and the abundance of vibrant flowers brightening the white walls. Chloe turns away from the glass. From her reflection. From the lights. Her heart swells.

She is there.

Ginger, Ryan and Chester are sitting in a circle.

In the centre is an upturned glass; surrounding it is the familiar sight of printed letters on small pieces of paper, and the words 'Hello', 'Goodbye', 'Yes' and 'No'. The three of them have one finger on the glass. Ginger's nails are pearly pink and take Chloe back to the dusty stage at the youth theatre.

'If you're here, Chloe, please talk to us.'

It's Ryan. Like it always was.

'She probably won't want to talk to *you*,' says Chester, lowering his eyelids in disdain at Ginger. 'If the poor girl *is* here, she'll bugger off once she sees it's you. That's if this even works.'

'It will,' says Ginger softly.

'I only agreed cos you're hot.' Chester looks at Ryan. 'Your new show's not bad either.'

'If we're gonna do this, we have to get on with it,' says Ryan, suppressing a smile. 'If we get caught in here, we'll be in the shit. Now we're all at the New Theatre this is breaking and entering.'

'We *had* to do it here,' says Ginger. 'Thank God they haven't changed the door codes.'

'I'm still not entirely sure,' admits Ryan, and takes his finger off the glass.

'Put it back on!' cries Ginger.

'The Ouija board is what started it all.' He sounds like the teen boy again. 'I think you've forgotten what happened to my friend Daniel.'

'I haven't.' Ginger looks as pale as the dressing-room wall.

'What happened to Daniel?' asks Chester, taking his finger away too.

No one speaks.

'He died,' says Chloe, but no one looks her way. 'But I don't think we can ever really blame the Ouija board. It's our own flaws and failings that led us all to this moment.'

With so much endless time to think, Chloe has realised Morgan is right. That troubled teenagers have no place playing with something they don't yet understand. Because the power lies within them, the ones who begin the game. After all a Ouija board is just an empty glass and pieces of paper without them. But as to why some suffer more afterwards, the answer to that is as much a mystery as any, and even with all the time in the world now, Chloe has no answer for it.

'OK, don't tell me,' snaps Chester. 'But tell me this – Chloe's been gone nearly eighteen months, so why tonight?'

Ginger glances at the *She Haunts Me* poster. 'I know she'll be here for her opening night. So put your fingers back on the glass.'

Ryan inhales deeply; and does. Chester follows.

'Her show was so fucking good,' says Chester. 'I cried my eyes out at the end. Wish I still worked here so I could see it every night. I'll be coming again.' He pauses. 'Still not sure why you asked *me* to do this with you?'

Ryan looks at Ginger. 'When we realised you were here tonight,' she says, 'we thought we should just ask. It made sense. Three is supposed to be best, you see. We were going to do it anyway. Chloe was fond of you. If she hates me, she might at least come to talk to you. And then I can—'

'Let's just do it,' interrupts Ryan. 'Chloe, if you're here, please make yourself known to us.'

Chloe stands up and moves closer to them. 'I'm here,' she says. No one responds. Of course. She's here, but not *there*.

Then Ginger frowns. 'Fuck,' she whispers. 'Can't you smell that? Her perfume. It's her. It's *her*. Chloe, can you hear us? Please respond.'

How is Chloe supposed to move the glass? Tell them, yes, she is here. *Remember how. Will it and it shall happen. Push.* The familiar words send heat along her spine. And she does it; she *pushes*. Not with her finger. Not with her body. With her heart.

And the glass moves.

Chester jumps back. Ginger and Ryan smile.

It touches the word 'Hello'.

'Hello,' cries Ginger. 'Is it really you, Chloe?'

'Might not be,' says Ryan.

'Fuck me,' Chester puts his finger back on the glass. 'You two moved that. You did, didn't you?'

They ignore him. 'How can we know it's you?' asks Ryan.

Chloe *pushes*.

SHE HAUNTS ME

Ginger sobs. 'It's her.'

'Anyone could mess with us and say that,' insists Ryan.

'This is crazy,' cries Chester. 'Are you two doing this? You're messing with my head.'

SWIM AND DONT LOOK BACK

'The song...' says Ginger.

'Everyone knows it,' says Ryan. 'They've been playing it everywhere, even before tonight's show. Could be anyone.'

HERE AND YET NOT HERE

'Chloe,' whispers Ginger.

THERE AND YET NOT THERE

'Ask her something only she knows,' Ryan tells Chester.

Chester pauses. Thinks. Then, 'Chloe,' he says softly. 'What was the last thing I ever said to you?'

TWITTER WILL BE THE FIRST ONE I TELL

Ryan and Ginger look expectantly at Chester. He nods, his eyes glistening. 'I always did say the most profound things, didn't I? If this is really you somehow, I miss you, Chloe. Shit, am I really talking to you? This is crazy. Life isn't the same without you.'

I MISS YOU TOO CHES

He nods, hand on chest. 'It's not the same at the New Theatre. I miss the DW. I even miss Cynthia. Hell, I miss Beth. That slag at Propaganda is my boyfriend now. Knew he'd commit in the end. Ryan's show is on, so I get see it loads. He's ace in it. Ginger's got a small role in it too, so we're all at the same theatre at the mo.' He pauses. 'Can you see all this stuff where you are, Chlo? Do you know that Ginger's mother killed Morgan?' Ginger looks down at her lap and doesn't respond. 'It all came out the week after you died. Shit, that was a shock. You were the first one I called ... and then I remembered. I can't—'

'I'm sorry,' interrupts Ginger. 'I'm *so* sorry, Chloe.'

'You're just sorry that killing her meant you never got to play Esme in this year's *Dust*,' says Ryan quietly.

'No. *No*. I *am* sorry.'

Chloe believes her. Is it because she wants to?

No. She *knows*. Like she always used to.

'You'd have had her fucking show if you could,' says Chester. 'It was trending you know, Chlo, the fact that she tried to nick it. #ScriptGate hasn't done her any harm, to be fair. No such thing as bad press turns out to be true. And she had the nerve to come and see it tonight!'

'I *had* to see it,' says Ginger, her voice reverent. 'Chloe, I remember when I heard you performing it that day, on the stage here. I told you it was beautiful. It was. I knew then that it was utterly magic. And I was consumed with jealousy and ambition. I wanted it for myself. I'm not making excuses, but my mum had pounded it into me that I had to succeed, at any cost. You know that, Chloe. You *knew* her. The success of me getting the role of Esme went to my head and I had to find something as big. And I knew that was your script.'

I NEVER MEANT TO HURT YOU

'I never meant to hurt *you*,' says Ginger.

IM SORRY ABOUT CUTTING YOU

'No, *I'm* sorry. Can you forgive me? I'm haunted by what I did. And I'm sorry.'

SHE HAUNTS ME

'Yes,' says Ginger. 'You do.'

Chloe realises that it's exhausting pushing the glass; using the heart is so much harder than using a finger. She is weak now. Just a few more.

GOOD LUCK RYAN

'Thank you,' he says.

BE HAPPY CHES

'Without you?' he says. 'Never.'

IM RIGHT HERE

He sniffs dramatically.

CHESTER TOMORROW PLEASE GO

The effort of pushing the glass is indescribably hard now. Chloe gives it everything she has.

AND TELL MY MUM

'Yes?' says Chester.

I SAW HER WATCHING MY SHOW

Push.

I DEDICATE IT TO HER

'I'll tell her,' he promises.
Chloe realises she can't push anymore.
'What about me?' cries Ginger.
They wait.
'Chloe! No! Please don't go without saying goodbye to me. I'm sorry, I really and truly am.'
Chloe walks around the three of them; a full and final circle.

Ryan and Chester take their fingers from the glass. Ryan says that Chloe has probably gone. Ginger begins to cry, sobbing, finger still on the glass, still hoping. Chloe stops behind her. She leans in to smell her hair. Nothing. She touches the curls, but they fall through her fingers. This is not where she wants to be. There but not there. She leans down and kisses Ginger's cheek. When she pulls away, she sees it is Jess. Sixteen-year-old Jess, her hair in plaits, her cheeks pink with the heat of a hot August night. Jess is frowning and touching her cheek. Chloe can no longer see Chester or Ryan. She moves the tiny ghost charm so it shivers – one last *push* – and Jess looks down at it.

She smiles and looks up, directly at Chloe.

'I'll always love you,' says Chloe. 'And I *do* forgive you.'

Then she closes her eyes.

She whispers, 'I am dust.'

And blacks out one final time.

Except it is silver.

ACKNOWLEDGMENTS

Thank you to my first readers who all, in their own ways, help shape the book. I depend on these wonderful people. You know who you are – my sisters Grace Wilkinson and Claire Lugar, and my friends John Marrs, Madeleine Black, and Matt Wesolowski.

When this book was in its infancy, my friend Dean Wilson tweeted about a dream he had where he and Madonna had written a song called 'Dust'. I got shivers. I knew it was supposed to be a musical. I asked him if he minded (which he didn't) and it became the show at the heart of the book. It was only fair that I should then name the playwright and theatre after him.

Thank you for the endless support from Anne Cater, Nina Pottell, Liz Robinson, Margaret Madden, Fiona Mills, Carrie Martin, Helen Jn Pierre, Laura Pearson, Sue Bond, Helen Boyce, Tracy Fenton, Claire Allan, Lisa Howells, Paul Burston, Susie Lynes, Louise Jensen, Louisa Treger, Gill Paul, Ellen Devonport, Frances Pearson, Deirdre O'Brien, Carol Lovekin, Chloe Deyes, Amelia Grimes, Michael Mann, and Alice Palmer.

A special mention and thank you to the THREE DAVES! Wakefield Dave, Durham Dave and Cake Dave. You know who you are.

Thank you to the groups that are my go-to place – TBC The Book Club, Book Connectors, The Prime Writers, and The Motherload Book Club. Thank you also to the Women of Words; Cass, Lynda, Michelle and Emily. Love you all.

Thank you to all those who came along on my last blog tour – Mac Reviews Books, Zooloo's Book Dairy, Steph's Book Blog, Book Social, DeeCee at It's All About The Books, Cal Turner Reviews, MADE UP Book Reviews, Passages To The Past,

Amanda at My Bookish Blog Spot, Beverley at Beverley Has Read, Hair Past A Freckle, Emma's Bookish Corner, Hayley at Rather Too Fond of Books, Portobello Book Blog, Claire Thinking, Rachael Read It, Jen Med's Book Reviews, Ellen Devonport, Bibliophile Book Club, BeadyJan's Books, Anne Williams, Joanne Robertson, Sandie's Book Shelves, Rae Reads, Kate at Everywhere and Nowhere, Books of all Kinds, Have Books Will Read, Novel Gossip, Novel Delights, Northern Reader, Emma R, Trish at Between My Lines, Sharon Bairden, A Little Book Problem, Sinfully Wicked Book Reviews, Joanna at Over The Rainbow, Donna's Book Blog, Varietats, Books And Me, Anne Cater, Kaisha at The Writing Garnet, Between The Pages Book Club, The Literary Shed, The Last Word, The Shelf of Unread Books, Claire Knight, Mr Gravy, the Bearded Book Blogger, Jacob at Hooked from Page One, Novel Deelights, Suze Reviews, Jaffa Reads Too, The Bookscoop, Books, Bucks, & Beyond, What Cathy Read Next, Herding Cats, On the Shelf Book Blog, Joy Kluver, Karen at My Reading Corner, If Only I Could Read Faster, Lisa at Segnalibro, Cheryl M-N's Book Blog, On the Shelf Reviews, The Big Fat Bookworm, The Reading Closet, Book Lover Worm, Booking Good Read, and Books Are My Cwtches.

Thank you, West Camel and Karen Sullivan, for the careful, thoughtful edits. Thank you to Mark at Kidethic for the eternally incredible covers. Thank you for all the love to #TeamOrenda. You are my family.

And thank you, always, to Karen Sullivan for having faith in my words, for letting me tell the story I have to, and for taking that chance every time.